LEGACY

BOOK ONE OF HONOUR'S STAND

MICAH R. MACCALLUM

WWW.MICAHRMACCALLUM.COM

Book Cover by Micah R. MacCallum

Illustrations by Micah R. MacCallum

Chapter Images Edited by Bob MacCallum and Micah MacCallum

First edition 2024

ISBN: 978-1-7383230-0-5 (ebook)

ISBN: 978-1-7383230-1-2 (print – Draft2Digital)

ISBN: 978-1-7383230-2-9 (print – IngramSpark)

To my parents

The following records have been transcribed by Aria Stueck, Archivist of Honour's Stand.

Editing, submission to guild registry, and cataloguing also completed by Aria Stueck.

Note to self (REMEMBER TO REMOVE FROM FINAL DOCUMENT): I deserve a raise, and an assistant.

Possible candidates: Yuina? Neva? Liatris or Isaac may also do well.

Jegrac – unlikely.

Certainly not Frost.

??? – revisit later

*also need fresh tea leaves!! Remind Isaac to buy more.

CHRONICLE 1
Recorded by Isaac Heathe

"Oh, and the end of the world just happens to be scheduled on your *only* day off? *Again?*"

She's tired of my excuses.

"Listen, Isaac, if you don't want to come home, just say so! Your father and I won't-"

"MOM. Stop acting like I have a choice! It's my *job*. The guild needs me! I can't-"

Our conversation is interrupted by the smack of a heavy spear. Peering over the counter, my gaze locks onto a market guard standing nearby. His boots clink as he approaches my hiding spot within this empty booth.

Not wanting to cause trouble, my hand rises to reveal the communication crystal in my grasp.

Clouds of dust seep through the gaps in the floorboards as he stomps away.

I pull the blue gem back to my face. It's silent on the other end - as if the connection has broken - but the subtle glow in the stone's centre suggests this argument won't end on its own.

"Sorry. I should go." I mutter. "Neva's probably looking for me, so..."

A sigh echoes against the clamour of the Nexus marketplace.

"Alright, Isaac," she concedes, "but try to come home soon. We miss you, and the house feels empty without you here, and I know you're busy, but, just - make time for us, okay?"

The wood of the abandoned stall creaks as I settle against it. My hand rises to flick an ant scaling a wrinkle on my dull brown slacks.

"I know, Mom. Thanks. Love you."

My eyes wander to the leaves above, squinting as splinters of sunlight pierce through. The crystal echoes: "Love you too, Izzy. Stay safe." It releases a gentle hum, shivering against my palm when I shove it back into the pouch on my waist.

Not wanting to leave quite yet, I linger here, alone with my thoughts, tucked beneath the shade of a solitary tree and cradled by boards lined with specks of chipped white paint.

The marketplace feels so far away, the sizzling and bubbling and clanging and haggling dampened by the walls around me, providing a quiet place to think. Comfort rests in the dirt and small patches of grass surrounding my feet, and in the faint scent of fresh herbs, oil, and sweet soaps tickling my nose.

Knuckles scratch against the coarse stubble lining my jaw as I search for ways to avoid (for today, *at least!*) this 'end-of-the-world' nonsense.

She just doesn't get it. Of course I want to go back to Borderik, but every morning there's a new quest or urgent prophecy about *a future WE have a responsibility to change* (Neva's words, not mine) and somehow I'm always guilted into staying.

So it's no surprise Mom and Dad think I'm avoiding them. Rescheduling once or twice is to be expected, but cancelling and changing plans several weeks in a row is pretty suspicious.

Not that griping about it will change anything.

Wiping the drool from my lips as the aroma of exotic, Orion-imported meat wafts into my nostrils, I step out into the bright, boisterous sunlight filling the Nexus market square. A nearby merchant calls to me, tempting me to visit his stall.

It couldn't hurt to stop for a little while, right? I've got time. The guild doesn't know where I am, and-

"Ah! Praise Morrowfir, we found him!"

I swallow a groan.

A man is crouched beneath the shade of another abandoned stall, his face tucked below the wide brim of his hat. Even though his features are hidden, I instantly recognize Jegrac's gnarled brown hair, the worn leather coat draped over his broad shoulders, and the giant black hound sniffing for crumbs in his long, thin beard.

"Good job, Pall! What a clever dog you are!" Jegrac says. "We must be the greatest trackers in all Eight Realms, huh, boy?!" Pall yaps loudly in agreement. "Alrighty then, as a reward, we'll fetch a treat after we talk to our Commander."

Jegrac's collar begins to wriggle, and a furry creature pops its head out from beneath the faded brown material. It's some kind of ferret, or maybe not, since most ferrets usually have two eyes, not three.

"We've been trying to get a hold of you, Commander," the Nomad continues, "forgot your guildstone again, huh? Better break that habit before it gets worse! Lucky for you, however, Neva suggested we search the marketplace, and once Pall caught onto your scent you were easy to find. Isn't that great?"

Hiding my annoyance, I force my lips into a grin and try to change the subject.

"Just you two?" I wonder aloud. "Strange. No offence, but I expected Neva to find me first."

Jegrac's head snaps upright, and he cranes his neck to carefully scan the area around us. A low, coarse laugh escapes his lips.

"Pity. Must have left her behind," Jegrac scoffs in his rumbling, rusty voice.

His disdain grows once his eyes graze over my plain pauldrons. His thick eyebrows furrow.

"I'm sure you have your reasons," he remarks, "but why hide our guild insignia in a place like this? You're our Commander. Have some dignity! Are you ashamed of Honour's Stand?"

"You know it's not that simple..." I start to say, but trail off. There's nothing to be gained from arguing with my stubborn companion.

Swallowing a sigh, I brush the illusion off my shoulder, revealing the decoration underneath.

"That wasn't too hard, was it?" Jegrac says, brightening a little. "Show some pride in who you are, and in your guild. We've got nothing to hide, right? So why lie?"

He's right, but the stares still come. Eyes in the crowd linger on my pauldrons, and I grasp my shoulder to obscure their vision.

"You worry too much, Commander." Jegrac shakes his head. "All you city folk are so self-conscious! But perhaps I shouldn't judge... even I want to hide my identity once in a while."

His eyes bore into me.

"But I can't."

Ears burning, my hand slips back down.

Jegrac nods in approval. "Let them stare, Commander! After a while, you barely notice the way they look at you."

His words sting. Considering what he must go through on a daily basis, what right do I have to complain?

"If I'm doing this, might as well do it right," I announce, wiping the illusion magic off the hilt of the sword strapped to my waist. The handle glimmers like oil on water as the trickery fades. "Don't tell Neva, but between you and me, I prefer to show this off."

A particularly stubborn patch of glamour covers up the image of a shattered sword resting beneath a brilliant golden shield, and it takes more effort than expected to scrub it off. "Just so you know, Jegrac, I don't think Neva's wrong about hiding this. Not... entirely. Sometimes it's the safest choice."

Jegrac shrugs. "Perhaps."

"Still," I add, "The safest choice isn't always the right one."

He grins.

Giving Pall one last pat, Jegrac straightens up and gestures in the direction of the market's exit.

It only takes a few quick steps to catch up, and I ruffle Pall's fur as Jegrac releases a quiet whistle. He pulls up his hat to push back his long brown hair, and then glances at the sky. We walk in silence, his eyes quietly tracking the birds above and Pall huffing happily as he trots between us. I keep a pleasant smile on my face and a watchful eye out for anything suspicious as we stroll through the familiar market square.

Most people ignore us, but a few citizens give me a friendly wave or a respectful nod when they notice the guild insignia. It's business as usual, except for the mercenaries lingering by stalls as additional protection, exchanging glares with the Nexus guards strolling through the marketplace on routine patrols. Their eyes burn holes into my shoulders, and hostile whispers stalk our backs, but I follow Jegrac's lead and ignore them.

A heavy thump echoes in my ears moments before my shoulder is knocked aside. The dirt embraces me with a hearty thud, and a voice behind me bellows: "HEY, YOU! GET BACK HERE!"

The ground slips away as I roll up and into a sprint, arms outstretched to tackle the offender, but my body shudders when a firm hand yanks me back.

"OW! *What the rift*, Jegrac?!"

I whirl towards him, curses dancing behind my tight grimace.

The words die in my throat.

Jegrac's face has drained from a bright tan to a sickly pale, his eyes wide as he stares past me, a drop of sweat dangling from the tip of his hooked nose. I bite back my anger, head snapping to follow his gaze.

The stranger who knocked me aside continues to shove through the crowd. His frenzied pace sends a girl tumbling into a merchant's cart, her fall softened as fresh produce squishes and bursts under her weight.

Shrugging off Jegrac's grip, I try to step forward, but he grabs me again, stronger this time, his hand clamped tightly around my wrist.

"*Wait,* Commander! Just - wait."

The stranger plants his feet, hands raised in surrender as blue and grey uniforms approach, flowing through the stream of merchants and customers trying to flee.

"Someone, please," the man cries, his brown cloak whipping up dust as he paces in the centre of the empty path, "HELP ME! Anyone? Please, someone!"

The grip on my arm tightens as the man catches sight of us. Tucked beneath the tattered hood is the sparse beard and tan complexion of a Nomad.

No wonder Jegrac stopped me.

The stranger is one of his own.

Jegrac's hand slides away, but mine rises to latch onto his shoulder before he can move. He hesitates, eyes narrowed at me, a furious question on his lips. But then he falls silent, rooted in place, fists bunched and trembling at his side.

"Commander," he hisses, "we can't let them take him. You know what they do to Nomads."

Pall releases a confused yip as he watches us, his body tense but still.

Something breaks in the stranger's eyes, and he presses his heels into the dirt, preparing to run.

"*Go,*" Jegrac whispers at him, his voice strained and desperate, "Reach the forest, and then you can-"

The world explodes in a flash of terrifying white light. Through squinted eyes, I watch the man crumple to the ground, and then my arms snap up to shield my face from a sudden wave of heat.

Blinking back stars, we watch him squirm, body smoking and twitching as a familiar face steps through the wall of guards.

"Take him away," the High Champion announces, adjusting his tie with one hand as the other runs through his slicked-back blonde hair. "The Council will deal with him."

"Yes, Solaris."

Blue and grey uniforms draw closer, weapons stowed, arms extended with rune-covered cuffs to escort the Nomad away.

A hoarse, rasping plea breaks through the silence that follows.

"*No,* you... can't... if my guild... if I could-"

Solaris aims a swift kick at the man's gut, lips set in a tight line as his victim groans in response.

"*Quiet.* I have no time for excuses. Just be glad you were caught before any riftspawn were summoned. Now bite your tongue, lower your head, and *cooperate.*"

My feet lurch back in disgust, and my shoulder bumps into something warm and unexpected. When I glance behind me, my eyes widen at the crowd starting to form, kept at bay by the presence of a High Champion and a captured criminal.

Arms raised, Solaris turns to address his audience.

"Celebrate, dear citizens! We have apprehended yet another Nomad responsible for the riftspawn attacks. You are once again safe to go about your day, armed with the knowledge that the Council and your High Champions guard the lives of everyone in Nexus. Yiatsu bless!"

The resounding cheers from the raucous crowd ring hollow and sickly sweet.

Jegrac stands beside me, eyes and teeth locked by anger, feet rooted in place by rage. All around us, citizens and merchants slowly return to their business, passing through the marketplace and over the soot-stained earth where the Nomad had been lying moments ago.

Nexus guards mingle with the crowd as it disperses, handing out masks and patches covered with filter runes while they remind everyone to be wary of the toxic corpses riftspawn often leave behind.

Bumped along by the flow of traffic, we restart our journey towards the market's exit.

"Commander," Jegrac snarls, drawing my attention, "you shouldn't have stopped me."

I shake my head.

"No, we-"

"We could have saved him! He needed our help, and we just-"

"What would you have done, Jegrac? Taken his place? Don't act like we could have stopped a High Champion. If we had interfered, we'd have only made things worse."

He falls silent, fuming, his anger emanating like heat from a furnace as we walk.

"Another *safe choice*," he spits back at me, "I'm tired of making safe choices, Isaac."

His words knock my response back into my throat.

Pall lets out a low whine, nudging his master's thigh, and Jegrac appears to soften, shoulders falling as he reaches down to give his dog a comforting pat.

"It's fine," he mutters under his breath. "I'll be fine. You're just trying to do what you think is right, Commander. I know. I'm just... tired. Of all this."

I search for the right words to say. By the time I find them, the conversation has ended.

"Mr. Heathe, is that you?" a voice bellows out from a nearby booth. "Come over here so I can get a better look at ya'!"

A jovial, round man waves at me from a stall a few steps away. His face is obscured by the vibrant and colourful fabrics hanging on racks around the booth, but he sounds familiar.

I turn to Jegrac, but he's already walking away.

"Go. We'll be waiting there." He points towards a hooded vendor selling a strange assortment of bones and animal parts. I nod. Despite his simmering anger, Jegrac will come running if this merchant is looking to cause trouble.

Pushing through the busy crowd, the man's grin widens as I draw near. He mutters a few quick instructions to the girl at his side before hobbling out from behind the stall.

"Yiatsu's blessings," I say politely. "How are you?"

The merchant smiles, the tips of his thick moustache tickling his eyes.

"Well enough! And thanks to you, my daughter and I are able to express our gratitude today!"

The man bows, placing a hand on his generous stomach as he shows me the top of his balding head.

Memories resurface, adding some clarity to his thanks; a flashback to a few weeks ago, out in Dahlia's Fields, where riftspawn stalk across grass with snarling black bodies. A small caravan rests in a ditch, scratched and scarred and nearly overrun, surrounded by mercenaries struggling to push back a tide of dark beasts.

For our guild, however? Just another routine fight; a pleasant change of pace on our journey to the Teeth.

All we did was show up at the right place, at the right time.

My mouth goes dry as I search for a response. It feels dishonest to take any credit, since all I'd done was stand by the road to babysit the caravan while the rest of the guild ran off to fight the monsters in the field.

After a moment of silence and a half-hearted "uh, well, you're welcome, sir," the merchant lifts his head and greets me once again with his giant grin.

"Call me Clifford, Mr. Heathe. And no need to be humble - it's comforting to know *some* guilds still take the time to help those in need."

I nod in agreement, not wanting to say more on the subject. Unfortunately, Clifford doesn't share my eagerness to move on to a different topic.

"Not many people would have stopped," he continues, a bit too loudly. "You'd be surprised how many of those 'honourable guilds' passed by before you did!"

My lips twitch, threatening to curve into a grimace. But I bite back my response; I know better than to comment on other guilds, especially in a place as public as this.

Clifford finally notices the discomfort on my face, and attempts to change the subject.

"Just wondering, the Nomad you were walking with - I recognize him. Was he with your guild, back in Dahlia's field? Well – in case you missed it – another one of those *Nomads* just got arrested! Glad to see it wasn't him."

Offering a careful nod, I brace myself as he continues to ramble.

"This may not be a popular opinion, but I think it's a real shame what's happening to his people." The merchant twines his moustache around his finger as he speaks. "Personally, though, I'm just glad none of the Watchmen were involved. Those masked fellows scare away a lot of potential customers whenever they show up."

He falls silent for a moment, his eyes distant.

"Well, either way, we're grateful." Clifford shuffles a little closer, beckoning for me to do the same. When I don't, he takes it as an offer to freely enter my personal space. His tepid breath caresses my face, but I endure it with a polite smile.

"I know being a guild leader can make things... complicated," he whispers. "Such dreadful business, how you're forced into this position, where you must choose between the safety of this city and the safety of your guild. Just remember: we're always watching. We see what you do, and we admire the decisions you folks make, aligning with the Nomads, despite what the Council might-"

The merchant pauses as a Nexus guard passes by. He straightens up with a wink and loudly declares, "And of course a well respected guild leader like yourself is always welcome at our humble store! I'll be sure to stock up on anything else you need in the future. We specialise in cloth, and my daughter is an excellent seamstress, so please keep us in mind!"

As the guard passes, Clifford grasps my hand and stares into my eyes, his smile hiding a strange, quiet intensity. Something is pressed into my hand; metal, flat, and round.

Realising it's a coin, I begin to protest - we are paid relatively well by the Council, and even though some members of our guild would be disappointed by my refusal, being able to help is enough of a reward. Clifford ignores me and wraps my fingers around the object.

"No, sir," he says firmly. "Take it, and *save* it. I insist." With a polite tip of the head, he saunters back behind his booth, watching with quiet pride as his daughter negotiates a profitable sale.

The coin clutched tightly in my grasp, I scan the heads of strangers until Jegrac's signature wide-brimmed hat enters my sight. He's still lingering by the stall he'd pointed out earlier. Pushing through the crowd, I peer down at the gift Clifford has forced upon me.

There are knicks and scratches sprinkled across the gold surface, and it's much too old to be from Nexus. It'd be hard to find a coin like this anywhere within our Realm... Aegis doesn't have the same history as the other lands.

Flipping it over, I discover a simple symbol carved into the back. Four horizontal scratches line up neatly on the blank surface.

"I wouldn't be looking at that right now," a voice chimes in my ear, and suddenly the coin is gone.

It's hard to hide my annoyance when Neva rests her grinning face on my shoulder.

She flashes the coin in her palm, letting it glint beneath the morning sun before it's tucked into her sleeve. Seeing my expression, Neva just laughs.

"You don't look like you're going to thank me," she says playfully. "How rude!"

My eyebrows rise along with my curiosity, though a sigh escapes my lips. Not really in the mood to play along, I stay silent, waiting for her to explain why she deserves my gratitude.

"Don't worry, Heathe! I'll give it back when you actually need it. Be grateful I'm taking it for safe-keeping, before some filthy thief snatches it away! I mean, look at you - I'm sure you'd be a mess without me. You didn't even notice someone snagged your purse!"

I clutch at the place where my bag of chargestones and jewels should be, but come up empty handed.

"*Yiatsu above,* are you serious?" I curse and scan the crowd. It's pointless; the thief is long gone.

Neva gives me a cheeky grin and dances over to my side, looping her arm into my elbow.

"Oh Isaac, you know me," she laughs, pulling a familiar purse out of the air and dangling it in my face, "I'm always looking out for my friends." As I snatch it back from her, she waves at Jegrac and Pall. The happy hound skips towards her, and she quickly pulls her hand away.

Gesturing for him to leave her alone, she commands, "No, Pall. No thank you."

Jegrac releases a low whistle, and the dog replies with a sad whimper, slouching back towards his waiting friend.

"Good. He's learning." Neva gives Jegrac a respectful nod, and then turns to face me. "Now! Let's walk and talk. No use standing around here when there's fun to be had elsewhere!"

Begrudgingly, I let her tug me along, with Jegrac and Pall looking somewhat amused as they follow behind. While we stroll, my eyes are drawn to the white paint lining Neva's fingers in an array of small dots, which shine even brighter against her gleaming black skin.

"Oh, that's nice," I say politely, hoping to distract Neva from talking about quests involving the end of the world. She follows my gaze, and then looks up at me with a pleasant grin.

"You think so?" She lifts her free hand to show off the paint, as well as the golden bangle looped tightly around her wrist. "Some shopkeeper offered to do it for free after selling me this beauty, and you know how I feel about pretty little things. And it matches my earrings, so I just *had* to have it!"

Tilting her head towards me, she lifts her wrist to her ears, comparing the bangle to the small strings of shimmering jewels that dangle down to her shoulders and stop short of the gold bands circling the base of her neck.

Scrambling for a comment, I manage: "Wow, you, uh, really do have a theme going on, huh?" I point at her eyes, which are decorated with what I think is gold zascara (or some other kind of Zorah cosmetic), and then up at her short, fluffy black afro, which is restrained by a headband glinting like rich honey beneath the summer sun.

Neva starts to reply, pauses to peer at me suspiciously, and then laughs. "Yes, well, I do my best to be rather distracting. Is that something you're working on?" She fixes me with an amused grin.

Then her mischievous black eyes find their way to my shoulder, her sharp gaze locking onto the exposed guild insignia.

Before I can explain, she whirls toward Jegrac.

"Seriously?" she snaps. "It's one thing for you to risk your life with that giant target on your back, but you don't need to pressure Isaac into joining your nonsense!"

The string of muffled curses exchanged by my guildmates causes a few marketeers to fumble their goods. They aim bewildered and angry stares at my companions.

"The Commander can make his own decisions," Jegrac finally mutters, "but I-"

"Fine. *Whatever.*" Neva huffs. "Just try not to get your idiot selves killed."

She waves away her annoyance with a shake of her head.

Glancing down at my hands, she comments: "It's a shame we couldn't ever paint something like this on you... it wouldn't show up on your skin, though I suppose if you worked a little bit harder on getting a tan it might be visible."

Her face brightens when her eyes catch on something new.

"Wait, is that what I think it is?!" She points at the device hanging by my side. I'd almost forgotten about it. Has it been recording this entire time?

Neva pokes me in the side, forcing out a response.

"Yeah, and - hey! Stop jabbing me. Yes, it's our chronicler. Aria gave it to me yesterday. Said it's about time we start using it again."

"Huh." Neva says dismissively, as she usually does when she's about to ask for something.

I sigh and unclip it from my belt.

"Here, just take-"

CHRONICLE 2
Recorded by Neva Oyii

In one smooth flourish the new accessory is looped onto my belt.

"By the way," I murmur, tugging Isaac along as he mumbles about how *he wasn't done talking*, "we're not going to Motamir today, so feel free to keep distracting me from something that's not going to happen. Though I must admit, I've been enjoying our conversation so far. Why don't you also comment on my clothes? I can do the same for you, if you'd like."

"No, please don't." Isaac protests. For a moment, he completely misses my remark about Motamir, but then he pauses, purses his lips, and looks at me with his eyebrows raised. He bites back a comment, shaking his head as he turns away.

While Isaac is distracted by our sudden change in plans, I scan the crowd. Several eyes dart away, though one guard is bold enough to keep staring at my exposed stomach. He locks eyes with me, a sheepish expression on his face, and I return his interest with a quick wink and little wave. He blushes.

If teasing Isaac wasn't so entertaining, the guard could earn my attention in exchange for a free drink and some conversation. But my friend finally speaks, and the man fades into the crowd.

"Are..." Isaac says suspiciously, and rightfully so, "are you serious?"

I do my best impression of an honest, endearing grin.

"Frost and Yuina left this morning to plug up Motamir and stop the apocalypse on our behalf, so *technically* we're free today."

His eyes light up, and a twinge of guilt digs into my side. But it's *his* fault for being so easily deceived, and in the end he'll get what *he* wants and I'll get what *I* want.

"By the way," he adds, "thanks for getting my purse back."

Oh, Isaac. Simple, naive Isaac. Not even considering that I'd taken his pouch moments before snatching the scratched coin. Given enough time to get over his initial panic, though, he'd have probably said some nonsense about how "if they took it, they must need it more than me" which would have guilted me into giving it back. Not that I'd ever keep such a light and inexpensive thing, anyways.

"Wait." His eyes narrow. "If there's no quest today, then... why are you here?"

I consider answering him seriously, but decide against it. It can wait.

"I was hoping to talk about your clothing choices for today," I tease. "Do you know what fashion is, Heathe?"

Keeping the grin on my face, my eyes wander over his wrinkled uniform. Most of the rips have been sewn - by hand, judging by the quality - while others have simple patches stitched on top.

I can't count the number of times he's refused my offers to visit a tailor to get some proper work done and the protective runes renewed. I'd even volunteered to cover the cost of dyeing the faded blue lines tracing the edges of his light brown shirt and pants, but he'd still said no. He'd much rather do it himself, apparently.

On the other hand, his chestplate, wristplates, and pauldrons are shiny and smooth, with any dings and nicks obscured by a layer of fresh polish. Tsk. If he put care into his clothes rather than his armour, he wouldn't be such a sorry sight!

But perhaps it's a part of his charm: you can tell who he is from the first glance. A simple man, with a simple buzzcut, and a simple set of gear that doesn't look pretty but gets the job done.

"Gaudy," an unwelcome voice chimes in from behind us, "flashy, provocative, and impractical. Is that fashion?"

I ignore Jegrac's pathetic attempt to annoy me.

"Anyways, *Isaac*," I clarify. "If you ever want advice on how to improve your image, I'd be happy to help."

Jegrac makes another snarky comment behind my back, mockingly asking for my help, and I shoot a quick glare at him.

"I'll keep that in mind." Isaac says. "If I'm ever looking to... stand out, you'll be the first person I go to."

Jegrac's laughter rumbles through the air, loud and coarse, and my annoyance grows. I should have known better than to talk about fashion with a man who only cares about his armour and his mutt-loving companion who willingly pairs a trench coat with an obnoxiously large hat.

All things considered, I recognize how I *might* look - to them, at least - a *little* overdressed for this grubby marketplace. But I already feel out of place due to my dark skin - which draws even more attention now that flashes of gold embellish my wrists, neck, ears, eyes, and ankles - so why not capitalise on it? My magnificence is further magnified by the specs of gold lining the hem of my black sleeved top, which rests above my midriff. Similar golden lines dot the top of my high waisted black pants and the expensive sheer-fabric dress that flows around my legs like a waterfall, swirling about as it gives brief glimpses of the short-heeled sandals hiding below.

I look *glorious*.

As a family steps aside to let us through, their eyes lock onto me. I hold my head high, scouring them with a regal gaze. A little girl stands amongst them, staring up at me, her mouth hanging open. She receives a nod from me, and a huge gasp escapes her tiny body as her parents yank her out of the way. Then she is gone, lost in the crowd behind us.

Jegrac, to my irritation, chooses to talk again.

"So," he chimes, "are you going to tell him, or should I?"

Isaac nearly trips over himself as he shouts, "I KNEW IT!" He turns to me, his mouth set in a thin line. "What did you do *this time?!*"

My eyebrows rise at the accusation, but Jegrac interrupts my snippy reply.

"It's nothing awful, and it's not anyone's fault, necessarily - the guild just had a request. Something small, and easily manageable. I'm certain we-"

"*Small?!*"

I glare at Jegrac, who has fallen into place on Isaac's other side as we step out from the bustling marketplace and onto the much wider street. "Jegrac, I know you're used to having nuisances around, but you're avoiding the biggest issue we should have with this so-called request: we're not being asked to do this. We're being *told!*"

He rolls his eyes in response, begging me to smack the disrespect off his face.

"Listen here, you-"

Isaac delays our argument, resting heavy hands on our shoulders.

"Can you two save this for later? Let's just deal with this so I can finally go home."

Jegrac and I share a glance. Silently, we agree to set things aside - for now.

We pause on the sidewalk as Isaac fumes silently, his annoyance shrouded by the giant shadows of the sleek monochrome buildings lining the shopping district. It's a welcome contrast to the marketplace, which stains the city's splendour like dirt on a diamond. Here, the soil is replaced by intricate white stones glimmering with hidden runes, and the air is no longer thickened by the scent of stalls and food and people crowded together on busy paths. The gentle ambience is diluted by the glowing orbs lazily drifting above our heads as they absorb the sounds, smells, and bugs straying too far into the city.

The glint of grey and blue tinted armour catches my eye, and a quick scan of the area reveals a surprising amount of Nexus guards, their spears and halberds tucked into nearby nooks and crannies as they linger by store entrances or on city benches. Polished helmets turn to glare at my companions, suspicious glances and whispers aimed at the obnoxious symbols displayed on their clothes and backs.

Isaac draws my attention with a sigh.

"Why are you leading me back to the guild hall?" he asks. "Just..." His arms fall back to his sides, and he goes quiet. His shoulders slump, finally admitting defeat.

For a brief moment, the pang of guilt returns. Isaac's been talking about visiting his family for the past month, and he's not looking forward to cancelling once again. I did warn him to not make any plans, but still - can't blame him for being optimistic.

"Let's take a portal," I suggest, pointing through the crowd and towards the spacious ring of glowing doorways at the end of the busy street. "We'll explain on the way."

Isaac releases another sigh and reluctantly falls into place beside me.

I share a concerned glance with Jegrac over the Commander's slumped head. *Say something*, I mouth at him. When he raises his hands in confusion, my glare sharpens. Since Jegrac *clearly* thinks this debacle *isn't that big of a deal*, the responsibility of talking falls on him.

Jegrac chews his lip for a moment.

"So, earlier today... a messenger from the Council stopped by."

Isaac perks up slightly.

"They came to *us*?" he asks.

"Yeah." Jegrac looks over at me, and I offer an encouraging nod.

"They want us to take in a new... recruit. Someone from outside of the guild."

"Like Ezekiel?"

I shake my head, smiling at the memory of the young boy who joined our guild at his parents' humble request. The little guy was so eager to get to spend a day with the members of an *actual guild*, even if it was a bit annoying having him tag along.

"No. Not at all. *They* want him to *join*." I snap. "Some noble's kid. They're *telling* us that he's joining. Not asking. Not requesting. Apparently we're supposed to ignore the rules and regulations of the guild charter to take on some charity case."

Isaac frowns.

"Well, that's not as bad as I thought it would be," he admits. As we approach the shopping sector's gatehub, I gesture for the families behind us to pass while we take out our guildstones. They rush by with a quick thanks, hauling an assortment of books, bags, lunchboxes, briefcases, and portal stones as they scramble towards the different gates.

"Ah. I forgot, there's one other detail," Jegrac says, "we've been asked to let this new recruit go on a quest. With us. Today."

"Also!" I interject, "If you haven't guessed already, we're supposed to be babysitting this kid for free. For at least a month! *A month!* Ezekiel was fine because we only had to babysit him for a day. Now we're getting some spoiled brat for who knows how long!"

It's Jegrac's turn to look upset.

"Thirteen years old is not a brat," he counters. "He's not a toddler."

"Yeah, well, he might as well be," I scoff. "Some rich kid who's never had to do anything for themselves is going to be tagging along on our next adventure, thinking it's going to be a family-friendly, magical little tale where no one dies and everyone lives happily ever after. Does that *honestly* sound like a good idea to either of you?!"

Jegrac and Isaac refuse to hold my glare, which tells me I'm right, even if they won't admit it.

"Guess it's time to meet the new recruit," Isaac sighs as he walks over to an open portal. He waits for the attendant to reset the gateway while Jegrac and I keep our distance, standing behind white lines that shimmer against the smooth black stone beneath our feet.

"These coordinates, please," Isaac says as he hands the attendant his guildstone. The woman nods and places the gem into the side of the empty doorway.

The portal bursts to life. It releases a dull hum as the entranceway warps and ripples like a mirage, filling the inside of the doorway with a thin haze. As the surface solidifies, the attendant hands the crystal back to Isaac and bows, gesturing towards the active gate.

"Time to go, then," he announces as he starts to step through the portal. "Is there anything else I'm supposed to know, before I meet this... kid?"

I shrug. If we missed something, he'll figure it out when he meets the newbie. Knowing Isaac, this entire situation will be interpreted as *an opportunity for learning, growth, and a chance to lead the next generation towards a greater future.*

Yuck.

With a final sigh, Isaac steps through the portal and out of sight.

As I hand the attendant my guildstone, my eyes flicker to a nearby guard. He's been staring at me for a while with a curious expression, and so I give him a wave. But when his lips remain set in a tight grimace, I follow his gaze and realise his eyes are locked on the device linked to my waist.

I unclip the chronicler from my belt.

"Here, it's your turn," I tell Jegrac, shoving it into his hands. "See ya'!"

CHRONICLE 3
Recorded by Jegrac

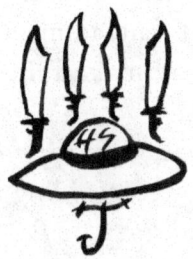

The smug, self-centred woman gives me a 'cute' little wave as she disappears through the blurry mesh leading to the guild hall. The surface of the portal ripples like an upset pond, a scene that could be calming and beautiful if it wasn't so unnatural.

Pall pushes his nose against my hand, and I give him a reassuring pat while we wait to use the nauseating gate.

"Oh dear!" the attendant gasps. "She forgot this!"

I choke down a laugh when she raises Neva's guildstone.

The well-polished jewel fits neatly in the attendant's soft and pampered hands, the subtle glow of the guild's insignia breaching the emerald's surface. The woman stares at me expectedly.

"Well, I'm sure she'll come back for it," I say with a grin.

She blinks in response, eyebrows raised, the gem still stretched towards me. After a sharp intake of breath, she folds her fingers over the luminous emerald and tucks it away.

"Okay then..." the woman says. "Your crystal, please?"

I dig through the pockets of my coat until a small green jewel finds its way into my palm.

"Thank you! This should only take a moment," the attendant announces as she takes the crystal from me. Her eyes narrow when she notices it's identical to the one Neva left behind, but she makes no comment.

I watch the sky as I wait, admiring the handful of birds brave enough to try and make a life in this city of empty metal and hostile glass.

Wind, coming down from the mountains, they tell me as they start to loop lower, avoiding the strong breeze that soon picks up overhead. *Prepare for the cold.*

I pull my coat a little tighter, making sure not to squeeze Neirut as he runs up my back. The three-eyed familiar scurries towards my ear, releasing a tiny squeak to alert me of an approaching presence.

"Excuse me? Sir. Please step away from the gate."

One of the Nexus guards approaches with a fake smile plastered on his face, his hand resting on the hilt of the sword at his side. "We're on the lookout for suspicious items, so I'd like to check out the tablet you've got there."

That blasted woman! So *this* is why Neva was so eager to hand the chronicler off to me!

Pall bristles at my side, and I release a quick, high pitched whistle only he can hear. My friend calms slightly, sitting back on his haunches and peering up at me, awaiting the next command.

"Certainly, sir."

The guard doesn't take the device from my outstretched hand, but looks over it carefully, poking at the small white crystals decorating the dark frame. He peers closely at the glowing blue runes hidden in the centre of each gem.

The attendant suddenly shrieks, her arms thrashing above her head. My legs grow tense, but then I notice the harmless beetle flitting around her. The guard's spear waves dangerously close to the woman's face, doing very little to scare off the creature and threatening to harm the person he is trying to protect.

Pressing my lips tight, I let out a low hum. The bug is lured away from further danger and takes solace on my hat.

It's a fragment of nature in this bustling, lifeless place; it does not deserve to be killed by fools who see it as a nuisance rather than a blessing.

The marketplace, at least, has trees for friendly birds and other creatures to rest, even if they are few and far between. But closer to the heart of the city, the freedom of grass is replaced by empty stone floors and shiny streets.

It's silent here, save for the sparse scavengers trying to make a living amongst the dead.

A place where only one species can thrive... it disturbs me.

"Doesn't seem to be anything suspicious," the guard finally grunts, "but I still have a few questions for a *Nomad* choosing to visit our city."

I steady my breathing and try to maintain my smile. Thankfully, the attendant steps forward, holding my guildstone up beside the one Neva had forgotten.

"He's part of a guild," she says. "His guildmate left this behind, so there's no need to question him any further, Carson. Let him go."

The guard listens carefully, but doesn't step back.

"You're talking about the foreigner who was in this line before him, right?" He scratches the stubble on his chin as he checks the glowing rocks. "It seems like something she'd remember. You don't find that odd?"

The attendant locks eyes with me, wordlessly communicating a message I don't quite understand, and then turns back to the guard.

"No, no, it's from the guy standing with them. The leader of their guild, I'd reckon. Isn't that right?" The question is directed at me, and she gives me another look. I start to catch on.

"Yes, of course!" I lie. "That's our Commander, always forgetting such simple things. Here, I'll take it back to him."

The guard steps away as the attendant drops Neva's crystal into my hand, and he finally releases the hilt of the sword on his hip.

"Well, on your way then," the guard says. "Next time, be sure to show off your guildstone right away, to prevent any future misunderstandings."

"Thanks for the warning." I bow to the attendant, who returns my gratitude with a sad smile.

Eager to leave, I give Pall a quick whistle and step into the portal, squeezing my eyes shut as it ripples over me. My stomach churns.

Opening my eyes again, I'm greeted by a familiar sight, and my gaze wanders up to the lush plants and playful critters lining the balcony of the *better* half of our vast guild hall. My nausea begins to settle as I check in on the different flowers, vines, ferns, and dwarf trees decorating the upper pathways. A few of the popular plants have been chewed bare by the small creatures flitting throughout our side of the hall, and I make a mental note of the ones that are the most barren. Liatris will want to know which plants need time to heal.

Neirut wiggles eagerly beneath my coat, and I lower my sleeve to the ground so that he can scamper across the shimmering white tiles of the guild hall. He scurries up a vined pillar to join his friends, squeaking eagerly about his return.

Following the balcony outlining the upper levels of the room, it's difficult to look at the *other* side of the hall, which sits sad and devoid of life. Boring, shiny decorations collect dust outside of Neva's room, accompanied by shelves bursting with her abundance of useless trinkets and fancy clothes. Yuina's area is bare beyond a handful of books and boxes she has yet to sort, and a thin layer of snow covers the railing near Frost's ice-encrusted door, where the air shimmers with a faint, deadly haze.

In the centre of the grand hall, Isaac and Liatris are talking with the new recruit.

Pall spots Liatris and lets out an eager bark, drawing her attention. A big smile sprouts across her thin face.

"Go ahead," I say, and he bounds towards her, tail wagging.

Liatris fixes the new recruit and Isaac with a quick grin before she sprints towards us, meeting my dog halfway. He licks her face eagerly.

"Good morning Jegrac!" she declares once she manages to pry herself free of the affectionate hound. "And I'm always happy to see you, Pall!"

Liatris raises the skirt of her simple yellow dress to wipe the slime off her green face. Her vibrant purple eyes thrum with excitement as she whispers, "Did you meet him yet? He said I'm the only dryad he knows!"

I'd seen the recruit this morning, briefly, before being coerced by Neva to join her on a hunt for the Commander.

He's looking around nervously, like a newborn fawn: scared, curious, and ignorant of the real world.

He stands there, stiff and uncomfortable, just like the oversized uniform hanging off his shoulders and hiding his hands beneath long sleeves. His eyes wander to the bannisters and various decorations spread throughout the guild hall, flickering back to Isaac as the Commander tries to hold a conversation with the nervous newbie.

Perhaps Neva has a point; he looks *weak*. While he doesn't fit the shoulders or arms of his uniform, he does manage to fill the stomach with a roundness that continues up to his cheeks and makes him look soft and harmless.

And yet, he may grow if we give him a chance.

Leaving Pall to enjoy Liatris's pampering, I casually approach the Commander and the new recruit. My pace is even and measured to keep our skittish guest from feeling the need to flee.

Before I've reached them a flash strikes the corner of my eye. Neva is standing by the balcony, wrapped in a bright blue dress that gleams against her skin.

She grabs the railing and nimbly hops over the bannister, her garments restrained by a careful hand as she drops onto the colourless tiles below, landing with a gentle tap as her heels touch the floor.

If it were me, I'd have tossed myself over the railing with Pall in my arms, rolling as I hit the ground to keep it from hitting back. That, or have chosen to take the nearby staircase like a *normal* person.

Peering at Neva, a tight, uncomfortable feeling twists inside my chest as she approaches. The lack of sound, the unnerving serenity as she carefully presses her dress around her, the quiet calculation behind her appearance and every action...

it's unsettling. Nature always provides clues about what to expect: a thud as something hits the earth, or the rustle of twigs and leaves as the wind changes. Neva, however, offers no hints. She is *unnatural*.

Regardless of my thoughts on the matter, her little show has the impact she wants. Liatris notices the new attire and eagerly rushes over to admire the vibrant fabric, Isaac looks somewhat impressed, and the new recruit's mouth hangs open.

Neva revels in the attention for a few moments, even offering Liatris some pointers in exchange for more compliments, and then waves at the Commander.

"Heathe, you live in Borderik, right?"

Isaac eyes her warily.

"Why?" he asks as she approaches. His grimace grows as Neva's smile widens.

"Hm. I thought so. How convenient!"

The Commander peers at her, crossing his arms across his chest, but doesn't interrupt.

"Well," Neva continues, "we have to do a quest, and you want to go home, right? So why not do both?"

Isaac trips over his words as he struggles to find a response.

"I'll have to let them know," he eventually mumbles, "because we can't just visit my family without warning. Let me make sure it's okay for *all* of us to visit, before we-"

Liatris releases a squeal of joy as she claps her hands. "Oh, Isaac, is this true? Will we get to meet the wonderful humans who sired you? Your progenitors? The man who planted your seed and the woman who helped you bloom?"

"Please, Liatris," Neva groans, "don't use the word 'seed' or 'sired' like that again."

The innocent sprite gives her a polite smile, feet tapping against the stone floor while she mulls over what Neva has said.

"Okay!" Liatris nods repeatedly when she finally speaks.

Neva turns to me.

"And Jegrac - haven't you hogged that thing for long enough?" she asks, pointing at the device attached to my side.

I hold it out before she can change her mind, eager to be rid of the strange apparatus.

CHRONICLE 4
Recorded by Neva Oyii

I dangle the chronicler between two steady fingers, careful of any dirt that might rub off on my clothes.

"Alrighty, time to get ready!" Liatris declares in an obnoxiously cheery voice, and Jegrac steps her way, beckoning for Pall to follow. The bubbly dryad turns to the newbie and says, "It was nice meeting you, Damian! I think we're gonna' be good friends. See you in a bit!"

The boy grins as he mumbles a barely audible reply. Liatris curtsies before skipping away, and Jegrac tilts his hat as he and his dog fall into step beside the dryad. Tipping my head to eavesdrop on their conversation as they go, I overhear the start of a brief and uninteresting discussion about the tacky plants and critters littering their side of the guild hall.

I also make a quick mental note of the boy's name; *Damian*.

"So, kid," I say to the newbie, "you ever been on a quest before?"

Damian's face lights up with pure, unfiltered excitement, wide eyes accompanied by an open-mouthed smile.

"No, but I'm ready!" he replies. "I've always wanted to travel outside of Nexus on my own."

Accepting his claims with a nod, I do a quick scan of the boy, taking stock of his softness and the high-quality tailoring on the oversized white shirt and the black dress pants hanging over the back of his shoes. The boy stands a little taller as my eyes return to his pudgy face.

"It's going to be dangerous," I warn, "so I hope you're prepared."

He straightens up, drawing his shoulders back and puffing out his chest as he announces: "My dad hired the best swordsmen in the land to tutor me, so I can handle it! I promise I won't be a burden." His cheeks flush with pride. Taking another glance, I bite back a question about how much training he's had when his body suggests a different story. Sure, he's not overweight, but he does have the rounded softness of someone who has never worked hard for a single meal.

Enh, whatever. No need to comment on it; if he survives his first fight, he'll gradually start to improve. And if he doesn't?

Well. In that case, Aria will have to find a way for us to carefully and quietly remove him from the guild.

Regardless of how I feel and how useless this child may be, we'll do our best to keep him alive so he can grow.

My attention shifts to the device in my hands; it's starting to hurt my fingers. I need to pass it off to someone else, along with the responsibilities accompanying it.

Seeing Damian gives me an idea.

"Kid, I've got a *special* job for you." My words are careful and precise, and Isaac raises an eyebrow as he rudely turns his mouth into a suspicious frown. The boy's face, however, lights up even more.

Keeping a firm grip, I lift the chronicler towards him, eager to be rid of it. Aria will want to check it before we go, and why should I have to deal with her? Damian ought to meet her. She can give him the blunt and honest welcome he deserves.

"Can you bring this to the kind old lady waiting just beyond those doors?" I ask in a sweet voice, gesturing towards the far end of the guild hall. "You'll find her waiting for you in the library downstairs. I'm sure she'll be happy to meet you! Here, go ahead. Take it."

Isaac snatches the chronicler before the kid can grab it.

CHRONICLE 5
Recorded by Isaac Heathe

"Neva! Stop offering the chronicler to non-guild members! Are you *trying* to piss Aria off *again?!* You *know* she hates having to erase and rewrite transcripts whenever you do this!"

Damian's eyes widen, shoulders slouching as he steps back, putting some distance between us. An apology dances on the tip of my tongue, but I swallow it back. Is the truth something worth apologising for? It's a reality this boy needs to accept - he's just a guest. Better he hear it now, rather than later.

Neva's lips curl into a smirk.

"Oh? Well, if you say so, *Commander*. You know best!"

She spins on her heel, her sapphire dress swirling as she walks away.

"Excuse me, sir," Damian asks in a small and timid voice, "but who is Aria?"

I answer his question with a smile and gesture towards the giant wooden doors at the end of the hall.

"Why don't we go meet her?"

Our footsteps echo as we walk, and when the silence grows awkward I attempt to continue our conversation by sharing some advice.

"Just remember, when it comes to Aria, the less you say, the better, and if you do say something, be polite." We stop in front of the massive, intricately carved doors blocking us from heading any further. One of them is propped open slightly, and Damian reaches around the door to give it a hearty tug.

It doesn't budge.

He pulls on it again, a little harder this time. When it still refuses to move, I reach over his head and pry the massive door open.

"Uh, thanks," Damian mutters as he pushes further into the depths of our guild hall. His ears are flushed red, and my gaze darts away when he looks back at me. I wave a hand to usher him onwards.

"I can barely open that door on my own, so I'm glad you helped," I say, trying to sound sincere. Damian's curly brown hair bobs up and down as he accepts my thanks.

Leaving the main room behind us, comfort waits in this smaller space, where the ceiling slopes down to a less intimidating height. On my tip-toes, I can just barely graze the ceiling with my fingertips (which I've done many times before, but *never* with an audience).

Damian perks up, words pouring out as he jabs at one of the pictures lining the smooth cerulean walls.

"Is that you?!" he asks a little too eagerly, his light brown eyes wide as they dart between myself and the framed image.

"Who made this for you? It's really good! And is it real? And, and...!"

His cheeks redden as he swallows back another question, falling silent as he waits for my response.

Leaning over his shoulder to peer at the parchment tucked behind the tarnished glass, I raise my sleeve to wipe away the dust. It's a painting from when I was only a few years older than our new recruit. A travelling artist had offered to draw us, showering us with praise and proclamations of inspiration after having witnessed a brave guild take down a horde of wyverns. Neva ended up buying his work, and had stored it in her room until Aria eventually claimed it for the guild's records. Then, like clockwork, the archivist had it framed and hung in this hall later that day.

It's a surprisingly detailed picture, portraying Neva, Yuina, and I posing by the beasts' remains, set against the scorched slope of Mount Motamir. Little fires add touches of red and orange to the brown and grey backdrop, contrasting with the violet and emerald scales of the slain creatures.

Frost had been there too, but he didn't bother sticking around after the job was done, much to the artist's disappointment. There are hints of him, though, in the melting pillars of ice sticking out from the dirt and stone behind us.

"It's a drawing from a long time ago," I say, the faint scent of smoke and ash tickling my nostrils as the memory plays out in my head, "and we didn't look so pristine after having slain a nest of wyverns! A lot more burned, with charred clothes, and tired smiles..."

Damian stares at me with such intense awe that heat rises up my neck and into my cheeks. The new recruit sprints from frame to frame, his eyes wide and his mouth agape as he absorbs the visual history spread throughout the hallway.

He's lucky; Aria has added even more decorations in the last few days, and the blue walls are obscured by articles, artifacts, and artwork that cover every available surface from the charcoal mahogany ceiling to the lined wooden floor. As I watch Damian, a smile begins to form on my face. He has a familiar eagerness, one I'd forgotten after years of adventuring.

I answer a few more of Damian's questions, until we reach the end of the hall. He stops in front of the staircase, his shoulders slouched and eyes downcast as he turns to me.

"I hope I'm not being a nuisance, sir. It's just - well, your guild, um..." His voice drops as his ears go red. "Sorry. It's not important."

He sprints down the stone steps before I can respond.

His heavy footsteps mingle with Aria's soft humming, which echoes up from the depths below. It's a good sign. She's (probably) not going to be *too* bothered by our interruption.

At the bottom of the steps, Damian lingers awkwardly by the entrance to the Archives, his hand resting on the ornate wooden door. A warm glow emanates from the crack in the entranceway, accompanied by the smell of old books and crumbling parchment.

When I finally catch up, Damian pushes the door open with a heavy creak, and then presses himself back against the grey stone to let me pass.

We walk out into the wide, circular room. I maneuver around a collapsed pillar of books collecting dust on the floor, raising a hand to keep Damian from following. The door groans as it closes, and Aria calls my name from somewhere amongst the shelves. I push past an overcrowded cabinet, scouring the room for our guild's archivist.

"Stop bumbling around like an ox, Isaac! Be patient, I'm almost there!"

Aria steps out from a gap hidden amongst rows of teetering documents and old tomes. Adjusting her spectacles, she peers past me, and her eyes lock onto the new recruit. I squeeze against a nearby cabinet as the older woman gently pushes me aside to hobble closer to Damian.

"Um, hello, ma'am," he says politely as she stares him down. "I'm Damian, the-"

She cuts him off with a curt wave. "Yes, yes, I know who you are. It's about time we met."

The room falls silent while Aria shuffles around the new recruit, sizing him up like a fish at the Nexus market. She grumbles something beneath her breath, shakes her head, and then her eyes snap to me.

"As for you," she declares, "why are YOU here?! Isn't there a gentleman bartender you ought to visit before leaving town again?"

Oh *rift*.

"No, there is NOT, Aria. He's just a friend. Also, my private life is none of your business!"

Heat rises in my cheeks, ignited further by the new recruit's bewildered stare.

"If you like him, Isaac, it's time to stop dragging your feet and-"

Aria notices the look on my face, and bites her tongue.

"Alright, alright, I get it. You're a grown man, and you need to make your own decisions. Just wanted to offer some advice, that's all. Didn't mean any offence."

Before I can reply, she shifts her attention back to Damian.

Aria frowns as she examines the startled boy. Pulling her shawl up onto her shoulders, she announces, "Well. This boy's dead."

"Aria!" I exclaim, horrified by her honesty.

Her wispy white hair drifts up and down as she limps back to her favourite, well-worn, over-cushioned chair. Aria pulls a tea cup from out of thin air and sips it as she glares at Damian.

He stares back at her, stunned.

"I brought the matter up to the Council as soon as we received their message, but I haven't been able to revoke any of this nonsense." She takes another long sip as she sinks deeper into the pillows engulfing her frail body, her brown robes blending into the colourless recliner. "I'll file a grievance claim, but this situation is unprecedented, so don't get your hopes up." She pauses, and then adds, "If you're truly worried about having this child's blood on your hands due to the whims of idiot nobles, there are a few things I haven't tried, if you're willing to take the risk..."

"No, it's alright." I interrupt. "Most of the us have accepted the Council's odd request, so don't bother. And Damian's eager to be here! Right, Damian?"

The boy nods, but it's hard to ignore his quivering lower lip.

"I see," Aria murmurs. "And Neva told you all about the quest she found, I assume?"

I shake my head. "All I know is that it's probably dangerous and is somehow conveniently close to where I live."

"*Probably* dangerous?" She lets out a soft chuckle. "Well, fair enough. At the very least, I will see if I can shorten his-" she pauses, looks at the boy, and corrects herself, "-if I can shorten *Damian's* time with us."

Aria stares over the edge of her porcelain cup.

"Listen closely, boy. I understand you've been coerced into this nonsense by your family and the unknowable motives of the Council, but you must recognize that your presence here puts pressure on all of us." She places her drink down, laces her thin fingers together in her lap, and leans forward.

"Despite what the Council and your father may say, you are *not* a part of this guild. And yet, every member of Honour's Stand will do whatever they can to keep you safe. Listen to them. If they tell you to stay out of the way, it is *your job* to stay out of the way. Do you understand?"

Damian stares at her with wide eyes. She clears her throat, and he straightens up, standing a little taller as he nods repeatedly.

"Yes, ma'am, I understand. I won't be a burden, I promise."

Aria leans back, pleased with his response.

"Good to hear," she says. Pulling the cup back into her hands, she gulps down the last of her tea.

"That's all," Aria announces. "As much as I enjoy the company, there are folders to file and transcripts to transfer, so I must cut this conversation short. Run along now, you two."

"Wait." I lift the chronicler towards her. "Don't you need to see this?"

Aria chuckles.

"Of course not!" the guild's archivist says as she waves it away. "I won't need any more data until you've completed your next quest. Bring it to me as soon as you get back, alright?"

She pauses, and then points at one of the larger crystals lining the outside of the device. It shines with a faint blue glow. "Just so you know, Isaac, there's no need to leave it on all the time. Do you remember how to turn the chronicler off?"

My finger rests on the sapphire stone.

"What, do I just press-"

CHRONICLE 6
Recorded by Jegrac

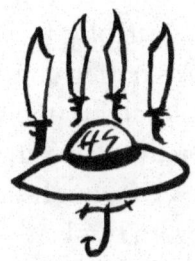

"See? It's on." The Commander withdraws his hand as the crystals lining the chronicler flicker with an unnatural blue glow.

Liatris stares over my shoulder with wide eyes, fingers extended to poke at the air as she pretends to turn on her own imaginary chronicler.

Letting the leather reins drop into Isaac's grasp, I twist to face Liatris, and she leans over the thin wooden board separating us from the inner comforts of the caravan. My coat pinches my side as I hoist the device closer to the dryad's face.

Her vibrant purple eyes light up, and a small green finger escapes the sleeves of her cloak to trace the jewels dotting the chronicler. A surprised, excited gasp slips out from between her lips as the stones glimmer in response to her touch.

"When can I wear it?" she asks.

I shrug. According to the Commander, each member of the guild is supposed to use it at some point. Aria also expects us to refrain from switching frequently, and to turn it off whenever we're doing something boring or mundane.

"Eventually, Liatris. But not yet."

Her shoulders begin to droop, and then rise once more as she shakes the gloom away. The abundant ferns decorating her head bounce in response.

While Liatris amuses herself with Aria's latest invention, my eyes wander past her, searching for Pall in the depths of our carriage. As expected, he's resting on the tattered rug near the back. My companion's loyalty to the frayed cloth makes me chuckle; Neva had offered Pall an extremely plush and fancy bed as a gift for Winter's Day, but he had stubbornly refused it in favour of the well-worn blanket.

Pall sneaks a glance at the boy seated across from him, and a pulse of suspicion carries through our bond. We're still getting used to the presence and scent of a stranger in our caravan, but I try to send a wave of calm back to the sceptical hound. His sharp green eyes dart towards me, and then drift shut, accepting the fragile assurance.

Damian doesn't notice this exchange, his attention snared by the many novelties and baubles surrounding him. His face is covered by the same dumb-struck awe he'd shown when first entering this cabin.

Though his stunned, slack-jawed response is easy to mock, his simple curiosity and interest in his surroundings isn't a surprise. From the outside, our carriage blends in with every other cart and wagon on the road; the wood is simple and un-painted, with a few knicks, scratches, and hastily added patches to cover up accidents and surprises from previous adventures. Even though the caravan is larger than most, there's nothing fancy or decadent to give the impression that anything of value is hidden inside.

Step through one of the side doors or under the dark curtain in the back, however, and the boring exterior is replaced by a beautiful disaster. Honestly, anyone unfamiliar with our guild might assume we took several different carriages and smashed them into an oddly cohesive mess. The benches lining either side of the walls have been claimed with unique furnishings, ornaments, and paint marking the territories of each member of the guild.

My attention is drawn away from admiring our reliable vehicle as we start to drift off the paved path and onto the gravel lining the side of the road. I release a low whistle, signalling to the horses tugging us along. Mayweather and Daisy reply with soft huffs, correcting our course as they trot back onto the stone trail. Isaac doesn't notice, his eyes distant and the reins loose in his hands.

He barely acknowledges me when I gently pry the ends of the long leather straps from his grasp before we can crash. A goofy grin covers his face, and the lecture about safety dies in my throat, tucked away for a better time. The Commander's attention is elsewhere; is he playing memories of his family in his head? As his lips move silently, it becomes clear he's thinking about what to say and do when he finally returns home.

I decide not to interrupt his happiness, but the Commander blinks when his fingers tighten around nothing. His daydream fades.

Isaac turns to me, and then notices Liatris, who is still enamoured by the chronicler. He reaches over to pull up the hood of her enormous grey cloak.

"Sorry, 'Tris, but we're still near the city, so it stays on," Isaac says. The dryad sticks out her lower lip in an adorable pout.

"You don't have to keep it on if you don't want to," Neva chimes in from the depths of the caravan. Liatris considers the suggestion, frowns, and then chooses to keep her floral face hidden.

"Has it been long enough yet?" the dryad whispers. "When is it my turn to wear the chronicler?"

Neva shuffles into the space beside Liatris and taps her on the shoulder.

"Not right now, that's for sure." She stops to squint beneath the bright sunlight, raising a pampered palm to shield her face from the mid-sun's glare. Pulling the patterned curtain down to cast a shadow across her face, she turns to the Commander and gestures at the road ahead. "Am I the only one who noticed? Please tell me one of you has already figured it out..."

I peer out at the wide pathway, which is littered with everything from beautiful to beaten horses, domesticated dogs, a variety of packbeasts, and endless streams of people heading to and from Nexus. Until now, my attention has been on the bugs and birds flitting through the air, listening quietly to the tales they tell, and admiring the brave bursts of green breaking through cracks in the weakening white road.

"Look at how the travellers are spaced out," Neva mutters. "There must be a security check hidden up ahead, or-"

A slight bump shakes the caravan as we pass through the edges of the illusion, and I grimace as magic washes over me.

"-it's right here."

My hand snaps up, covering my nose and mouth. The sickly sweet smell of repellent and incense forces me to swallow back bile and take careful breaths through my fingers. Pall whimpers behind me, but the whine disappears when Liatris blankets him in soothing murmurs, her gentle hands tucked against his ears.

As he begins to calm, so do I. Hoping to distract myself from the unnatural sensations pressing into my skin, I scour the area up ahead. Two white tents flank the widened path, and bright sunlight obscures the shimmering runes painted into the colourless cloth. Beneath the massive shadows of the tents, a few Nexus guards lead a cart onto a freshly terraformed patch while another carriage passes by on the main road.

"Thank Yiatsu for this new system," Isaac sighs as we inch closer to the checkpoint. "It took us forever to get through last time!"

He's right. Thanks to the craftsmanship of some talented geomancers, the white asphalt has widened far enough to fit 4 carts side by side. It also explains why we didn't notice things sooner. Unlike the previous checkpoints we've encountered, multiple vehicles and travellers can now be investigated at the same time.

Directly ahead of us, the guards throw open the curtain at the back of a caravan, peeking inside to chat with passengers.

The Commander swears under his breath, and I share his concern. Why are they acting so diligent? But then the reason catches my eye, a glimmer within a sea of dull pauldrons and unpolished spears.

A familiar white and gold emblem flickers into sight, and my hands drop to the daggers tucked in my belt. That's a mistake, however - my stomach churns in protest, and I'm forced to re-cover my exposed nose and mouth.

The use of white and gold is revered and restricted, and the simple symbol of a sword within a shield can only mean one thing.

A High Champion is here.

Isaac takes a sharp breath, his face pale and his eyes wide. He leans back into the cart to warn the rest of the guild, but Neva angrily cuts him off.

"I know what you're going to ask," she snaps, "but if Liatris doesn't want it, I'm not doing it."

The dryad's face is fixed with a steady frown, but she silently shuffles to the bench in the middle of the caravan. Pall lets out a sullen whine when she leaves him, and his misery amplifies as ripples through our bond.

I know exactly how he feels.

It's heartbreaking how Liatris no longer protests. She clearly hates having to do this.

Neva releases an exasperated huff as she settles into place across from Liatris. She rubs her fingers together to warm her magic, and then whispers sternly to Damian: "If anyone asks, we're all human. It saves time, so don't say anything else."

"She's serious, so keep your mouth shut," I add, and the boy nods. Liatris sits up a little too straight as Neva carefully applies her unnatural but necessary magic over the dryad's beautiful mass of ferns and vines, transforming it into boring human hair. Her fingers trace down to Liatris's face, and the verdant lines covering her features like weathered bark fade and warp into peachy-white skin. She looks like any other human citizen of Nexus, although her eyes remain a vibrant violet.

"I hate doing this," Liatris sighs.

Neva takes the dryad's hand, continuing to cast a veil over her emerald complexion.

"How many times do I have to tell you?" she mutters, her voice rising with hostility as it lowers into a growl. "Say *no*. If you're willing to fight, we have your back. But I'm not going to answer for you."

Pall trots over from his bed at the back of the caravan to snuggle his head into Liatris's lap, and she welcomes the gesture. Neva, however, yanks her hands away. The dryad scratches behind his ears as Neva readjusts her bracelet, her fingers flickering with excess magic as she changes the stones dotting her jewellery from white to blue.

Isaac nudges me.

"I'll remain up here, if you want to go join Pall," he whispers. "You can keep an eye on Damian, too. He could probably use the support."

Grateful for the chance to avoid the scrutiny of the upcoming security check, I clamber into the back to join the rest of the guild. I carefully step over Neva's legs, which are extended onto the oversized footrest she always tries to shove beneath her well-cushioned and excessively decorated bench. She sits with her eyes closed, her breathing even, with one of her many fictional adventuring novels closed in her lap, manicured fingers tucked between the well-worn pages.

"Is this really the time to sleep?" I remark. Neva only manages a glare, indicating that it's best to leave her alone. The pressure from keeping up multiple glamours must be weighing heavily on her mind.

Liatris has moved to our bench at the back of the caravan, where she rests beneath the skylight Isaac installed for her plants. Pall lies between our feet in his makeshift bed, rising for a quick pat as I settle into place across from Neva and beside Liatris.

"Good boy," I say, ruffling his fur before leaning back against the wooden boards. Content, my faithful companion rests his head on my boots, burying his nose in the familiar scent. Just like me, he's struggling against the invasive and revolting magic filling the air.

Glancing at Liatris, I find her staring up at the sun with empty eyes, the halo of light casting a sickening spotlight over her unfamiliar face.

Hopefully, this stop will be quick and painless, so we can be gone and done with this place where a dryad needs to hide herself from the spite and shame of people who make no effort to understand her. Without the glamour, the bright beam of the skylight would have made her face a glorious sight; a denizen of lush fields with emerald-green skin, enjoying life amongst the many plants she has raised and chosen as her companions for this adventure.

But for now, her smile is gone. She endures this, so it can return.

Isaac slows the cart, adopting a polite, cheery voice as he makes conversation with the guards. In any other situation, his words would be easy to hear, but in the centre of this glamour my energy is turned inward to settle my churning stomach, accompanied by ragged and uneven breaths.

Familiar phrases break through my concentration, a stranger's voice echoing in my ears... *this is just routine, sir; yes, it has to do with the riftspawn summonings; you're a Nexus citizen, I'm assuming? Ah, thank you, we will return your guild-stone in just a moment... a Commander? I see, well, we won't keep you for too long. Do you have...?"*

Before they finish the question, Neva is already at the front of the caravan, a folded piece of parchment and her guildstone offered to Isaac as he starts to turn back, a question on his lips. He blinks, surprised, and then thanks her. He passes the items forward as he resumes his casual dialogue with the guards.

Pall whimpers, and I reach down to place a comforting hand upon his back.

"We'll be done soon, boy," I say. "Just a little longer."

But as Isaac starts to say goodbye, and the guard thanks *Honour's Stand* for being so cooperative, another voice interrupts. Isaac's tone changes from polite to guarded.

"*Oh rift*," Neva swears beneath her breath, "two of them."

The curtain at the end of the carriage is yanked open, and I bite down on a few curses of my own as two High Champions stare back at me.

Through teary eyes, I manage to spot the white and gold emblems adorning the man's wrists and the woman's crown right before the stench of repulsor magic sends me reeling. Pall starts to hack as quietly as he can, and I swallow back bile while fixing a polite grimace to my face for the two strangers sizing up our guild.

Morrowfir, give us strength, I plead silently. Pall and I will not be able to endure this assault on our senses for much longer.

A man with a stretched, joyless smile watches us with pale blue eyes, his thin lips pressed tight as his empty gaze lingers on Liatris for a disturbingly long time. From this close, breathing through my nose is pure agony - he smells like a funeral, and without his glamours, he'd probably look like a corpse. His rubbery skin is pulled tight, with the paleness of a being that skirts away from the sun. I try not to twitch when he leans deeper into the caravan, the scent of embalming fluids and cleansers flooding my nostrils, forcing me to squeeze my eyes shut to will away an encroaching headache.

With sickening reverence, Damian whispers a name under his breath; *Foivos*.

Behind Foivos is the other High Champion, who looks much healthier than her ghastly peer. She lingers at the outskirts of the carriage, glancing over each of us in turn. A disappointed look rests on her stern face, and she cranes her neck as if trying to peer past us.

"Don't bother, Rahma. He's not here."

The woman's face sinks, her shoulders dropping as she takes one more hopeful peek into the caravan. Unlike the man, her scent is comforting, and I pray to Morrowfir she will move closer, so the musk of fresh earth and tilled soil will overpower the moist miasma thickening the air.

Rahma crosses her arms and steps aside, her figure no longer hidden behind her cadaverous companion. Dark clay and silt blend in with her brown skin and stain her emerald sari with smudges and handprints, and her scowl is tight, just like the chestnut bun at the back of her head.

Foivos climbs up and into the caravan, surveying us with a thin smile as he steps toward Liatris.

Before we can stop him, his arms dart out and he clasps Liatris's hand, his sunken eyes narrowing. The glamoured dryad gasps, but she says nothing, and Neva slides her foot towards her, reaching for Liatris's bare feet.

She's too late. The foul man fills our carriage with the stench of glamour as he pushes against the magic Neva had carefully crafted.

The peach skin fades, and Liatris stiffens when her green bark starts to break through. Foivos stares at it, a curious expression crossing his face. His eyes narrow.

"Something the matter?" Rahma asks. She leans towards us.

A dagger slips into my hand as the bench creaks beneath my shifting weight, and Pall starts to bear his fangs. Neva moves too, shuffling calmly to the edge of her seat, a quiet glint of metal tucked into her palm. Isaac lingers outside of this scene, hand on the hilt of his sword, eyes darting between us, waiting for someone to make the first move.

Damian, however, remains oblivious to our growing hostility, his mouth open and his gaze enamoured by the High Champions invading our space.

Before my blade can slip between his ribs, Foivos snatches Liatris's other hand and places it on top of where the glamour has disappeared, hiding her true skin from sight. He stares in her eyes for a moment, then looks to Neva, his non-existent eyebrows arched high, and he shuffles back.

He turns to Rahma and shakes his head.

"Sorry, my mistake," he declares, "just another false alarm."

"Don't be a creep," Rahma mutters as she steps away from the caravan. "Besides, if Frost isn't here, this is a waste of time. Let them go."

After giving Liatris one last look, Foivos nods, and pulls the curtain closed behind him.

The wooden wall braces my weight as the tension dissolves, and I sink against it, letting out a sigh of relief.

We sit in silence as Isaac exchanges a few forced pleasantries with the High Champions, and the wheels below us creak when the horses start moving forward.

Before we are far enough away to safely start a conversation, Damian pipes up: "Wow, I can't believe it!" His face is alight as he turns to each of us, eventually settling on Liatris, who stares back at him with a sad but welcoming smile. "We got to see Foivos the Pure and Rahma of the Earth! I can't... I just... wow. Two High Champions!"

Neva ignores him, standing up and pushing one of Liatris's many potted plants aside so she can sit. She grabs Liatris's hand, quickly pressing another glamour on top of the one Foivos had removed, concealing the bark once more.

"What the *rift* was that?" Neva hisses as she studies her work, her lip raised and teeth pressed into a snarl. "Damn it! I should have been more careful. Why didn't I put an extra layer on top? And how did I not see this? That crusty old man wouldn't have been able to remove it if I'd-"

"It's okay, Neva," Liatris says as cheerfully as she can. "How could you have known that a High Champion would be here?"

"*It's my job to know!*" Neva snaps, and Liatris jumps in her seat.

She remains there for a few more moments, fuming, and then firmly shakes her head before stalking back to her bench. Liatris and I share a worried glance, but neither of us dare to push the issue any further. There will be time later to discuss Foivos and his strange reaction to the dryad's skin, and to figure out whether or not we should be concerned.

We fall into an uneasy silence. I give Pall a pat, and then clamber back to the empty space beside the Commander, since I want to be as close as possible to fresh air and freedom. We should pass the threshold soon, and I'm eager to leave this glamoured dome.

As we draw further away from the Nexus guards and the High Champions, I spot the thin wire that snakes over the road and separates the inside of this glamour from the reality outside. Following the length of the winding black line, I glare at the illusionists sitting in the field, holding onto the wire as sweat beads down their faces and soaks through their violet robes. Amongst them are revulsors, cloaked in a sickly green and red to symbolise a specialisation in magic meant for warding away living things. More illusionists and revulsors sit in the field on the opposite side, also clutching the thrumming black wire.

And then they are gone, along with the pressure, and I can breathe freely again. The aroma of grass and the rustle of nature rushes back, and the world springs to life with a great buzzing and chirping, harmonising with the whispers of leaves on the wind.

Isaac gently guides the horses onto a less trodden pathway cutting through the prairie, the wheels of the cart releasing a soft groan of protest as we move from the unnatural smoothness of the main road and onto cultivated dirt and stone. Here, the weeds have become braver, forming desperate patches of green in the areas where wheels and hooves rarely tread.

As I settle back for the long road ahead, my eyelids grow heavy, beckoning me to keep them closed. Placing my hands into my pockets, Aria's strange device bumps against my left wrist.

Peeking at it through the shadows of my wide-brimmed hat, I find the jewel the Commander had pressed earlier.

CHRONICLE 7
Recorded by Isaac Heathe

"It's what Aria would want, right?"

Liatris withdraws her fingers from the device on my belt.

Her face lights up along with the gems dotting the chronicler, and a gentle vibration tickles my thigh as Aria's creation emits a faint hum.

"Thank you, 'Tris." I reply. The dryad's smile blossoms even wider.

She returns to admiring the passing scenery, her elbows resting on the cushioned barrier dividing us from the horses.

"What forest is that?" she asks, waving at the trees lining the edge of the field, which draw closer and closer the further we get from the city.

I shrug.

"If you want a proper answer, you'll have to ask Yuina when she gets back from her quest with Frost. But I do remember my parents always warning me about passing the treeline... they told me the forest belonged to the Nomads."

Liatris raises her uncanny brown eyebrows; for some reason, the dryad has yet to scrub the illusion magic off her face.

"Oh! Like Jegrac?" she exclaims. "But as a sapling, didn't you want to meet his people? And what if his tribe had been there? You could have become friends while sprouting!"

Her questions are innocent and naive, but they hit hard, reopening scars from conversations and arguments shouted over my shoulder and across the dinner table. Echoes spill into my ears, whispers of a time when I was younger, angrier, and much less polite. The memories fade as I remind myself to appreciate how peaceful our family gatherings have become, now that I've learned to swallow comments that highlight the growing divide between my personal experience and the prejudices of an isolated town.

Liatris stares at me, head tilted as she waits for a response. Looking into those wide violet eyes, part of me wants to declare I'd known better and had fought to maintain the friendships made beyond the treeline, but I'd be lying. Before I left Borderik, there was no reason to question what I was told.

So instead, I offer her a flimsy excuse.

"Not every Nomad is like Jegrac," I say, "so my parents were just being careful. I think."

She squints at me, her piercing gaze threatening to uncover the weak excuse for my family's ignorance. But she lets it go and starts shifting uncomfortably in her seat.

"I'm getting sore from all this sitting," Liatris complains. "Can we stop?"

This question, thankfully, is easier to answer.

"Sure. Why not?"

"We *just* stopped at the last town," Neva comments from the roof of our carriage. "Can't we wait a little longer?"

The curtain behind us whacks our shoulders as it is flung aside.

"Pall and the horses would enjoy running through the fields," Jegrac counters, leaning past our heads and out of the caravan, "A short break couldn't hurt."

Acknowledging the sturdy beasts in front of me and the pleading look on Liatris's face, I steer the horses towards the side of the trail.

"Hey, Liatris. We've gotten far enough away from the city, so you can take that off." Neva leans over the roof above us and gestures at the dryad's face. "Honestly, you could have removed it a while ago. Did you forget how? Prime your hands with magic, and then wipe it away."

Liatris presses her fingers together, a gentle green glow sprouting from beneath the layer of peach skin as she furiously scrubs at the glamours hiding her true self.

"I'll take over," Jegrac says, slipping the reins out of my grasp. He turns to Liatris, giving her a playful shove. "Go on, girl. Get outta' here!"

The dryad grabs my sleeve, tugging me off my seat as she hops onto the road. Stumbling behind her, we sprint down the short incline and leap over the ditch lined with loose stones and damp soil.

Damian and Pall follow shortly thereafter, joining us at the edge of the field. The air thrums with life, long strands of grass brushing my shins and ankles as we walk into the bustling emerald sea. A bright orange butterfly flutters past Liatris's nose, and she giggles, admiring the flitting insects flowing and swirling around our heads. I stare out towards the forest to scour the trees. The shadows give no indication of an impending threat, and Neva will warn us if something dangerous is headed our way, so worrying is pointless. My armour begins to loosen as I toy with the clasps, my shoulders and chest relaxing once the pressure disappears.

Liatris's grin widens while she starts chasing after another butterfly, but then her feet come to a sudden halt, an unknown force holding her in place like a rag doll. She turns, staring up at me through her mossy eyelashes. "Isaac, please, can I..."

A painful tremor seeps into her voice, a restraint she has yet to overcome.

"Of course, 'Tris! You don't have to ask. Just go!"

Before the words have even left my lips she's sprinted into the grass, the plants waving wildly as they greet their new friend.

"Wow, so this is where Dahlia's Field ends?" Damian exclaims. He takes a few careful steps into the clearing. "I've never been out here before! We only take the main road when travelling. This is a nice change."

His light brown eyes survey the field as a beetle buzzes by his head, and he bolts out of the way, startled by the large insect. The bug floats by, undeterred, but the boy's ears and cheeks fill with a vibrant red. He coughs, fixes his collar, and attempts to change the subject.

"So, where exactly are we headed?" he asks. "If we're not taking a gate, then your town must not be a Nexus Community, right? Or do you live too close to the Outskirts? Or in Orion? Wait, no, Orion is to the south, and we're heading west, so... where are we going?"

Jegrac releases a rumbling laugh, his amusement following our horses when they gallop past. The beasts share his joy, enthralled by the freedom to roam the fields until the Nomad calls them back. Jegrac's chuckles turn bitter with each step he takes down the hill.

"A Nexus Community?" Jegrac scoffs, a bushy eyebrow arched high as he examines the new recruit. "I bet you think all these towns are begging to trade in a unique name and history for a colony number and a Nexus-appointed governor. And who wouldn't want to give up independence and freedom for that?"

Damian returns his cynicism with a blank stare. "But if you're a part of Nexus, you get direct support from the guilds, and you no longer have to make requests through a second party, *and* Nexus even sets up an outpost for shopping and other services right in town...! Of course they want to join us."

Jegrac shakes his head, dumbfounded by the boy's ignorance. Unfortunately, Damian's answer isn't a surprise; a kid who's never left Nexus to explore the rest of the Realms - or even the local land of Aegis - can only see things from one side, just like most citizens in the city.

"Listen, it's not that simple," I say, placing a hand on Damian's shoulder. "Some places would rather be independent."

"Sure, they think that," he argues, undeterred, "but they don't know what's good for them! Or what they're missing out on!"

Jegrac sighs, and then crouches in the grass beside the new recruit. Pulling two clenched fists out of his pockets, ripples travel through the flowing green as all manner of hidden and well-informed creatures scurry towards and around his outstretched hands, sharing their secrets in exchange for a quick bite to eat.

"So what you're saying is the Council should just make decisions *for them*? For *us*? Just like how they make choices for everyone in Nexus! And for *your* greater good, you've been convinced into accepting a lesser evil. But let's not continue this conversation. There's no point. You're not ready to learn. Not yet."

Damian chews his lip, likely biting back a rude response.

"I'm going for a walk," he eventually grumbles. He turns to me and adds, "I won't go far."

Jegrac raises his eyebrows as the boy walks away, and gives me a worried look. Even though we're both concerned, neither of us make a move to follow Damian as he stomps away.

"I'd like to leave soon," Neva shouts from atop the caravan. "Isaac! How long is this going to take?"

Happy to remove myself from this awkward situation, I hop over the ditch and scale back up the small hill until the grass blends in with the gravel of the road. The carriage is parked on the other side.

"Good to see you're feeling better," I say, shielding my eyes from the summer sun while I peer up at the roof. "Had any visions we should know about?"

Neva gives me an unamused look as her head rises, her elbows resting on a plush pink cushion so she can prop herself up to glare at me. She's changed into a new outfit (or, perhaps, has placed a glamour over her old one); it's the usual sapphire-blue two-piece swimsuit she wears when sunbathing.

"I wish," she replies. Her proud shoulders slump, and for a brief moment exhaustion douses her features in a weary grey. It quickly disappears, however; glamours shift into place to hide her fatigue.

"But now that we're out of Nexus, the future isn't as cloudy, so I can let you know when something interesting is about to happen." She pauses, her eyes watching something no one else can see, and a smile creeps onto her face. "Eventually."

She notices my anxious expression, laughs, and then rolls onto her back and out of sight.

"Don't worry, it's nothing we can't handle," Neva calls from her sanctum. She lifts an arm to give me a quick wave, signalling an end to our conversation.

Unfortunately, it also shuts down any further discussion about Foivos and his reaction to Liatris, which we still haven't properly addressed. Everyone seems to think nothing of it, but it worries me.

For now, though, his motives will have to remain a mystery.

Turning back to the field, it's hard not to admire the view. Liatris dances within the swaying ocean of green, her yellow dress twirling like a leaf on the wind as she frolics alongside Pall. Beyond her, Mayweather and Daisy gallop near the shadows of the forest. Jegrac is still crouched in the grass at the bottom of the hill, the wind carrying his whispers up and out of reach. Whatever information he is sharing, it evades my ears.

Off to the right, Damian has started to walk back towards us. Good to know he didn't wander too far.

An unexpected shift in the forest catches my attention, and a deer springs forth, prancing out from the brush and into the overgrown meadow.

Watching it run, my eyes wander to the horses, who are beginning to trot towards us.

"Jegrac, you didn't have to call them back so soon," I say, taking three quick steps down the hill, "we still have time."

The wide-brimmed hat perks up, the rippling grass spreading out and away from him as he stands, marking an end to feeding time for little creatures with secrets to share.

"I... didn't call them." Jegrac scans the field, his eyes darting up to the skies. The birds above send a message as they scatter, and he yells: "*Liatris!*"

The dryad pauses in her gallivanting, turning to us with a smile on her face. It fades to match our expressions when the line of trees explodes in a torrent of bark and fur.

The field bursts to life as all manner of forest creatures scamper our way, the sea of green churning as a cascade of hooves, fangs, and claws shove towards Liatris's exposed back. My throat tightens and my feet pull me forward, but Jegrac's hand presses against my chest, stopping my charge.

His fingers dig into my skin as a monstrous bison stomps dangerously close to the dryad, casting her fragile figure in its massive shadow.

But then the grass reaches up in desperation, pulling Liatris into its embrace, and the plants rise and thread together, forming a shield to block the stampede.

Damian sprints back to us, his face blanched white as he stares at the mass of animals closing in. He shuffles from foot to foot, shaking his legs to keep the swarm of mice, ferrets, and squirrels from clinging to his shoes as they scurry by.

"What's happening?" He waves at the surging horde of beasts, his voice rising to a shrill squeak. "They're gonna' crush us!"

Jegrac steps forward and raises his arms. Pall springs from the grass, turning with his master to face the encroaching crowd, the hound's body shaking as something builds deep within him.

Pall's jaws part to release a piercing howl, and the effect is instant, rippling through the charging beasts. They scatter, hulking grizzlies and skittish stags flowing around us and the caravan, careening away from Pall.

"Morrowfir's blessing will keep us safe," Jegrac declares. "Their fear does not make them our enemy, and we can use that fear to guide them on a better path."

Damian relaxes slightly as the animals pass by, but he still stares wide-eyed at the empty, trampled field behind them. Stepping in front of him, my body becomes a shield between the new recruit and the reason for this sudden stampede.

A low, guttural scream rips through the silence, accompanied by a smattering of birds bursting from the depths of the trees. Jegrac stiffens at the sound, his hand falling to rest on Pall's head, who growls quietly at his side.

"What? It's just riftspawn," Neva says as she steps past us. "I was hoping for something more entertaining, but this'll have to do!" She pulls a fan out of thin air and brandishes it in the bright sunlight, the wooden slats snapping as it unfolds. The blades lining the edge of her weapon glimmer with a deadly sheen.

Staring at the writhing masses slinking out of the trees, a shiver crawls along my spine. Trails of smoke hiss from warped black bodies as vicious claws and misplaced limbs carve the trees and dirt in the riftspawn's path.

"Abominations, disturbing Morrowfir's natural order," Jegrac snarls. His foot slides back when the creatures begin to slink across the field, and he glances over at the horses, who pace restlessly by the caravan.

"Guard them for us," I suggest, placing a sturdy hand on his back to guide his worry away. He whispers his thanks, and then whistles for Pall to follow him up the slope.

Damian gasps, jabbing a finger at the writhing clump of grass growing by my feet. The strands of greenery sprout until they reach my knees, twining together like a blanket, and then wither away as Liatris unfolds herself from their grasp. The slithering plants clutch at her hands and feet as she shakes herself free.

She stands, brushing off the stubborn weeds still clinging to wrists and ankles, and stares out into the field.

I follow her gaze, scanning the area where the black masses have congregated upon a pair of deer that couldn't get away in time. A quick count of the hulking creatures adds up to ten, though they could split into more soon.

"Head back to the caravan, you two, and stand by." I turn to Neva. "If you're ready, we'd better-"

She's not there.

My attention snaps back to the riftspawn.

An odd haze drifts through the air, lingering on the outskirts of the feeding beasts. Their feast is interrupted as a surge of black blood spurts from the necks of two riftspawn, sending the others into a frenzy. The creatures consume the injured, serrated fangs tearing chunks from their wounded brethren. Whether an act of mercy or hunger, the moment is quick, the sight is sickening, and it becomes quite clear Neva's already gotten busy.

"You couldn't have waited just a little longer?" I snarl, swearing under my breath as I tighten my armour and draw my sword.

Before stepping away, my hand falls onto the device Aria assigned to me. Without a second thought, I unclip the chronicler from my belt.

"Liatris! Keep this safe!" I shout, and toss it over my shoulder.

CHRONICLE 8
Recorded by Damian Cappell

I fumble with the device, but manage to keep it and my dignity intact.

When I look up, Mr. Heathe is already halfway across the field, completely unaware of his mistake and too far away to correct it.

"Up we go," the dryad chimes behind me, and I shove the chronicler towards her.

Liatris stares at it for a moment, and then smiles.

"You caught it, so you keep it," she says, pushing my hands away. "You're part of our guild too. No, Damian, really. I insist! Keep it, for now."

I struggle to clip the tablet onto my belt, and it nearly drops to the ground for the second time.

After way too many embarrassing attempts to secure the metal hook, the device finally attaches, and I scramble up the hill after Liatris.

The Nomad lingers by the horses, whispering to them as he reattaches thin black reins and sturdy harnesses to the powerful beasts. He notices my stare and gives me a curt nod. I avert my gaze, hiding my burning cheeks as Liatris leads me through the side door of the guild's carriage.

The dryad darts to one of the small oval windows facing towards the field, peering at it while she attempts to scrub away the dust and grime blocking her view. Ignoring her, I settle down in the empty seat beside Neva's well-furnished area, shoving aside the large cushions intruding onto my part of the bench.

I place a particularly invasive pillow on the small ornate cupboard Neva uses as a footrest, and peer through the scarred glass at the collection of novels inside. Most of them are books I've read, though a few rarer titles catch my eye.

"Hey, Damian," the dryad declares in her sugary sweet voice. "We can get a better view from the roof!" She drags Neva's miniature cabinet to the centre of the caravan, and then hops onto it, straining to reach the runes embedded in the ceiling. When her fingers graze the glowing blue symbols, a hatch appears. It slides out of the way as Liatris bends her knees.

With a mighty leap, she clambers up and through the gap in the ceiling.

I peer at the empty space as her feet disappear. Taking a careful step onto the footrest, I strain to reach the wooden slats lining the hole in the roof.

My arms burn when I try to pull myself up, and my head barely passes my wrists before I'm forced to drop back down.

Liatris's limber form flashes in my mind, and I try again, this time bracing my legs to jump towards the gap, tugging myself upwards as the footrest topples over with a solid thud.

My elbows thrash as my fingers slip, but then the dryad's hand grabs me, her grip sturdy and firm. Any embarrassment is swept away by the shocking feelings of her skin; it's rough and textured like bark. Thankfully, patches of green moss give her fingers and palm a welcome softness.

I dangle over the toppled container, the tips of my toes grazing the surface of the ornate wood.

Liatris hoists me up with relative ease.

Once I'm on the roof, I take a moment to catch my breath.

My gratitude withers in my throat as the roars of riftspawn echo across the field. My head snaps up, eyes straining and chest tight at the opportunity to witness a fight between monsters and the members of this guild.

Earlier, I'd counted only eleven of the terrifying creatures, but now their numbers have tripled. Swarms of black terrors flood the field, some clashing with Isaac while others lurk just beyond the reach of his deadly blade. In their midst, riftspawn stumble and burst from an unknown cause, tar-like liquid spurting out as vicious gashes are carved into unsuspecting bodies.

More astonishing, however, is the sea of riftspawn remains littering the edge of the forest.

This guild works quickly.

My eyes catch sight of the dark-skinned foreigner, Neva, who flashes into existence for a brief moment, her fans slicked with black tar. She hops from one foot to the other before dancing back out of sight, leaving the beasts confused and bewildered as they slash and claw at the air around them.

Just a few steps away, Mr. Heathe fights with much less grace but a very similar ferocity. His giant blade strikes with resounding crunches and snaps as it plows through the horde of monsters.

"So," Liatris says in her cheery voice, "how old are you, in human years?"

I try to focus on what she's saying, but my eyes refuse to leave the carnage in the field.

"Uh, what?"

The dryad swings her legs over the side of the roof as she settles into place beside me. Something soft bumps against my side, and I look down to see an embroidered blue and gold pillow.

"Neva won't mind," Liatris whispers, "she lets me use it, so you can, too."

I settle on top of the cushion, mimicking her position, the heels of my boots thumping against the caravan's wall.

Liatris tugs on my sleeve.

"You didn't answer my question," she insists. "How old are you?"

Out in the tar-slicked grass, Isaac cleaves a riftspawn in half as Neva snaps into existence behind him, her fans carving through a creature clawing at the Commander's back.

"I'm almost fourteen," I reply, giving the dryad a quick glance. Her bright violet eyes are trained on my face, and I lean away, trying to focus on the fight in the field.

A riftspawn breaks away from the group and begins to lumber in our direction.

"Wow, that's older than I thought!" Liatris lets out an audible gasp.

A low whistle resounds from somewhere below us, and the Nomad's pet darts across the field, jaws snapping and fur bristling as the hound charges towards the other beast.

"How old do you think I am?" I ask as the dog tears through the riftspawn, leaving behind a ragged black corpse.

"Almost fourteen," the dryad declares, "that's how old you are!"

My annoyance starts to overtake my fear, and I turn to face Liatris.

"No, how old did you think I was, before you knew my actual age?"

She pauses.

"Maybe... five or six?"

Startled, my head shakes as I stare at Liatris in disbelief. Her hands dart up to cover her mouth.

"Oh, I didn't mean to be rude! Human ages are so confusing, and five years is a long time and, well, you all grow so fast."

"I'm not a baby," I snap, and Liatris's eyes widen.

My gaze drops to the space between us.

No wonder they all look down on me. They think I'm just a kid.

The dryad slips her hand over mine, but I pull away. We sit in awkward silence for a few moments, as the clanging and slashing and screeching in the field becomes background ambience for the quiet tension between us.

Glancing up at her, I'm surprised to see slumped shoulders and crestfallen eyes.

"You know, sometimes I think the guild treats me like a baby," she mutters. "But I guess they should. I've only been alive for fifty-eight years."

My mouth drops.

"That's *old!*" I blurt out. "And - wait - you're fifty-eight? That's - what, wait - no, you - you can't be older than twenty! Are you serious?"

Liatris shoves me gently.

"Oh, stop it!" She giggles. "You're teasing me, right? Neva once told me it's a compliment when people say you look young, so thank you. And fifty-eight isn't very old for a dryad! I mean, compared to humans, it might seem like a significant number, but we dryads sprout slowly and aren't fully grown until the end of our thirtieth human year."

The ferns on her head rustle as her laughter rings out, and I can't help but smile, even though I wasn't joking.

Calming herself after a few more chuckles, Liatris points towards the field. "Look, Damian! They're finally done."

Following her gaze, I gasp at the massacre of bubbling black corpses. Isaac and Neva stand in the midst of the writhing bodies, swatches of colour amidst the sea of darkness. The strange beasts have already begun to dissolve, the shadowy smears staining the air and earth, their horrid abundance of limbs and claws and vicious fangs seeping and evaporating back to the rift from which they came.

Peering over the side of the carriage, my breath catches at the sight of more corpses at the bottom of the hill, twitching and burbling on the ground by the Nomad and his dog. The man sits amongst the bodies, cleaning a set of blackened blades with strands of grass while his hound hacks up steaming chunks of riftspawn flesh. The wide-brimmed hat tilts back, and the Nomad gives us a wave.

"Glad you've got my back, Liatris," he says, moving a dagger to gesture at a nearby carcass.

Some of the riftspawn remains have patches of green sprouting on and through them, with plants wrapped around sizzling necks and limbs, the vines and roots scarred by desperate claws. Liatris nods, and the Nomad turns away.

Shifting my attention back to the depths of the field, Isaac is already walking towards the caravan, and Neva is nowhere to be seen. The commander of Honour's Stand flicks chunks of black gunk off his dented armour as he drags his feet closer and closer. Once he's within shouting distance, he asks: "Everyone okay?"

He's staring at me, so I offer a limp thumbs up.

The roof trembles as Liatris hops off the side of the caravan, the grass bending to bear the weight of her fall, propelling her forward as she sprints to Isaac. He smiles when she draws close, saying something I can't hear. She nods and looks over her shoulder at me.

Not wanting to miss anything important, I shimmy back down into the caravan from the hatch in the roof, landing a lot less gracefully than I would have liked on the hard wooden floor below. As I make my way out the side door, whispers from the members of Honour's Stand carry up the hill and into my ears.

Something tickles my throat, but I swallow it so I won't interrupt the guild's conversation.

"All we can do is wait until Neva returns," Isaac says, "but we can't stay here for too long! I want to get home before nightfall."

Liatris doesn't reply, her mournful violet eyes peering out at the bubbling black bodies littering the field, splotches of ink upon a beautiful jade sea. She shakes her head, letting out a heavy sigh as she kneels down to tend to the grass struggling beneath a rapidly dissolving claw.

"Leave it." The Nomad is by her side, tapping her shoulder. His dog pushes his snout under the hook of the dryad's arm. "You can't save them, Liatris. The rift has bled too much. But do not lose hope, because Morrowfir will…"

He pauses to correct himself: "Because *nature* will find a way to survive, as it always does, with or without our help."

Continuing to swallow as quietly as possible, my neck constricts, my breaths ragged and strained. I clear my throat behind my hands, not wanting to break the silence the dryad and Nomad share.

It only makes things worse. My eyes water as heavy coughs rattle my skull.

Blinking away tears, something spills from my lips. Chunks from the clog in my throat are finally coming loose. Still hacking, I wave Isaac's concerned hand away, offering a strained smile before doubling over in another fit. A trembling hand rises to wipe my mouth, and my eyes widen at the black, bubbling liquid slathered across my thumb.

I gag, horrified, my throat continuing to fill, the throbbing in my head growing unbearably loud, my arm reaching out to grab someone, anyone, but then my legs give way, crumbling as the world fades.

CHRONICLE 9
Recorded by Isaac Heathe

I pull the chronicler from the sleeping boy's belt, checking for any cracks or scratches from his sudden collapse.

"It'll stop his withering for a day or two, but it's not a permanent solution," Liatris announces as she places another plant by Damian's face. Stretching over the boy, she pats his back, and he coughs out small wisps of black smog. The thick smoke drifts towards and then into the outstretched leaves of the potted fern. "Poor thing, having to suffer like this. He must have been breathing in toxic air the entire time we were talking, and I didn't even..."

She falls silent, choking on a sob.

"Don't blame yourself, Liatris." Jegrac interrupts. "None of us could have known. After all the recent riftspawn attacks in Nexus, why would a kid - and a *noble's* kid, of all people - be left vulnerable to their remains? Right now, he's just lucky to be under your care. This would have ended very poorly if he'd been travelling with any other guild."

Settling back on the bench at the front of the caravan, I secure the chronicler on my waist and add: "He's right, 'Tris. You've done well."

"If we're sharing gratitudes," Liatris declares, "then I'd like to thank Jegrac for raising such a smart dog. If Damian had fallen directly into the riftspawn's blood..."

She shudders.

Jegrac offers a half-hearted grin as he rubs Pall's tummy, the giant black hound splayed across his lap and enjoying the attention. He'd taken the brunt of Damian's collapse, darting under the boy before he could land in a sizzling puddle of black remains.

The new recruit is sprawled on his side in the middle of the floor, his limp body resting on one of Neva's pure white blankets.

Liatris turns to me.

"What do we do now?" she asks.

I shrug.

"Best we can do is find a riftspecialist. If Yuina was here, she'd probably patch him up on her own... so hopefully we bump into her on the way to Borderik."

"Have you called her guildstone?"

"Already tried. No luck."

"Aw. Okay, then. What about your family? Will they be able to help us?"

"Probably not. They were never interested in magic, beyond when it was mentioned in sermons, and even then they preferred to talk about Yiatsu rather than the rift." I picture my dad telling Damian to just 'walk it off' as my mother announces 'some fresh air would do him good.'

"Sorry, Liatris. I don't think my parents will be much help."

The leaves decorating the dryad's head go limp, and she slumps back to her bench. The mess of ferns and vines perk up again beneath the halo of light.

Jegrac sighs wistfully.

"So we'll just have to find a riftspecialist," he mutters as Pall settles onto his blanket with a content huff. "I doubt they're common out here."

I nod. "Thankfully, there's one more town between us and Borderik, so we can try our luck there."

The rustle of the curtain at the back of the caravan interrupts our conversation.

"What happened here?" Neva chimes as she climbs inside. She pauses to admire the scene, smirking at the collection of potted plants surrounding Damian's unconscious figure.

"Neva! You're back!" Liatris blurts out. "Where were you?"

Our elusive guildmate ignores the dryad, her lips pressed into a tight frown when she recognizes Damian's makeshift bed and the black smears on the expensive-looking fabric. Her stare burns a hole into the stained blanket, but then she rolls her eyes, shakes away her annoyance, and points down at the boy.

"Honestly, I'm shocked. Or, I suppose, *not* shocked at all, considering how unprepared he's been this entire time. What were his guardians thinking, sending him out here without a single blessing or enchantment or at *least* some protection runes sewn into his clothes? It's suspicious. Right? Am I the only one thinking about how odd this is?"

I shake my head. "Maybe his parents didn't consider those things. You know how nobles are: completely disconnected from the real world. I doubt they expected their son to be in any real danger..."

Neva stares me down, her lips set in a tight line.

"What?"

For the second time in a short while, she rolls her eyes.

"Seriously, Isaac, you didn't notice?" She lowers herself onto Yuina's bench, shoving aside one of the dusty tomes so she can face the spot where Damian had been sitting throughout our journey so far. Her knees rest by the handle of the side door.

Reaching down, Neva pulls up the small grey satchel tucked beneath the seat.

"Look at this," she says. "It's everything he brought. And there's no hidden compartment or glamoured pockets; trust me, I checked. Two books, a canteen, some half-charged currency, and a change of clothes. That's it! Seriously, anyone else find this to be really, *really* strange?"

I look down at the new recruit, who shudders in his sleep. Black smoke continues to leak from his mouth and nose.

Why did the Council insist we take this woefully unprepared boy on a dangerous adventure?

"Judging by your stunned silence, we're all finding this to be a little suspicious, right? Good. Because I've got something else to talk about." Neva pulls a small object from the pocket of her pantsuit. "I found this." The item glints as it weaves through her fingers, and then she tosses it to me.

It's smooth and worn, with bumps and ridges decorating the surface of the old currency. Flipping it over, there are four lines carved into the ancient gold plating, just like the coin Clifford had given me this morning.

Passing it back to her, I shrug. The merchant hadn't offered an explanation as to why this object was important, though it's unsettling how another one was found here, amidst the riftspawn.

"We'll have to wait for Yuina, then," Neva sighs, lifting the coin for Jegrac and Liatris to see, "unless...?"

The other members of Honour's Stand shake their heads.

Tucking the coin back into her pocket, she steps carefully around the boy and into her usual spot, leaning over to pull a book out of the small cabinet in the middle of the floor.

"What else did you find?" I ask.

Neva ignores my question, instead choosing to hoist her footrest over Damian's unconscious body, letting it settle on the other side. She tosses a pillow onto her miniature cabinet, throws her legs over it, and then finally turns her attention back to me.

"A camp. You need to visit it before we go," she mutters. Neva focuses on her fingers, twining and then tucking them into her lap. "Didn't see any survivors, or a rift, so whoever or whatever was summoning riftspawn is either dead or gone."

She extends a weary hand towards Jegrac, her face aimed at him but her eyes elsewhere, searching for something.

"Go with him," she mutters, her stare distant and sad. "It's a Nomad camp. Though you'll have to hurry, if you want to get there first."

"How long until-"

"It's hazy, but you've got time. The Nexus clean-up crew won't arrive until the sun sets." Her sight returns to the present, focusing on Jegrac, her mouth set in a tight grimace. "Prepare yourself, because it's a brutal scene. But this way, at least, you can give your people a proper burial."

Jegrac gives a curt nod, his eyes narrowed and his fists clenched. He turns to leave, but hesitates when Liatris rises to clutch his sleeve.

"Let me help," she begs. "I can part the earth, to ease the burden of burying the dead."

A conflicted look crosses Jegrac's face, but his green eyes soften at Liatris's gentle touch.

"My brethren have suffered too, Jegrac. Human life is not the only casualty in this massacre, so please don't tell me to stay."

The Nomad holds the dryad's hand in his own, his eyes solemn and weary. Then he reaches under their bench to pull out a pair of shovels, tossing them through the curtain in the back. The tools clatter against the road. As he heads out the side door, he glances at his hound.

"Pall, stay here and guard the boy. We'll be back soon."

His dog lets out an anxious whine, but settles into place at Damian's side.

"Neva, keep an eye on him, okay?"

She doesn't respond, her attention on the book in her lap, but after a few beats of silence she gives him a wave. That seems to be enough for Jegrac, and he turns to me.

"I'll get Mayweather and Daisy ready. Meet us at the edge of the meadow, Isaac."

"Be back before sunset," Neva calls out after him. I stand, preparing to leave.

Neva stops me, her hand raised. Not bothering to look up, she points at the device on my waist, her finger resting on the glowing blue jewel.

"You're going with them, so I'll turn this off now so you don't forget. This is not something Aria needs to know about, and she shouldn't have to review what you see. We can turn it back on when this dreadful business is done."

CHRONICLE 10
Recorded by Jegrac

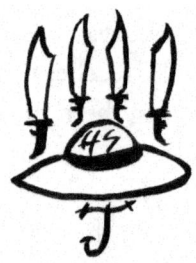

"**Y**ou heard what Neva said, right? Aria shouldn't have to transcribe this massacre. Turn it off, Jegrac."

The Commander attempts to peer at the chronicler in my hand, his lips set in a disappointed frown that bounces along with his horse's pace. The expression disappears when he's forced to duck under a branch, and Daisy maintains her speed despite his struggle to stay balanced.

Liatris shifts against my back, her arms tightening around my waist as Mayweather gallops over the remains of the forest, tracing the blackened dirt and soil leading us towards my people's camp.

"Come on, Isaac, can't you let this slide?" she says. "*Someone* needs to record what happened here to honour the victims of this tragedy. Who better to do it than a fellow Nomad?"

I glance at the Commander, waiting for his response.

He chews his lower lip for a few moments, and then sighs.

"Fine," he mutters, "but if it's as bad as Neva said..."

Brushing away his concerns, I give Mayweather a little encouragement, sending a few sparks of magic through our bond, and she picks up the pace. After a quick whistle, Daisy does the same.

"She must be over-exaggerating. Wouldn't be the first time, right? And we're resilient folk, us Nomads. No offence, Commander, but you worry too much."

Isaac sets his mouth in a thin line, but doesn't respond. Maybe he's convinced. Or he suspects I'm trying to convince myself that Neva is wrong.

As I said: she's just over-exaggerating.

She has to be.

The shovel weighs heavily on my shoulder as the horses begin to slow, the air thick with toxic smog yet eerily void of sound.

No birds. No rustling branches. No fluttering leaves.

Only soot and ash mixed with bubbling puddles of tar.

Liatris gasps, her body shuddering when Mayweather hops over a fallen oak. She whispers a solemn prayer for the mighty tree, fingers pinching my sides as she buries her face into my back.

And then we reach the camp.

I glimpse it for only a moment: a sea of red and black smeared across the earth. The smell hits next, something horrid and foul and burnt, despite the filter runes on my neck struggling to stifle the stench.

My hand snaps down to my waist, thumbing for the chronicler's off gem.

Moss-covered fingers slip over mine, the gentle touch forcing me to hesitate.

"Are you sure?" Liatris whispers into my back.

I shake my head, unable to respond.

There are things in this world no one should have to see. This is a burden I will carry on my own, for my people.

CHRONICLE 11
Recorded by Neva Oyii

"For the night, mind taking this with you?"

The chronicler flickers on as Isaac wearily passes it to me. His eyes are still heavy from the massacre in the forest.

"Yeah, I've got it," I say, hopping out the back of the caravan. Gravel crunches beneath my boots. "I'll take it with me while I search for a riftspecialist. We're close to the Outskirts, right? They must be common around here."

A gruff voice calls out from the other side of the carriage.

"Neva! Help me with this blasted thing. I think it's broken."

I saunter over to Jegrac, taking a moment to admire the old man's persistence. The runes etched into the door carve through the darkness with a faint blue light, competing with the dim glow of a nearby inn and the windows decorating various shops lining the road.

Jegrac pokes at the symbols and fails to activate the security system; the colour remains a defiant blue. He mutters something rude under his breath, implying I hadn't charged the magical battery before we'd left.

Stifling a smug grin, I say: "You know Liatris is still in the caravan, right?"

My advice falls on deaf ears as Jegrac continues to prod and swear at the runes, completely unaware of the dryad halting his progress. Thankfully, it sounds like she's almost done.

"There! Just had to say goodnight to my friends," Liatris announces. She steps out the side door and pushes it shut with a gentle click. "You can lock up now."

Jegrac rubs his fingers together in an obvious imitation of my magical priming pattern and presses his hands against the glowing characters.

As expected, nothing changes.

His dog brushes up against him, letting out a sullen whine.

I want to whine too. Rolling my eyes is giving me a headache.

"How many times do I have to teach you this lesson, old man?" I reach across Jegrac to cover the two outer symbols, taking care not to elbow him in the face. "Start with these two, and *then* touch the middle one. And keep your fingers still! Don't take your hands off until *after* the light fades."

When Jegrac makes no attempt to interrupt or ask a stupid question, I continue: "And just so you know, this process takes *zero* magical energy. Sure, sometimes I place a glamour to keep these symbols hidden, but it's not a requirement. We've talked about this before, right?"

Jegrac's sharp green eyes hone in on my fingers as I activate the security system in a very slow and deliberate manner.

When it's done, he frowns.

"That's it?"

The Nomad reaches out to touch the fading runes, but I slap his hand away.

He shakes his head, letting out a rude snort.

"This is much too simple. Any thief with half a brain could figure that out!"

"Oh, is that so?" I remark. "Just like how *you* were able to 'figure it out'?"

I bite back the rest of my snappy response, since any further comments will lead to more inane questions about the security system, magical energy signatures, and how enchantments can solidify a flimsy curtain into a wall of iron.

Thankfully, Isaac interrupts before Jegrac can.

"Is it okay to leave Damian in there?" he asks, staring at the caravan's wooden door. "What if he wakes up? Will it trigger the alarm?"

Liatris shakes her head. "I wouldn't worry. He'll be out for a while, and if we need to get back inside, you or Neva can deactivate it. I might be able to, I think, but I don't want to set it off by accident."

Jegrac keeps silent, noting the absence of his name with a grunt.

"Well!" I declare, clapping my hands together. "I'd love to stick around, but there's other business to attend to!" I point towards the lively saloon across the road, where muffled music and a chorus of voices break the stillness of this quiet town. Now it's Jegrac's turn to roll his eyes.

"Are you going to come inside?" Liatris asks him. The Nomad shakes his head, pulling a rustic satchel off the ground and onto his shoulders.

"Appreciate the offer, as always, but Pall and I will find a place to rest in the forest. I'll see you all in the morning."

With a polite nod, Jegrac swivels on his heels and strolls towards the trees, the giant black hound scampering to his side as they disappear into the night.

Liatris yawns, not bothering to stifle it as she stretches her arms up into the air. Isaac pats her shoulder, and starts leading her towards the Inn.

He stops a few steps away, turning to look at me.

"Neva, listen - if you need to join us later, I've paid for an extra room." He pauses, and adds: "They seem clean, so..."

He notices the look on my face and promptly shuts his mouth.

"Ugh, no thanks," I reply, glancing over my shoulder at the bar. "I'll find a better place to sleep."

Isaac nods. He struggles to keep his eyes open, but he doesn't leave, so I give him an encouraging smile.

"I'll be fine, Isaac. Go get some rest."

He stares at me for a moment, his lips pursed.

Before he can lecture me, I say, "Yes, I'll be careful, and no, I'm not going to do anything stupid. You realise I'm not running off to have fun, right? Damian needs a healer!"

Isaac's face twists as he tries not to roll his eyes. He fails, and I grin.

"And, of course, my *very important task* may require me to cosy up with the locals, have a few drinks, dance on a table... but it's all for Damian! Why, it's practically a quest! Are you proud of the courageous sacrifices I am making for our guild, oh benevolent Commander?"

Isaac turns towards the Inn halfway through my spiel, trudging along with a drowsy Liatris in tow.

"Goodnight Neva," he calls as he lumbers up the stone steps. I give a wave, stick out my tongue at his back, and then spin away, doing my best to resist the urge to skip across the road.

My shadow grows long as the tavern draws near, and tiny coughs of dirt swirl around my feet. My boots tap upon the creaking wooden patio, the hilts of my bladed fans caressing my fingertips as I scan the area. Horses drink from troughs while others pace freely in a nearby stable. Huddled figures linger around the open door with backs exposed and weapons either sheathed or absent.

I listen halfheartedly to light conversations about work, the farm, who they want to dance with, and other topics that briefly catch my attention and tell me more about this quaint little town. A faint musk tickles my nose amongst the embers dancing in the night air, the smell of smoke shared amongst friends as emptied glasses clink a familiar tune.

Faces turn, following my path to the front door. Staring down my admirers, I'm met with friendly smiles and curious waves. A few people even muster up a 'hello' or 'Yiatsu bless'. It's a warm welcome, and my guard starts to lower.

The musicians stumble over their notes as I cross the threshold, but then hastily resume their upbeat song with a modicum of professionalism.

Forging a path towards the open bar, whispers follow my trail, slipping past the hands of patrons crowding around worn wooden tables and lingering by the edge of the dance floor.

Priming my fingers, I brush the glamour off my shoulder, revealing my guild tattoo. It's a relief to finally uncover it - even though hiding this symbol is a necessary act, it becomes a bit tedious after a while.

"Busy night," I say to the bartender, slipping onto a red stool streaked with white rips and tears.

The man nods, tipping his head. His thinning grey hair flops downwards, revealing a bald patch on top. He sizes me up, his bushy brows furrowed, and then a smile erupts under his thick moustache when he notices the symbol on my shoulder.

"Ah, an adventurer! Planning to drink someone under the table tonight?" His brown eyes twinkle.

I pretend to glance around the room.

"Everyone else seems to have gotten a head start..." I offer a courteous smile, and then a genuine grin, falling into a rhythm of familiar banter with the tavern keeper. "I'd better start catching up, don't you think?"

My hand rifles through my glamoured purse, searching for a chargestone barely tinged with colour. "You take these?" I ask. The Nexus currency glimmers between my fingers.

The man shrugs.

"Feels like a mistake not to, though if you have anything else to offer, I'll take that instead."

Having been in enough bars to know how bartering works in a small town, I peer around the room.

Sun Shulls drift lazily along the low ceiling, the magical balls of light slipping between wooden bars and bumping against heads bobbing along with the music. Some of the glowing orbs have managed to escape onto the dance floor, where they can roam high above the people milling in front of the small stage.

My gaze settles on some noisy patrons, who clamber around tables and slosh their drinks onto the floor. I gesture at the more rambunctious part of the crowd.

"What do I get for taking them outside to cool off?"

The bartender laughs.

"A kind offer, miss, but my wife's already on it."

As if on cue, a large woman stomps toward some of the rowdier customers, who have their foreheads pressed together as they hurl insults. Wiping her hands on the tattered brown apron clutching her burly figure, the woman lifts two hefty hands and grabs the men's ears. The crowd laughs as she yanks them outside.

"What we could use," the tavern keeper announces as his wife reenters to a smattering of applause, "is a singer." He gestures at the woman standing on the wooden stage near the back of the dance floor. Despite the desperate attempts of the other musicians to salvage this public disaster, the song sounds awful. "My wife - bless her heart - thought of a wonderfully horrid idea, which involves random audience members going up to sing their own songs with the band. Unfortunately, people actually started accepting her offer."

I restrain my eagerness as the stage calls to me.

"Your band, can they play Stompin' Dahlia? Or 'A High High Champion'? I can do more, but those are the two I know best."

The man fumbles with the glass in his hands, and I place a finger against it, steadying the mug so it doesn't tumble to the floor. The bartender nods his thanks as he says, "If you could sing either of those, I'd really appreciate it."

He pauses, and then carefully adds, "*If* you can sing."

Moments later, I'm stepping onto the stage, gently gesturing for the previous performer to remove herself before she can massacre another song. Every eye is glued to me, taking in my incredibly dark skin, beautiful smile, and elegant sapphire dress. I let them stare. Shadows dart in and out of the door as members of the crowd run outside to grab their friends. Glancing over my shoulder to give some cues to the band, they sit up eagerly in response. After humming a few notes to demonstrate my vocal range for the musicians preparing to support me, I turn back to my audience, reach up to massage my throat, and send magic trickling down into my lungs.

When my lips part to belt out the first few lines of Stompin' Dahlia with a rich, powerful force, shock and awe ripple through the stunned crowd, and then the dance floor bursts to life with excited cheers and a chorus of enthusiastic voices. My grin widens and my eyes drift shut as I savour each note and the adoration of my audience, which carries out sweet and strong.

Between numbers the bartender sends me a drink, accompanied by water, which is downed quickly as the band starts to play, calling me back to centre stage.

The songs last forever, but not long enough, and eventually I give a polite bow, stepping away to let a brave (and very drunk) farmer follow my act. A few people reach out to shake my hand as I head back to the bar.

The tavern keeper and his wife are waiting for me, and she generously administers a full glass of ale, the heavy mug scraping across the wooden counter. I shake my head, declining the offer.

"Too strong for ya'?" she asks.

"Got anything better?" I slide onto an empty stool.

"If you're asking for one of those fancy Zorah wines, then no."

"A shame, then, since this isn't strong enough to trick me into thinking it's good."

The woman laughs, clapping her husband on the shoulder. Her long curly hair jiggles along with her stout arms as she walks away, calling over a few younger barmaids to repeat what I've just said.

"So, you from Nexus?" The bartender asks as he pulls a platter through the window to the kitchen. He places a tray of assorted meats, cheeses, vegetables, and fresh fruits in front of me. "You must be, if you're part of the guild staying at the Inn."

I nod, nibbling away at some celery as he speaks.

"Well." His voice lowers, eyes narrowing above his polite smile. "There's a rumour going 'round that you brought a Nomad into our town."

My carefree grin threatens to slip off my face, and my nails dig into my palm.

"That may be true," I muse aloud, elbows resting on the counter as I lean forward, "but Jegrac is an important part of our guild."

The man's fingers tighten around the glass in his hands, and I challenge his stare with an innocent expression.

"I can bring him with me next time, if you'd like." Leaning back to put some space between us, I shrug my shoulders. "Though let me warn you, he's not much of a drinker. And you certainly don't want to hear him sing."

The bartender gives a hefty grunt, his arms crossed over his stout chest as he scowls at me.

"I expected folks from Nexus to be a little more careful," he says. "After those Nomads opened a portal in the middle of your city, I'm surprised any guild would be foolish enough to harbour one of *them*."

"Another rumour," I reply.

The man places the glass onto the counter with a deft thud.

"Fair enough," he remarks, "but the riftspawn always come from the forest, and the only people living there are Nomads. We just want to keep our families safe."

Not wanting to press the issue any further, I simply nod.

The sharpness returns to the man's voice as he adds, "And one other thing! If you're here to talk the town into becoming one of your Nexus communities, you'd best be on your way."

His wife cuts him off, resting a hand on his shoulder.

"Don't be silly, Gordon. That's not why she's here," she remarks. "Why, Cresley mentioned that one of the Heathe boys is staying at the Inn! You know the family, right, Gordon? Wilson and Marie Heathe, from Borderik. Good people. Very kind."

Her husband deflates a little at the mention of Isaac's last name.

"He's our guild leader," I announce, my appetite returning as the conversation grows lighter. Reaching for a sliced apple, the bartender pushes the platter a little closer to me in a gesture of good will. The smell of cinnamon tickles my nose. "Isaac gets to come home, and we complete a quest along the way."

"An adventurer?" the woman exclaims, eyes widening. "Why, I'd heard rumours about how the Heathe's oldest son had left the family farm, but didn't know if they were true." She pauses, and then quickly says, "No offence, of course."

I shrug. Her statement affects Isaac, not me, and there's no point in being offended on his behalf.

She smiles, her round and rosy cheeks puffing out as she turns to address a waitress clamouring for support with another rowdy patron. She offers me a quick wave and gives her husband a pat on the shoulder before tramping off.

The bartender attempts to follow his wife, but I tap the counter, calling him back. "I have to ask: does your town have a riftspecialist?"

He nods, standing tall to scan the room.

"Oh yes, he's in high demand these days. Unfortunately, Dr. Conley is in the neighbouring town right now - you know Borderik? You'll see him if you're heading that way."

Noting the disappointment on my face, he adds, "Ah! But you're in luck. His apprentice is still in town. See that table in the corner, near the edge of the dance floor?"

I follow his gaze, settling on a scrawny-looking man seated amidst a crowd of young farmers. His pink and teal armband is easy to spot, signalling his role as a riftspecialist. I'd been so wrapped up in this conversation and my performance that he'd somehow slipped into the bar without me noticing.

"Thanks," I say, giving the tavern keeper a genuine smile. Even if he's a little misguided, he seems to mean well.

I bid him goodnight, standing to politely shake his hand, and the device on my waist clunks against a nearby stool. I run my fingers over it absentmindedly, searching for the off button. The night's not over yet, and I'm sure Aria isn't interested in some of the fun I plan to have.

CHRONICLE 12
Recorded by Isaac Heathe

A jolt strikes my chest as the chronicler slides off Neva's empty bench and into my hand. The feeling recedes once my foot bumps against a bag of clothes sloppily tucked out of the way; Neva must have stopped by the caravan to freshen up before running off to some stranger's house for more entertainment. She'll arrive right before we leave, as per usual.

Liatris pushes past me with a large potted fern clutched in her arms. She hoists the plant through the hatch and onto the roof before hopping up after it, her feet tapping the boards above my head. The sound is followed by the scraping and scratching of ceramic on wood. Liatris claps her hands, satisfied, and then drops back into the caravan, scurrying about like a squirrel as she prepares to move another one of her floral friends.

Taking care not to step on Damian's comatose body, I move from Neva's area to settle down on the bench near the front of the caravan, leaning forward to peer at the runes scrawled on the boy's forehead in a messy font. The quality isn't great, but our new recruit does look a little healthier and a lot less pallid, so it'll have to do for now.

Liatris lands with a thump, her legs braced on either side of Damian to keep her from bumping into him, and she picks up another one of her massive ferns. The dryad doesn't even notice my attempts to help, ignoring my outstretched arms as she lifts the plant through the hatch with ease.

"No sign of Neva yet, but I'll keep you posted," Jegrac announces from the front of our carriage.

Shuffling against the wooden bar, I throw my arm over it, raising the other to lift the curtain out of the way. The black fabric latches onto the hook above my head, allowing me to observe Jegrac as he adjusts Mayweather's harness. The white and brown speckled horse nuzzles against him, while Daisy chews on the edges of his wide-brimmed hat.

"Not much of a surprise," I reply. "She'll get here eventually, I'm sure. Right before we leave."

Jegrac nods, his eyes trained on the horses. Peering past him, the town is drenched in morning sunshine, a freshly cracked yolk settling on buildings and dyeing the earth with a yellow haze. The air is scented with dew and freshly woken grass, reminding me of home, early mornings, and simpler routines.

A familiar image flashes behind my eyes; mom is in the kitchen preparing a meal with Sam, who does his best to keep up despite barely being able to reach the counter. Her apron is dusted with flour, her curly brown hair tucked behind her ears as she putters about, shuffling sizzling pans and bubbling pots on a humble stove.

Through the window overlooking the crowded sink, Alexis can be spotted tending to the horses in the stable, but then the vision blurs, and now she's by the pasture, checking on the cows and sharing stories with the neighbouring farm folk. Markus is out in the fields, too far to see clearly, a tiny spec beyond the faded red barn.

And then there's me. Seated at the table in a chair that feels too small, too cramped, too mundane. Making another fumbled attempt at polite conversation with my mother as she once again asks why I can't stay for another day. My answer isn't what she wants to hear, and we fall back into awkward silence.

The memory leads into another, shaken by a clatter as a door slams against the wall, my father stomping inside, complaining about lazy farmhands. He abruptly closes his mouth when his eyes settle on me, and his grimace is replaced with a strangely tight smile before he whirls away. The offer to help dies in my throat.

I squeeze my eyes shut, shoving the thoughts aside. It'll be different this time. It has to be.

My fingers tap against the wooden box beneath my bench, a reminder of my duties as a member of Honour's Stand. Once we're moving again, someone has to make breakfast, and no one wants Neva's charred nonsense, Jegrac's scavenged mystery meat, or Liatris's water and sunlight in a bowl, so it's my responsibility to make sure everyone gets fed.

Taking a quick mental inventory of what we've packed, a plan begins to form: eggs, bacon, and toast for Neva, Jegrac, and I, fresh water for Liatris, and I'll also get some coffee brewing since *someone* will be tired and cranky when she finally arrives. Might as well add a blend of vegetables, rice, and beans in case Yuina shows up later, and frozen juice on a stick for Frost.

The thought of food sends a rumble through my stomach, accompanied by an eagerness to leave. Liatris has grown quiet on the roof, her bench finally empty, the sound of her patter replaced by the soft murmur of the waking world. Chirps and the buzzing of little creatures grow louder as a familiar voice rings in my ears.

"If we want to heal him, we should get going."

Neva climbs into the back of the caravan, her black eyes weary as the curtain drops behind her. She's noticeably unkempt and untidy; while her natural beauty and quick glamours keep her from being an absolute mess, her hair looks like a tangled nest of black wool, and her simple red skirt and grey sweater have a few wrinkles poking through their vibrant designs.

"Glad you're finally here!" I exclaim. A grunt echoes through our cabin as the bar behind me shifts; Jegrac has settled against it, whistling low and long until he's met with a thump and an eager bark.

Neva tosses her purse onto the floor with a solid thunk and tugs a large grey bag onto her bench. She roots through it, holds up different garments, peers at them, and then shakes her head as she shoves them back inside. The irritation in her voice rises while she continues to reject clothes and outfits with increasingly violent force.

"Yeah, you country folk, always getting up early." A sapphire dress smacks against the wood of the wall as it is cast aside. "My companions from last night didn't have the decency to wake me, so there I was-" a purple blouse nearly rips when it's pushed back into the bag "-all alone in some stranger's house, rudely awakened by some-" a pair of black slacks squirm in her fist "-stupid, unattended mutt!"

Neva's voice softens as she pulls out a package wrapped in brown paper.

"However, one gentleman was courteous enough to leave me a note, but if and *when* I see him again, he's on *thin ice*." She holds up a folded piece of paper, and then leans across the caravan door to tuck it inside a book on Yuina's bench. "There, a nice little surprise for her."

Jegrac starts to clear his throat, but she interrupts before he can comment.

"HEY! I'm *here*, so don't complain! I barely had time to shower and freshen up, since you're all *so* eager to get up and go at this Yiatsu-forsaken time, which is so irrationally early I'm surprised anyone's awake. Keep your mouth shut, because I'm not in the mood to suffer fools."

Jegrac follows her advice, although a quiet chuckle rumbles through him and the board separating us. He whistles to Daisy and Mayweather, and soon the creaking wheels are accompanied by a low hum, the floorboards thrumming as magical energy spreads out towards the sides of the cart, vibrant runes dyeing the floor with flickers of blue and white. The carriage responds to the sudden movement, and the horses pick up the pace as their load becomes noticeably lighter, assisted by enchantments that allow our wheels to turn on their own. A hearty bark echoes through the walls of the caravan, a sure sign Pall is running alongside us.

Nestled on her bench near the back of the carriage, Neva pulls out a bowl, a comb she has yet to break, and a beige-coloured cream from one of her many bags. She knocks on the wall, and like clockwork Liatris drops through the ceiling to take the metal basin from Neva, hopping over to the rain barrel to fill the container with fresh water. Neva takes it from her and grumbles quietly to herself as she starts the arduous process of untangling the frizzled mess on top of her head.

Eager to escape, Liatris slips back onto the roof, carefully closing the hatch behind her. Jegrac lets the curtain at the front of the carriage drop, shielding himself from any scathing comments and the temptation to make a snarky remark.

Any attempts at conversation will be met with a hostile glare, so my attention turns to the prospect of a hearty breakfast.

I take care not to kick Damian in the head as I settle on the floor, and nudge him away with my feet to prevent any future harm.

The smooth white icebox glides soundlessly across the boards, and my hands reach back under the bench to drag a large wooden container into place beside it.

My fingers dance across the surface of the colourless storage device, and the lid slides open with a satisfying click. A blast of cold air hits my face.

"Coffee," Neva grumbles.

Shifting my attention to the wooden box, I pull out a variety of mugs, bowls, and cutlery. Once they've been secured, the container is sealed and pushed out of sight so I have room to withdraw the wide black case holding the other breakfast supplies.

With as much care as possible I place Neva's expensive coffee-making-machine onto the floor, tapping the small silver button on the bottom of the large metal cylinder. A few aggravated whispers scratch my ears as my grumpy companion shuffles about, and then a cold canister of water pokes my cheek. The side of my face gets soaked in the process, but I bite my tongue.

Unintelligible muttering stalks Neva back to her seat as the liquid pours into the top of the coffee machine. With the most important menu item out of the way, my attention turns to setting up the rest of the cooking station. After some shuffling and hoisting of a great many things, the metal platter on the bench begins warming with a sharp click, followed by the sizzling of butter in an iron skillet. The air fills with the aroma of frying eggs, brewing coffee, and fresh toast. The smells give way to the crackle of bacon, which competes with the other delicious fragrances. A beam of light fills the carriage as Jegrac peeks through the front curtain to take a hearty sniff.

My mind drifts back to thoughts of home. Mom had been pleased about my change in schedule, although her excitement had come to a sudden halt with the explanation that most of the guild would be joining me. Oddly enough, she hasn't bothered to contact me since then, and any attempts to reach her have ended in failure.

She must be busy preparing the house for unexpected guests.

Neva interrupts my musing as she settles on Yuina's bench, quietly filling her mug before sipping away at it.

"Is it ready?" she eventually asks, a hint of eagerness breaking through her cranky shell. Moments later, she is happily mowing down on a full plate of peppered eggs, crispy bacon, and buttered toast. The two of us eat in silence for a little while, and Neva opens up the curtain at the back, letting the cool morning breeze and the scent of fresh dew linger amongst the scrape of metal on ceramic and the satisfied munching of a hearty breakfast. We watch the road as it rolls away, my eyes wandering to the sturdy trees and flittering bugs and birds beyond the dusty trail we leave behind.

Jegrac hasn't asked for anything yet; he probably hunted down some manner of wild beast earlier, long before the rest of us had woken up.

After a while, Liatris drops down from the ceiling with a plant in her hands. It's one of her 'divas', a fragile and particular flora requiring extra attention and care. She wrinkles her nose, hooks the pot into a container hanging from the ceiling, and then scurries back to the roof. Her absence is brief as she continues her routine, dropping down with more hardy plants to secure within the confines of the caravan.

Once the last of her ferns, flowers, and other greenery are in place, she hops up and out of sight.

Neva passes me her plate, along with the basin she'd been using earlier. It's empty, the water having been unceremoniously tossed from the back of the carriage and into the dirt whistling away behind us.

She settles back on her bench, pulling out a book as she adjusts the hem of her sleeveless dress, tugging on it so the edge touches her ankles. It's a brilliant and vibrant blend of purple, pink, and red; the fuschia and magenta lines meld amongst speckled bursts of rose and ruby.

The glamours on her face have been adjusted to include a variety of Zorah cosmetics, with hints of fuschia on and around her eyelids, accompanied by striking white lines that sharpen her eyes. In a surprising transformation from the poofy mess this morning, there are now sleek and glossy braids curving up from her forehead into a spiral that leads to the flawless bun resting on top.

Neva's planning to make a good first impression, though it's unlikely anyone in Borderik has forgotten her. She leaves an impact wherever we go, and many of the people in my small hometown - including my parents - remember her fondly.

Refilling the basin, my hands grow soapy and soft as I scrub various pots, plates, and cutlery, drying each item with a towel before carefully placing them back into the wooden box. When my work is finally done, I shove the containers under the bench with a hefty grunt.

"Heavy fog up ahead," Liatris calls out. "My goodness, look at it rise... how alluring!"

Jegrac's voice echoes through the caravan.

"Turn your machines off, Isaac. I can smell smoke."

"Yeah, burn down the caravan when we're *not* inside, Commander," Neva smirks. "But with your track record, why don't I take a glimpse forward to make sure you don't..."

Glancing over my shoulder to remark how *that happened over a year ago and it wasn't even THAT bad*, the words catch in my throat when the smile drops off Neva's face.

"Oh no..." she whispers, fingers digging into the bench as she watches something none of us can see.

Before she can explain, Jegrac releases a high-pitched whistle. Mayweather and Daisy reply with fierce whinnies, and the caravan bucks when the horses break into a gallop.

Neva whirls on her bench to smack the wall, accessing a hidden panel. The floor ignites, a spiderweb of runes and symbols stretching across the bottom of the cabin. The wheels hiss as they pick up speed to match the horses' frenzied pace, spurning us on even faster.

Not bothering to ask what's going on, my attention turns to the remaining kitchen supplies, packing them away as quickly as possible.

Neva settles down on the floor in front of her bench, gently pushing Damian's legs aside so she can stretch. Her breathing is steady and measured while she prepares to fight, each muscle straining and flexing as they bristle with glamours seeping from her skin. With each exhale, her body shimmers and distorts, a living mirage.

Pall bounds alongside the caravan, and Jegrac reaches over to hoist the hound onto the front seat.

Kicking the last frying pan into place under the bench, I sit up to check the clasps of my armour. My shaking hands make it a near-impossible task.

We're too close to Borderik. To home.

My home.

Sweat trickles down my nose.

Borderik should be just ahead. My family is just ahead, waiting beneath the rising smoke.

Wood scrapes under my nails as I force my gaze through the back of the caravan.

I'm greeted by a familiar sight, though it's hard to recognize at first. The landmark house on the edge of town has been replaced with ash and tar, the garden now a smouldering black pit, the field laced with a poisonous, lingering haze. We can't be on the outskirts of Borderik already, can we?

But the shattered mailbox with a soot-stained flower decal confirms we're by the Vonnebank family's home - our old neighbours, until they moved to the other side of town.

The wreckage blurs as we race by, and bile rises at the sight of a few charred lumps lining the driveway, surrounded by bubbling remains of riftspawn. Toxic corpses drip from the skeleton of a nearby shed, sizzling black tar choking the grass and staining the dirt.

Ducking my head, my eyes squeeze shut, and my breaths come slow and ragged. The bench shifts when Neva moves to my side, her thigh grazing mine while we sit in silence. She doesn't say anything, but she doesn't have to. And even though the air feels thick and heavy, her presence calms my trembling hands.

"Two on the right," Jegrac announces, and a stomp echoes across the roof. Liatris grunts, and her exertion is followed by a loud thump and a soft crunch from somewhere outside of our caravan.

"Three behind!" Liatris shouts.

A gentle hand pats me on the back, and the bench shifts once more as Neva steps away. Her dress lands on the floor with a flutter, followed by shuffling as she yanks on pants and a sweater with invisible hands. Her footsteps stop for a brief moment, hesitating, waiting for me to look her way, but my eyes stay shut, as if this temporary darkness can lock out the painful reality outside. After one more gentle pat on my shoulder, Neva releases a soft huff and springs towards the back of the carriage.

"I'll hide the rear," she declares, her voice accompanied by the thud of her feet against the wall and then a light tap as she settles on the roof.

My eyes press into my palms, and a muttered apology escapes my lips.

"*Sorry. I'm so sorry.*"

I'm met with the quiet thump of curtains on either side, which muffle the screeching and sizzling outside the caravan.

"When you're ready," Neva's voice calls from above. Her words are a direction, a command. An offering.

I nod. Silence is the only response I can give.

Gripping my knees, I force my eyes open, staring blankly at the map over Yuina's station, my gaze unfocused as my breathing slows. The shuddering starts to leave my shoulders, retreating back into my chest.

Something brushes my shoulder, and I slam back against the wall. Jerking my head, the tension dissolves once I notice Jegrac's tan sleeve reaching under the curtain.

"Give it to me," he says, "the chronicler."

He doesn't have to ask twice. The device slips in my hands as a cold sweat slicks the hook, but eventually it comes free, trembling in my grasp. Jegrac's steady fingers wrap around the chronicler as I pass it to him.

CHRONICLE 13
Recorded by Jegrac

"Almost done glamouring the back. Moving on to the left side!" Neva declares, her voice strained with effort and weakened by the rushing wind. "You two okay defending the caravan on your own? I can take a break from this if you need support."

Pall manages a muffled bark through the reins clenched tightly between his fangs.

"The three of us will be fine," I shout back. "On our left, Liatris!"

A horrifying screech rips into my ears when another riftspawn notices us, lumbering across the desolate fields with heavy steps, unnatural claws tearing the dirt and drawing closer and closer at an alarming speed. The road weaves, and the horses grunt in response, hooves carving thunderous steps into the dirt road as the wheels shudder from the sudden turn.

Biting down another shiver, my hand rises to aim a steel dagger at the creature.

The air carries hints and suggestions on where to strike, pillars of smoke weaving a pattern for my blade to find. In one swift motion, the blade flies from my fingertips and buries into the skull of the approaching beast.

My confidence rises as tar squelches into the soil, the mass of flailing limbs dissolving into the earth.

With renewed vigour, two more riftspawn fall prey to my strikes, dropping out of sight as we race past.

Pressing my lips together, I release a low hum. The blade in my hand thrums in response, signalling the other weapons to do the same.

A small shadow flashes above me, and a dagger drops into my hand, splattering sizzling black riftblood across the bench as it lands. Other knives soon follow, the birds responding to my whistle of thanks with screeches and shrieks before they whirl away.

"He really can't hear us?" Liatris whispers from her perch atop the caravan. "Or any of this? Good. That's good, right? He must be so worried about his family. And his people. Oh, Isaac..."

"Give him time," Neva snaps. "He doesn't need your pity."

An angry huff echoes above my head, but the dryad stays silent.

"Besides," Neva continues, "we'll save his town after we've saved ourselves, so just keep covering me. I'm gonna' seer for a bit, to give us a heads up about what we'll be facing next."

A nearby riftspawn crumbles from a well-placed dagger as Neva's voice fades. Her eyes look elsewhere, searching for a future where we all survive.

Liatris and I continue to protect the horses as they gallop along the ravaged and blackened path, trying not to flinch when the air thickens with soot and ash.

"Okay, I've seen enough," Neva declares, and she hops down to the empty space between Pall and I. My hound jolts upright when she lands. Not wasting time, Neva yanks open the curtain and yells: "They're fine, Isaac! A little bruised and looking worse for wear, but we'll find them eventually. So get off your lazy butt and come help us survive!"

She releases the curtain, letting it fall with a loud thump.

My nose wrinkles as the thick smell of glamours blends with the smoke and upturned soil. Neva reaches a steady hand over Pall and onto the side of the caravan, fingers trembling, her magic rippling across the wooden walls.

I continue my deadly game of fetch with the birds, daggers slicked with riftspawn blood as they cycle back and forth from the tarred creatures to me. Pall's snout dips, exhaustion catching him while he wrestles with the reins, struggling to keep the frenzied horses in check.

Neva climbs back onto the roof, her fingers weaving lines of colour in the air as our carriage slowly drowns in her artificial camouflage. The snapping of bones and the rustling of vines and roots dwindle; half of the caravan is now hidden from sight. An encroaching riftspawn is knocked down by my hurled blade and then crushed into the dirt as grass rises to strangle the beast.

Liatris and I flow in tandem, the rhythm of my daggers punctuated by plants that twist and warp to grip the creatures attempting to mow us down.

"Almost done," Neva huffs, "one side left. Or right. Ha! ...Yiatsu above, what a stupid joke."

"Isaac would've liked it," I grunt. Liatris's laughter is followed by Neva's annoyed sigh.

The air fills with the screeching of birds as I snatch more daggers from their grasp. Listening for a change in the wind or the bugs frantically flitting by, my ears catch the crunch and squelch of riftspawn bodies, the panting of the horses, and the steady thrum of wheels gyrating against the ground.

Eventually the attacks begin to slow, our tempo decreasing as Neva finishes her work. Tilting my head, the thud and hiss of riftspawn resound when they start to chase us, but their massive footsteps dull after they fall behind.

"The horses will be visible from the front," Neva mutters, "but if we can keep a steady pace, we'll look like an unappealing haze drifting down the road."

We travel in uneasy silence, my daggers clutched tight in my hands, but thankfully the journey becomes a little less frantic. Any offending riftspawn are dragged and hurtled out of our way by Liatris's brethren, and Pall rests his weary head once control of the reins returns to me.

The houses start to whisk by more frequently, some still standing while others lie ruined and overrun by riftspawn. Screeches and growls carry on the wind, growing louder and more condensed the closer we get to the town. A street lies directly ahead of us, bare beyond overturned cobblestones and streaks of tar and blood. Listening carefully, an eerie silence lingers beyond the crackle of fire, the occasional shudder of a building collapsing, and the continuous hissing from the blackened puddles lining the road.

The life in this town is being strangled by unnatural beasts and spreading flames.

"The church!" Neva shouts. "On our right, take that path!"

Pall releases a fierce bark when I yank the reins in response to our seer's sudden command. Mayweather and Daisy whinny angrily, but manage to twist sharply around the corner, nearly clipping into a bent street sign. The carriage wobbles dangerously, its well-worn wood hissing and groaning as the magic imbued throughout the cabin struggles to keep us stable. Pall moves to my side, the two of us leaning out of the caravan to keep it from flipping. With a thud, the wheels hit the ground running, the horses straining as we rush along at a steady pace.

The curtain rustles against my back, and then Isaac's head appears, stretched out between Pall and I to stare straight ahead.

"Of course, the church!" he exclaims. "Oh, thank Yiatsu! At least some of the town must have taken shelter inside..."

Judging by the crowd of riftspawn surrounding the building, he's right. Another involuntary shiver runs through me, so I try to focus elsewhere when my breathing quickens. The birds above fly freely through the dome of light enveloping the sanctuary, while the monsters below are held back by an unknown force.

With enough space to park the caravan on the untouched grass, we just have to get through this horde and then-

The tar-filled beasts stop clawing at the shimmering barrier, their smooth black skin boiling and popping with eager splatters as they turn to acknowledge us. A new, unguarded prey, heading straight towards them.

Sharing the reins with Pall, he rubs his sore mouth with a paw before gripping the leather with his fangs.

"Brace yourselves!" I shout. My seat thrums as Neva prepares to slow the caravan, the runes lining the wooden walls tingeing our surroundings with a soft blue hue. After a sharp whistle, Pall and I tug on the reins, the horses releasing frightened cries as the wave of snapping and crashing black bodies draws closer, a wall of teeth and claws blocking our path to the sanctum. The wheels of the caravan screech in protest when they drag against the dirt.

The Commander leaps from the carriage, his sword drawn and his face steeled. He rushes ahead, slicing through riftspawn and carving a path to the doors of the church, where spears poke through the forcefield at the distracted beasts.

Hopping out of the caravan, I place myself between Mayweather and Daisy, my hands on their manes, fingers tingling as my bond extends out to them, attempting to imbue the terrified mounts with a sense of calm. If they panic, we'll be stuck here. We follow the trail of corpses, doubling in size due to Neva, who weaves in and out of the swarm with devastating efficiency, leaving bubbling carcasses in her wake. Pall darts amongst the riftspawn as well, tearing and gnashing at any creatures foolish enough to come too close.

We draw nearer to the front steps of the church, a few measured paces away from the glowing barrier.

"Liatris, you ready? The soil should be safe in there, if you're able to-"

The dryad is already on the move, her small form flanked by Isaac, Neva, and Pall, who carve a wide swath through the crowd to let her pass.

The wall of light gives way, allowing me to sigh in relief once the blackened beasts become muffled and distant. Neva and Isaac fall back to clear away a few more riftspawn, and Liatris's legs buckle, her knees digging down into the grass. The plants reach up to her, embracing the dryad to pull her hands into the dirt. Her wrists sink below the ground, and she lowers her forehead to connect with the earth.

A mighty groan erupts from the trees surrounding the church, and they shift and stir, the weight of thick trunks and heavy roots warping in response to the dryad's call. The giants of the soil turn to embrace the old stone walls, the ancient building shuddering as the plants move in tandem. A mangled tidal wave of green and brown rises behind the caravan to form a rigid fortress of bark and leaves.

As the entwining wall of branches, vines, and other flora push back the tide of riftspawn, I undo the clasps on Mayweather and Daisy's reins, freeing the horses to wander and catch their breath within the safety of our small enclosure. Neva finishes off the remaining beasts trapped within our organic fortress, and the Commander disappears into the caravan, returning with Damian draped over his arms.

"I did it," a quiet voice announces.

Liatris peers through the mass of emerald ferns dangling over her weary violet eyes, offering me a smile before collapsing into the grass.

My hands dig into the soil, prying her limp body from the firm grasp of the plants below. Lifting her with as much care as possible, the dryad is hoisted gently over my shoulder.

Her breathing is soft against my back, though it quickens when a whisper of thanks escapes her lips. I shrug gently in response, and head towards the church to find her a place to rest.

Stepping through the entranceway, the scent of stale sweat and dried blood hits me first, followed by the must of old wood and ancient stone. People fill every corner of this space, huddled in small groups on the pews that have not been used to barricade the walls and windows, lingering around the priest and priestess locked in prayer, and standing guard by the door with rusted spears and repurposed farm tools.

Children's laughter echoes out from a doorway behind the altar, accompanied by the barks and mewls of family pets. Pall nudges my thigh, and I wave forward with my free hand. He sprints off, eager to join the frolicking downstairs.

"The wall, will it hold?" A woman asks, her voice strained as she peers past me, her fingers wrapping around the arm of my coat. "Father Garith and Sister Holly have been maintaining the barrier for hours. Please, tell us!"

Liatris mumbles something into my back.

"It won't disappear until my companion wills it," I say, and Liatris relaxes.

The air shifts to release a collective sigh, and the citizens of this town lean back against the walls and the benches, finally lowering their guard. The woman rushes past me to inform the clergy of the protections now in place.

"My friend needs to rest," I declare to the surrounding mob, my eyes scouring the old building. My attention flickers to the birds hiding in the corner of the high ceiling, chittering away as they duck behind the wooden rafters. Then my gaze wanders down to the limp bodies on the floor by the altar, where groaning and whimpering figures nestle on fur coats and ragged blankets.

Isaac brushes my shoulder, striding past, and I fall into step behind him.

A prickle creeps up my back as heads turn to follow me, hostile stares and suspicious glances out in the open, no longer hidden behind polite smiles and careful words.

My eyes are locked straight ahead, my breaths even and measured despite the whispers festering around Liatris and I.

A hand grips my shoulder, yanking me back. My gut tightens as I stumble.

But that same hand keeps my body stable, and a man with a strangely familiar face excuses himself, slipping by to reach the Commander.

"Isaac...?" His hardened face softens as the Commander's eyes widen.

The stranger attempts to embrace the Commander, his lumbering arms reaching out and wide for a big bear hug, but they falter when Damian lets out a faint wheeze.

"Hey, Dad," Isaac says. His smile fades. "Mom and Sam and the others, are they-"

His father clasps the Commander's shoulder, nodding slowly.

"We're fine. We're *all* fine, Isaac. I'm just glad to see you made it here safely. Your mother-"

Neva interrupts them, slipping her arms under the boy held aloft by Isaac.

"I'll take Damian so you two can catch up." She jerks her head towards the makeshift infirmary, gesturing for me to follow. "Good to see you're alright, Wilson." Isaac's father blinks in response, and then grins.

"Hey, Neva!" he shouts at her back. "Glad to see you haven't changed; still getting our son in and out of trouble!"

She laughs while she walks away.

I accompany her, and the eyes follow us, but the prickling at the back of my neck fades as the crowd's attention shifts. Faces switch from suspicion to shock, fear to curiosity, wariness to wonder. Neva's glamorous sapphire dress shimmers and ripples like the surface of a pond, and a hidden gratitude swells within my chest as people begin to focus on our ridiculously entrancing seer.

When and *how* she had time to change, I have no idea, but I'm glad she did.

Her appearance draws their attention away from me, and some of the citizens even recognize her, offering friendly waves and stammered greetings.

In the corner of the church, two makeshift beds have already been set up for us. Neva turns to a red haired gentleman in a white smock, his vibrant pink and teal armband sliding down to the crook of his elbow as he adjusts a bandage on a nearby patient.

"Dr. Conley?" she asks. The man tilts his head at the sound of his name. "Your apprentice said you could help us. He stabilised this boy, but not enough for a full recovery."

The riftspecialist moves into place beside Neva as she settles Damian down onto a ragged piece of cloth. Dr. Conley adjusts his spectacles and examines the weird white symbols sketched across the boy's forehead, neck, and chest.

He shifts his weight onto his heels before waving at his apprentice's work.

"Yes, I see what you mean. It's sloppy and meant to be a temporary solution, rather than a permanent one. Hmm. I'll have to review these runes with Mel next time I see him." He turns to us. "This'll take me a while to fix, unless either of you happen to have a one-eighth chargestone to spare. Need to tune up my instruments to get this child out of stasis and ready for a new set of enchantments; my magic reserves are all tapped out."

"That's all you need?" Neva asks, rifling through an invisible purse. "Take a half chargestone, at least. No, really, I insist. Whatever it takes to heal this kid."

I help Liatris onto the other makeshift bed, her limp arms falling away and sprawling like wilted leaves on the stone floor.

Neva and the riftspecialist begin a conversation beyond my understanding, so I look elsewhere, searching for an excuse to get back outside.

My only escape is the loosely barricaded entranceway.

Staring past the toppled benches and the scarred remains of what must have been the front door, the path to the wall of plants is clear; the shimmering barrier is gone. Nearby, a priest talks with the Commander in hushed tones, while a priestess rests her hand on a woman's bloody arm. No one is staring at me.

Sending a pulse of magic through the unseen, intangible thread binding Pall and I together, it travels into the basement beneath my feet.

My trusty companion sends an attentive spark back to me, and I reply with calm reassurance. He returns to frolicking with the children hidden down below.

Armed with the knowledge that Pall is fine, I walk towards the door and try to collect a variety of excuses about why I need to go back outside. As I approach, the man in gold and blue robes of the Order of Yiatsu falls silent, peering over Isaac's shoulder with narrowed eyes. The Commander turns to wave at me, and the priest breathes a sigh of relief before continuing to speak.

"-isn't the first attack," he mutters, "so thankfully, we were prepared."

Isaac shakes his head, turning to the man who looks a lot like him. If Isaac was a little shorter - and had a face hardened by time - it would be impossible to tell the two of them apart.

"Dad, why didn't you call? The guild could have been here sooner, if you'd just-"

His father silences Isaac with a pat on the shoulder, and rubs his stubby beard with a well-calloused and thick hand before responding in a deep, husky voice.

"If we needed your help, we would have asked for it," he replies, "but we were expecting this debacle, as Garith was just saying!"

The priest clears his throat and mutters *Father Garith,* but he's ignored.

"And, of course, there were signs. Nomads were-" Isaac's father pauses, glancing at me from the corner of his eye before continuing, "-spotted out in the forest, and you know the, uh, how do I put this... the *rumours* about their connections to riftspawn."

He lets out a gruff cough.

"Besides, we're farm folk. We're independent. We solve our own problems! Though we're certainly grateful for your help so far."

Isaac sighs, opens his mouth to speak, and then closes it again when Neva steps past me.

"*So far* is right," she announces, casually working her way into the conversation. "This many riftspawn in one place means only one thing: a portal, leading directly into the rift."

The priest's head wobbles as he struggles to make sense of her gaudy figure, flashy attire, and the words spilling from her mouth.

"But you're in luck!" Neva declares. "I've shut gates like this before, so you can hang back while I get to work. You've all got families to protect or whatever, right?"

Her haughty black eyes survey the men in front of her and - to my surprise - she stops at me.

A manicured nail jabs at the chronicler.

"Also, I'll be taking *that* with me," she says, "Aria enjoys archiving *actual* adventures, not debates about the morality of Nomads, rude assumptions, and unproven *rumours.*"

I hold it out to her, but she doesn't take it right away, instead turning to address Isaac, his father, and the priest.

"By the way, which one of you put in the request?"

Isaac's father looks like he's been shot.

"*Excuse me?*" he stammers, his face flushed as he glowers at the priest, who shrivels under the man's intense glare. "Garith, you didn't dare-"

"Oh, don't blame him," says a familiar voice. We turn to look at the woman crouched by the priestess. "It was me, Wilson."

Isaac's father looks like he's been shot a second time.

"Marie, what are you- what- I don't-"

She silences him with a glare, and then stands, taking restrained but eager steps towards the Commander.

"Izzy, welcome home! And - oh! Oh my. Isaac... how long has it been since you bought new clothes? Why, look at that nasty patchwork! Once this nonsense is over I'll have to fix you up good and proper."

The Commander smiles sheepishly as he draws the woman into a tight hug.

"Good to see you, Mom. Glad to know you're safe."

Her shoulders settle, and she melts into the embrace, pulling her son close. After a few moments, she pushes him away and turns to Neva.

"And welcome back, Neva. Thanks for looking after our boy." Her stubby fingers fix the crumpled apron wrapped around her wide waist, and then her elbow digs into her husband's side. He gives an awkward nod. When her arm comes threateningly close to his ribs again, he quickly adds: "Yes, you have our thanks. For what you've done, and what you're going to do. I'm sure you'll want to be paid, as always, so-"

She gives him a jab for the last remark, and he falls silent.

Then she turns to me, the warmth in her face shifting, the smile slipping for a beat, no longer than the flutter of a hummingbird's wings, but I still see it.

"So, you know how to close the rift?" she asks, her head bobbing as she peers at me. "I figured one might open up after those Nomads were caught lurking outside of town – although there were other signs, like the faint smog trickling through the trees, and that odd, acidic smell on the wind. Still, I'm glad your guild responded to my request!" A thick and calloused finger points at the chronicler, which is still in my outstretched hand. "I'm guessing that's what Nomads use to open and close riftportals?"

Before I can respond, Neva interrupts, her voice tight and brimming with annoyance.

"As I already said, *I'll* take care of it," she snaps, reaching to take Aria's device out of my hands, "and yes, we expect to be paid."

CHRONICLE 14
Recorded by Neva Oyii

G lares burn my back as I storm out of the church, but honestly? They can all die mad. After I've closed the riftportal, I'll worry about their closed minds. Right now, I have a barrier to overcome. The whispers fade as my attention turns to the wall of plants blocking my path, where gnarled branches twist to form improvised footholds, and bushels of bright green leaves obscure wooden rungs.

"Hey, Neva? You sure don't want help? I could accompany you, if you need a hand."

Jegrac steps beside me and stares up at the warped trees and vines, his face shadowed by the vast structure.

"If you're eager to be drenched in glamours and magic, then sure, join the fun!" I tease.

He grimaces.

"A horrid suggestion, though it might be better than staying here," Jegrac admits. He strokes his beard. "But I can't leave Liatris on her own. I doubt these folk have ever treated a dryad before. I should stay."

He disappears into the carriage for a moment, leaving me to survey the structure until he returns with a large watering can.

"One last thing, and then I'll leave you be," Jegrac says. "Right now, the caravan's empty. Might be a good idea to rest and regain some energy before heading out."

I brush off his concerns with a laugh.

"You worry too much, old man."

Despite my bravado, I still take a moment to step into the caravan and swap my dress and heels for a simple sweater, pants, and a pair of sturdy boots. With my outfit set and ready to go, I face the looming obstacle once more.

Bracing my legs, I hop onto the verdant barrier, starting my ascent up the tangled mess of leaves and wood.

As I leap towards the top of the enormous wall, the world sweeps out below me, the ground drifting away while the smeared grey sky lingers just out of reach. My mind goes blank as the rough bark helps me rise, my eyes searching for the next foot or handhold to help me scale even higher. The roof of the church passes by, and suddenly the peak of this living structure is only a few careful hops away.

Clambering through the last layer of branches, I slip over the side to admire the view. Smouldering buildings paint a beach of brown, black, and grey before sweeping out into a sea of trees. Peering beyond the forest, the outline of The Teeth is faintly visible, great white bases piercing clouds as mountains disappear into the sky. Staring off to the east, a hint of disappointment thrums inside my chest; the towers and stone walls of Nexus are nowhere to be seen. Instead, the land is filled with rolling plains, crowded trees, and dirt roads tracing a path back to the city.

Shifting my attention back to the forest, a steady stream of riftspawn slink out from the shadows, heading towards the church. Looking past them, I note where the smog is thickest. Squinting to dull the harsh light of the sun, a flash of red gleams amongst the ash-soaked green. A tent, perhaps?

Wanting more certainty, I refocus my gaze, magic thrumming behind my eyes. The world refracts like shattered glass, bending and shifting in a kaleidoscope of colour.

The present gives way to the future.

My teeth grind as a familiar white haze obscures my vision; it should have cleared up by now, but the milky cloud remains, muddling my ability to seer.

Thankfully, some areas are still visible. Blurred, perhaps, but still visible.

My eyes throb as I concentrate.

Details come into focus, pushing through the fog: a camp of some kind, with... a Nomad, I think? A hand emerges from the shimmering white mist, with a tan strikingly similar in tone to Jegrac's complexion. It's wrapped in the sleeve of a threaded brown robe. Peering past the outstretched limb, something pulses, and after a beat of intense effort the haze gives way to a black mass that bleeds riftspawn. Screeching beasts crawling out of the bubbling tar and into our realm.

The divination isn't very comforting, but it'll have to do for now.

A deep breath brings the present rushing back. Branches cradle my slumped figure, and I squeeze my eyes shut as prickling stars jab at the edges of my vision.

After a well-deserved pause, I turn my attention to the other problem I have yet to solve. Rows of riftspawn swarm the wall, held back by the thorns and writhing vines waiting to rip apart the next beast foolish enough to get close.

As the creatures lurch and crawl about the perimeter, a disturbing trend drums a heavy beat into my heart. Mangled heads keep rising to stare at the forest, beady black eyes aimed in the direction of the red camp.

They're waiting for something.

Suppressing a shiver, I rub my arms and legs, priming my magic. Exhaustion trickles through my veins as my body starts to disappear, engulfed in glamours that hide it from sight. Gritting my teeth, my foot latches on a nearby vine, and my descent begins.

Peering down through my invisible chest, a flood of relief courses through me when the riftspawn don't react to my presence.

A flicker of worry worms into my thoughts: will Liatris's magic eventually register me as a threat? No point in taking that risk; the eviscerated beasts below convince me to find a different path.

Off to my right, a solemn branch extends towards a tree unclaimed by the dryad's call. I climb towards it.

Thick wood darts past as my boots secure a new foothold, and after a quick survey of the area I slide down the trunk of the tree. Before reaching the base of the mighty plant, I leap, taking great care to put space between myself and the riftspawn wandering through the field.

The ground is smeared black, and it oozes with each step as the road draws closer.

Borderik is quiet and still, the silence broken only by the occasional crackle of small fires and the hissing and popping of bubbles on the skin of nearby beasts. Tar soaked streets lie surprisingly empty, and many buildings appear to be stable and untouched, odd coincidences beside smoking ruins filled with charred wood.

My attention turns to the forest.

More black beasts lurk in the shadows of the trees, feasting on wildlife as they lumber in the general direction of the church, drawn onward by the screeches and shrieks of their brethren. A surge of magic floods the ends of my heels to the tips of my toes, silencing my steps as a glamoured hand rubs my throat to hide my breathing. I weave among the riftspawn, keeping my eyes forward, searching for the camp from my vision.

When a hand squelches beneath my boot, it takes me a moment to recognize the vibrant red liquid spurting from the place where the wrist should be. My teeth sink into my lips, and I swallow a horrified gasp.

A blackened claw steps on a nearby branch, releasing a sharp crack and a reminder not to linger. Guttural growls creep through the trees as riftspawn draw closer. Can the beasts sense me nearby? My fingers grasp the branches of a nearby tree, pulling me up and into a sanctuary of leaves. Riftspawn slink past, baring rows of fangs at the disembodied hand. But then the beasts stop short, heads jerking as if tugged back, and they turn away to stalk deeper into the forest.

Travelling by foot no longer seems like a good choice.

A thick branch resists my tentative shove, and once it manages to hold my weight without creaking, I leap across it and into the next tree.

Shuffling around the massive trunk, my heart quickens at the sight on the other side.

The forest ends abruptly, cut short by a patch of land filled with ruined tents. The slaughtered structures surround a large, bubbling mass.

The riftspawn are more plentiful here, brooding in a ring around the camp, cutting slow swaths over corpses painting the ragged earth and soiled cloths with splotches of red and black.

Corpses?

I sink deeper into the shadow of the trees, fearing my beating heart will overpower the glamours silencing it.

They're not feasting.

The riftspawn have left the bodies of the Nomads alone.

Again?

It's a horribly familiar scene. A mirror image of the previous massacre, back in Dahlia's fields. Corpses, torn apart and streaked with red scars, but inexplicably left alone.

Why?

It doesn't make sense. Riftspawn are ravenous. They're not picky eaters.

Accusations, rumours, and whispers squirm in my ears, blaming the Nomads for the attacks, pointing fingers at Jegrac and his people, besmirching their names and declaring them outsiders and terrorists.

And then I see *them*.

Three hooded figures, swathed in black robes, facing towards the portal with their backs to me. The hot sweat running down my neck turns to ice as a white and gold emblem flashes on one of the stranger's shoulders.

A High Champion, here? Did the Council send them to support us - to close the portal on our behalf?

I should reveal myself. See what I can do to help.

No. Not yet.

Something's... off. Can't quite say *what*, exactly, but my gut tells me to watch and wait for now.

The hooded figures nod to each other, signalling the end of a conversation. The unidentified High Champion walks away, and the riftspawn part to let them pass. The shadows of the trees swallow the white and gold symbol, leaving the other two strangers standing guard by the bubbling mass.

Slipping down the tree, my eyes scour the camp, trying to make sense of what's going on.

The stained soil oozes tar as my boots soundlessly hit the ground, and a sickened laugh threatens to escape my throat.

Quest complete. Technically. The demand to 'investigate the Nomads in the woods' finally has an answer: *they died. Brutally, inexplicably, and unfairly.*

Just like last time.

No, wait - not quite. The massacre we discovered during our journey to Borderik was a tragedy. This, however, looks intentional.

In the midst of the ash and ruins are strange clues, ones that suggest foul play. Weapons are scattered about, stained with black blood. Some bodies reach for a blade, faces startled and twisted in horror, while others are peaceful and solemn, as if completely unaware of their fate.

A gruesome image burns in my eyes before I can look away: a small hand grips a toothbrush, the fragile limb stuck beneath a woman's mangled corpse. Bile starts to rise, so I focus my attention and thoughts elsewhere, turning to the hooded figures lingering by the tar tumour in the dirt.

The absence of the mysterious High Champion is a welcome relief. It's a title only offered to those the Council deems worthy, so bearers of such a name are often a pain to deal with.

With the High Champion gone and the portal left open, a deluge of troubling questions rise to take their place.

How did this massacre happen? Why are the riftspawn circling quietly around the outer edge of the camp instead of attacking? Why hasn't the gate into the Rift been closed yet?

I've never witnessed *anything* like this before.

It doesn't make sense.

Darting back into the solace of the leaves, my mind begins to wander.

Is this part of an investigation? Research? Does the Council even know about these strange riftspawn and this unknown High Champion?

And then, a worse thought.

Is this the result of a Nomad ritual? Could the rumours be true?

A pang of guilt strikes my chest, but the accusations are already forming, suspicions worming their way into my head.

Beyond Jegrac's strange connection to animals and his distaste for anything fashionable, he and his people are a mystery to me. Not that we'd ever had much conversation beyond topics related to the guild, but even so he'd often characterise most Nomads as good people. And even if *some* of his folk are corrupt, that doesn't mean they'd-

One of the strangers swats at a fly, shrugging back their cloak as they turn around.

My stomach drops.

Tan skin is visible for a brief moment, but too long to excuse it as a trick of the light. The other figure turns, hood tilting back while they make a comment to their companion, chin jutting out to reveal a similar complexion.

The branch creaks beneath me as my feet push towards the edge, hoping for a closer look, a sign that I'm wrong.

Please let me be wrong.

A shadow passes beneath my perch.

The lurching beasts have begun to slink away from the camp, drawing closer to the treeline. The leaves help mask my presence, rustling quietly as I slip beneath their careful embrace. Shuffling a little higher amongst the branches, I put more distance between myself and the riftspawn below.

A second glance indicates they have yet to notice the invisible woman in the tree above. Their attention is locked on something else.

Following their gaze, a damp thump echoes in my ears as the edge of the camp darkens with rows of riftspawn, all watching the hooded strangers and the boiling black bubble in the middle of the ruined settlement.

Bladed fans slip into my hands as the portal pops; it releases a dull squelch and sprays ooze into the air. Wooden hilts dig into my palms as the horror begins to unfold.

The Nomads notice the change much too late, their screams swallowed by the giant mass in the middle of the camp. It expands suddenly, covering feet then legs then arms then necks then terrified faces with tar.

In the blink of an eye, the strangers are gone.

The pool of darkness continues to expand, hissing, popping, and burping out splotches of ink as it grows, crawling towards the treeline at a rapid pace.

It's tempting to run, to search for reinforcements, but something compels me to stay - curiosity, perhaps? My heart thrums in my ears as my hands drum on the handles of my fans, a dreadful yet excited anticipation filling my stomach. The portal continues to swell, and the centre of the black mass grows.

And then the pool of darkness bursts. A long limb ruptures the surface, bladed claws dwarfing the ruins of a nearby tent when it slams against the ground. Blackened nails dig into stained soil as more tarred legs burst from the growth, a quick count of eight different appendages straining to pull a tremendous body out of the tar. The remains of the portal drip from the skin of this gigantic creature, and the large drops sizzle upon the ground.

What is this thing?

Riftspawn aren't supposed to be this big...

The creature's round, bulbous body splits open at the top, black slabs of bubbling skin peeling back like a rotting orange to reveal rows of serrated teeth. My hands rise to my ears, shielding them from the piercing bellow erupting from the beast. Leaves scatter, and I'm shoved back. The tree's trunk braces me with a solid thump.

The wind changes.

Branches shift, loose foliage whipping and spiralling through the air in a beeline towards the fanged maw. My cover is quickly shredded to ash, suctioned directly into the creature's gaping mouth. Black mist flows towards the giant riftspawn as well, sprayed from the backs of its brethren lingering below my perch. The dark smoke whirls into the arachnid-like beast, and my feet stagger, one hand pulled forward as the other reaches back to latch onto the rough bark behind me.

My eyes widen when my nails catch my eye.

I can see my fingers.

Clasping my hand to rub more magic into place, I rapidly conjure a new glamour. It refuses to stick, immediately whisked up and into the beast, disappearing along with more of my invisibility.

Resisting the riftspider's ravenous inhale is futile. It takes everything I can to shrink back amongst the disappearing leaves, my body pressed against the swaying trunk of this massive tree. The magic hiding me from sight has faded.

The wind stops.

Not wasting any time, bark scratches against my hands as I swing around to the other side of this barren oak, steadying my feet to leap from the branches and hit the ground running. My remaining magic surges under my skin rather than on top, strengthening each strained limb.

My knees lock, and a ragged gasp escapes my throat. But I catch myself with a steady hand, keeping my pace as I stagger upright, spurned on by the snapping of twigs and the squishing of blackened soil as screeching riftspawn notice me for the first time.

The raucous noise is accompanied by a larger crunch, the shuffling of many limbs, and a chorus of ground-shaking stomps.

I don't have to look over my shoulder to know the riftspider has begun its pursuit.

I'd rather not look.

The temptation to hide grows stronger, but my remaining energy are meagre sparks flickering at my fingertips, my eyelids dragging down as my dwindling magic struggles to keep me moving.

Glamours are no longer an option.

My shoulder smacks against a nearby tree, ache punching the inevitable bruise, and I stumble forward. Exhaustion has already started darkening the world around me.

I want to hide.

I can't.

The last dregs of my magic pull inward, the glamours contouring my face and clothes disappearing and flowing back into my skin, temporarily pushing my weariness away.

Each new step is a little easier, and my legs fill with renewed strength, my bladed fans still clutched tightly in my palms. My eyes rise to scan the web of scarred trees, tracing a careful path through them. Once the route is clear, I stare out into the void, blindly watching the world crack into pieces so a new future can unfold. The haze is still there, obscuring my vision, but I catch glimpses of what's to come if I return to Borderik for support: a smouldering town and a church in ruins.

Time to change plans.

The heels of my boots dig into the dirt, and I whirl about to charge back into the fray. If leading these beasts towards Borderik doesn't end well, then my only option is to fight.

Kicking off a nearby tree, my fans trace two silver lines in the air, carving deadly slashes in the necks of the pursuing riftspawn. Magic floods my lungs as black blood paints the dirt, each breath calm and precise as corpses crumple at my feet.

The ground shakes, and an approaching shadow catches my eye. Humongous arachnid legs snap trees like twigs as the riftspider draws closer, each thunderous step sending splinters and soil up into the air.

Slicing through another riftspawn, I search for a way to use my limited magic and energy to slay the approaching threat. Scaling up a giant bubbling limb doesn't seem like a good idea, especially with the beast's body hefted high above the treeline. The tallest branches barely scrape its dark underbelly.

Glamouring it to death isn't an option, so what the *rift* am I supposed to do?

My resolve falters, and the thought of leading it back to Borderik returns. The temptation fades, however - it's not worth the risk. As a fan stabs through the skull of a charging riftspawn, I consider my other options.

Going against the warnings in my vision is foolish, but... aw, *rift*. If only Yuina and Frost were here, or Liatris wasn't incapacitated! At least then we might stand a chance. But without the support of our guild's strongest members, the chance of civilian casualties is too high.

I concentrate, preparing to take another glimpse into the future, but then my legs are swept away as a massive claw slams into a nearby tree. The impact sends a tremor through the ground, knocking me off my feet.

The sky is blotted out by a bubbling darkness.

The riftspider has finally arrived.

Draped in shadow, a drop of black liquid hisses against the dirt as I rise to face the threat lingering above my head.

Tall spindly limbs cover my escape; pillars for a cage of living tar. My eyes flicker towards the surrounding trees, where rows of riftspawn linger at the edge of our makeshift arena, not wanting to disturb the riftspider's meal.

The body hovering overhead floats lazily on outstretched legs, threatening to slam down, and I brace myself, calves filling with magic as my muscles tighten. I prepare to leap out of harm's way.

In the midst of the black, the beast's skin splits open to reveal a giant red eye, which blinks at me.

Crouching, my glare turns into a grimace when my heel nearly gives way, forcing a hand into the dirt to steady myself.

The riftspider and I stare at each other, prey sizing up predator. It's too high for me to reach, but the lidless eye looks like the perfect place to strike.

My breath billows in front of my face, soft grey puffs exhaled much faster than I'd like. Raising a weary arm, it takes everything I have to hoist up my fan, the metal glinting as it trembles.

If it's going to eat me, I'll kill it in the process.

Somehow.

"Come on," I snarl. "Don't keep me waiting."

The beast blinks once more, and then the squelch of twisting flesh shrieks out. The eye turns away, the entire bulb rotating until a gaping maw is directly overhead, rows of sharp teeth wriggling in eager anticipation of their imminent feast.

Sucking a deep breath into my burning lungs, I extend my fans to their full length, muscles screaming for me to let them fall.

Aria. If you find the chronicler and have to read this, I hope it's because I survived. But if not? Oh well. Make my final story a good one, okay?

And to the guild... I'm sorry. Especially to you, Isaac. I hope you and your family and your people are safe.

I hope this wasn't all in vain.

A tear burns down my cheek as my thoughts darken.

Sorry, mama.

Your prophecy was wrong, in the end.

I failed.

This is as far as I can go.

My pained sigh breaks the silence, and a wispy cloud rises through the cold summer air.

Will we meet again on the other side? Do you-

I blink.

Cold?

The air is cold?

The dirt hardens beneath my feet, a great shiver running through the riftspider as little white specs coagulate amongst the dripping tar.

Snowflakes sting my skin, planting sharp, soft kisses as they die.

An awful squelching sound fills my ears, and the bulbous body starts to rotate again, the mouth spinning away so the unblinking red eye can peer out at the surrounding forest.

A strange haze rises among the trees as the sun declares war on winter.

I blink again.

It happens in an instant, ice creeping up each limb with such speed and ferocity that the beast has no time to react, a cage of frozen glass tearing along the blackened tar and encasing it in a glacial tomb.

The riftspider shatters with a great, terrifying crack.

Raising my fans to protect my head, a shriek escapes. The bodies of nearby riftspawn implode, bursts of black blood jutting out and freezing like shards of glistening onyx. The creatures collapse, screams dying in their throats when they turn to ice, frozen and still.

And then, amidst the corpses, a familiar child appears, cloaked in robes whiter than carved bone. A colourless hand dangles beneath a chalky sleeve, thin fingers wrapped tightly around the ankle of the body dragging behind.

A flood of emotions accompany his arrival: relief, then horror, then outrage, then gratitude, and then exhaustion.

Frost watches with indifferent silver eyes as the earth shifts beneath my feet. He tilts his head as his body does the same, flipping along with the trees as the ground presses against my face and the world starts to fade. The last thing I see are his bare feet, drifting through the snow.

CHRONICLE 15
Recorded by Frost

S he shifts in my arms, and the device nudges my shoulder.

It refuses to be shrugged away.

Since the chronicler won't budge, I'm tempted to just drop this woman and leave her behind. Unfortunately, Yuina will be annoyed if she is harmed, so I endure.

Neva mumbles something in her sleep, but I do not listen. My focus is on the frigid magic locked beneath my skin, shoving against my wards and threatening to escape.

A branch snaps beneath my foot, breaking my concentration for an instant. A surge of cold leaks into the open air.

The seer shivers.

Annoyed, I pull the chill back inside of me, restraining the deadly frost.

Neva trembles again.

Ugh.

What a pain.

The woman tosses and turns in her sleep, and I take advantage of her restlessness to bump the device away.

CHRONICLE 16
Recorded by Neva Oyii

I wake surrounded by corpses.

My head is mired in a dull haze, forcing me to blink away sleep until the carnage comes into focus. Familiar red cloth is scattered on streaks of blood seeping into blackened soil, accompanied by shattered beasts sprouting flowers of ice.

My eyes snap to the centre of the camp, searching for the rift portal.

Relief floods through me; the space is empty, a patch of bare soil with no trace of the bubbling mass.

"Neva." Frost punctures the silence with his quiet voice.

The pale child sits by the treeline, perched cross-legged on a pile of riftspawn tangled together in a frozen sculpture. I stare back at him, rubbing my arms as a cold wind flows out from his throne of corpses.

An oversized silver cloak dwarfs the boy's thin body, carving a trail in the snow falling around his bare feet. He slides down the glacial remains until he reaches the ground, keeping his distance from me. With a sharp breath, the chill retreats, shimmering in a deadly haze around the porcelain-white figure.

"I closed three." he declares, his voice dry and his silver eyes void of emotion. "Check for more."

I stifle a yawn as my legs shift into a more comfortable position.

Frost stares at me, unamused by my drowsy stupor.

A snarky reply dances on the tip of my tongue, but I know better than to push my luck with him.

Taking a deep breath, I shut my eyes, gathering magic under my eyelids with renewed vigour.

Opening them once more, the world has shifted. The irritating mist lingers, but it's a little less intense, fading to reveal a humble wooden table set with an assortment of dishes and half-finished meals. The fog widens, unveiling the members of Honour's Stand crowded together on uncomfortable-looking chairs, scarfing down food while making pleasant conversation with the rest of Isaac's family.

It's a cute scene, but not at all related to what Frost wants to know. I keep seering.

My vision cracks and folds into the edge of a cliff. The forest spreads out below, revealing lumps of black amongst the trees and towers of crystallised ice rising from the bodies of riftspiders.

A disembodied voice mutters '*I'm never climbing anything again*' and curses between ragged breaths.

It only takes a quick scan to confirm every riftportal has been closed.

Squeezing my eyes shut, I return to the present.

Frost's eyes are locked on me with his creepy, unblinking gaze.

"We're in the clear," I declare. Rubbing my arms, I hop up and take a few defensive steps away from the child, desperate for warmth.

Frost slides down the ice and walks away.

The cold recedes as he heads into the forest, verdant leaves curling in his wake. He disappears amongst the trees.

Taking a moment to massage the numbness out of my skin, I swear under my breath before sprinting after Frost. He's already put some distance between us, a trail of snow and slush marking his steady path through the woods.

Magic thrums from fingertips to toes thanks to my nap, and the ground races past, thudding beneath my feet as I close the gap between myself and Frost. A chill in the air signals I'm starting to catch up, and soon a silver cloak is visible a few steps ahead.

Weaving through the trees as icicles form on outstretched and ravaged branches, I call out: "Frost! Where the *rift* are you going?"

He doesn't stop to acknowledge my presence, though the top of his head tilts slightly.

"I'm bored." His oversized sleeves flow behind him as he glides across a sheet of ice carved through plants and soil. "Motamir was boring too," he states. His emotionless voice is tinged with annoyance, sounding a little too much like an accusation.

After a few beats of silence, he relents. "Yuina found an artefact. So it was not a complete waste of time."

He stops, forcing me to dig my heels into the dirt before the cold can bite at my skin. I hop back to maintain a safe distance between us.

Frost glances over his shoulder, half-lidded eyes piercing through the snow sprinkling around his pale silhouette.

Taking a careful step forward, he points at a corpse nestled amongst a bed of blackened leaves.

"Look," he says.

The boy turns away, ice forming under his bare feet as he slides out of sight, his fragile figure slipping into the shadows.

Once the chill of winter is gone, I approach the body.

It's another hooded figure, wrapped in a tattered black robe. The man's face is unfamiliar, though his brows are thick and his features are sharply defined. His skin is dyed with snow but clearly tinged with the same complexion as most Nomads.

Glancing over the corpse, I wonder how Jegrac will take the news. Perhaps these deaths won't come as a surprise after the massacre in Dahlia's Forest, but the confirmation of his people's involvement with the riftspawn? He's not going to take that lightly.

It's an anger I struggle to understand at times - why feel responsible for the actions of other Nomads? It's not *his* fault some of them are corrupt.

A weary sigh escapes.

Should I even tell Jegrac about what happened here? No matter how I present this information, it's only going to make him feel worse.

Aw, *rift*.

I don't need a prophecy to picture the look on his face when I tell him about the Nomads guarding the riftportal. Such knowledge will tear him apart. But-

I hesitate.

None of this makes any sense based on what I know of Jegrac and his people. Most Nomads have a strange and irrational love for nature and life and Morrowfir and whatever it is they pray to when they're annoyed or horrified.

Riftspawn, on the other hand, only exist to destroy. Plants, animals, people, insects... nothing is left untouched, even after death.

Strange thoughts tickle the back of my mind. An itchy feeling, as if I keep drawing the wrong conclusions. Something is off. But *what?*

A memory plagues me, centred around the two Nomads lingering by the portal. They'd certainly looked the part, and yet... why did they seem so odd? So unnatural?

Jegrac's annoying voice rings in my ears, interrupting my observations with an invasive echo. It's a familiar lecture about killing spiders in the guild hall, another one of his many self-righteous speeches about how the *children of Morrowfir are all precious* and *we have a duty to preserve life.*

If that's what Nomads believe, then *why had the person guarding the riftportal tried to swat a bug?*

Hmm.

Not all of Jegrac's people *have* to be devoted to nature, right?

I look down at the body by my feet.

I could just walk away. Ignorance is bliss, isn't it?

For a moment, my feet scuff the ground, threatening to leave my growing suspicion behind.

I crouch to get a better look at the corpse.

My fingers pause a few inches from the dead man's face. Touching his head feels invasive - even if he's no longer alive - so my attention slips down the length of his sleeve and onto his hand.

Priming some basic magical energy, I press against the cold, clammy skin, pushing away unseen glamours.

Nothing changes, and I breathe a sigh of relief, thankful to be wrong.

But something compels me to stay.

I have to try again. Just in case.

I reach down once more.

This time, my mind traces back to the humiliation with Foivos, when he'd uncovered Liatris's illusion with a deception of his own, the two glamours countering each other in a way I'd never seen before.

Magic seeps from my fingertips, pushing against the surface of the dead man's skin. Rather than working to remove a glamour, I focus on replacing it with a layer of glass.

Nothing happens.

A sigh escapes my lips. Why was I worried about such a silly thing? Of course the Nomads are to blame. Who else would it be? And who would have anything to gain from such a grand conspiracy, really? Nexus? As if the Council would let-

The tan starts to fade, revealing white skin underneath.

Oh.

Oh no.

I can't stop myself. My hand rises to the man's face, brushing his cold cheek. A pale splotch blooms underneath my fingertips, glamours waning as my breath grows short.

Settling back on my heels, I swallow the lump in my throat.

Admittedly, this is very, *very* suspicious. But I've only uncovered *one* person. And even if this is part of something greater, who's at fault? Why would anyone want to hurt Nomads or endanger townsfolk like Isaac's family?

And why would a High Champion be involved?

I stand, peering down at the white splotches staining the lifeless body.

The light striking through the trees refracts and bends as I look beyond, searching for answers. Scouring the images before me, my eyes burn as they peer through the haze, the white mist thickening each time I attempt to seer an explanation for these events.

A pressure strikes my pupils, the clouds swelling until a burst of pain forces me to look away.

I stumble, one hand pressed against my head as the other grasps at a nearby tree to steady myself.

What the rift?

A wet line trickles down my cheek, and I wipe it away, revealing a red smear along the length of my index finger.

"Well," I say, wiping the blood on my sweater, "that's new."

Turning back to the town, I pull up my shirt to gently dab away any crimson stains. My fingers glamour the blood out of sight as I pace through the forest, taking careful steps around the sizzling remains of slain riftspawn.

Borderik draws closer, and the ice littering many of the corpses is replaced by clean slashes carved through bubbling bodies.

I quicken my pace, taking care not to step on the deep wounds splitting the dirt.

The soil thrums, each cut vibrating with lingering magic.

Oh! Yuina is here! Perfect. If anyone can figure out why the Nomads are being framed, it'd be our guild's historian.

My steps quicken as the church's steeple peeks through the top of the trees. Just a little further to go.

The ditch beside the main road greets me, one final hurdle to climb before I can rejoin the guild. Peering across it and into the open doors of the church, Isaac and the others can be seen milling about inside.

The tangle of plants and trees still cradles the walls of the building, though it has slipped away from the entrance. Jegrac's horses have also disappeared, and a quick scan of the nearby field reveals their mighty forms frolicking amongst rotting black carcasses.

Enormous riftspiders are strewn across the meadow, severed legs rising like melted chimneys, coughing smoke from the tips of each spire.

I pause at the edge of the ditch, gathering my strength to leap over the muddy water lining the bottom of the small trench.

Almost there.

My knees buckle as a violent force slams against my lower back, accompanied by a punch that knocks the breath from my lungs. I gasp for air, hands grasping at the blade rupturing my stomach.

"You've seen too much," a voice snarls in my ear. "Should've walked away after failing the first time, *Neva*."

The steel is ripped out, and I stumble forward, water soiling my boots as I stagger up the ditch and onto the road, one hand sopping wet with blood to cover the wound at my side, the other slipping around a bladed fan.

Grass itches my arms and prods the hole in my back as I fall against it, shoulders collapsing against the sparse gravel.

My grip falters at the sight of a gold and white band, flashing in the sunlight beside a curved dagger dripping with blood.

The High Champion's face is obscured by glamours, their skin painted in a cruel mockery of Jegrac's people and their features sharpened into an androgynous face. It's an obvious illusion; the Council would never promote a Nomad.

I grit my teeth, force magical energy into my gaping wound, and then gasp as torn skin and bruised flesh begin melding back together.

The High Champion lunges forward, blade piercing the air as I kick my legs off the side of the ravine and somersault onto the road.

My side hurts like *rift*, but I've felt worse. Straightening my back, I stretch my limbs, toy with my fans, and look down at the hooded figure. Their brows are furrowed, noticeably annoyed by my refusal to die quietly.

Good.

"You know, it's amazing what an hour of rest can do," I say, gathering my strength. "Ready for a dirt nap? Apparently mud works wonders on your pores - show me that face of yours, and we can get to work."

My skin tingles as glamours spread across my body, and I draw my foot back into a proper fighting stance.

The High Champion moves, and my weight shifts onto my toes so I can leap around any incoming strikes. Instead, the stranger starts to shrink away, retreating into the shadows of the trees.

"I don't have time to deal with this," they snap.

Magic flickers over my eyes, and I catch a glimpse of myself sitting in the caravan. A grin spreads across my face.

"What a pity! But don't worry, I just checked my schedule; looks like I've got time to spare, so please, stay a little longer. Here, I'll even put on a show to make it worth your while."

Glamours pour through my skin, covering my entire being and hiding me from sight. The High Champion stumbles back, eyes wild and searching for a prey they can no longer see. Their hands rise, and the ground shifts in response, spikes of earth and stone piercing the air, narrowly missing my feet. The dirt shudders as I leap across the ditch and land at my opponent's side.

The stranger turns in response, eyes narrowed but un-focused. They gesture again and the earth responds with more protrusions, but it's too late. The High Champion tries to dodge my attacks, the ground rising to knock them away from my outstretched fans.

Twisting midair, I hear a satisfying gasp of pain when my blades slice cleanly across an exposed leg. Having secured a solid strike, my arms reach up from my roll to grab a nearby branch, swinging myself up and into a sanctuary of leaves.

The High Champion swears as they grasp at the blood trickling down to their brown sandals. Their head twists as they search for me.

Hah! - one little cut, and their confidence shatters?

Wiping my fans on a nearby leaf, I take care to hide the crimson stains.

With my glamours thrumming at full force, I am not simply *invisible -* to the threat below, I no longer exist.

They won't know how I killed them, but they *will* know it was *me.*

Unfortunately, I can't kill *them.*

Murdering a High Champion could bring the wrath of the entire Council down on our heads. It's not worth the risk.

Voices call from across the road, people spilling out of the church to point at the warped earth and the stranger clutching their leg.

"*Yiatsu above -* how *dare* you!" the High Champion spits, their voice distorted and warped by the glowing red runes lining their neck. "I'm going to enjoy breaking you and your filthy guild."

Leaving the shelter of my glamours behind, I jump down, facing my opponent head-on.

"Excuse me? Why are *you* upset?" My hands press against my hips like I'm scolding a child. "I'm the one who got stabbed! Don't throw a fit just because *we* did our job and protected these people!"

I grab hold of the stunned silence and blaze through the rest of my lecture.

"Are you throwing a tantrum because you got hurt? What, gonna' go whine and complain to the Council about a *scratch*? Don't bother - my actions count as *self-defence*. You attacked first! But I'm a kind, generous, *forgiving* person, so I'll make you a deal - if you accept defeat and leave quietly, we can pretend this never happened."

The High Champion snarls.

My hands tighten around my bladed fans, ready to fight again, but after a long moment the stranger sighs and sheathes their sword.

"You know what - *fine.* Take this victory. You're not worth killing anyways, and we can afford to give up this insignificant town. Borderik isn't our *only* option."

Folding their arms, the stranger falls down into the earth. The soil squelches as it swallows the hooded figure whole.

Once the High Champion disappears, my legs buckle, threatening to give way. Fans slip into hidden pouches on my thighs as I stagger back to the ditch, a hand pressed against the wound on my side.

Jegrac reaches me before I fall, lending his shoulder to keep the ground from rushing up to meet me. There are questions in his eyes, about his people, about the rift, but now is not the time. He'll have to wait.

"Here," I say, passing the chronicler to him. "Take this. I need to lie down for a while."

CHRONICLE 17
Recorded by Jegrac

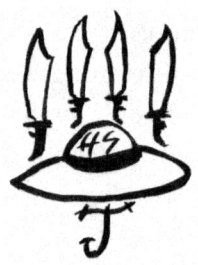

Neva stumbles as we climb the ravine, and I offer my shoulder for support. She attempts to stand on her own when we reach the road, and my eyes lock onto the bright red flower soaking through the back of her sweater.

"Morrowfir above! Neva, are you-"

She clamps a hand over my mouth.

"I'm fine," the seer hisses, "just need to rest. Focus my magic. I'll handle it."

Questions burn in my throat: *What happened? What did you see? Who summoned the riftspawn?*

One last question scalds my tongue when I swallow it down.

Are my people to blame?

It shouldn't be hard to just ask; knowing Neva, she'll probably laugh and say *What? No, stop being silly! No bitter and furious Nomads were involved in any of the riftspawn attacks. It's just a coincidence.*

Fear sews my mouth shut.

The truth will have to wait.

Isaac reaches us first, closely followed by Pall. My faithful hound offers a concerned whimper when he sniffs Neva, but she shoves his snout away.

"Handle *what*, exactly?" Isaac asks. He pauses, and then gives Neva a concerned look. "I might not have Jegrac's nose, but I recognize the smell of blood. You okay?"

She gives him a weak smile, and pulls out a fan splattered with red streaks.

"Don't worry, it's not mine," Neva declares as she limps over to our caravan. "Anyways, I'm looking like quite the mess, so give me some privacy while I freshen up a bit."

The Commander steps aside to let her pass, glances at me with wide eyes, and then follows her across the road. I fall into place behind them, with Pall trotting along at my side.

My courage rises enough to ask an easy question.

"Morrowfir protect us," I mutter as I scour her dishevelled figure for other wounds, "but that person earlier, were they...?"

"A High Champion? Yes. Unfortunately." Neva climbs onto the wooden bar at the back of the caravan, stifles a pained grunt, and tumbles through the dark curtain. Isaac holds it open while we watch her settle amongst a bed of blue and gold pillows, her bloodied hand groping for something hidden beneath the bench.

The air grows cold. Turning, I spot a familiar boy lingering by the road.

"Who?" Frost says. His emotionless voice is tinged with an unsettling eagerness.

Neva shrugs.

"They glamoured their face, so I don't know, and I can't even tell you where they went. Though they couldn't have gone very far..."

Frost tilts his head.

"Excellent," he states, "I was getting bored."

Isaac turns, his lips parting to call the boy back, but Frost has already drifted into the forest. Relief floods my chest when the cursed child leaves, but the feeling is soon shoved aside by dread. His unnatural presence will wreak havoc on the lives lingering amongst the blackened soil and scarred trees, and the bitter cold will trick and terrify all manner of forest creatures with the unexpected onslaught of winter.

The Commander clasps my shoulder.

"Why don't we go check on Yuina?" he suggests. Neva offers him a grateful smile, and then her eyes drift shut, one hand nursing the red stain on her side while the other hangs off the bench. Her sigh of relief is cut short as the cloth wall drops between us.

"She'll be fine," I say when Isaac hesitates. "Let's go save your fellow townsfolk from Yuina, before her curiosity drives them mad."

He nods and shuffles away faster than expected, swapping between sprinting and walking until finally settling on a light jog. The Commander calls to his family before he's even stepped through the church door.

Oh, I see. So now *I'm* in charge of drawing Yuina away from the relics inside this ancient building? *Thanks*, Commander. How *kind* of you to dump this responsibility on me.

The small circular stones dotting the path up to the church are smooth, solid, and a wonderful distraction. My pace slows as I take careful, methodical steps on each carved rock. I'm not eager to pass through the entranceway of this temple, where another onslaught of suspicious stares and hostile whispers wait on the other side.

Pall gives me a reassuring push, forcing a stumble forward and a quickened pace. He releases a soft bark, encouraging his master to stop dragging his feet.

I give my loyal companion a quick pat, and he nuzzles my leg in response.

It's all I need; even if the Commander, Neva, and Liatris aren't with me, I'm not alone.

Slinking through the doorway, barely anyone turns my way. Their attention is locked on Yuina, who stands near the altar, her arms crossed and her thin brown eyes sharp and narrowed at the priest blocking her way.

"It'll only be for a moment," she argues, gesturing past the man and at the giant goblet in the middle of the stone dias, "and you can have it back once my cataloguing is complete. You understand the significance of this spiritual relic, right?"

The priest stays rooted in place, his arms spread wide in a pathetic attempt to obscure her view.

"While we are grateful for your assistance with the riftspawn, this is not a trinket for outsiders to gawk at!"

Yuina's long black ponytail sways against her back as she shakes her head.

"You are making a *mistake*," she mutters, hands on her hips, "but I will not push this issue any further, out of respect for our Commander and his family."

She unclips one of the notebooks hooked on her belt and pulls a piece of charcoal from a pouch strapped to her thigh. The small writing tool glimmers with a soft grey light.

"Now then! If you can just step aside, I will make a quick sketch of this item for my record and then be on my way."

When the man remains steadfast, she adds, "It will not be touched. You have my word."

He doesn't move.

Yuina sighs, and then tilts her head at the priestess standing nearby.

"Is there *anything* in your scriptures forbidding outsiders from drawing relics? In my studies of your religion, I have yet to come across such a thing, but perhaps I'm mistaken...?"

When the woman gives the priest an uncertain glance, Yuina rolls her eyes. Standing to her full height, she stares over the man's balding head and begins to sketch, her charcoal scratching long lines on parchment paper.

She raises an eyebrow as the priest steps back towards the altar, shrouding the chalice with his frail body.

"Yuina," I say, and she whirls towards me, her angular eyes sharpening. Her stoic expression is framed by a few strands of black hair, which have slipped out from her ponytail to cradle the sides of her face.

"Oh. Jegrac." she replies, taking a precise step in my direction, her brown boots tapping against the stone floor. "Are you here to talk some sense into this man?"

She tucks the notebook under her arm, the bladeless hilts strapped to her wrists swinging like spiders on threads as she gestures at the priest behind her.

I pause and mull over how to answer.

Yuina's right: the priest is overreacting. It's just a metal cup. But we're here as guests, not tourists, and our role right now is to keep a low profile and avoid conflict. It's what the Commander would want.

"Didn't you get enough sketches at the last temple we visited?" My words are even, polite, and teasing, and the clergy relaxes as Yuina's lips press into a thin line. "Why don't we let these fine people focus on their rituals to cleanse the area of riftblood, while we head back to the caravan? They clearly don't want you looking at this... relic, so why not find something else to do? I bet Neva's eager to talk with you; let's go see how she's doing."

Yuina smiles, but her eyes are furious.

The priest sniffs. "Finally, a man of reason," he declares, "so, my dear, if you could just-"

Yuina whirls on him.

"Your actions are an affront to historians everywhere," she declares, "and you ought to be ashamed of your ignorance, *not* proud of it!"

The priest gives her a haughty glance, sizing Yuina up from head to toe, and then sinks against the altar once he gets a proper look at her.

At first glance our guild's scholar is tall and slender like a reed, but muscular lines lurk beneath her grey dress shirt and tan pants. The large, light brown backpack slung over her shoulder has a noticeable heft and weight to it, and the notebooks attached to her belt or poking out from the pouches strapped to her legs obscure a powerful figure.

With an irritated huff, Yuina stalks away, grabbing my sleeve to tug me along with her. After a few awkward steps I plant my feet, forcing us to stop. She glares at me.

"Neva would've had my back," Yuina mutters, each word laced with venom. "If you're not planning to help, keep your comments to yourself!"

I shake my head, hoping to diffuse the bristling hostility in the woman's precise, pointed tone.

"We're here for the Commander."

Yuina snorts.

"You might be," she scoffs, but then she calms a little, her rage subsiding as her eyes drift to the ceiling, studying architecture and runes I've never been able to appreciate.

"Neva *is* in the caravan," I say. "Doubt she's up for a conversation, though. Just fought a High Champion earlier, and is taking some time to recover."

"Huh." Yuina's gaze remains upward, not even blinking to acknowledge what I've said.

"Don't you want to ask Neva about her battle?" I ask, trying to hide my bewilderment. "I thought you'd be..."

"Interested?" Yuina gazes down her nose at me. "No. One High Champion is enough, thank you. Now leave me be."

Pall nuzzles her hip, and she gives him an absentminded pat on the head. It satisfies him, and he hops back to my side.

Taking a cue from the diligent historian at my side, I turn my gaze upwards to glimpse birds fluttering amongst the rafters. Tracing their path along the ceiling, a sparrow fumbles with the small branch in its beak, and the twig drops to the floor where Liatris and Damian are resting. My eyes widen when the dryad begins to stir.

Suppressing the urge to sprint, my steps quicken as Liatris sits up, blinks, and stretches her arms. Her mouth widens to release a fierce yawn.

It takes the dryad a moment to get her bearings, her eyes squeezing away sleep, and then she smiles and shakes herself awake. The ferns atop her head uncurl, the vibrant green bouquet springing to life once again.

"I! NEED! SUNSHINE!" Liatris roars. The dryad hops off the makeshift bed, her feet patting on the stone floor as she rushes towards the door.

She stumbles, and I reach to catch her, but Liatris just uses the momentum to move faster, sprinting out the building to leap into the light of the afternoon. A smile spreads across my face as she dances beneath the sun, pausing every so often to nurse fallen flowers and trampled grass, her fingers sparkling with emerald magic.

"It's no chalice, but my observations of the runes hidden within this intricate structure will have to suffice," Yuina declares, hands on her hips as her eyebrows arch. "Shall we visit Neva?"

I glance at the Commander, who is sitting on an overturned pew with his family, talking in hushed tones.

"Should we let-"

Yuina shakes her head, whisking the thought away with a flick of her hand.

"Give Isaac some space. We'll see him later! And right now, he's probably quite eager to finally have some time away from his responsibilities and the guild. If we learn anything new, he can hear about it when we regroup."

Yuina points a long, slim finger at the device on my waist.

"Speaking of responsibilities," she says, "may I? Aria would certainly appreciate a variety of perspectives."

As we walk towards Liatris, I follow Yuina's lead and try to ignore the cautious stares and hostile glares following us out the door. Passing the chronicler to our historian, I turn and look back at Isaac, who offers me a smile that doesn't reach his eyes.

I don't have to eavesdrop to know his family is talking about us.

About me.

CHRONICLE 18
Recorded by Kaneko Yuina

My hands grasp for an empty pouch, a list forming in my head as I tap the different items in each pocket. *Notebook, nexus chargestones, notebook, strange coin, spare notebook, chalk, vials, riftspawn samples, emergency notebook ... ah!* The chronicler slips into a sleeve on my shin, and I kick to adjust to the new weight.

Once I'm comfortable with the added burden, I resume my steady pace towards the exit of this religious facility. A sniff and a grunt at my back confirm Jegrac and his obedient pet have fallen into place behind me.

"Yuina," he says, "was that cup *actually* special, or were you just trying to make a scene?"

Biting back a snippy reply, my eyes trace the runes surrounding the church's doorway, hoping to smother my annoyance with curiosity. I blink when harsh sunlight hits my face, the entranceway disappearing as the stone floor beneath our feet is replaced by soft grass.

"Yes, *of course!* And if you'd backed me up, that religious fanatic would've backed down! Out of respect for the Commander, however, I restrained myself."

For now. When I get a second chance, Neva will be coming back with me. Actually, I'll invite Frost instead. He'll be volatile enough to knock the clergyman out of the way.

That fool should have just stepped aside when I'd asked nicely.

But it's fine. Eventually, the relic's ancient Aegis script will be mine.

A shiver of excitement rushes through my fingers, and I flex each one as thoughts surge about the practical applications of the symbols embedded in the old chalice. Before I'd been rudely interrupted, the character for *good health* (two bold lines covered by a circular shape) had flickered on the rim of the artefact. When Isaac lets me tailor his clothes later - as he often does - I'll sneak some runes inside his collar. He'll be my active field test of their effectiveness!

My plotting is interrupted when our dryad dances over to us, her violet eyes sparkling once she notices me.

"Oh, I've missed you, Yuina!" she exclaims. "How was your quest? Did you save the world again?"

It's hard to suppress my smile at her endearing demeanour, and my gaze wanders to the ferns swaying on her head amidst the still summer air. Focusing on the green lines inside each thin leaf, I spot the soft emerald glow hidden within, a sign of Liatris's ability to draw magic and energy from sunshine. Unfortunately, my knowledge on such a thing is limited, since our dryad has yet to lend me one of her headpieces for future experimentation.

Regardless of my ignorance, however, the process is fascinating to watch, and Liatris notices, sheepishly covering her head with her small hands.

Not wanting to embarrass her any further, my attention shifts to the caravan, tracking the runes hidden throughout the ancient wood. Admiring my handiwork, I follow Jegrac and Liatris to the side door, running a hand over some particularly complicated symbols that register magical signatures, noting the addition of an unfamiliar mark. Squinting, it takes a few attempts to translate it - *Damian?*

The slumbering figure in the church, perhaps? He was tucked on the cot beside our dryad and clothed in a noble's attire, clashing against the homely and rustic feel of other individuals in the ancient building.

Isaac had mentioned him when I'd first arrived, but my attention had been elsewhere. The old church was much more interesting than some inconsequential kid.

Liatris and Jegrac slip inside while I start a routine check of the runes decorating our carriage, taking care to fix the fading ones. I'm tempted to update the older symbols with my magically-charged chalk, but then Neva shouts something unintelligible and undoubtedly rude, indicating it'd be wise not to test her patience right now.

My fingers rest on the door handle as my eyes wander to the forest, searching for any signs of Frost. His atmospheric haze is nowhere to be seen.

Ah, too bad. Hopefully he's off fighting a High Champion, or has found some other way to enjoy himself. He's been so bored lately. I'd prefer his cravings for entertainment be satiated soon, before they become my problem.

Shutting the caravan door behind me, I glance around the cabin to check for any changes in the last few days. Blankets are crumpled in the middle of the floor, and Liatris has added even more plants to her conservatory, but otherwise everything else is as expected.

Or not. A satchel rests under the empty part of Neva's bench, and a spear lies nearby, piquing my interest for a moment. The curiosity subsides when the steel remains bland and lifeless. *Tsk.* Another boring Nexus weapon. It certainly looks fancy enough to trick a noble into buying it, but the simple craftsmanship is not worth my time.

"Took you long enough," Neva grumbles.

Ah, yes. *Neva.* A specimen worthy of my attention, and a good friend. Today our seer is wrapped in an intricate silver robe, which flickers with dark grey runes and ripples with magical energy. At first, it's hard to discern the exact symbolic nature of the shimmering lines, but eventually I manage to decipher a simple script for *health* and *healing.*

"Yuina, you're the only person in the world who can creep me out with their stare," she says as I examine her white headwrap, which pushes up a puff of curled dark hair into a makeshift halo.

My eyes wander down to her sandals, where multiple straps twine around her feet and ankles. Neva snaps her fingers, drawing my attention up to her face. She's added a white design on her eyelids to sharpen her features, and I peer closely at her cosmetics. It's an interesting look, though impractical - but with the runes for *sight* and *clarity* scrawled overtop, perhaps it could-

"You're not allowed to touch me," Neva interrupts, "so don't even think about it."

"Okay. Another time then," I reply. The seer rolls her eyes.

"Anyways," she says, "you wanna' know who-"

She hesitates.

"Wait. Before I forget..." Neva shares a glance with Jegrac and Liatris, sending a chill down my spine.

"Brace yourself, Yuina," Jegrac says, picking up the conversation, "because one of the High Champions knows that Liatris is a dryad."

Curious.

But who? Hmm. Since we're all alive and unbothered, it couldn't have been Solaris or Rahma. Strike, perhaps? Toxil? No, of course not - Liatris would have been glamoured!

"Foivos." I declare. Neva raises an eyebrow, but doesn't disagree.

"That's... not great," I mutter, "but let me check with Frost when he gets back. Maybe the Council sent him a heads up about the situation. However, since Liatris is still with us, let's assume we're safe for now."

My hands press against the stray hairs framing my face and push out a sigh.

"All things considered, the timing of this event is in our favour. The relationship between Nexus and Orion is currently unstable, so I doubt the Council will report Liatris to any authorities from the Dunes. Especially after that rogue guild rebelled against the Elders! But if the situation changes... hm. Worst case scenario, the Council might try to capture our dryad, and use her as a peace offering or a bargaining chip. *Might*, mind you. Probably not. I think."

"Good, so we have nothing to worry about!" Neva says sarcastically. "And since we've got *that* out of the way... y'all wanna' know who's been opening the rifts?"

Jegrac stiffens.

Neva notices, and she waves a hand at his face.

"Oh, calm down, Jegrac. Sure, the strangers by the riftportal looked like Nomads, but they weren't *real* Nomads."

My heartbeat quickens when Jegrac sits up even further, face flushed and brow furrowed. He doesn't hide his glare as he rounds on Neva.

"Careful, girl," Jegrac snarls, "I'm not in the mood for games. Tell me: *are we responsible?*"

Neva blinks.

"Watch your tone, old man. Are you even listening? They *looked* like Nomads, but they *weren't* Nomads." She raises a forearm to press a glamour onto her skin, lightening the black tone until it reflects Jegrac's tan colour. "See? You get it?"

He takes a moment, lips tight, eyes flickering to me as I gasp.

She has to be joking.

"Neva, you're certain?"

She nods.

A thump echoes through the caravan as Jegrac falls back in his seat, head buried in his hands.

"By Morrowfir..." he mutters. Pall gives a concerned whine.

Liatris watches, concerned but confused. She looks at me, eyebrows raised, but I can't be bothered to explain anything to her - my mind is churning.

"Alright, Neva, let's assume this isn't a coincidence or a one-off event. Which, mind you, we have yet to prove. Right? Right. And another important question: *why?*" The words spill out, a torrent of roiling thoughts breaking forth in response to this strange but terrible news. "Hmm. Some people dislike Nomads, yes, but to do something on this scale, and to even open a rift in the first place... only a few individuals are capable of something like that..."

It's improbable. Highly unlikely. Ridiculous to consider!

But *not* impossible.

"Wait." I press my hands together, attempting to organise my thoughts on my fingertips. "Before we get further - did you learn who or what is responsible for the glamours used to make Jegrac's people into a scapegoat? What happened, exactly?"

Neva shrugs.

"You know what I know," she says. "Wish I knew more, but lately all of my visions have been obscured by an obnoxious white haze. Also! Getting stabbed by a faceless High Champion has sapped the last of my magic, so don't expect me to seer for a while."

Jegrac whispers to Liatris, explaining the situation while also debating with himself about why someone would be disguised as a Nomad.

Neva settles back and closes her eyes. Sparks flicker like tiny bubbles around her face, magic accumulating to search for a future only she can see. Her brow starts to furrow, and a tear draws a bloody red line down her cheek.

She gasps, rubs the crimson stain away, and takes a deep breath before trying again.

Disturbing her attempts is a poor idea, so instead I scour my many pockets for a blank notebook. Yanking coiled parchment from a pouch on my thigh, the pages rustle until they flip to an empty page.

Fascinating, I scrawl. *When Aria told us to meet the guild here, I didn't expect so much entertainment. Definitely an improvement over a boring apocalypse caused by an eruption in Motamir! Slaying disgruntled cultists and fire giants is pretty routine, but this? Well! To commemorate this occasion, a new journal has been started: 'The Nomad-Riftspawn Conspiracy! An Ongoing Saga.'*

Chalk taps against my chin.

Title pending.

"Hey, Yuina. Look at this."

Neva interrupts my writing, her hand extended towards me. Leaning forward, I peer at the object clutched in her grasp, and snatch it away as she turns her palm. The tarnished gold glints, as if teasing me; as if it's just a trick of the light.

Tracing the horizontal slashes with trembling hands, my excitement grows.

Another coin! Here?

The object clinks, and the metal slides apart.

TWO of them?!

Rummaging through another set of pouches, my fingers latch onto a familiar item, and I raise the coin Frost had discovered on our way here.

A quick examination provides a list of startling similarities. The currency clicks and clacks in my grasp as it slides about, offering glimpses of secrets and a hidden message.

I hesitate.

My thoughts have become quite loud.

Ears ringing from the sudden silence, I glance up at my guildmates.

Four sets of eyes are locked onto me. Liatris shuffles to the edge of her seat, Neva's foot taps impatiently against the floorboards, Pall gives a quiet bark, and Jegrac shushes him, his gaze trained on the coins in my hand.

Ah. They want answers?

Holding one of the gold objects up to the skylight, I pretend to study it.

"It's currency from Orion, *the Oasis in the Desert*. A place we're all familiar with, I'm sure." My comment is aimed at Liatris, to make her feel included in our conversation, but her smile quivers. Ah. She's not fond of her homeland? A fascinating revelation, to unpack at a later time.

I continue.

"These coins don't have much value outside the Dunes, but are in direct competition with chargestones. Well, they used to be, before the frequent riftspawn attacks began happening throughout Aegis. Nowadays most traditional marketplaces won't accept anything from outside of Nexus."

My audience nods, and I turn the coin so the four slashes face them.

"These lines, however? Horizontally or vertically, the meaning changes. Unfortunately, this symbol holds no significance in Orion scriptures and culture."

Jegrac sighs.

"You said all that, and then concluded with a point about how it's all nonsense?" He frowns. "Yuina, why are we wasting time on this? My people-"

Neva shushes him. He glares at her, but bites his tongue.

"Yes, the lines have no significance t*o people from the Dunes*," I continue, "but these four lines mean something here, in Aegis. According to religious scriptures the number four is deadly and dangerous! Early writings from the church of Yiatsu depict riftlords visiting our realm in sets of four. Assuming you believe in nonsense like that, these four lines could represent a lot of things. Four is also the number of days it took Yiatsu to banish them."

Jegrac refuses to look impressed.

"So the coins are connected to riftspawn?" he snorts. "Is that it?"

I shrug.

"If we travel to Orion, we could get more answers, but the curious part is *why* someone would bother carving this set of lines over and over again throughout Aegis. Why here? And why now?"

Neva perks up.

"Wait a moment," she exclaims, "Isaac was handed one of these coins! From a merchant in the Nexus marketplace."

My eyebrows rise.

Interesting. Could the Council be involved, somehow? Or citizens, or a guild? I doubt it, but...

A loud knock on the side door interrupts my thoughts.

Jegrac kicks the wood aside, revealing one of the clergy-women. The hems of her blue and gold robes are lined with superficial runes for *faith, hope, and Yiatsu*, which glimmer beneath the sun. Her eyes flicker around the caravan as she cranes her neck to look inside, and after a few beats of silence she says: "Hello there, all..."

Her gaze lingers on Jegrac and Liatris, and she stares a bit too intensely at my face before turning to Neva.

"Your boy is awake," the priestess announces.

Her disregard for the rest of us is insulting, but I relent, since Neva *has* visited this town many times before, and people feel comfortable talking to her. I doubt this woman is intentionally ignoring everyone else in the caravan.

Her refusal to meet my eyes, however - or even look at anyone other than our seer - suggests otherwise.

Jegrac stands, and the woman stumbles back.

"Excuse me," he says, and Liatris hops up, following him out of the caravan. The door swings shut behind her, hiding the priestess from view.

Ah. Problem solved.

My attention shifts to Neva.

"So."

I hold up one of my books, and a mischievous grin spreads across her face.

"Been having fun, I take it?"

Neva tries to hide her glee beneath a confused expression, but it gives way when she starts to laugh.

"What, you didn't like it?" Neva exclaims. "I thought it was very sweet! Go on, add it to your records."

I set the book aside and slide closer to my incorrigible friend. She tosses a few pillows off the end of her bench, beckoning for me to sit. She doesn't have to ask twice.

Neva opens her robe, and my breath catches as she lifts the white shirt underneath. A small red bandage is stained red and covered with faint blue runes for *health* and *wellness*.

"Had to borrow this without asking. Sorry." she mutters. "Not that it matters, since it seems to be a dud." With a pained groan she yanks it off, the symbols flickering as the parchment detaches from her skin. My grimace grows at the sight of blotchy purple bruising surrounding a pulsing red wound.

"Must have been an enchanted blade, since it still looks like this. May I?"

My hands start to poke at her delicate skin, but they're pulled back when Neva flinches.

She never flinches.

This is *serious*.

Slipping a scrap of paper out from the pouch on my side, I sketch a few new runes, adding symbols for *dispersal, swiftness, healing, and resilience.* As an afterthought, the sign for *numbing* is scratched in the middle.

I seal the bandage into place over her gaping flesh, and Neva relaxes, hands open and shoulders slumping even further.

"You should fix my eyes next," she says. Neva stares at me with her black irises, which glimmer with specks of white amidst the beautiful darkness.

She blinks. "*Rift.* No change. If only I had the energy, it'd be possible to push through this layer of fog, but... oh well." A soft sigh blows against my face. My cheeks burn as I pull away.

Neva smirks.

"At least you're still predictable. How was Motamir?"

I'd much rather talk about her crippled vision, but she seems eager to change topics. My questions will have to be set aside for now.

"Couple of cultists, riftspawn, a lot of lava, and some furious fire giants. More of the same, I suppose. The zealots were using these books to try and summon a riftlord, and there were fascinating runes hidden within their ancient texts. Which was great!"

Neva raises an eyebrow, but doesn't interrupt. I ignore her unimpressed grunt and keep talking.

"Ah. Yes, we also stopped Motamir from erupting, but honestly, Neva, couldn't another guild have handled it?"

I pause.

"For once?"

Neva frowns, her eyebrows rising in shock and then lowering in annoyance.

Hmm. Probably should have kept that comment to myself.

"Yuina, did Isaac say something to you? Because lately, he's been questioning my ability to seer - not directly, mind you, but it's in his tone - and now here you are, acting like some other run-of-the mill guild could just waltz in and-"

Liatris tumbles onto the caravan floor, the door swinging against the wall with a heavy thud as she scrambles upright.

"Neva! Yuina!" she exclaims. "We're going for a walk!"

A weary sigh echoes through the caravan.

"Alright, enough of this." Neva waves a hand at my face, her lips set in a thin line. With a sharp intake of breath she starts to stand, but hesitates halfway, reaching out to steady herself against my shoulder. "Ouch. Ooh."

She sinks back down onto the bench.

"You two go ahead, I'll catch up."

Liatris and I share a concerned glance.

Before the dryad can speak, Neva snaps: "GET! OUT!"

She doesn't have to tell us twice.

The rest of the guild is waiting on the stone pathway leading to the main road. Locals stagger past in huddled groups, flanking children wrapped in soot-stained pyjamas. Smudged bandanas cover noses and mouths, accompanied by hastily scrawled runes on collars and necks.

Curious eyes glance at Liatris and I when we approach, but sharpen to glares once Jegrac comes into view. Others smile at Isaac while hobbling by, and then give us polite waves as they trudge back towards their homes. Or, perhaps, towards the smoking craters where their homes once stood.

At the bottom of the path, whispers carry on the wind as mouths gape at the silver child standing in the shadow of the trees, his pale feet nestled in a bed of freshly fallen snow.

Frost notices my stare and tilts his head. I shrug in response, and a chill carries up the hill. He doesn't like having to wait.

When Liatris and I draw closer, the newbie catches my eye. He's recovered, and now lingers just outside of our haphazard circle. Liatris beckons for him to join us.

"Excuse me, but, uh - why are we staying here?" the kid blurts out. "Your quest is complete, right? The portal is shut! What are we waiting for?"

No one speaks up right away, so I use this opportunity to introduce myself and answer his question.

"Here, let me explain." I interject. "Yuina, by the way."

He nods, lips curving into a wavering smile.

"I can narrow the answer down to three reasons." I count each point with a little tap in the air. "First: our guild has a responsibility to survey this town before we leave. Basic protocol, especially with anything riftspawn related. Ensures we haven't missed any monsters still lingering in the area. Second: Isaac wants to visit his family, so we're stuck here until that happens. Third - and this is the most important reason: our newest member just recovered. I applaud your eagerness to travel again, but we can't have you relapsing while we're on the road. Riftspecialists are actually quite rare outside of Nexus, and your death is a risk we can't afford to take."

He blinks.

"Oh. Uh, okay."

Damian pauses, and then adds: "It's, um, nice to meet you too, miss Yuina."

I offer him my hand, and he takes it, a little too eagerly, his palm clammy and his grip weak.

Wiping his sweat on the back of my pants, I poke a thumb at the boy lingering amongst the trees.

"He probably won't introduce himself, but that's Frost. You'll get along with him, as long as you leave him alone."

Damian gulps, eyes wide and head bobbing up and down as he stares at Frost's back.

"Also," I say, holding the chronicler out to my guildmates, "I've recorded my share, so it's someone else's turn."

No one moves to take it, so-

CHRONICLE 19
Recorded by Isaac Heathe

S he shoves it into my hands.

"Alright, if you insist." I mutter.

The device clicks onto my belt as Yuina suggests we survey the town. Nodding, I glance at the church steps to wave at my family. Father Garith has their attention, but Markus notices my gesture and points towards me. A moment later my mother cups her hands around her mouth and yells: "We'll see you all at dinner, Izzy!"

Offering a quick thumbs up, I turn and follow the guild down the hill.

One of the caravan doors swings shut with a soft thump. Neva emerges from the depths of the cabin, wrapped in the red, pink, and purple dress she was wearing this morning. A large grey coat is draped over her arms, and she tosses the thick grey fur to Yuina. After a gentle sprint to catch up, she matches our steady pace towards the road.

When we set foot on the crumbling gravel, Frost steps closer. The air turns brisk and cold. Yuina sinks deeper into her coat as he approaches; the giant garment dwarfs her body. Jegrac and Liatris move to the far side of the path, with the Nomad doing his best to shield our dryad from the bitter chill.

Damian shuffles to my side, while Neva walks behind us.

I listen half-heartedly to my guildmates' conversations, but my eyes wander, tracing buildings that were once an important part of my life. Most of the structures are stable but scarred.

My breath catches in my throat at the sight of the bakery, which has become a smoking ruin, its embers sizzling and dying as Frost passes by. In a nearby alley, the owner and his family huddle together, pleading with Sister Holly in hushed tones. They perk up when a shiver passes through them, and their gazes flick towards the silver child.

My memories of the bakery are few and far between; it was added long after I'd left Borderik. The baker and his family will be fine, however, even if their livelihood is in shambles. The town will step up - as it always does - to support those in need.

When we draw closer to the village square my anxiousness returns.

Buildings and businesses have been decimated, smeared with soot and dripping with remnants of the rift. A crater rests where the general store used to be, and Mr. Lauwell's family crowds around the old man, who sits on an overturned stump, his head buried in his hands. A pang of nostalgia beats in my chest; Markus and I spent a lot of our hard-earned allowance on candy and treats from that place, and Mr. Lauwell always gave us more than we could afford.

But he's not the only one suffering. Mr. Lauwell is just one of many figures lingering beside ravaged wrecks and smoking piles of blackened wood and stone.

I know Yuina tried to keep collateral damage to a minimum, but the stores here are decimated, just like the small apartments up above. As we near, I receive humble waves and exhausted nods, which quickly change to wrapped arms and confused shivers, wide eyes tracking the pale boy and his frigid atmosphere.

Frost doesn't acknowledge their bewildered and harsh gazes, but Yuina leans over to whisper at him. He tilts his head, shrugs his shoulders, and then the air grows warmer. He pays no mind to the change, his attention locked on the road ahead, his glacial features cold and empty.

Every so often, however, his eyes flicker to Yuina as she fills the silence with a rant about the *history of Aegis* and *why we should visit the Outskirts before we leave*. The stoic child mutters short and simple replies, mostly variations of the word 'no.'

Shifting to the other side of the road, Liatris walks barefoot on the remains of feeble lawns and gardens while Pall and Jegrac flank her. A trail of greenery blossoms beneath her feet, each footstep reviving the blackened dirt with a smattering of emerald life. Jegrac mentions the animals suffering in the forest, and Liatris gives him a sad, slow nod.

"So what's going to happen to this town?" Damian asks, shoving my thoughts away. I stifle a smile as he meanders around a black stain on the ground, giving it more leeway than necessary. His eyes widen, and then his hands snap up to cover his nose and mouth.

"Hey, kid. You can put those down." Neva snorts as she steps into place beside me. "Your clothes have runes now and Frost's presence is a natural filter, so even if the riftspecialist made a mistake, you'll be fine."

"And speaking of runes, I'll be spreading them throughout town if anyone wants to help." Yuina says. "When you're not rebuilding Borderik, come assist me with inscribing riftspawn protections and failsafes into the remaining buildings."

"Huh," I mutter. "We're not going back to Nexus tomorrow?"

"We all assumed you'd want to stay," Jegrac pipes up, "to spend some time with your family. Furthermore, I could use this opportunity to bury my people and investigate their camps."

"Ah, yes, we have to do that too," Yuina declares. "I am also planning to get a proper look at this town's relics and history. Hopefully a priest or priestess will finally set aside their ignorance and let me get my hands on that chalice and those fascinating runes, especially after I *generously* offered to strengthen the church's wards."

"Some of us are still recovering," Neva adds, "which I would rather do when the caravan isn't bumping around."

Frost stays silent, but his lack of objection suggests he's fine with staying here.

"Okay, sure, but... will we be safe here?" Damian toys with a piece of bandage stuck to his ear. "A High Champion attacked your guild. They even attacked *you* directly!" He points at Neva.

She shrugs.

His wide eyes snap onto me. "Isaac, sir! We, uh, we have to return to Nexus and report this right away! They'll protect us. The Council-"

Yuina dismisses his clamour with a wave.

"Buddy. Calm down. We'll be fine," she says, "and even if they come back - which I highly doubt will happen - it won't be a problem. Frost is here."

Damian's voice rises.

"It's a *High Champion!*" he exclaims, stopping in place, his voice strained as he begs us to listen. "Don't you understand? If they're after us, the Council must be too!" His breaths come quick and sharp as he clutches his head. "They- we- no, no, if they, if they come back-"

"Ugh, *shut up.*" Frost suddenly drawls, peering at Damian through half-lidded eyes. His expression shifts from emotionless to unamused. "You *stupid* child."

Yuina frowns, and looks past him to address Damian, who stands startled, slack-jawed, and stumbling as he tries to salvage a response.

"Oof. Sorry, kid. Frost is not *trying* to be mean. Not really!" She pats her frigid companion carefully on the shoulder, and then yanks her fingers back before the cold can nip at them. "He's just annoyed that the other High Champion ran away."

The child's frostbitten glare drifts over to Yuina, silencing her.

"Don't speak for me," he snaps. "Our guild is no place for the weak."

His piercing eyes fixate on me as he adds, "*One* is enough."

Heat rushes up my neck and reddens my cheeks, and I start to stammer out a response, but Neva cuts me off.

"Damian doesn't know about you, Frost, so dial it back a little." Her hand presses against my back, her gaze locked on the snow-glazed boy. "And you can't talk to *your* Commander like that! You know better."

A chilling wind rises as the ground beneath Frost cracks, white lines jutting out from the ice surrounding his bare feet.

Then he breathes in, slowly, and the cold recedes.

His eyes turn to Damian, who cowers beneath the weight of Frost's harsh, judgemental stare.

"Isaac is not powerful," he declares, "but he is important. And, compared to most people, he is sturdy and strong."

Huh. That's the first apology I've ever gotten from Frost. At least, I think it's an apology.

Probably not.

Whatever. I'll take what I can get.

"Also. You are a fool to think those Nexus lap dogs are a threat." Frost sighs. "I should know. I'm one of them."

Damian twists his lips, staring at the other child as he pieces together Frost's words. After a few beats of silence he gasps, his eyes widening.

"Wait, are... are you a High Champion?!" Damian's face warps as he struggles to hide his shock. "No. No way! But, I've never seen you, uh, on... I mean, in the Nexpapers, you're not, uh... wait. Is this a joke?"

"It's true," I say, patting his shoulder. "He's number thirteen."

"And also the youngest champion ever!" Yuina pipes up, beaming. A hint of a smile flickers on Frost's face as she continues to rant about her companion. "Though I understand your confusion; part of his deal with the Council is that 'number thirteen' stays out of the spotlight. Which works well for us; makes it easier to travel, and Frost naturally drives away annoying spectators. Unlike the other High Champions, he's not interested in being popular."

"But, he's..." Damian peeks at me, and whispers, "Isaac, he's... so, well... so *rude!*"

Frost's glare silences the new recruit.

"Politeness is not a prerequisite for becoming a High Champion." He scoffs. "All that matters is strength."

He pauses, then adds: "It also helps if the Council recognizes you as a threat."

Damian stares at the boy for a few more moments, struggling to find a response. After a few stammered attempts to talk, he manages to ask in a sheepish tone: "Excuse me, sir? Can I see your Champion's insignia?"

Frost turns away, and Damian's shoulders slump.

"Please?" the boy squeaks out.

The High Champion sighs, and tilts his head at Yuina. Hiding her grin, she tosses a crumpled white and gold armband at the new recruit.

"He'll need it back eventually," Yuina calls as the two of them walk away, "but you can keep it for now!"

As they leave, Jegrac and Liatris approach. The dryad keeps her distance, shivering from the lingering cold.

"That went well enough," Jegrac laughs. "Frost must have missed you, Isaac. After all, he did compliment you. At least, I think he did, right?"

"Oh, yes indeed!' Liatris exclaims. She takes a quick breath, raising her hands to test the air, and then skips closer as the chill recedes beneath the setting sun.

Pall hops towards Damian, who continues to admire the armband with a fierce reverence, cradling it in his shaking hands. The dog rubs against the boy's leg, and he pauses to give him a quick pat. Satisfied, Pall returns to his master.

"Anyone else ready to wrap up their tour of this sad little town? We'll be wandering around here when we're helping these people rebuild, so I'm good to go." Neva declares. "And one other important question - are we accepting Marie's invitation to supper? I'm sure *the Commander* doesn't mind."

I sigh.

"Do I even have a choice?"

Neva laughs, looping her arm in mine. Her weight shifts as she leans against me for support.

I stumble from the unexpected burden, but brace my legs to lighten her load. She's using me to help her walk. Has she been hiding her weariness this entire time?

Perhaps a day of rest and a hearty meal will be good for all of us.

Especially her.

Shaking my head, I walk along with my guild as I start to turn off the chronicler. The next few days are going to be especially busy, so there's no point in leaving it on right now.

***

"Isaac, you simply *have* to record this! It's an event worth cataloguing!" Yuina teases as she switches the chronicler on. "Aria's never met your family, so at least let her read about them!"

She slaps my hand away when I try to turn the device off.

"Hey!" I exclaim, leaning away from the finger shoved in my face. I bite back a snippy reply about how *Aria doesn't need to hear my family complain about my role as a Commander.*

There's also an extremely high chance this event will go very, very poorly, which is why I'd rather not have it "catalogued."

But Yuina stares at me, one hand on her hip, the other raised in case I try to turn the chronicler off again. We stand in an awkward stalemate outside of my childhood home, poised under the tree where the grass is thinnest.

We used to have a swing here. The thought slips through my head.

I wonder what happened.

The memory distracts me long enough for my rebellious spark to die out, and I sigh.

"Alright, you win." I hold the chronicler out to Yuina, so she can take over.

She laughs.

"Hah! No thanks." Yuina pushes the device away. "I just had it. Hand it off to someone else!"

The chronicler is snatched out of my hand as Neva arrives, her eyebrows knit and mouth set in a thin line as she takes it away.

CHRONICLE 20
Recorded by Neva Oyii

"There, problem solved." I shift my dress so the chronicler can disappear into the hidden pouch on my thigh. "Now, can we get going already? Our guild is waiting."

Isaac glances past me, admiring the figures hovering by the front steps, waiting for him to lead them inside.

"Wow," he declares, "You're all very... *dressed up* for a humble family dinner. You didn't have to-"

My fingers snap in his face, bringing the prattle to an abrupt end.

"It's your family, Isaac. We want to make a good impression." With a gentle flourish, magic ripples across my brilliant red dress. The expensive garment compliments my silhouette, further embellished by the crimson waves foaming around my upper arms and chest. I adjust the ruby-crested necklace painting a gorgeous gold circle around my neck, and let Yuina continue my lecture.

"Yeah, wouldn't want anyone thinking we're some regular, *boring*, ordinary guild," she announces, placing a gentle hand on his shoulder. "I mean, I certainly didn't put on my *fanciest* cargo pants and whitest blouse for *nothing!*"

The two of them chuckle, though I certainly don't share their amusement. After aiming another disapproving glare at Yuina's outfit, I shake my head in horror.

She looks like an evergreen topped with snow.

And as expected, Isaac is somehow worse! No, wait - not entirely. His faded blue dress shirt is *somewhat* tolerable now that it's been ironed - thanks to his mother's touch - and his brown slacks may have seen better days, but at least they're in better condition than usual.

Walking back to the caravan, worries about the guild whisper in my ears: *what will Isaac's family think?* They've been polite whenever the Commander and I have stopped by, but what about the rest of Honour's Stand?

A quick glance over my sordid companions suggests this might be a mistake.

At least Liatris looks cute in the sundress I bought for her. The ferns decorating her head are pushed back and pressed down, and a tiny wreath has blossomed pearls of white and violet to dot the green. She wouldn't let me glamour her, but had been okay with a few illusions over her sunshine-yellow dress. The subtle detailing glimmers as she swirls in it.

"They won't mind my presence, will they?" Jegrac asks, adjusting the wrists of his surprisingly clean trench coat. His beard and hair look freshly combed, and the hound at his side has received a similar makeover, his fur glossy and smooth.

Isaac starts to nod, pauses when he sees the look on Jegrac's face, and then shrugs.

"They don't have a choice," he finally decides. That's enough for Jegrac, who rolls his shoulders back and turns to compliment the dress *I* picked out *for* Liatris. Biting my tongue, I shift my attention to Damian, who is lingering by the caravan. The boy is dressed in simple but expensive fabrics: a teal polo shirt and sleek black pants. It's one of the two outfits he packed, which would usually be rather shortsighted for a trip like this, but expensive clothes are often laced with delicate runes to keep the material in near-mint condition. He should be fine.

Unfortunately, Damian's magic garments can't prevent the nervous sweat glistening on his forehead.

Isaac turns towards the front steps of the old farm house, and we fall into place behind him with me at his side, Liatris skipping along after us, and Yuina tugging Jegrac along. Frost climbs onto the roof of the caravan, silently rejecting Marie's invitation. The temperature sinks as the High Champion starts to relax, and the sudden cold chases Damian up the stairs behind us.

We stop on the porch to admire the scars from the riftspawn's recent attack. Souvenirs of a tough battle are scattered on a broken bench at the far end of the porch, where shattered farm tools and darkened blades decorate the weathered wood.

A warmth emanates from behind the door, and movement in the nearby window catches my eye as curtains drop. A small face disappears from sight; Samuel, perhaps? If it is, he's certainly grown since I saw him last.

The door slips open, creaking on its hinges as the comforting aromas of butter and garlic and something fried slip outside, accompanied by the sizzle of food on a stove.

Isaac's mother greets us, wiping her hands on the stained white apron covering her patterned dress. It looks like a tablecloth; simple in design, but practical, and well suited for this family.

"Well!" Mrs. Heathe announces, "It's good to finally meet you all. And hello there, Frost!" She offers a spirited wave at the High Champion, her arm nearly smacking me in the face as she attempts to draw his attention.

The boy doesn't answer, but this doesn't deter Mrs. Heathe, who calls out to him again.

"Yoo-hoo! Frost? Hello?"

The High Champion's frigid sigh can be felt from here, and he slowly raises his hand in return.

Pleased with herself, Marie starts to speak, but she pauses when she nearly trips over the child hiding behind her.

A pair of shy eyes peek around her waist, belonging to the same boy who was staring at us through the window. He watches us warily, but then his face lights up when he notices Frost.

"No, Samuel," Isaac says before the child can speak. He steps past his mother and gently takes the boy's hand. "Why don't you show me your room? I heard a rumour you're sleeping all by yourself now! Is that true?"

His little brother giggles eagerly, taking the lead and pulling Isaac up the stairs. The Commander gives us an apologetic wave as he abandons us, forcing the guild and I to deal with his family on our own.

After her sons scurry away, Isaac's mother turns to me with a wide smile.

The grin falters, slipping off her face.

Oh. Should I have thrown something over my bare shoulders?

The ridiculous thought passes as quickly as it came, and I extend a hand in an attempt to reconcile her disapproval.

Her expression returns to a welcoming smile, the shadow on her face dismissed when she looks up at my eyes.

"Good to see you again, Neva," she says, and my shoulders stiffen as her arms wrap around me, her head tucked beneath my chin to pull me into a hug. I pat her on the back, startled by the sudden contact. After an eternity the woman finally steps back to let me breathe. "It's been a while, hasn't it? And look at you, more beautiful than ever! Alexis will be eager to talk with you, I'm sure. Entertain her questions about fashion, won't you? It'll mean a lot to her."

She shuffles aside, gesturing for me to pass as she adds: "Now, come on in, dear, and make yourself at home. Dinner is almost ready to be served! You know the way - just straight down the hall."

I give her a polite nod.

"Thank you, Mrs. Heathe."

Isaac's mother ushers me inside.

"Oh *please*, call me Marie! You're practically family at this point."

Before I can respond, she's already turned to the rest of the guild, leaving me standing in the hall. It hasn't changed much since I was last here. Mismatched paint covers bruises dealt by a busy household, while the dull yellow walls boast a handful of new pictures scattered throughout the hallway.

I settle on the nearby steps, fingers hesitating on the straps of my shoes. Stealing a glance at Marie, it's clear that barefoot or socks is the way to go. It makes sense - after being out in the fields all day, you wouldn't want anyone tracking mud and grime through the house.

The stairs creak beneath me as I pry my heels from my feet.

"Hello!" Liatris exclaims. Her exuberance causes Isaac's mother to take a small step back, and her head shakes when she's caught off guard by the dryad's consequential hug.

Hah! Have a taste of your own medicine.

But Marie's shoulders relax, and she returns the embrace, wrapping her thick arms around the wiry sprite, engulfing her.

Ugh. Annoying.

Jegrac steps forward, tipping his hat.

"Good evening, ma'am," he mutters, lingering in the doorway as though waiting for an invitation to come inside. Yuina rolls her eyes and pushes him forward.

Marie grins at them.

"So, this is the rest of Isaac's guild?" She pauses, her face lighting up as Yuina hands over a decorative white bag. "Oh, sweetie, you didn't have to!"

Yuina laughs, pushing the gift forward until Isaac's mother is forced to accept it.

"It's nothing much, just some odds and ends from the Nexus Marketplace. I hope your family enjoys it!" She draws one leg back to offer a regal curtsy, pulling out the sides of her gaudy shorts as Isaac's mother offers an awkward bow in return. "I don't know if you remember me, Mrs. Heathe, but it's good to see you again. And in case you forgot, I'm Yuina."

Marie clucks her tongue as she ushers everyone inside.

"Of course I remember you, Yuina! But please, save the introduction until the whole family is here - otherwise, we'll be saying names all night!"

Scouring the muddied boots and dirty shoes scattered on the black mat by the entranceway, I decide to hang my heels on an empty hook amongst the coats and hats on the wall.

"Should we invite him in?" Marie asks as she peers at Frost. The frozen figure sits silent and still beneath the dim glow of the setting sun. Yuina shakes her head and assures Isaac's mother: "No, he'd rather be outside."

Marie looks concerned, but when she turns away a flicker of relief crosses her face.

"Well," she announces, "come along, then! Your timing is perfect. We should be ready to eat very soon."

I shuffle out of the way as she takes a few quick hops up the stairs to holler "Markus! Sam! Izzy! Dinner's ready!" The sound of scuffling feet echoes from the upper level of the house, but no one appears.

"...Alexis, can you go get your brothers, please?"

Someone grumbles in response, and then Isaac's sister appears in the hallway. Her face lights up when she notices me.

"Neva!" she exclaims. Her eyes widen, highlighting her attempts to replicate a look I'd worn during my last visit to Isaac's family farm. I nod, stifling my grin as she scrutinises me; her lips open in surprise as her gaze lingers on the red and gold design I've painted over my eyelids. Something registers in her face, and she tucks some stray blonde hairs behind an ear, one hand reaching down to carefully adjust her dress.

"Uh, since you're here, I'd better get changed," she declares, cheeks bright and red.

I offer her a pleasant smile.

"Good to see you, Alexis."

She ducks her head, gives a shy nod, and then sprints up the stairs.

Isaac's mother calls us from within the kitchen, so I lead the group forward since no one else is going to take the initiative. Once we move into the dining room, I gawk at how little this place has changed since my last visit.

The table is stretched to fit our entire group, the wooden chairs pressed firmly against the walls and cabinets surrounding this humble setting. Scanning the seating arrangements, I claim a spot at the head of the table before anyone else can. It's one of the only areas with a little extra room, and the chance of getting bumped by people travelling from the dining room to the kitchen is low.

Isaac's father looks up from his place by the sink to offer a cordial wave, small bubbles lingering in the air as he returns to his task.

"Come in, come in," he says. "Make yourselves at home. I know it's nothing fancy, but it's what we've got."

"Wilson, we're just happy to be here," I reply, settling into my chair. I kick the nearby seats away from the table to give Liatris and Jegrac a clue. The two of them awkwardly shuffle into place, sitting up to keep the old chairs from squeaking out complaints.

I point at a seat across the table, and Damian squeezes past the cabinet to sit just like Liatris and Jegrac, trying a little too hard to make a good impression.

Yuina steps towards the kitchen, but Marie brandishes a ladle at her.

"Oh no, don't you try to help - you're a guest, Ms. Yuina, so stay away."

Bubbling dishes and the clatter of utensils, pots, and pans accompany the muffled voices and footsteps echoing above our heads.

"Neva, I've got a request, if you don't mind me asking." Mr. Heathe says, leaving the dishes to dry on a simple wire rack by the sink. He rests his elbows on the counter as he tries to make conversation. "Could you do that *seeing into the future* thing, you know, seering or whatever," -he waves his hands at the air as he speaks- "for peace of mind, so we know our town is safe?"

I nod, surprised he hadn't asked this sooner.

"Yeah. Actually, I've already looked. Shouldn't be any more attacks! And don't worry, we'll be sticking around for a while, so if anything happens our guild will handle it."

Mr. Heathe breathes a sigh of relief, and a hidden tension leaves his shoulders.

"Thank goodness," he says, "because there's a lot of work to be done, and we can't afford another interruption." He turns to address Liatris, Damian, and Jegrac. "You might not know this, but Borderik is a farming community first and foremost! Rebuilding our town is important, yes, but we also have fields and livestock in desperate need of attention."

Marie interrupts the conversation with a soft thwack, her hand slapping the counter.

"Enough talk about riftspawn and work, Wilson! I'm sure our guests have had enough of such topics." She clicks her tongue, gives her husband a *look*, and returns to minding the stove.

"Alright, a different question, then," Mr. Heathe announces, his eyes returning to me, "has Isaac, uh... met anyone?"

I laugh.

"If you're wondering if he's made any progress with that bartender, then no. He did mention he's planning on asking him out, but you know how Isaac is."

"What bartender?" Yuina asks, all eyes in the room suddenly on me.

My hands go up, deflecting any further questions.

"You'll have to ask him," I reply.

Isaac's parents share a glance, their eyebrows raised.

"A bartender?" his mother exclaims. "Oh dear. I was hoping to introduce Izzy to our new farmhand, Jacob. Lovely boy, from a good family!"

She pauses, twists her lips, and then turns to me.

"Neva, this gentleman from Nexus - it doesn't sound like anything too serious. Would Isaac be offended if he met-"

"I've said too much!" My hands rise to my mouth, drawing a pinched thumb and finger across it. "Talk to our Commander about it later, when I'm not here!"

Yuina comes to my rescue, declaring: "Mrs. Heathe, this smells delicious! Why don't we pair it with something? We've got wine and juice from Zorah and the Pillars in the caravan, why don't I-"

Jegrac stands, chair skirting on the stained white tiles as he declares, "I'll get it!" He strides towards the door, shouting over his shoulder: "I'd best check on Pall, too. Don't mind me! I'll be back."

The front door swings shut with a tender clang.

Mr. Heathe raises an eyebrow, staring at Jegrac's empty chair.

"Never been this close to a Nomad before," he says to no one in particular, and Yuina stiffens alongside Marie, who stops to glare at her husband.

The man freezes, standing a little taller as he realises how he might sound. He stumbles for the right words, and I decide to intervene before he says something he might regret.

"You've realised he's not what you expected; he doesn't match what you've been told."

Isaac's father nods.

"And," I add, "it's tough to admit you're wrong."

His brows furrow, eyes peering at me, unpacking everything that's just been said.

Eventually, he just shrugs.

"Part of being human?"

Marie shoves her way into the conversation, hefting a large soup pot onto the crowded table with a solid thump. As the delicious aroma fills the room, she says: "Yes, well, Isaac isn't always right either, you know."

She raises her head, turning away before I can defend our Commander's honour. Not that I really care about such a thing, but still, her *tone* annoys me.

"And speaking of Izzy: *where* are those children of mine? Wilson, dear, will you go upstairs and figure out what's going on?"

Her husband marches out of the kitchen, shuffling around Yuina and Liatris while apologising profusely for bumping the backs of their chairs. He pauses at the bottom of the steps and draws in a long breath.

Marie exclaims: "No, go *get* them, don't just shout from down here - I could have done that! Go fetch your kids!"

Mr. Heathe sprints up the steps.

We're graced with silence for a brief, blissful moment, but it disappears as heavy feet pound down the stairs. Samuel hops down onto the floor, his poofy blonde hair bouncing along with him, and he turns, little button nose pointing to Isaac, who comes tumbling down after him. The boy reaches out, and his big brother takes his hand, letting Samuel lead him to the table.

"Hi!" Liatris says, enamoured by the small child. He peers at her, uncertain, and then grins.

"You are Lie-ah-triss!" he declares, and she nods, causing him to clap, which causes her to clap, which just makes him clap more.

Yuina laughs at the look on my face.

"Neh-vah!" he announces, pointing at me, his blue eyes wider than his bright smile. I nod, amused by his presence.

The front door creaks open, and Samuel turns around, nearly bumping into Markus as he lumbers past. Jegrac enters as well, laden with bags and bottles. Markus glances over his shoulder, and then ducks his head under a lantern on the ceiling as he walks back to the Nomad.

Markus flexes his broad shoulders as he lightens Jegrac's burden, hefting a few heavy bottles of wine while blowing strands of stray brown hair out of his eyes. He notices me and lets out a low whistle.

"Ey, Neva! Looking good!"

Isaac and Sam excuse themselves as they try to pass, and I adjust my seat so they don't bump into me.

Glancing at Markus's bare feet, overalls, and stained blue shirt, I cock an eyebrow.

"Wish I could say the same, but you seem to share Isaac's fashion sense... too bad his 'big-city-flab' keeps him from wearing it as well as you."

My chair shakes when Isaac kicks it under the table. Markus's laughter joins mine.

"Never change, Neva," he muses while he avoids his mother's ladle. He lets the bottles in his hands settle on the counter, and his cheeky grin widens as he gives Isaac the same once-over I offered him.

"Don't worry, big brother. I still think you're beautiful, even if you're fat."

"I'm not-" Isaac sputters, but Samuel stands on his chair, shouting, "ISAAC IS NOT FAT! HE IS STRONG! HE IS AN ADVENTURER!"

The boy places his hands on his hips, posing, before getting pulled back down by the Commander.

"We're just teasing," I say, winking at Isaac, "you're in good shape, just not... *farmhand* shape."

"Round is a shape," Markus adds, and he dances away from his mother's ladle again, finding solace in a seat on the other side of the table, directly across from Yuina and Jegrac. Out of the corner of my eye, I notice Damian is now sitting a little taller, stomach pulled in slightly, his ears tinged red.

Marie smacks her hand against the counter, causing Liatris and Samuel to jump.

"I won't have any more of that talk in this house," she snaps, keeping her stern gaze from focusing on Isaac and, more importantly, Damian, "so if you're going to be calling anyone fat, Markus, keep in mind that I'm larger than all of you. Watch what you say!"

Her husband lumbers down the stairs, brightening when he notices the table is full of food and family.

"Oh good! Just Alexis left. ALEXIS!" he bellows up the stairs, to a muffled "I'm coming! Stop yelling at me!"

Wilson joins his wife in the kitchen, puttering about as Markus begins to prattle eagerly to his big brother about how things have been going in town, sharing random gossip about strangers the two of them must have known as kids. Isaac listens intently, saying *what* and *no way, seriously* every so often.

While I eavesdrop on their conversation, I catch Samuel squinting at Damian. The older boy attempts to ignore the child's stare, but can't stop stealing furtive glances back at him.

"Wait a second..." Samuel asks, "Who are YOU?"

Damian's head lurches.

"Uh, what?" he replies, eyes wide.

"Well," Samuel continues, "I know Neh-vah, You-ee-nah, and everyone else-" he points at me, and then his hand waves along the table, "-and I even know about Ah-ree-ah, but she's supposed to be a cranky old lady, so... *who are you?*"

Marie and Wilson move a little closer, but don't chastise Samuel. They must have been wondering about the shy-looking noble as well.

Isaac comes to Damian's rescue.

"He's our new recruit!" the Commander declares, reaching around Samuel to pat Damian on the shoulder. "Just joined us a few days ago!"

"Recruited... from where?" Wilson asks.

"The Council," Isaac replies. "It's a long story."

Any further conversation is interrupted by a hoot from Markus, drawing attention to Alexis as she enters the room. Her makeup has been sharpened and her blonde hair is pulled back into a ponytail, and a decorated blue gown is wrapped around her sturdy figure. A quick glance at the hemming suggests it's handmade. If it's her handiwork, I'm impressed.

"I hope you're not planning to eat in *that*," Marie mutters, but she bites back any further comments as her daughter glares with a perfect blend of fury and desperation.

Marie sighs.

"Well, as long as you're the one cleaning it, I suppose it's fine - we have guests, so formal is preferred over frumpy!" She aims a disapproving *look* at her sons, who are all wearing casual clothes.

"Ugh, enough about fashion!" Markus bellows, turning to his family. "I'm starving. Let's eat! And crack open that wine. After today, I could use a drink!"

Mr. Heathe wags a finger at him before standing to go gather a pot off the stove. Marie follows suit, and we settle in for a hearty meal.

Dinner, surprisingly enough, is a relatively calm and peaceful event.

On one side of the table, Jegrac listens to Isaac, Yuina, Markus, and Mr. Heathe discuss the use of mystical tools and techniques when farming, each participant eager to debate the value of technology and magic in various agricultural tasks. Every so often, someone mentions the riftspawn attack, but Marie silences them with a firm reminder that such talk is prohibited at the dinner table, for tonight at *least*.

On our side, Alexis finally finds the courage to ask me about my current cosmetic choices, and allows me to advise her while Liatris eagerly adds inane but adorable comments every so often, trying her best to contribute to our conversation.

Across from us, Damian is stuck with Samuel. After some awkward silence, the boy's eager questions about Nexus and our adventure and what it's like to be in a guild with *adults* engages the new recruit, and the two of them start to talk.

The evening's chatter is pleasant enough to keep me engaged, until Liatris starts asking Alexis unnecessary questions about living on a farm. With nothing to anchor my attention, it drifts towards the other side of the table.

"Yes, Yuina, I'll admit you have a point - but these runes and gizmos and gadgets are only useful with someone controlling them! So, as I said before - magic will never overcome hard work and effort."

Wilson leans back in his chair, arms crossed with a smug grin on his face.

Yuina rolls her eyes.

"While a caster *is* almost always necessary, you still haven't answered my original question!" Her knife and fork clink against her plate as she carefully sets them aside, freeing her hands for a more active debate. "We're not discussing the importance of people. On that, we seem to be aligned. Perhaps we should just agree to disagree, since we're talking in circles."

"Well," Marcus snorts, "it would be nice to have some extra help these days, especially after this whole debacle with..." -he censors himself before Marie's ladle can interject- "...uh. So! On a different note: it's great your guild is sticking around for a while."

"Yes, yes!" Wilson adds, "A shame you can't stay longer!"

Isaac's plate scrapes across the table as he pushes it away.

"We have other things to do, unfortunately. As Commander, I have to-"

"Oh, come on, Izzy!" Marie interjects with a loud, forced laugh. "What could be more important than-"

The sharp clatter of Isaac's chair screeching across the floor cuts her off.

"Excuse me, everyone, but I need to stretch my legs. Sorry. I'll be back."

Under his breath - but loud enough for everyone to hear - he mutters: "...once this conversation is over."

Isaac slips away, and then his mother stands, following him up the stairs, whispering and pleading in a tone too quiet to overhear. Markus and Wilson fall silent, and Yuina fills the void with an attempt to continue their conversation, ignoring the concerned glance Isaac's father shares with his second-oldest son.

"Excuse me," I say, "but I need to use the restroom. If I recall correctly, it's the second room at the top of the stairs, right?"

Alexis nods. I walk out of the kitchen, maintaining a casual and uninterested gait as the steps creak and the sound of conversation melts away.

The upper hallway is dimly lit, due to the night light tucked against the wall and the dull gleam from a half-shut door on the far side.

Hushed voices echo through the quiet space, and it would be wise to just walk away, but my magic arrives before it can be stopped, sparks crackling in my ears and carrying whispers to me as Isaac begins to respond.

"-said before, no, I can't! Why do you keep-"

"Your father is getting older, Isaac. We could use more help on the farm..."

"I know, Mom, but Markus is enjoying it, and I don't want to step on his toes! Besides-"

"Izzy, please, you know he'd be thrilled to have you back home. Don't be-"

"You *know* I can't just *leave* the guild. I'm the Commander! They need me. It's my responsibility. I know you and Dad would rather I be on the farm, but-"

"But *what?* Your friends are more important than your family?! We've been patient, Isaac, but eventually you need to come home and start your life on the farm. It's our legacy; generations of farmers are waiting for your return. It's *your* legacy."

Isaac sighs.

"I don't get it. Why is *this* such a big deal?"

An empty laugh echoes through the hall.

"I mean, come *on, M*om! You and Dad were able to accept me when I came out, which *clearly* wasn't easy for the two of you, so... why does my *career* choice matter? You got over the fact that your oldest son is *gay*, right? How is any of *this* a bigger deal?"

He lets out a huff.

"Mom. Why do you care so much about what *I* do with *my* life?"

Marie's voice softens, and the magic in my ears sparks to hear her careful whispers.

"My mother - Yiatsu bless her soul - wanted to be an adventurer too, you know."

"...you're not answering my question."

"Hush! I'm getting to it, just listen."

After a beat, the Commander strains out: "Alright. *Fine.*"

Marie clears her throat.

"Your grandmother, well... she wasn't as lucky as you, Isaac. She abandoned our family and your grandfather, and her legacy, just to die in a ditch. She could have stayed to live a peaceful and secure life on our farm, but she left all of us behind to chase some dream." The final word is spat, bitter and angry, leaving a foul taste in my mouth.

"It's not a *dream.*" Isaac's voice starts sharp and angry, but fades into disappointing uncertainty. "The guild needs me, Mom. I can't leave-"

"They're nice people, honey, but really, they're not... *your people.* And I don't want you getting hurt because of them!"

Isaac starts to object, but Marie can't stop herself. Each word is punctured by pain, growing louder the longer she speaks.

"Your father and I accepted you *because* it's part of who you are, Izzy. It's part of your identity. But this, Isaac? This is a *choice*! And if you make this choice - if you make *the wrong choice* - you're going to abandon us one way or another. You will be leaving your family behind, Isaac!"

Her voice breaks, and the stunned silence is staccatoed by sobs.

"You're going to leave me behind, *just like Mama.*"

It goes quiet again.

"I'm not going to die, Mom."

Marie sniffles.

"You can't guarantee that, Izzy."

She's not wrong.

"No, Mom, you're right. I could die. But you also can't guarantee I'll be happy if I stay. Because I won't be. I *know* being here isn't what I want to do with my life."

Another sigh.

More silence.

"Isaac, listen-"

"I don't want to hear it, Mom! No! We have this conversation every time I come home, and my answer is always the same. I'm not taking over the farm. What I am going to do, however, is go downstairs and pretend this conversation never happened. "

The door opens with a creak, spilling light into the hallway.

"Izzy. Wait."

He doesn't hesitate, but then she adds: "Your father, he-"

The footsteps pause.

"He *what?*"

"I- well, he wouldn't want you to know, but it happened before you arrived."

"What happened, Mom? Is this another one of your stories, to make me feel guilty about wanting to live my own life?"

Marie doesn't say anything, and Isaac sighs.

"Fine. Tell me. What did Dad say this time?"

A beat of silence, and then: "He's hurt, Izzy. Badly."

My head snaps up. *This is new.*

The Commander appears to share the same thought. Suspicion floods his tone.

"If this is true, why hasn't he mentioned it yet? He could have followed us up here, to also try guilting me into staying! So why not-"

"He's hiding it because you don't want to be here, Isaac! He's never going to tell you because we all know you *hate coming home!*"

As her voice rises, so does Isaac's, words colliding in a torrent of fury.

"If Dad *actually* wanted me here, *he'd* be the one inviting me to visit. You keep saying he does, but not once has he-'

"YES! FINE! YOU'RE RIGHT! But not because he doesn't want you here, Issac! It's because he's a proud, stupid, caring man, and he's been willing to give up *his dreams* for his selfish son, and he'll never say a thing about it because of his stupid pride. You're not the only person in this family, Isaac! Your choice to run off and play 'adventurer' affects *all of us!*"

"I-"

"It's easy for YOU, being the one who gets to walk away. But we have to watch YOUR BACK every time you leave, and I thought it would get easier, but it *never has*. If you're fine with leaving us behind - if you *want* to abandon your family - then FINE. I don't want a SON who doesn't WANT TO BE HERE!"

A gasp, then a stunned, painful, quiet sigh.

The door slams against the wall as Isaac storms out, stomping across the carpet, his brow knotted and his eyes aflame.

He sees me, sitting at the top of the stairs. He's not pleased.

His rage begins to boil over, mouth opening to hiss out a retort, but it snaps shut when he notices the look on my face.

He hesitates.

In the quiet, we have a conversation. Neither of us speak.

His anger isn't aimed at me, but I take it in stride, returning his gaze, refusing to back down.

And, as always, it begins to disappear, mere droplets in an ocean, drifting away.

I don't know why it works, but it does.

He rubs his tears away, and although the hall gets misty, I maintain my stare.

He knows what I'd give to argue with my mother again. To talk with her.

The silence lasts for a little longer as he begins to calm.

I nod, slowly, carefully, and he returns the gesture, un-clenching his fists as he draws in a deep breath.

Isaac turns, straightens his shoulders, and walks back into the room.

"Mom," he says, pausing as she chokes back a sob.

"*Mom,*" he repeats, a little softer this time. The crying slows, allowing him to speak.

"I'm not Grandma."

A sniffle, and then: "I know. I know you're not. I just...."

"You worry about me."

"Yeah."

"You have to let me go, Mom."

"I- no, really, I have, Isaac. I'm trying."

"Okay."

The temptation is too much, and I lean a little further into the hall. Their shadows are at an impasse, separated by inherited rejection, guilt, and pain.

The quiet seeps in.

And then-

"I'm sorry, Izzy. I get so scared, not knowing if your next visit might be your last, and... oh, Yiatsu, I'm such an awful mother. I'm sorry I said those things. I didn't mean it."

"It's okay. I'm not always the best son, either."

"You don't-"

"No, it's true. I could call more. And..."

He trails off.

"Well. I'm not leaving the guild. Not yet. But... I've been thinking about it lately. "

"You do what you have to do, Isaac. I just want you to be safe."

"I will be. You and Dad don't have to protect me anymore. The guild looks after me."

Silence again, for a little while. My bones ache from sitting, but I can't move - not yet. So instead I wait, statuesque and still, just like the figures at the end of the hall, who still have yet to breach the space between them.

"Is it easy to leave?"

The question is fragile, balanced on a razor's edge, threatening to break. Isaac takes his time finding an answer.

"No. I know what I'm choosing to leave behind. But it feels like the right decision, every time. I still miss home, and you, and the rest of the family, and helping out around the house and on the farm."

A chuckle.

"Oh, I'm *sure* you miss having to do chores."

Isaac's laughter rings through the hall.

"Don't worry, I've got more than my fair share back in Nexus. Neva and the others work me pretty hard, you know."

"Yeah."

" ..."

"I love you, Izzy."

"I love you more, Mom."

"Okay. Thanks. Sorry."

A hand is offered, like the hilt of a shattered blade; an attempt to right years of wrongs. It lingers, traced by light and cast across the floor, trembling, waiting for the son's response.

The hand is taken.

"Don't apologise. Just... try to have a little more faith in me, and in my friends."

"Yes. Yes, I will, Isaac. I will... try."

"Is there anything else I should know?"

"It's a bit off topic, but..."

"Oh no. I know that look. Mom-!"

"Wait, let me tell you about him first! Because this boy, Jacob - he started working for us a little while ago, and - wait, no, I should introduce him as *this man,* Jacob, who-"

Magic dissipates from my ears, turning whispered apologies and quiet conversation into muffled noises. I can't hear them anymore, but the shadows in the hall draw close, merging into one, locked in a quiet embrace.

I tip-toe down the stairs, taking care to avoid the steps at the bottom with a quick leap, bracing my legs to silence my fall.

Before returning to the kitchen, I linger in the hall and pretend to admire the pictures on the walls. Alexis beckons for me to return, but I wave her away. She shrugs and turns back to Liatris.

A creak draws my attention.

Peeking over my shoulder, Isaac and Marie descend, her arm slipping off his elbow as they approach. Quiet smiles linger on their faces.

"Well!" Mrs. Heathe announces, "Who's hungry for some dessert?"

Isaac barely glances at me when he falls into place at my side.

"You have a lovely home." My comment is casual and restrained as I gesture at the framed image. In the picture, Isaac is much younger, seated on the porch for a family photo alongside the rest of the Heathes - although Samuel is hidden within his mother's oversized belly.

He nods.

"It's nice to be back here," Isaac says, nodding at Marie when she calls us back to the dining room. As we near the end of the hall, he leans over and whispers, "but to be honest, I can't wait to go *home.*"

I grin despite the nagging thoughts keeping it from widening. I try to brush them away; our Commander has faith in us, so I should have more faith in him.

He chose the guild.

He always chooses the guild.

For some reason, this reassurance doesn't feel as great as it should.

Would he still stay with us if he wasn't our Commander?

My hand taps Isaac's back, and he pauses in the doorway.

When he looks at me, the question dies in my throat.

He's been through enough. We can talk another time.

"Here." I hand the chronicler to him, my finger hovering over the glowing blue jewel. "Turn it on later or hand it off to somebody else, just make sure we record *something* while we're here, okay?"

CHRONICLE 21
Recorded by Jegrac

"W hat do you mean IT'S BEEN OFF THIS EN-
TIRE TIME?!"

Neva jabs at the Commander's chest as he shrinks back
into his seat. "Do you know how *cranky* Aria is going to
be when she finds out we missed two entire days? No one
wants to deal with that! Especially not me! I like getting
paid!"

The wooden bar presses against my shoulder when I
brush the curtain aside. Hopefully I can offer the Commander some support.

"Come on, Neva! Give him a break. He-"

Her glare suggests I'd better focus on the road. Not
wanting to risk her ire, I slink out of sight, giving Isaac an
apologetic shrug before ducking away.

"Jegrac, why is Isaac in so much trouble?" Liatris whispers from her perch at my side. "What did he do?"

The curtain drops behind us, muffling Neva's angry tirade. A twinge of guilt pokes my side; protecting Liatris and I from the seer's rage has left Yuina and Damian trapped inside.

Reaching through our bond, I attempt to call Pall up to the front, but he's too busy enjoying his nap. Makes sense; Neva's upset but not *furious*, so the noise shouldn't bother my hound's sensitive ears. And if it does, he'll let me know.

"Sounds like he forgot to turn the chronicler back on," I explain, adjusting the reins so Mayweather and Daisy weave around a pothole in the weathered road, "which means Aria will have no record of the last two days."

Liatris raises an eyebrow, the thin moss shaping a wave of confusion above her violet gaze, which darts nervously to the dark curtain at our backs.

"Is it that important?" she asks. "All we did was fix up the town and help in the fields..."

I shrug.

"According to Aria, it's vital information, and she hates having to fill gaps in our recordings. Has to do with quest completion, apparently. Can't get paid without proof."

The shouting slows, giving Isaac a chance to mumble out a response, and then the shouting returns, this time entwined with Yuina's scoffs and snarky remarks. Something about *the importance of evidence* and *how we're making Aria's job harder*, and *that you only had one task and you completely forgot it! We're lucky Jegrac asked about the chronicler, and - no, don't try to change the subject, you had it, so it's your responsibility!*

"Hey," Liatris says, pulling my attention away from the flurry behind us, "do you feel it? The air, the plants, they call for rain."

I stare out at the thinning sunlight, searching for clues. The impending darkness stares back at me, silencing wildlife as the clouds grow thicker, choking out birds and forcing them to swoop lower.

Hints of rain arrive long before it does - the scent of damp soil, which permeates the heavy air, and a faint patter, which arrives moments before the torrent descends, pelting our skin. Beautiful droplets thrum a gentle pattern against the caravan's roof.

An annoyed huff whispers out a billowing gust of snow as Frost moves towards the back of the carriage. The rain crystallises when it reaches him, drifting past his position on top of the caravan.

Liatris shivers as the cold passes, but then her arms reach up, rising like her brilliant smile, embracing the downpour bouncing off the ferns on her head. Her actions soak the right side of my face, despite the safety of my wide-brimmed hat.

My hands linger by the folded extension above our heads, but upon seeing the dryad's enjoyment, I let it go to embrace the storm with her.

We enjoy the ride, basking in the rhythm of the rain. Liatris is vibrant, rejoicing alongside the plants, but for me, the forest has quieted, a temporary pause amongst the wonderfully raucous chaos of nature, little creatures and resilient critters forced to take shelter in deep grass and cosy dens.

"I'm gonna' cook some of the food we got from Borderik," Isaac interrupts, poking his head through the curtain, "and we should probably stop for a bit. Do you, Neva, and Yuina mind checking the caravan's condition? We've been on the road for a while now. You okay if we take a break, Jegrac?"

Not sure why he's asking me; sounds like we're planning to stop regardless of my response. Still, I offer him a courteous nod. The Commander slips away, and I lead the horses towards a bank of grass a little ways off the main path, hopping from the cart as we crawl to a halt. Turning back to the caravan, my hands begin toying with Mayweather and Daisy's harnesses.

I pause.

"Hey. Liatris?"

She breaks her quiet contemplation to tilt her head at me.

"Yes, Jegrac?"

"You want this?"

Her eyes widen when I lift the chronicler towards her, and she starts to reach for it, but hesitates. Her fingers linger above the black surface.

"Are... are you sure, Jegrac? I don't think Neva wants me to touch it." she chews her verdant lip.

"When you're ready, start recording," I reply. "Just don't leave it off for too long. You saw what happened to the Commander! Don't make the same mistake."

The leaves on her head sway when she nods, and my thumb rests upon the glowing jewel as vibrant green hands eagerly yank the device away from me.

CHRONICLE 22
Recorded by Liatris Summerstep

F ather Sky is crying. He has been, for a long time now. But my little cousins reach out with joy as the tears fall; Father Sky is happy to cry, and the flowers take his weeping in stride.

My less floral friends, however, do not share this joy.

"Wipe that smirk off your face, Liatris. You look like a twat."

Neva's voice sounds strangely sharp as she enters the caravan. Her ebony bark glistens with tiny droplets, which she shakes towards the smirking Jegrac following behind her.

The little buds on the top of her head - she had called them *twists* earlier this morning - have blossomed into a beautiful frizzy garden that sits like moss on a mushroom. I want to touch it, but know better than to try. She doesn't like uninvited fingers in her hair.

"Surprise, everyone - it's still raining!" Jegrac remarks with a grin, and I laugh, because my friend is finally happy again. Neva glares at me, because she is mean.

Since the two of them have returned, Mayweather and Daisy must be fed and ready to go, and Neva's strange magic must have activated the wheels and walls of the caravan.

Once our companions have settled my body lurches with squeamish nausea as the bark and wood of this decorated corpse begin to jostle and turn in unsettling ways.

I cradle little Aspleni, clutching the crudely painted pot and concentrating on my friendly fern, struggling to hide my discomfort. My guildmates don't need to know how much this caravan upsets me.

It makes me miss travelling with Frost and Yuina; while they may be cold and distant compared to the rest of my companions (who are just so *kind!*), I secretly wish to trade that kindness for the feeling of grass and friendly plants rushing beneath my feet as we sprint through the fields.

The beautiful bracken in my lap rests its tender green tufts on my hands, whispering silent comforts only I am allowed to hear. I thank Aspleni and ignore Neva's comment about how I'm *talking to the plants again*.

Feeling a little more at ease, I sneak another glance at Jegrac, who has lost his laughter. He sulks on the floor of our dreadful wooden carriage, with Pall resting his head on the man's thigh. I usually talk with the wise Nomad after my potted acquaintances have had enough of our unsaid conversations, but Jegrac has seemed distant lately. Perhaps witnessing so many horrible things in the forest has silenced his joy.

A shiver creeps around my ear as the screams of elder oaks and maples echo in my mind, the trees crying out as bark is carved by dreadful claws, forced to die without a natural purpose to an unnatural force, rotted from the inside and warped beyond any use to future offspring wishing to grow from their remains.

The Mother may seem cruel, certainly, but the death of all things is meant to have a purpose. It brings life.

From the Rift, however, nothing good springs forth.

Sometimes, when left alone with my thoughts, I wonder if it would be better to have never left the Glass. Had I stayed, my mind would be free of this dreadful knowledge.

Aspleni notices my discontent and wraps its soft leaves around my hands, assuring me that everything is alright. That I am safe.

Not wanting to dwell on feelings of pain and misery, I readjust my smile and think of kinder thoughts to share with my patient plant.

My mind goes to Isaac, a polite young man; respectful, compassionate, and always looking out for me. His people have been so lovely, even with their strange pauses and careful looks after every word they say. It was truly wonderful to meet the progenitors of Isaac, and the saplings with whom he shares a name.

Family. A word foreign to dryads, but precious to humans - such an odd concept!

Plants only share the bristling love and ruthless care of Mother and Father Sky. My dryad relatives - who I can barely remember - probably share the selfish indifference of our floral friends.

Thoughts of home draw me back to a sadder place, but I brush them aside for now. Carefully scooting along the bench, I arrive at the front of the caravan. Isaac sits on the other side, guiding the horses with less grace and patience than Jegrac.

"Isaac," I whisper, and he sits up a little taller, as if I have scared away his solemn concentration. He turns to me with a warm look upon his face.

"Hey, 'Tris. Come sit up here for a while! You enjoy the rain, right?"

I dart through the cabin to put Aspleni back in its place, and then hop over the bar to take a seat at Isaac's side.

The air thrums with life, and I savour every breath, delighting in the abundance of nature.

I sit in silence beside my friend, my mind and gaze wandering as the rain washes over my outstretched hands.

Here, in this freedom, this blessed downpour, I quietly mourn for the dryads back home. While the desert and the Oasis of Orion were wonderful places to grow and sprout, the elders always told me it was my duty to be free, to explore the world, to live a life none of them could - to live without roots.

Regret tinges my heart, but it disappears as the pleasure of the plants spreads back into place. One day, my people will see this sight.

One day.

The downpour pauses as Yuina's umbrella casts a shadow on our heads. She leans over us, grinning from her perch on the roof.

"Loving the weather, Liatris?"

When I see her, I smile, shouting a cheerful '*yes!*' while hoping her glacial companion is not following close behind. Frost is somewhere above us, preferably at the back of the caravan, where he can send waves of snow onto the road and simply wound plants with the shocking cold, rather than kill them outright.

Isaac says something else, and I nod even though his words don't reach my ears. Happiness covers my face, obscuring the anxiety hidden underneath. Thankfully, the boy does not appear, and my attention turns back to the beautiful scene ahead of us when Yuina slips out of sight.

Oh?

I almost miss the shift in the air.

The change is barely noticeable at first, the joy of the trees merging with a lingering sorrow. But then the giants of the soil begin to wail, a rough melody within the thrumming rain, which hits much harder now, sharpening from a caress to a violent torrent. The road ahead is obscured by the storm.

An ominous grey lingers beyond the walls of water.

A cloud of silver and black, sizzling up into the sky.

"No. Not again!" Isaac gasps, eyes wide as his grip on the reins tightens, "Smoke? Here?"

The curtain smacks the back of my head when Neva throws it aside.

"Oh, *no*," she says, "no no no NO *NO!*"

Her face contorts, as if struck by an unbearable pain.

"*No.*" she whispers again. "Oh *rift*. What have I done?"

Jegrac appears beside her, and I shuffle aside so the two of them can stare past me.

"It's fine, Neva. The people of this town must be holed up in their church," he mutters, though a tremor fills his voice. "And why are you blaming yourself? None of this is your fault. We can't save everyone - but even still, the people in this town must be okay. Riftspawn attacks are nothing new out here, right?"

My friend releases a sharp whistle, and the horses pick up speed, the rain pummelling against us as we rush forward. We could climb back inside, to protect ourselves, but no one moves.

I squint through the torrent of rain soaking through us and drumming heavy thuds against the caravan's weathered roof.

As we draw closer, the plants grow disturbingly quiet. The land is silent and still, despite the rhythm of Father Sky's tears, the panting of the horses, and the growing hiss from the depths of the town somewhere behind the rain.

Neva's breathing grows louder, ragged, and I shift to caress her knuckles, which grip the bar between us. She pries her fingers free, as if my touch burns, but then reaches for my hand. Her eyes stay locked on the road.

I follow her gaze, watching as ruined buildings begin to line the road. My head reels when a horrible, charred stench mixes in with the aroma of wet dirt and burning wood.

"Here," I say, offering the chronicler to Neva. She takes it quietly, her face twisting as she draws in short, pained breaths. We hold it together, a shared link between friends; a bridge between our anxiety.

"I should have known," she murmurs, "I could have stopped this. If I'd just looked a little further, for a little longer, they could have lived. *I let these people die.*"

Staring out at the town, the church catches my eye - a pile of shattered stone and scorched pillars. The sanctuary is overrun with riftspawn remains.

Nearby, the road has been disrupted, the earth rising to form warped and twisted spikes of dirt.

Neva's grip tightens.

She recognizes the protrusions. I feel like I should, too - the giant thorns of soil appeared in Isaac's hometown, didn't they?

The memories are swept aside when our seer releases a pained, furious whisper.

"Of course they wouldn't stop after Borderik! That High Champion wasn't planning to end things there - they just went and found another town to destroy!"

She spits her words with such ferocity I instinctively draw my hand away, scared by the hatred in her voice.

"*They warned me!* Why didn't I realise sooner? I'm supposed to know these things, but, the haze - I can't... why? *WHY?!*"

Neva leaps off the cart before anyone can respond, taking the device with her as she sprints into the storm.

CHRONICLE 23
Recorded by Neva Oyii

When I was little, my mother would return from the funerals of warriors and tell me of a great, terrible game we all must play.

Life is a race against time.

Because no matter how fast you run, how furiously you fight, how hard you yell and scream and rage against the inevitable - none of it ever changes how the race ends.

Time always wins.

People always die.

We lose guild members. I sacrifice to save others. We arrive a little too late to protect citizens from certain demise, and help pick up the pieces for those left behind.

When I was 15, my people disappeared.

I should be immune to grief. Death is a familiar friend, after all. In my visions he warns me of futures we can prevent and endings we cannot change.

Sometimes, tragedy is inevitable despite our best attempts.

But this?

I didn't foresee any of *this*.

If this haze was gone - if I'd tried a little harder - *if I'd been stronger* - would this town still exist?

It doesn't matter.

I didn't save anyone.

They died because of ME.

If only I'd understood the High Champion's warning; *THIS was their 'other option' - they were talking about other towns!*

Voices echo through the rain, interrupting my thoughts. The frantic calls are obscured, dimmed by the torrent soaking through my skin and splashing against my glamours.

I ignore them. I want to be alone.

Through heavy, dripping eyelashes, the ruined bar enters my sight. Riftspawn remains smudge my sandals, hissing as rain splatters across the dark ooze. The murky liquid ripples with each arduous step, dark stains seeping into crumpled wood.

The building - this town - is decimated, the structures crushed and the ground smeared black. Tar clings to my ankles and weighs me down, as if warning me, whispering: *'go no further. There is no joy to be found in this place.'*

And yet here I am, still searching for something within the shadows of shattered wood and cracked pillars.

Answers, perhaps? Hope? A survivor?

None of those things will be found here.

What remains are pieces of glass, the handle of a mug, and an object poking through rippling riftblood. A golden sheen glimmers beneath the black substance threatening to swallow it whole.

I already know what it is long before the cold metal is resting in my palm.

Another coin?

Again?

Why?

A nearby splatter draws my attention upwards. Yuina steps through the rain, her umbrella dragging behind as she rushes towards me. Her other hand grips an empty hilt, shimmers drifting from the place where the blade should be.

Before she can say anything, I raise the coin. Thin eyebrows scrunch together, and she bites back her lecture to trace the scarred object with her fingers.

She opens her mouth to say something, pauses to chew on her words, and then locks eyes with me.

"You found it *here?* This can't be a coincidence." Yuina taps her chin. "Unfortunately, we can't draw any conclusions yet. Not until we've gotten more info from Isaac's merchant friend in Nexus. Still, it strikes me as rather odd that Isaac was given one of these coins in the first place. Especially with these items showing up whenever we come across a riftspawn attack."

She frowns.

"Hopefully the merchant is still alive..."

Yuina shakes her head, then shouts into the rain: "I FOUND HER!"

A clamour breaks our shared silence as the rest of the guild nears; shapes form behind the wall of water.

A hand slips into mine, and Yuina pulls me forward.

"Alright, Neva. We'd better go."

I don't move.

Untangling from her grasp, my feet stay rooted in place, the tar and rain mingling around my boots, squelching as I wait to sink into the swirling darkness.

Yuina twists her lips, glances over me, and then yells: "STOP! GO AWAY! NEVA IS FINE! CHECK FOR RIFTSPAWN OR SOMETHING! GO! SOMEWHERE! ELSE!"

The noise stops, our guildmates lingering just out of view, silhouettes against the storm.

After a bit of confused grumbling, they fade into the portrait of heavy rain.

Yuina's staring at me, even though I can't bear to make eye contact with her. She stands still for a moment, and then closes the distance between us, her shoulder brushing mine.

"Neva," she asks, "what's wrong?"

The words are locked in my throat, so I just stare up into the sky, letting the rain wash the quiet, terrifying thoughts away.

Yuina waits, the umbrella tucked at her side. She looks away, but every so often I can feel her gaze flicker to me.

Wiping my face with the bottom of my palms, Yuina takes it as an invitation to move even closer, bumping her hip against mine to casually knock me out of my stupor.

She raises her umbrella and shields us from the clouds leaking on our heads.

"Hey," she says quietly. "What's wrong, Neva? You're usually the composed one. Our seer. Why be bothered by something you already *knew* was meant to happen?"

The words won't come.

I manage to shake my head.

Yuina frowns. Catching a glimpse of her from the corner of my eye, I notice how her brow is furrowed, her gaze is locked straight ahead, and her face is knit tight in thought.

"Ah." she murmurs. "It's because you *couldn't* foresee it, right? Or... is it because you didn't check?"

My silence is the final dam keeping me from breaking, so instead I just lean against her. Yuina takes the cue to wrap an arm around my shoulder.

"I know you spend a lot of time looking forward, trying to save everyone. Which is noble. Or whatever you might call it - selfless? Heroic? But the moment you lose your sight, you get upset?"

When I don't respond right away, she adds, "Are you pouting?"

I elbow her in the ribs.

"Ow. Okay, sorry, let me try again. Listen, Neva, you can't blame yourself. None of this is your fault."

Her voice softens. "And even if it was - which we both know isn't true - *you're allowed to be sad*. You know that, right?"

I rest my head on her shoulder.

She's right. I know she is. If I spent all my time looking forward, I'd never be able to save anyone.

The High Champion did this, not me. It's silly to feel guilty about something I couldn't change.

I should be fine.

And yet, the awful feeling remains.

Why?

It's not like I have a connection to this town.

Was I truly looking forward to performing in this dinky little bar again?

No.

Of course not.

But...

It shouldn't hurt this much. These deaths can't be the reason why my heart feels so heavy.

Is it because I didn't have a vision?

Is it because my weakness is the reason these people died? Could I have stopped this tragedy from happening?

No.

While I'm upset by these events, they were beyond my control. *It's something else.*

Yuina interrupts, granting me a welcome break from my thoughts.

"Hey," she says softly, "feel free to correct me if I'm wrong, but if you're dealing with guilt because of your recent struggles with seeing the future, don't worry - you're so much more than *just* a seer. I mean, look at you! You're smart. Confident! Powerful. Capable and proud. You are *so much more*, Neva. Don't forget that."

She's right. I know she's right.

But it still hurts.

Because-

The words find me, spilling out before I can understand what's being said.

"*I can't lose this power*," I whisper. "It's all I have."

Silence lingers for a long moment, the truth hanging in the air.

Then Yuina lets out a loud snort.

"*Excuse me?!*" she exclaims, "Neva, have you been ignoring me this entire time? As I *already* said: you've got your looks, your glamours, your charisma, your character... and you can fight! You have us. You're not worthless, just because you're missing one skill."

I shake my head.

"No. I was listening. I know." I continue to speak, the dam finally broken. My honesty shoves through, refusing to stop, despite my best attempts. "It's just... lately, I've been thinking about my family a lot. Seeing Isaac's parents certainly didn't help. Brought up memories and feelings I'd forgotten. Or had tried to forget."

Yuina holds my shoulder tightly, pulling me towards her. She's quiet, letting me talk about things I've kept bottled up for so long.

"My ability to seer is the only thing I have left of *them*. Of my family. Of my mother. She taught me this skill. Even though I wasn't interested in following her footsteps or learning this part of our legacy, she managed!"

A pained chuckle escapes my lips. I can almost remember her voice, insisting I follow tradition and become an oracle.

"It was her final gift to me. Before... well. You know. *Before*."

Yuina's chin brushes against my hair when she rests her head upon mine.

"Your legacy, huh?" she mutters.

I nod.

We remain together, huddled in our small sanctuary from the rain, for a quiet moment.

Eventually, Yuina whispers softly against my ear.

"Neva. You're allowed to be sad."

My chest heaves as my breathing starts to quicken, threatening to break into a sob.

Aw, rift.

Yuina falls silent, and I untangle myself for a moment to stand alone, arms wrapped around my shoulders, holding myself together. She keeps her distance, but continues to speak.

"I know it happened a long time ago, and you think it shouldn't bother you anymore, but... that's *not how grief works*. It cannot be outrun or beaten or avoided; we all have to face it eventually. And then face it again. And *again*. But each time, it weakens. No, perhaps that's not quite true - perhaps we grow stronger. Slowly but surely, we learn to live with it. Bear the burden, and transform it into something new."

Yuina doesn't notice my stare, her eyes distant.

I'm not sure if she's still talking to me, or to herself.

"We will always miss the people we love," she whispers. "Even if time has passed - no matter how strong we get - we will always grieve, because we cannot stop loving them. It is not a punishment, nor a curse. It is what remains; it is life defeating death. Grief is love, and love is eternal."

Yuina pauses, blinks, and then turns her attention back to me.

"Sorry for the lecture. All I'm trying to say is this: don't be so hard on yourself, okay?"

The silence returns.

This time, however, it's a welcome pause.

After a few deep breaths, I ask: "You'll stay here with me, right? For just a little longer?"

She says nothing, but pulls me even closer.

My head rises, and I watch the raindrops streak like falling stars across the top of our umbrella.

I try to picture my parents. Their faces are blurred, their voices just out of earshot, as if obscured by the pounding rain. The memory hurts, digging even deeper than the wound in my side. My eyes squeeze shut to will the pain away.

Yuina's right. I miss them.

I hate that I can't seer properly.

And I'm sad these people died.

But buried deep underneath all of these feelings, I miss my home. My family. My people.

It hurts.

But...

It hurts because the love still remains, even after all this time.

Even though they're gone.

Gentle, ethereal hands press against my back, urging me onwards. Lingering whispers from faded spectres repeat familiar phrases; words spoken to their daughter each and every time she tried to give up.

Continue, little seer, even when you cannot see the path ahead of you.

And so I will keep moving forward, constantly, consistently, even while glancing back at everything I've left behind.

My lungs fill, and my face buries into Yuina's shoulder as I scream, emotions boiling over, my strength and fury and grief and pain bursting from my chest. As the sadness goes, peace finally arrives to take its place, so I can move on. *Again.*

"Ow." Yuina says, rubbing her ear.

I ignore her.

"Okay," I announce. "We can go."

Water laps at our heels as we push through the storm.

Keeping my head high, I steel a fist against my hip, and peer over my shoulder at the ruined bar and the remains of the unknown patrons.

Sorry I couldn't save you.

But I will do what I can to make things right.

So... rest now.

And live on, in the memories of the ones you loved.

Leaving the bartender and his wife behind, I reach down to my side and silence the chronicler.

Chronicle 24
Recorded by Jegrac

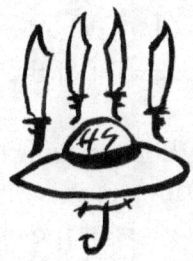

"It's been a while since anyone used the chronicler," Neva declares, her words directed at the device in my hands, "but the trip was uneventful and dull, so we didn't bother recording anything, which means there's no need for *any archivists* to get mad about the gap in our transcripts!"

Yuina pops her head into the caravan.

"Ah, covering your butts for when Aria realises we forgot about that thing?"

Pall perks up as she enters.

"Oh, that reminds me," Neva says to the chronicler, "Yuina demanded we stop recording, as it is - and I quote - *important we force Aria to figure stuff out once in a while, because she is getting old, and it will keep her wits sharp.*"

"Hey!"

"She also said we should-"

Yuina lunges for her, but Neva's already dancing out of the way, hopping through the curtain at the front of the cabin. Her laughter echoes as she is chased into the guild hall.

Pall trots towards me, panting happily.

"Hey, bud. Guess it's just you and me now." I loop the chronicler onto my belt and then pick up the delicate potted flowers Liatris asked me to bring inside. When she gets back from the marketplace with the Commander, we'll have to assess the balcony and make a list of the plants in need of extra care.

Using the heel of my boot to swing the door out of the way, I stumble back when Damian suddenly appears. He attempts to shuffle around me, mutters an apology when he bumps into Pall, and then takes the satchel he'd left behind and throws it over his shoulder.

I step aside so he can exit. To my surprise, the boy lingers. *He wants to help?*

When he continues to hesitate - with one hand resting on the door handle even though he makes no move to leave - I take the hint.

"Lend me a hand, will you? Need to take in two more plants, so do you mind - yeah, over there - no, the one with the scarlet..." I pause, searching for a description he'll understand, "...with the red and white spikes on top. Similar to a flower, but with thin green leaves. Yes, that one! Also, the green and yellow fern - no, look to the right - there we go! Excellent. Now, walk carefully - you don't want to drop either of these fragile beauties."

The boy nods, falling into place behind me as we travel up the walkway to the guild hall. Our silence is accompanied by a pleasant breeze and Pall's quiet panting, syncopated against the tapping of our boots upon rows of grey tiles.

"Excuse me, Jegrac, sir? Is it safe to have your guild's insignia out right now?" Damian asks. "Aren't you worried?"

I shake my head.

"We're in a safe place. No one will attack us here," I reassure him, "and we have allies nearby. The risk of reinforcement is a strong deterrent to would-be threats."

"My dad doesn't like guilds," Damian blurts out, "but he always tells me they're an essential part of the economy and of Nexus or whatever. Uh, and sometimes he talks about how the guilds are the *only thing* citizens from all Eight Realms don't take for granted."

"Huh. Neat." I say. "And what about you?" When Damian looks confused, I add: "You're part of a guild now, right? Even if it's just temporary. Have your views changed at all?"

The boy chews his lip.

"I dunno. They're alright, I guess? And you guys are cool! Plus, guilds help people, which is good. And you get to go on adventures and travel all over the place. That's really awesome."

It's tempting to correct him, but I swallow my comments. He's been chastised enough, and he's saying something nice, so it's not worth the hassle. And - to his credit - he's *partially* correct. Most guilds travel a lot, but not all of them. Some stay rooted in specific areas, since merchant and business oriented guilds have no need to embark on quests.

The conversation starts to fizzle out, so I do my best to mimic Isaac and attempt cordial small talk.

"So... what does your family do for a living? The Cappells, right?"

Damian nods.

"Yeah, that's us! Uh, how do I explain it... we support Nexus, I guess? For example, my dad invests in a ton of weaponsmiths. He provides funding and rents out buildings designed by my mom. Nothing exciting though, not like what you guys get to do! Oh, and we also get orders from the Council to supply armour and swords and stuff to the Nexus guards, but the blacksmiths do all the *actual* work."

"Hey, still sounds pretty impressive," I reply as we step through the giant doors leading into the guild hall. The gateway in the corner of the massive room thrums with magical energy, an uncomfortable rhythm against the twittering birds and the chittering critters scurrying about the upper levels of the hall.

Pall prances across the spotless white floor, but his eager huffing shifts into a whine. His snout shakes.

My stomach turns as a horrid stench floods my nostrils. It's strangely familiar, and very strong. The air shimmers as we walk, and then-

Glamours?

Who would-

Cold steel pressures my throat as a horde of people flicker into view. Neva and Yuina are locked within the bristling crowd, held still by hostile blades. Their faces are a sharp contrast to our current circumstances: Neva looks bored, while Yuina admires our captors with wide, excited eyes (much to the chagrin of the guard behind her).

The grey and blue uniforms force a gasp from my chest.

Nexus guards? Here?

My attempts to find answers are silenced by the cold metal against my neck, and I swallow my questions. Pall starts growling, but a quick whistle stops him from starting any trouble. His hackles lower, and he sends a wordless message through our bond: he is waiting for my command. Pall's eyes lock onto the ankles of the man aiming a spear at his back.

A signature, sickly smell enters my nostrils, and after a quick scour of the room, I pinpoint the source.

Foivos leers down at us from the balcony, fouling our home with his stench. Rahma lingers near the putrid man, her arms resting on the balustrade, legs shuffling as her eyes dart towards the snow-crusted door on the far side of the upper level, a hint of a smile playing on her face.

Foivos speaks, his words haughty and precise, snipping through the silence.

"As I was saying - the Council and the City of Nexus are charging you, the members of Honour's Stand, for the following crimes: harbouring a dangerous creature, facilitating and enabling a terrorist, kidnapping, conspiring against the Council, and disturbing the peace."

Neva and Yuina share an annoyed glance.

The lingering silence gives me time to sort my thoughts and figure out an explanation for each accusation. First of all, the *creature?* Could be Liatris, since she's a dryad. Frost might be the more accurate answer, but the Council wouldn't dare provoke him, so it has to be her.

As for the supposed terrorist... it must be me. They need someone to blame for the riftspawn attacks in Greyton and Borderik. They need a scapegoat. If the truth came out about a High Champion being involved in the rift summonings, people might realise the Nomads are actually innocent.

The only accusation that doesn't make sense is kidnapping. We've been with the same folk this entire journey, so who did we-

When my head snaps toward Damian, I find him staring at the ground, his ears a bright, burning red. He peeks up at me, his face flushed.

"I - look, I'm sorry, Jegrac. I didn't know!"

"Oh, hush, boy," Rahma muses from above, "you played your part perfectly. And don't worry - we'll undo any brainwashing done by these terrible *criminals*. Once their associates arrive, you'll be free, and these Nomad sympathisers will be locked away where they belong!"

"Rahma! Don't antagonise them," Foivos scolds, "we were instructed to avoid any and all unnecessary casualties. Let's not start a fight with *this* guild."

His companion rolls her eyes and presses her lips into a tight smile.

Her grin widens when the air grows cold.

Our attention shifts to the other side of the hall.

Frost is coming.

Neva whispers to the guard beside her: "Your blade - put it on Yuina's back, not her throat. Hide it where he won't-"

She's cut off when her captor hisses: "Traitors have no right to talk!"

A few uniformed men and women stalk towards the black wire sustaining this giant glamour, their blades poised and ready. Two purple-swathed figures crouch in the far corner of the room, hands gripping the dark twine circling the outer edges of the hall and blanketing us in deceit. My eyes drift, searching for the red armbands of specialists trained to drive away bugs, birds, and all manner of good things. I come up empty.

No revulsors? My gaze wanders up to our plant-covered balcony, where many small critters and birds hide amongst the foliage.

Good. My living weapons are standing by.

As Frost draws near, the tension in the room grows. I make a quick tally of our current foes - at least 20 guards, including the ones up on the balcony, along with the two High Champions, who pose a more significant threat.

My eyes also catch an odd sight: giant boulders litter the bottom of each wall. The massive stones appear to serve little purpose beyond adding chunks of brown and grey to this canvas of white, but I take them into consideration as well - why bother placing these rocks so carefully, if not for some secret, nefarious reason?

My attention snaps back to the side door as Frost passes through the edge of the glamour. His eyebrows rise at the thin blades pressed against his throat.

The boy tilts his head as stares of awe, fear, and trepidation wash over him. Rahma gives him an eager wave, but the boy's gaze drifts over her, scanning the room with great disinterest.

His empty eyes sharpen with a glacial, bitter hatred when he spots the dagger by Yuina's neck.

"Aw, *rift*." Neva sighs. "Should've listened to me when you had the chance..."

The guards surrounding the boy slop to the ground with crisp *thunks* as bloodied chunks of ice separate heads from necks, and the hall bursts to life. The blade against my throat goes slack, and I release a fierce whistle. A flurry of black smears dart into the man behind me, forcing him to tumble away as he screams and smacks at the mob of birds pecking his face and eyes.

Pall falls into place at my side. Nearby, his captor howls, clutching his ankle as he writhes around on the floor.

The temperature in the hall sinks dangerously low when Frost walks past. He glowers at the High Champions on the balcony.

"Wait, dear Frost! Did you forget? You're one of us," Foivos declares, extending a hand towards the boy. "If you choose to side against your guild, I am sure the Council will-"

He ducks when a blade of ice pierces the space his head had been moments ago.

"Frost, please! Be reasonable! We can-"

But the conversation is already over. Shards of ice explode against his body, and he dances back.

Frost's expression shifts from indifference to annoyance. Neva swears under her breath.

The two High Champions barely have time to exchange a worried glance before Foivos's arm snaps in half, split by a blade of ice rupturing through his elbow. He screams and stumbles back. Rahma manages to duck out of the way, though her cheek splits open with a nasty gash as a frozen dagger slices past her face.

Her eyes light up when Foivos falls against the wall behind him, and she rises, grinning at her fellow High Champion.

"Finally, a good excuse for self-defence!" Rahma exclaims. She snaps her fingers with a loud crack, and a great rumbling fills the hall. Staring past the guards lying around Yuina and Neva's feet, my eyes widen as the massive boulders begin to move, rolling onto each other to form hulking titans of stone.

Neva dances out of the way when a rock golem attempts to strike her, its giant fist drawing up a cloud of white dust. Cursing under her breath, Neva rubs a hand against her forearm and then pauses to stare at her skin. When the glamour doesn't appear, her head snaps towards the illusionists hiding in the corner of the room, still clutching the black wire. She sprints over to them, fans glinting menacingly, but they're gone before she arrives, feet skirting as they race out the front door. Satisfied, Neva slices the wire apart and begins glamouring herself out of sight.

"Damian! Go!" I shout, and he peeks out from his hiding spot in the corner of the room. He follows my gesture to the doors leading down to the archives. The boy sprints under the balcony supporting Rahma and Foivos, his hand rising to offer a generous salute before ducking behind the wooden barrier.

"Alright. We'll handle *this*," Yuina announces, pointing at the golems. "So, Neva and Frost, you mind taking care of those two nuisances?" She nocks her head towards the High Champions, and our companions nod.

The empty hilts laced to Yuina's wrists are brandished and ready, the thin handles clutched in her fingers like pieces of chalk as she sketches something into the air. A glowing blue rune floats in place, bracing the weight of the stone fist slamming against it with a sturdy *thud*. "Jegrac! Get over here and help!"

I follow her command, dispatching wave after wave of birds and creatures at the remaining guards while Yuina defends us from a barrage of heavy punches. Frost and Neva march past, undeterred, gazes locked on the High Champions up above.

A soft, powerful voice punctuates our conflict, and we freeze.

"All of you. Please. Stop."

The words are strained, but strong, and even Frost pauses at Aria's call. The ornate wooden doors barring the back of the hall swing open, revealing more guards, as well as a tall blonde man in a black suit. My stomach drops at the sight of the shiny golden armband clashing against his tuxedo, and my blades fumble through my fingers and clatter on the floor when I notice the hand pressed against Aria's frail neck. Damian is held captive as well, tugged along by the man's grip on his bicep, the black gloves wrapped tightly around the boy's arm.

The High Champion sneers, contorting his handsome face with a hideous, haughty expression.

"I'd listen to her if I were you," he scoffs.

"We had this under control, Solaris!" Rahma shouts, her tone angry yet tinged with gratitude. "You didn't have to interfere!"

Solaris doesn't look up at her. Instead, his eyes remain locked on me. They brim with hatred, sending a shiver down my spine.

The High Champion starts to glow, his skin emanating a faint light, but it fades when he notices Frost's outstretched hand. Solaris starts to speak, hesitating when the boy's fingers flex. He steps back, shaking his head, and glances at Yuina.

"Remarkable, Frost. You want to fight in a place like this?" he says. "We might cause some... *collateral damage*."

The boy pauses, registering Solaris's threat. Then his gaze sharpens. Snow flutters down from the ceiling, swirling about the room as the child's aura bursts forth. Solaris frowns, and a wave of heat washes over us, shoving against the whirling cold.

Before either of them can strike, Yuina calls out: "He's right, Frost. Let's play along. For now."

Our High Champion glances at her, hand partially raised and covered with a deadly haze, magic brimming within the spiralling snowflakes at his fingertips. But then he steps back, shrugging his shoulders as he walks over to his companion's side. She gives him a nod, and we turn together to face Solaris.

"They're complying, Rahma," the man declares. She sighs and snaps her fingers. Her stone golems lumber back to the walls and crumble into piles of lifeless boulders.

The man's shoulders relax, and he gestures to the guards at his side.

"Search them for weapons, and then runelock their wrists and necks. Have them prepared for transportation as well," he commands. "Honour's Stand will be on trial tomorrow morning, so let's make this quick."

Sweat trickles down the guards' foreheads as they anxiously click cuffs around my wrists and neck. Their hands shuffle through my clothes and pat my sides before confiscating the daggers hidden within.

Pall whines as a tight collar slides over his throat, and then releases a muffled whimper when his jaw is muzzled shut. I send sparks of comfort to him through our bond and try to mask my uneasiness.

If my companion notices, he pretends not to, and obediently follows the guard leading him out the side door of our guild hall.

"Excuse me," a man mutters as he unclips the chronicler from my side.

CHRONICLE 25
Recorded by ???

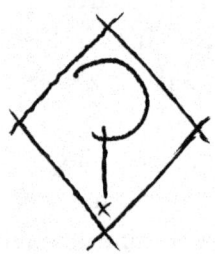

"And *what* exactly d'ya think this *thing* is supposed to be?"

Devona peers at the slab in my hand as she pokes the glowing stones.

I shrug and turn the device over. The back is smooth, covered in an onyx material that clacks beneath my nails. Flipping it again, our faces are reflected in the dark glass rectangle amidst the glimmering blue jewels.

"Oof, such an unflattering angle," Devona mutters, leaning away from me. Her curly brown hair settles on the pauldrons of her uniform as she steps away. My fellow guard heads towards the lockers on the other side of the room to examine herself in the mirror.

My attention turns back to the object in my hand. The rhythmic shimmering of the tiny stones fascinates me. Would Laura like this? Her birthday *is* coming up, so maybe I'll claim this item when my shift ends.

"Anyone say *why* this stuff is in here?" I ask, glancing over the collection of items and weapons scattered across the tables in our break room.

Devona shrugs as she walks back to my side, carefully adjusting her belt so the baton doesn't clunk against a nearby desk. She runs her hands over the hilt of a weathered sword.

"Must belong to a guild; Kevin just mentioned that we locked another one of those groups up in the main holding cell. Sounds like more work for us, but hey, at least we get free stuff!"

Her fingers linger over a familiar symbol, and she lifts the hilt so I can get a better look.

A shield, shattering a sword.

"You recognize this?"

Before I can reply, the door on the other side of the room swings open.

Kevin stumbles in, collapsing on a chair that squeals in protest. The furniture's cries are smothered by the large body draped over it.

"Hey," he says, rubbing the top of his balding head, "doesn't your shift start soon, Reggie? Might want to clock in early. Those High Champions are sniffing around again, looking for people to blame. Don't remember their names, but you know them - the sun man, the pale guy, and... the, uh, rock lady? Be prepared for another rough evening, cause it looks like they're not going anywhere any time soon."

Devona sighs.

"Ugh, they're still here?" She groans, standing tall as she checks the clock framed against the bland grey walls. "Oh, look at the time. Better get back to it."

I glance at the table, searching for an empty space to place this device. My hand hovers above the desk, frozen by the strange gurgle and solid thump that suddenly fills the room.

It's a terrifying sound.

A shiver creeps up my arm.

The temperature in the room drops. Goosebumps itch across my skin.

A white fog crosses my face, each ragged breath marked by a small cloud.

My hand grips the baton on my waist, heels digging into the floor as the weapon flies up and out, aimed at the unknown threat. The puddle of blood forming beneath my feet is slick and surprising, forcing my back against the table as I-

CHRONICLE 26
Recorded by Kaneko Yuina

"You didn't need to kill them, Frost."

With a sigh, I tuck the chronicler into an empty pouch on my thigh.

Tiptoeing around the puddles of blood dotting the grimy floor, my hands fold in a silent, apologetic prayer.

If these frozen corpses could still speak, would they forgive us? Not that *I've* done anything wrong; it's just a shame these guards were in the wrong place at the wrong time.

Regardless, this slaughter is because of the Council - they're the ones foolish enough to try locking up a volatile High Champion.

They chose to aggravate him. Now *they* have to deal with the consequences.

Unfortunately, the rest of the guild will disagree and likely pin this entire massacre on me - again - as if I'm the one doing it! All because *I* didn't impede my companion's rampage.

But I digress.

Leaving the bodies behind, my attention returns to Frost. The young High Champion lingers by a table at the back of the room, his fingers hovering over an assortment of weapons and trinkets. Hoisting a satchel onto the wooden surface with a soft thump, he begins to unceremoniously shove our guild's "confiscated items" into the bag.

Frost stops to toss me a familiar grey pouch. I snatch it from the air with a muttered thanks and peer inside.

"*Pillars above*! These morons broke my chalk!"

I scour the room for a waste bin and then throw the shattered pieces away. A chill brushes my neck, drawing me back to Frost. My bladeless hilts dangle from his outstretched fingers.

Taking care not to touch the boy's frigid skin, the precious writing tools return to my wrists once their thin cords bind them in place.

Frost continues collecting items from the tables spread throughout the room, so I use this opportunity to examine our surroundings. It's a disappointing sight; the only splash of colour is the bright red decorating the floor. The walls and ceiling are a dull grey, covered by posters with mundane instructions for prison guards to ignore while on break.

My eyes catch on the large map sprawled across a nearby bulletin board. It's identical to one tucked in my back pocket - which I've already memorised - so my attention drifts onwards.

Lockers line the side of the room closest to the door. Most of them are closed, but one hangs open, and my curiosity draws me to it. After a few careful steps over the bodies sprawled across the tiled floor, I peek inside.

It's filled with ordinary things; Orion cloves for fresh breath, an empty bag, a handful of drained chargestones, and a crumpled picture taped to the inside of the small metal door. A cold twinge pierces my chest at the sight of a man in the centre of the photo, flanked by two young girls and a woman kissing his cheek.

A quick glance over the corpses confirms he won't be going home tonight.

Frost's voice draws my attention away from this sad little tragedy.

"Yuina?"

His words are tinged with a wisp of emotion, and my head snaps towards him. Did he see the photo?

If he did, he clearly doesn't care. Frost is already halfway out the door, unfazed by the blood pooling towards his feet as he glides away. The seeping substance crystallises before it can reach him, tracing steps of crimson glass across the room.

I'm tempted to call him back, to make him wait - to test his limits, just to see how he'll react - but he's already gone.

So instead I stay silent as always and simply follow his lead.

Our walk is rather relaxing, with my companion interrupting his carnage every so often to ask for directions. Since Frost is clearing the way, I'm free to analyse and admire the inner workings of this prison.

Peering through the blood, each wall hides subtle runes glimmering with symbols for *resilience* and *warding*. Others lie beneath, drifting to the surface with rough translations of *draining* and *suppression*.

Ah. Is this why my attempts to use magic have been so taxing?

Another victim crumples while attempting to shock the boy with a lightning incantation, and I pause to examine their remains. Sparks of remnant magic fizzle in the woman's palms, drawing my attention to her wrists. A simple metal bracelet is buried in her sleeve, embedded with runes I don't recognize. The material is cold, sticking to my skin as it slips off the corpse.

Waving the bangle to flick off any traces of blood, it slips into place beside the cords on my wrists.

The effect is instantaneous. Magic runs freely through my veins, crackling with energy and sparkling across my fingertips.

"Frost!" I call out, tossing the bracelet to him. It slides onto his arm, and the chill in the air grows stronger.

Our journey picks up speed as he carves through guards with renewed ferocity, allowing me to enjoy my thoughts and observations in relative peace. It takes some effort to push the startled screams and gurgles and snaps and cracks out of sight and out of mind, but I manage.

It's gotten easier over time.

Eventually rows of empty cells signal the start of the temporary holding area. The guild must be close!

A hint of worry breaks through my examination of the rune-embedded architecture. Isaac's inevitable lecture becomes an annoying possibility the closer we get to reuniting with the guild, and while Neva and Aria might turn a blind eye to these casualties, Jegrac and Liatris will certainly feel the need to say something about *the value of all living things* and *how murder is almost always wrong*.

Ugh.

Voices echo down the hallway, a sign of more ignorant guards wandering to their deaths.

Perhaps I should at least try *convincing Frost to use his other abilities. Even if the Council ignores his actions due to his High Champion status, they could still pin his crimes on the rest of the guild.*

Taking a deep breath, my feet stomp against the floor as I push through the intense cold surrounding Frost. He registers my presence and tries to stifle the biting chill with a sharp inhale.

"Listen. I know these people deserve to die," I lie through chattering teeth, "but can't you just charm them out of the way? They'll be more useful alive, right?"

The boy pauses, tilting his head as he peers back at me.

When he doesn't respond right away, my head is drenched with the sinking feeling that I've overestimated our relationship. His source of entertainment and support is talking back and overstepping her bounds.

Perhaps it would be better to let him continue on his merry way and reconcile with the consequences later.

But before I can retract my statement, he mutters: "*Fine.*"

As if on cue, a squad rounds the corner. The guards talk and chat with each other while they step in front of Frost, and they don't notice him at first, glancing once, then again, until finally staring in shock and confusion, their eyes darting to the golden band around the boy's arm. Instantly, shoulders straighten and arms rise to salute. But then mouths gape and weapons are clasped when they stare past us; the guards gasp and choke, sickened by the massacre in our wake.

Frost runs a hand through his silver hair.

A cold flurry whirls around his frail figure, and I hop back, my bladeless hilts scrawling runes for *resistance* and *unfeeling* onto my skin.

The air shifts from hostile to welcoming.

The strangers shake their heads like horses shooing away flies, their breaths growing short and their words fumbled as Frost begins to snare them. His magic threatens to seep through my wards; the siren's call whispering something unintelligible and enticing and familiar...

My foot slides forward, lured across the ice. I can almost hear it. Just a few steps more, and-

Pain erupts as the runes sear my skin in protest, overpowering the urge to listen. My eyes press shut, shoving the call away. After an eternity of silence, Frost's voice breaks through.

"It's done," he says, and I find myself staring at an empty hall. Swallowing a shiver, I nod.

At least *now* our journey will be uninterrupted. Those guards will do everything in their power to protect Frost and keep us from being caught.

Better to have lives ruined by a charm than cut short by a shard of ice, right?

Frost's lips twitch into a faint frown, before resetting to an emotionless straight line.

"I'm not doing that again," he snaps.

Then he glides away, his words hanging in the air behind him.

We walk in silence for a little longer, but my curiosity starts to overcome my sensibility and the question slips out before it can be stopped: "*Why?!* You could have done this as soon as we escaped. Not that I'm doubting your choices, Frost, but enchanting the first set of guards we met would have made our journey a lot easier."

Frost says nothing. Perhaps he doesn't want to tell me. Or, he finds answering to be too much of a bother. Which is fine - if the answer was important, he'd let me know.

I return to my examination of the runes glimmering within the grey stone walls and ceiling, but my ears stay perked, awaiting a possible reply.

We round another corner, and a sharp crack fills the corridor as two stone golems shatter, split apart by chunks of ice.

Frost sighs. He glances back at me, though I pretend not to notice.

"It makes me... *uncomfortable*," he murmurs.

I hide my curiosity behind a moment of silence, and then ask: "*Why?* You've charmed people before. Do you always feel... *uncomfortable*... afterwards?"

He shrugs.

"It's unpleasant, being reminded of who I am."

I can't stop myself.

"Not to be repetitive, but - *why?*"

As I gesture at the hall leading us towards the guild's cell, Frost snarls.

"Because it reminds me of my family."

The chance to pry further slips away when a great clamour interrupts our conversation. The noise comes from behind the barrier at the end of the hall, where a clear surface flickers with runes, shadowing the faces of our guildmates.

"Yuina, is that you? Great work! I'm glad to see you and Frost are safe."

"Hey, please tell me that's not - *oh Yiatsu, no! Frost, what did you do now?!*"

"They took Pall, Yuina. We have to find him. Don't worry, he's not hurt, but he *is* scared!"

"Finally, you're here! Let's offer some well-earned payback to the fools who locked us up! After we rescue Aria, of course. Oy, Yuina, hurry up! On this side, there's a panel-"

"Wait... have you two been tracking blood through the-"

"QUIET." Frost commands, and the shouting stops.

He steps aside, allowing me to reach the chargestones embedded in the wall beside the barrier. To my dismay, there's nothing to press or click. The glimmering black gems are held in place by small metal talons erupting from a white square.

A glamour, perhaps?

Running my fingers over the smooth surface doesn't reveal any useful clues, and the stones powering the barrier are locked in place by magic, burning my skin when I attempt to pry one loose.

After a moment of contemplation, I pull a piece of chalk out of the pouch on my side. Rubbing the end of the blue charcoal to sharpen and imbue it with magic, one hand rests against the wall to steady myself as the other sketches an ancient symbol for *unlock*. Once the last line is drawn the barrier flickers out of existence.

Okay. Simple enough.

Not one to waste time, Frost is already stepping towards the guild.

"Wrists." he demands, and Neva tentatively drags herself forward, arms stretched out warily when the boy points at her. A shard of ice forms in the middle of the cuffs, and they drop onto the floor with a sharp clang. Flexing her fingers, Neva reaches up to toy with her collar, sliding it off after some careful manoeuvring. The clatter of metal is accompanied by more clangs as the rest of the group is freed from their restraints.

"Alright! Everyone ready?" Neva declares. "Yuina and Frost, here's the plan: Isaac and I will get Aria while everyone else figures out how to escape from this awful place."

Jegrac calls to us from his position at the end of the hall.

"My connection to Pall is strained, but I've got a vague understanding of his thoughts: he can smell Mayweather and Daisy, along with - how do I describe this... 'something unfamiliar, smeared with dust and the musk of time'. Wait! He recognizes one more scent - it's the caravan!" Jegrac grins as he scans the corridors for guards. "We'd better get moving while the halls are clear. Pall's waiting for us!"

Liatris sniffs, her eyes narrowed as she stares at Frost. She turns to Neva, her mouth opening in protest.

"Are you sure you don't need my help? I could-"

Neva cuts her off with a quick snap. "No! Definitely not! You and Jegrac are the ones in the most danger. I know you're not a fan of Frost, but the safest place to be is by his side."

Our seer turns to the Commander and winks. "Besides, Isaac has the most experience being stealthed by me, so he's the best option for a rescue mission. You, however, need to stay with the group."

Neva shifts her attention to me.

"Oh, and Yuina? We need to talk, so if you've got the chronicler, hand it to Isaac before coming with me." She eyes Liatris, who starts to follow us. "No, *just Yuina*. We don't need an audience."

CHRONICLE 27
Recorded by Isaac Heathe

Neva's voice is harsh, urgent, and too quiet to hear. Yuina's eyes go wide, and she steels her expression, her jaw clenched tight. Our historian whispers something back, nods, and then sprints down the hall after the rest of the guild.

I rub my wrists and neck, glad to be rid of the restraints. My skin is sore but not broken, and a surge of energy fills my body, driven by a creeping anxiety about the path ahead.

"Hey, look at us!" the seer declares, rubbing her hands together as sparks of glamour drift through the air like colourful, glimmering snowflakes. "Neva and Isaac, back at it again. Just like old times."

I offer her my arm so she can get to work. The illusion is cold, but Neva ignores my shivers and slides her hands over mine. The magic clings to my skin like a wet glove.

"Ugh. Just like old times," I reply. Neva grins.

"Bet you're glad you left that boring farm to become an adventurer, huh?"

I try to mimic her smile.

When her fingers begin tracing magic across my face, her eyes soften.

"You don't have to answer this, but... you ever wonder if your parents were right? Especially Marie." Her words are doused with a deep bitterness, despite how carefully she tries to hide it. "If things were different - if we'd never met - you could have had a normal life as a farmer in Borderik."

She pauses for a long moment.

"Isaac, do you ever regret meeting me?"

The question startles me, and I fumble out a response: "What?! Neva, why would I-"

She places her hand over my mouth, cutting me off.

"Sorry," she says, "I shouldn't have asked."

Voices echo down the hallway, silencing any further conversation. Neva takes my hands, squeezes her eyes shut, and then draws in one long breath, her shoulders rising. The glamour comes quicker now, shrouding us and removing our presence from the hall. She keeps her fingers locked in mine and guides me to the far corner of the corridor moments before a group of guards pass by, their weapons raised and ready as they escort a familiar figure down the hall.

Heat sweeps over us when Solaris arrives. A furious glare twists his handsome features into a sinister grimace.

"Why does the Council hire such *incompetent fools?!*" he snarls, shoving aside the wardens standing in his way. He darts into the empty cell, his eyes ablaze. Sweat coalesces on my forehead as a humid stench hits my nostrils.

We're not the only ones enduring the heat; the men and women accompanying Solaris are soaked and weary.

Neva breaks through my thoughts when she squeezes my hand and tugs me away from this sweltering scene.

The High Champion's rage burns at our backs, but quickly fades while we sprint through the halls, leaving the simmering man and his sweaty entourage behind.

The prison is strangely quiet, with the occasional guard expressing very little interest in the disappearance of our guild. Snippets of conversation slip through my ears; Frost's name is mentioned rather frequently and with a suspicious amount of passion, but any other references to *Honour's Stand* are notably absent.

Swallowing the lump in my throat, I distract myself from our High Champion's misdemeanours by emptying my thoughts. Neva appears to know where we're going, which makes it easier to zone out.

Has her sight returned? If it has, she's made no mention of it. I want to ask, but lately her visions seem to be a sensitive subject, so I keep my curiosity to myself.

We rush past slumped figures lurking behind flickering barriers, and a familiar face catches my eye.

Clifford's daughter is hunched in the corner of a cell, her head pressed back against a colourless wall, empty eyes staring through ragged strands of unwashed hair.

"Wait," I whisper, yanking Neva back. "*Look.*"

She stops.

"That's her!" Waving my arm towards the merchant's daughter, I wait for Neva to respond.

I can't see her, but she's definitely rolling her eyes.

"Seriously, Isaac? You're gonna' have to clarify - we're invisible, remember?!"

"Oh. Right. Yes, you're right. I'm getting used to being glamoured again. Sorry. Um, in the cell on the left, the girl there - she's Clifford's daughter."

I'm met with silence, and then an annoyed mutter: "Okay... and Clifford is...?"

"You know, the merchant! Right before we got arrested, I was in the marketplace trying to find him. We met Clifford and his daughter a few weeks ago when we protected them from riftspawn."

Neva sighs. She clearly has no idea who this person is, so I try to be more direct. "Fine. You don't need to remember. But her father gave me one of those coins with four scratches; she might know why!"

Neva draws in a sharp breath and yanks me towards the barrier.

"Hey!" she hisses. "Can you hear me?"

The girl doesn't respond. Empty eyes remain locked on the shimmering surface between us.

Perhaps she doesn't recognize Neva's voice?

"Miss," I whisper, "we're friends of your father. Clifford. What happened? Why are you here?"

The girl registers nothing. She remains still and silent, as though carved from stone.

"She can't hear us," Neva mutters. The seer pulls me away, even though my feet refuse to budge. An irritated huff echoes in the quiet hall. "C'mon, Isaac! We can free her on the way back, if she's still here. Right now, our priority is Aria. Let's not keep her waiting."

My chest tightens. We both know rescuing her isn't worth the risk; freeing Clifford's daughter would only add to our guild's growing list of crimes.

To protect Honour's Stand, we have to leave her behind.

The glimmering runes lining the walls race past, and despite my protests Neva refuses to slow down, steadily leading us closer and closer to our archivist with each frenzied step.

My heart skips a beat, and a horrible image fills my head.

I blink it away, but the brutal scene is already burned into my eyes.

They wouldn't hurt Aria, would they? She may be mentally resilient, but her body is fragile and weathered by time.

I shake the thought aside and tighten a hand around the hilt of my blade.

We'll be there soon, Aria. Just hold on a little longer.

A wall slams against my back when Neva suddenly shoves me against it. I bite down a curse, silencing myself while the ground trembles beneath the weight of the two gigantic stone golems lumbering around the corner. We shuffle out of the way, becoming as flat as possible until they have finally passed.

"Rahma?" I wonder aloud. Neva squeezes my hand, reminding me to be quiet.

We continue for a while longer. The journey is quick but uneventful, and eventually we reach a simple wooden door at the top of a stone staircase.

Without hesitating, Neva shoves it aside. Several guards hop to their feet from couches and cushioned chairs lining the well-furnished, cosy room, their eyes and weapons aimed at the empty doorway.

A crackling fireplace casts the room in a warm glow. The light source is nestled between two recliners, where Damian and Aria are swathed in fluffy blankets and soft pillows.

The archivist raises a wispy eyebrow as she stares through us, rising higher to catch a glimpse down the stairs. A smile crosses her face, and the fuzzy white robes draped over her frail body sink into a nest of velvet.

She takes a sip of tea and returns to scribbling in the ledger on her lap.

"Be gentle," Aria murmurs. "They've done nothing wrong."

The guards stare at her and raise their eyebrows.

"It's just an old door, ma'am. This happens all the time. Shoddy craftsmanship."

One of the guards rolls her shoulders as she drags her feet towards us, the spear in her hand drifting through the air. "Don't worry, I'll handle it."

"Worry? Oh, no, my dear," Aria laughs, "I'm not worried at all."

Neva's grip slips away, taking the glamours along with her, and the guard's head rattles with disbelief when I suddenly become a very visceral and real part of the room.

"What?! Oh! Isaac!" Damian exclaims, his eyes growing wide. He clamps a hand over his mouth before he can blurt out anything else.

"Wait a- uh, who the *rift* are-" the woman starts to exclaim, but a blurred shadow knocks her to the ground. Neva flickers into sight, whirling towards a guard who barely has time to unsheathe his sword. His legs are swept out from under him by a well-placed kick, and he hits the ground hard. With a snap Neva disappears again, and then moments later two other guards are knocked to the floor. The remaining man swipes a dagger wildly in the air, hoping to catch the invisible woman. His desperation makes him an easy target, and he crumples beneath the hilt of my sword.

When the room calms, I turn to Aria.

She still has yet to look our way. Damian, however, continues to watch us with wide eyes. An eager smile covers his face.

The archivist keeps working in the notebook on her lap, and so I ask: "Aria. Are you alright?"

She nods, and then empties her drink in one long, blissful gulp before tossing it aside.

Brushing off her blankets, the old woman reaches for Damian, who stares at her for a few confused blinks before hopping to his feet. Taking her arm, the boy helps our archivist pry herself out of her cushioned chair.

"About time!" Aria remarks, scuttling over to my side. "I've had enough adventure for today, and I'm ready to go home. If you're here, then I'm assuming the rest of the guild has been tasked with finding an escape route. Good. Well done, you two."

Before I can respond, her attention drops to the chronicler on my belt, her thin fingers fumbling with the buckle before falling back to her side with a sigh.

"Be a dear, will you?" Aria asks, and I unclip the device for her. It rests upon her outstretched palms, and she cradles it.

Her exhausted smile softens as she takes it from me.

CHRONICLE 28
Recorded by Aria Stueck

"Great. You done? Come on, Aria! The guild's waiting!" Neva snaps. Her impatience amuses me; I'm allowed to take as long as I want to get ready. The temptation to slow down is alluring, but the opportunity for such mischief has long passed. My guildmates look to me for wisdom, so instead I rest a gentle hand on her forearm. Neva rolls her eyes, but her voice softens when she adds, "Yes, I'm glad you're safe. Obviously. So, can we leave now?!"

She glances down at me, her eyebrows arched and her lips set in a tight line. I give the seer another kind pat, which she shrugs away. Swallowing my amusement, my gaze wanders to Isaac, who waits politely by the steps, his elbow extended towards me.

Not wanting to test Neva any further, I shuffle over to our Commander. He greets me with a kind smile as he locks arms with me, granting a stability I've sorely missed.

While we prepare to leave, my eyes drift over the men and women slumbering on the floor.

They were pleasant enough (though a little *too* sympathetic) and apparently quite aware of my connections to the Council, which explains their abundant politeness.

When they wake up in this empty room, I sincerely hope a mild headache is the only consequence they have to face.

But such worries are not mine to bear.

My thoughts turn elsewhere as my hands tighten around the chronicler clutched to my chest. An electric eagerness builds at my impending return to the depths of the archives; cataloguing the latest adventure of Honour's Stand will be quite the feat!

The daydreams drift away, however, and are quickly replaced by the fact that we have yet to leave.

A glance over my shoulder explains why.

Ah.

Goodness. We're not quite done, are we?

Damian lingers by the fireplace, his long shadow cast across the crimson carpet, a hand gripping the arm of the recliner to tether himself in place. Despite the anchor, an uncertain foot edges towards us.

Oh, this poor boy! Cast unwittingly into our guild as a means to frame and lock away a group of outcasts who dared to challenge the Council's authority. A simple pawn, to be thrown away at a moment's notice.

This entire time, he's been used. A piece on the board with no agency - forced to join us, forced to follow our rules, and then forced to come here.

But now? Finally, the game has changed.

He gets to make a choice.

"Well, Damian?" I ask. "Are you coming with us?"

He steps forward, but his hand lingers on the armrest. My question dangles in the air, luring him forward, but he restrains himself. He pauses, looks down at the unconscious figures decorating the floor, and then back up at us.

If we left without him, perhaps it would be a kindness - this boy must still have people who care about him in some capacity. Abandoning Damian is the easiest answer; he remains a pampered noble and our guild stops putting him in danger.

If he doesn't follow us, we won't be at fault when he inevitably gets hurt.

Before I can say anything, however, he turns to Isaac.

Our Commander draws in a long, careful breath before he speaks. His words are heavy. Isaac knows he cannot make the decision for the boy, and we're all aware of what Damian will lose if he joins us.

"Staying is the safest choice," the Commander says. Damian's shoulders drop.

Isaac steps forward, tugging me towards the boy, but I plant my feet. He glances at me, eyebrows raised. I shake my head.

The Commander won't do it intentionally, but his words could sway Damian, which will rob the child of his independence and agency. The decision *must* be his own - not the result of our Commander's influence.

Isaac shouldn't help him.

My eyes shift towards the person who should.

Neva simply sticks out her lower lip and tries to ignore my meaningful stare.

Hmph. So, she wants more *direct* prompting?

"Your advice could help him decide, Neva. It has to be you."

Her glare sharpens, but I continue: "Isaac is kind, but kind words don't always lead to the best decisions. Right now, this child needs someone who will be *honest*. Out of everyone here, you're the person who will guide him towards a decision he won't regret - whatever that may be."

Neva huffs, venting her annoyance at me, although her eyes remain locked on the boy. She peers at Damian and his quiet, lonely figure, drenched in the glow of the fireplace. Crackling embers and shifting logs add sharp staccatos to the silence filling the room.

Eventually, our seer shakes her head.

"He should stay."

Isaac steps forward, preparing to interrupt, to argue - to lie for the sake of this boy - but I stop him with a gentle pat on the arm.

Neva sighs.

"But the safest choice isn't always the right one." Her words are precise, targeted, and aimed directly at the boy. He raises his head as she speaks. "Damian. Listen. It doesn't matter what *we* tell you. If *we're* choosing the path *for* you, it'll never be the right one. You have to choose. For *yourself*."

Her voice, though cold, is tinged with a brimming sadness. A solemn undercurrent tears beneath each solemn syllable.

"*If* you join us, you'll gain *some* things: adventures, quest rewards, good companions, excitement - but it all comes at a cost. Leaving with us means leaving your family behind. And you've got a good life, one not worth losing! Even if things aren't perfect at home, it's much harder to maintain a good relationship with your parents as an adventurer-" she pauses to glance at Isaac, who shrugs- "and you'll avoid a lot of misery if you go back to being a noble."

The boy's eyes start to water.

"I know," Damian mutters, "but going home might not be the right decision." He deflates a little, shoulders and head bending, as if threatening to fold in on himself. "My parents used me to frame your guild! And I could have gotten... no! I *did* get hurt! I almost died."

A sob wracks him, shaking the child with a violent shudder.

"Did they *want* me to suffer? Just to give the Council another crime to hold against you?"

He goes quiet, voice dropping to a whisper, terrified of his own words.

"And yet - despite everything - I don't want to lose them. Being a noble doesn't matter, but... I'm scared of no longer being their son."

Wading through the misery filling the room, Neva steps towards the boy and offers a gentle reply.

"You miss the people you love, even when you probably shouldn't."

She pauses.

"However, your family could also be waiting for you to come home. Worried sick, regretting what they've done, wondering if you're okay. But you won't know until you ask them."

Our seer presses a hand to her forehead, massaging her temples. Then she reaches out and taps the bottom of Damian's chin, lifting his face so he's forced to meet her gaze.

"Except this isn't about them. This is about *you*. If you want to join us, then *join us*. If you want to go home, then *go home*."

She twists her lips, eyes shifting as a quiet thought passes.

"You could also choose to stick around for a little longer, and *then* decide if Honour's Stand is the right guild for you.

Keep in mind, though, that we are *currently* convicted criminals in the middle of an escape attempt, so it might not be the best time to join."

She clasps the boy's shoulders, and he shakes beneath the weight of her grasp. "Damian, we will accept you for who *you* are - whatever and whoever you may be, or may become. We fight and bicker and don't always see eye to eye, but at the end of the day our guild is a family. If you can put up with us, you might as well join us."

"So. Damian." Neva says. "What do *you* want to do?"

Silence hangs in the air, waiting to be broken.

Damian is a statue, eyes trained on his feet, hands pressed against his sides.

We wait.

Isaac opens his mouth to say something, but my elbow digs into his side to force the words back down his throat. When he glances at me, I simply shake my head: *no.*

The boy must decide on his own.

Neva looks over her shoulder at us, her mouth set in a thin line. But then she notices our wide eyes, and her head snaps back towards Damian as he clenches his fists, plants his feet firmly into the ground, and raises his head.

"I know what I want."

Neva raises an eyebrow, but doesn't interrupt. The quiet coaxes an answer out of the boy.

"My family is important to me, and yeah, they're not the greatest parents, but... I know they love me, in their own way. It doesn't feel right to leave without saying goodbye."

"Fair enough," Neva replies.

Damian steps aside to address us, his gaze strong and his voice rising to match his confident stance.

"Isaac, sir!" he declares, and the Commander stiffens at the mention of his name, "I want to keep in touch with my family, just like you, so... could you help me with that? When we're away from Nexus. I know being an adventurer means leaving my parents behind, but.... I don't want to let them go completely. You've managed to stay connected to your family, which is what I want. Will you show me how to do that?"

The boy's confidence wavers, and he adds, "Um, if it's not too much work, I mean. If that's okay! I want to be like you."

Isaac blinks, and then eventually manages an awkward thumbs-up.

Neva smirks and pats Damian on the head.

"Look at you - just joined moments ago and you're *already* demanding things from our Commander! You're gonna' fit right in, kid."

Neva grins at Isaac's halfhearted glare before turning back to Damian.

"Anyways, Mr. *New Recruit*, your first task as a member of Honour's Stand is to help Aria down the stairs. Shouldn't be *too* challenging, right?"

With a sharp laugh, Neva glimmers out of sight, her footsteps echoing as she runs off. Isaac gives me a humble bow, clasps Damian on the shoulder, and rushes after her.

When the boy hesitates, I link my elbow around his arm and shuffle forward, leading him onward. As expected, the stairs are quite the trial despite the rune-infused bandages wrapped around my knees and pressed against my back. Yuina will have to rewrite them later.

My mind wanders back to days long past, reminiscing on when I could be the one leading the charge. Thankfully, the boy doesn't attempt stilted small talk this time; he has thoughts of his own to chew on.

With nothing to distract me, a bitter fondness seeps into my heart.

It's tough to watch this next generation carry on without me.

A fantasy plays behind my eyes, and I entertain it, if only for a little while.

Would the guild have gotten along with my younger self? A simple scholar and a forgettable clerk for the Guild Registry, just like my father before me - would I have been a part of Honour's Stand, back when my body could keep up?

Hmph.

Perhaps it is too greedy to wish for such a thing.

And, to be frank, what point is there in being ungrateful? I have the privilege of transcribing their journeys, recording their quests, and glimpsing brilliant snapshots of their remarkable adventures.

Shouldn't that be enough for an old archivist like me?

Perhaps.

But I digress.

The halls of this prison are bleak and boring, blurring together as I retreat into more pressing thoughts, checking off a mental list of things to do and documents to file. After we escape from this place, we won't be free until we convince the Council of our innocence. That, or become the kind of threat they would never dare pursue.

The latter option is tempting; it's what works for the High Champions, after all. Or what *used to work* - Frost's status didn't stop him from getting locked up like the rest of us.

We'll have to prove our innocence, then.

The guild will find a way.

Our journey is rather uneventful, relatively speaking. Pain flares up every so often, along with the soreness that moved into my hip one summer and decided to settle down. Damian is gentle, if somewhat clumsy, and he manages to make the trip easier, though not by much.

After a while, we arrive. White walls extend into a dimly lit, spacious garage with a cold grey floor decorated by bound and unconscious guards. The guild rises to greet me: Jegrac extends a hand to lead me into the caravan while Pall nuzzles against me - gently - as he's been taught. His fur is soft beneath my hand.

I scour the faces of my guild, admiring their reactions. Yuina, bless her soul, is already peering down at my ankles, brandishing new bandages and chalk. Liatris stands by the horses, offering me a small wave. Frost looks at me, snorts, and then turns away.

Kuh. Rude little brat.

I ignore him.

"Welcome back, Aria," Jegrac says, his tone respectful and his arm outstretched to offer more support. "Oh, Damian - you're coming with us? That's... unexpected, but good. Pall was starting to miss you!"

Leaning against the door to stabilise myself, I carefully step inside, searching for a comfortable spot to rest. Jegrac moves closer, attempting to help, so I place the chronicler in his hand before waving him away.

CHRONICLE 29
Recorded by Jegrac

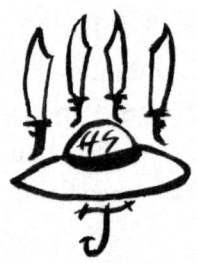

Aria's dismissal hangs in the air as she slips into the carriage, and Damian gives me a respectful nod before following her inside. I sigh and slip the chronicler into my jacket.

A sharp hiss draws my attention to Neva, who stands nearby with her hands on her hips. Despite her hostile stance, Pall continues to affectionately nuzzle her leg, while Yuina fusses over the seer, flitting about the irritated woman. Neva keeps shifting her glare from Yuina to Pall, clearly overwhelmed by the attention but unable to get in a word of protest as the historian covers Neva's cuts and bruises with glimmering gauze.

"Stop complaining! Yes, it's uncomfortable, but it'll strengthen and replenish your magic reserves, so put up with the discomfort for just a little bit longer."

Neva's voice rises in response.

I take that as my cue to walk away.

My journey doesn't get me very far; Mayweather and Daisy stamp their hooves, beckoning me to come closer. Each short huff repeats the question: *why haven't we left yet?*

Unfortunately, I can only run my hands through their manes to comfort them. I share their eagerness to escape this foul place, but the decision is not one I can make alone.

Liatris lingers nearby, wringing her hands and shaking her head before turning to me.

"Jegrac, what's next?" she asks. "Where are we going?"

"Home, I expect. But..." I gesture at Yuina, Neva, and Pall as they approach.

Then I notice the looks on their faces, and a chill runs down my spine.

A brimming hostility fills the air, strengthened by the way Yuina's fingers toy with the empty hilts hanging off her wrists, and the glimmering blades tucked behind Neva's back.

My foot slides back as I offer a tepid wave. But their glares remain, locked on Liatris and I. Tight grins rest beneath narrowed eyes, barely flinching when Isaac starts moving towards us, as if to intervene, but then Neva snaps her fingers and jabs them at the caravan.

He hesitates.

I catch his eye, wondering if he can explain what's going on.

Will he come to my aid, as the guild suddenly turns on me?

Instead, the Commander gives me a weak smile and retreats into the caravan.

The door locks shut behind him.

We're on our own.

"It's time, Frost," Yuina declares, and the child breaks away from his post by the garage's entrance. The High Champion stares at her, head tilted, and then nods.

With a wave of his hand, tendrils of ice crawl up and over every door in this massive room.

He's locking us in here.

Why?

To shake away the thought, I force my mind elsewhere - to search for the answers I keep missing - but my guildmates edge towards me and a quiet terror creeps in...

Liatris's grip tightens around my wrist as she ducks behind me. She trembles against my back, and I reach for her, to comfort her.

Mayweather snorts when we bump against her.

With the horses at our backs, we have nowhere to run.

My most faithful ally darts past Neva and Yuina to take his place at my side. Pall releases a confused bark, frightened by the strange hostility drifting towards us.

"Liatris." Neva commands. "Step away from Jegrac. Now."

Her words drip with malice.

The dryad gasps, shakes her head, and presses closer to me. My hound growls at first, but then dips down into a whine. His snout taps my knee as he begs for guidance - he doesn't want to hurt my friends.

Neither do I.

My daggers clatter against the stone floor, and I raise my hands, palms open and exposed.

"Listen, let's talk this out," I say. My eyes start watering as my guildmates draw closer. "I'm sure this is just a misunderstanding. If we can all calm down, and figure out what's happening, together..."

But the glares don't disappear.

They still don't trust me? After all this time?

"Did I - *did we* - do something wrong, Neva?"

She doesn't respond, and simply tightens her grip on her bladed fans.

I try a different angle. Desperation claws at my throat.

"Yuina, what is this? You *know* me - whatever is happening - whatever you think I am responsible for - you *know* it's not true. Please, I..."

The Historian's eyes flicker, a great pain coursing through them, but the hesitation lasts for a quick, careful breath before sharpening once more.

"STOP! Please! Leave him alone!" Liatris screeches. "Even if he's a Nomad, he's still your ally! This man is your guild-mate!"

They ignore her.

Yuina stares at me, her mouth set in a thin line, lips pressed tight to restrain a vicious secret. The empty hilts clenched between her fingers flicker with magical energy, and her eyebrows scrunch, a conflicted expression crossing her face.

"Jegrac. Let Liatris go."

Neva releases a hiss to silence Yuina, but it's too late. I understand.

They see me as a threat. A liability.

I am holding Liatris captive by keeping her near me - to them, she is an innocent shield I've manipulated to protect myself.

Yuina is right. This is between me and the guild. No need to get anyone else involved.

I will settle this misunderstanding on my own.

Patting the back of the dryad's smooth hand, I gently pry it off my shoulder.

"I'll be fine, Liatris. Really."

She hesitates, violet eyes wide and unblinking, her lip trembling, but after a moment she nods and steps away.

My attention turns to Pall, reaching through our bond, willing him to leave my side.

It takes a rather forceful lie to encourage my loyal hound to abandon me, but eventually he slinks away, ears low and eyes downcast.

Liatris opens her mouth to speak, but I raise a hand to silence her.

I must deal with this. Alone.

Liatris frowns, steps back, and then stumbles out of sight.

Neva snaps into existence between us, obscuring my view as she slams the dryad onto the floor with a violent thud. The illusion standing at Yuina's side shatters like glass; the real Neva straddles the victim crumpled beneath her.

Ice cracks and creaks when Frost hurtles towards the ceiling, propelled upwards by a frozen pillar. He sneers from his perch above us, his pale hands pressed against the ceiling as deadly stalactites form around him. Their sharp ends shiver as they twist to face the dryad.

Neva presses her knee into Liatris's chest, forcing a strained grasp through the hand wrapped tightly around the dryad's throat.

My feet lock in place, despite the voices in my head screaming to help her.

But then she catches sight of me, her vibrant violet eyes filled with terror and begging me to rescue her.

My fingernails dig into my wrist, restraining the urge to free my friend.

And then she speaks, her words breaking through my hesitation - *what am I doing? Why am I still standing here?*

"Jegrac, *please...! They're hurting me!*" Liatris wails, and my fingers clutch at the empty space where my daggers used to be. Before I can kneel to grab my blades, Yuina blocks my path, her legs bent and hilts raised as she steps in the way.

"Sorry, Jegrac, but you need to back off." Yuina frowns at me, idly traces glowing runes in the air while she talks. "We wanted to share our plan earlier, but we couldn't risk you being taken hostage. I'm sorry."

The rage and confusion fades a little. Yuina's gentle brown eyes are filled with unspoken apologies - and a quiet, genuine remorse.

Protests die in my throat. None of this makes sense, but at the very least, my guildmates seem to be on my side.

But what about Liatris? What are they planning to do with her?

A creeping hostility draws my attention, angry sparks jolting through my bond with Pall.

I respond with caution, and my companion's snout shakes at the shared emotion.

He hesitates, back bristling and teeth bared, but eventually he settles down.

I understand his rage. If they don't let Liatris go soon, we will act.

Yuina notices my frustration, and sighs.

"Jegrac, that's not who you think it is," she mutters. "At least, Neva's pretty sure it's not, and she's usually right, so..."

She chews her lips, and then turns along with me to watch Liatris writhe beneath Neva.

"NOW," the seer snarls, "stay still and *shut up*."

Liatris releases a piercing scream, but the sound is snipped off as Neva's grip tightens. Pall springs onto his haunches, mirroring my own stance as my eyes flicker towards the daggers on the ground a quick leap away. Yuina grimaces, shakes her head at me, and then points at the two guild members grappling on the ground.

"Really, Jegrac? You're the one who's closest to her! Hasn't Liatris seemed rather strange lately? We can't be the only ones who noticed."

Yuina places a gentle hand on my back.

"Just... try not to panic after this. We're not going to abandon her. Remember that."

My fury evaporates when Liatris's neck starts to fade. It happens slowly at first, as if a crude trick of the light, but then the beautiful verdant skin peels away with a violent fervour, revealing a dreadful, pale mold underneath.

An awful squelch echoes throughout the garage as the dryad's body stretches and swells into someone else. Someone horrible. Someone familiar.

The air fills with a sweet stench, riper than an abandoned fruit: sour, rotten, and decayed.

"Tsk. You weren't supposed to find out *this soon*," Foivos wheezes as Neva raises her fan, the blade poised and ready to strike. "But you're too late! The dryad is ours."

Neva tightens her grip, forcing a pained wheeze out of the pale High Champion.

"*Tell us where she is.* NOW."

The foul man gasps for air.

Snow spirals down, shrouding Foivos and Neva in a gale of white. My head snaps up to recoil at Frost's face, which is blanketed with vicious glee. His excitement chills the room as his frozen stalactites quiver, eager to pierce the High Champion's flesh.

"Yes. Speak. Is she with Rahma? Or anyone else worth my time?" Frost leans over the edge of his perch, his voice rising when he exclaims: "Ooh! I bet she's guarded by Solaris! Ah, YES! Finally, an *opportunity!*"

Foivos manages a weak nod, and Frost's twisted grin widens. The pillar of ice shatters in a brilliant torrent of white, and the boy plummets down to Neva's side, landing with a quiet tap, his silver eyes locked on the other High Champion.

"They'll come for *you*, won't they?" he says, rubbing his hands together, the air bristling with glacial malice. "And the others might decide to interfere, and - oh, *finally!* - an actual challenge...! One where I'll have no option but to retaliate and kill, in a desperate act of self-defence."

Frost releases a gentle laugh. The sound crinkles like ice beneath a violent heel.

A shiver crawls along my spine. He sounds like a child - because he *is* a child - but his excitement mirrors a cruelty far beyond his years.

Foivos attempts to respond, but his words become a mangled gasp when Neva tightens her grip.

"ENOUGH. Stop wasting time. *Where. Is. She?*" Her words are tense, pinched, and ready to snap. "Tell us. NOW."

A squelch erupts from the ghoulish figure.

The foul man is chuckling.

"Inside," he wheezes, "guarded by other High Champions, in a place you will never reach."

Neva's palm is quick and precise, smacking the man's forehead so he ricochets against the stone floor with a solid thunk. With Foivos unconscious, she stands, turning to look at Yuina, Pall, and I.

"Well, you heard him. Looks like our escape will have to wait. We-"

"-CAN'T do that!" Aria calls from within the caravan, "At least, not all of us."

Damian stands by the carriage door, propping it open so the Archivist's voice echoes towards us. As Neva steps away from the collapsed High Champion, Frost shuffles a little closer, flexing his fingers and covering the man's chest in a layer of glistening ice. His eyebrows rise before he lands a solid kick on Foivos's forearm, and his terrifying grin sharpens when a prosthetic limb is knocked away.

"*Good.*" Frost whispers. "I didn't miss."

Not wanting to witness the boy's horrid performance, I slip into the caravan along with the rest of the guild, shutting the door behind me with a soft click.

Neva stifles an annoyed grunt, scowling at the blankets and pillows stolen to create the old woman's opulent nest. Pall barks at Aria, spinning a slow circle before settling down beneath her outstretched legs, sandwiched between the bench and Neva's small cabinet.

Once I'm settled in my usual spot, Aria starts to speak.

"Until the Council stops pursuing us, this won't end," she mutters, "and we're in no position to start a full-blown rebellion - at least, *not yet* - so we need to find a way to resolve this debacle peacefully."

"What are our options?" Isaac asks. "We can't just-" he winces when a strange squelch slips through the wooden walls of the cabin.

Yuina hops to her feet.

"Yeah, yeah, I know. Let me deal with him," she mutters. "Tell me the plan when I get back."

She slams the door behind her.

Neva hums quietly to herself, drawing our attention as she leans against the bar at the back of the cabin.

"Study the evidence, find the solution. It's what Yuina would say if she was here, so let's work through what we know." She drums her hands against her knees as she settles down on the floor with her legs crossed. "First: someone is glamouring rift summoners and framing Nomads, and at least one of the High Champions is involved. Second: we still don't know *why* our guild was targeted, but it's probably due to Liatris and Jegrac." She glances at Aria. "Or is it because we know too much? Which is a strange reason to frame our guild... other than a few personal testimonies, what proof do we have? It'd be our word against theirs. And I doubt we're the first group to uncover this bizarre conspiracy; where are the others?"

Aria shakes her head. "Isn't it obvious? The *others* have already been silenced, in one way or another."

An uneasy quiet settles over the caravan.

"So," I say, clenching my fists so tight my fingers sting, "all we have is Neva's word about what she saw, and nothing else?" A sigh slips through my tight grimace. "So, now what - we just give up? Is this how it ends?"

Isaac pats my shoulder.

"Don't cut our story short, Jegrac," he declares, though his weary eyes betray him, "we'll figure something out."

Aria glances at the Commander and frowns. But then she gasps, the pillow in her lap flopping to the floor when she bolts upright.

"Oh, Isaac!" the Archivist exclaims, "You've given me a great idea!" Aria claps her hands, eyes alight as she turns to our seer. "How did I not consider this sooner? Neva, were you wearing the chronicler when you witnessed the fake Nomads and their riftportal?!"

Neva nods.

"Yes, I had it, but..."

Her eyes widen.

"Ah! Of course! *Yiatsu above*, do you really think...?" A wide grin spreads across her face. "Aria, if we can get the chronicler back to the guild hall, we might have exactly what we need to prove our innocence!" She claps her hands together, and the sound rings through the caravan. "The Council won't accept it as legitimate - at least, not at *first* - but they've always demanded transcripts from us. They'll *have* to recognize it!"

Aria clicks her tongue. "And I can send copies to other guilds, just in case. As collateral."

The bench creaks beneath Isaac as he leans forward, eager to join this conversation.

"Sounds like you two have a plan. What do we need to do?" he asks.

I also shuffle to the edge of my seat, ready for Aria's instructions.

"We'll have to split up." the Archivist declares. "While some of us return to the guild hall, the others will rescue Liatris. Neither task will be easy, since the Council is sure to have both places heavily guarded, but I'm certain we can handle it."

Neva hops onto her feet.

"We should start by rescuing Liatris together, and *then* head to the guild hall. Once there, Aria can transfer the chronicler's recordings onto a proper transcript while we protect her. After that, we visit the Council, prove our innocence, get a good night's sleep, and find a brand new quest for tomorrow!"

With a swift kick, Neva knocks the door aside and slips through. Isaac trails along behind her as Pall leaps past him, and I brush the rear curtain aside, lifting a leg to scale the small wooden barrier. A gentle hand presses against my back, forcing me to hesitate.

"Jegrac?" Aria's voice is doused with concern. "I'm sure the events earlier were quite unnerving, even *if* it was all an illusion. Are you alright?"

I fall silent. What does she want to hear? That I'm fine? *I can't lie to her.* But it doesn't matter - this is my weight to bear.

When I don't reply, she simply shakes her head. "Sorry, Jegrac. Neva and Yuina had no choice but to keep you in the dark - they couldn't risk Foivos realising they'd seen through his disguise. Hopefully you're not too bothered by everything that's happened. Not just here, but... *everything.* If only we could fix this whole situation, with you, your people, and the Council, but..."

Pushing my misery aside, I offer Aria a reassuring smile. She raises an eyebrow, clearly unconvinced, but I bow through the curtain moments before she starts to speak.

Her words slip through before the cloth can cut them off.

"We're trying, Jegrac. And we'll keep trying. I'm sorry we can't do more than that."

Anger rises in my throat. *She doesn't need to apologise on the guild's behalf. Or even on Nexus's behalf.*

It's not her fault. She *knows* it's not her fault.

But I understand her guilt. She's a part of this city, of this realm, where the system is designed to hurt and scar people like me.

My ears twitch when something crunches and splinters on the far side of this vast garage. Turning, my eyebrows rise at the wreckage before me; the floor is now decorated with the fresh remains of carts and carriages. Frost lingers amongst the ruins, muttering under his breath as he continues to ravage the empty vehicles.

Nearby, the rest of the guild argues around a bloodied but breathing rag. Foivos burbles on the ground, covered in

Yuina's hastily scribbled parchment and patches. He looks like he's made of paper rather than flesh.

"*Rift below - TEAMS?!*" Neva snaps, her voice sharpening as I approach, "That's your brilliant idea?! We need to stick together! Oh, but of course y'all wanna split up. Ridiculous! I oughta'-"

Isaac interjects.

"I KNOW, Neva! But the Council will be looking for us, and we don't have the strength to fend off several High Champions or - *Yiatsu forbid!* - any Watchmen pursuing us *after* we've rescued Liatris. It's a safer choice to try accomplishing two things at once *before* they catch on. Aria and her group will get the transcripts while we get Liatris. What, you have a better plan?"

Neva snarls, but lowers her hands.

"Alright. Fine! So then why don't we just send Frost to clear out the guild hall? He doesn't need a chaperone."

She rolls her eyes at our stunned faces.

"*Okay,* stupid idea, I get it. So we'll send Yuina with him, too. And since Aria's going, we might as well toss the new recruit into the mix. It's the safest place for him to be."

Neva turns to me.

"With everyone else assigned to babysitting the old lady and the kid, the three of us will be responsible for saving our dryad."

She stops and glances down at Pall. "Sorry, the *four* of us."

Neva sighs as she walks away, but then whirls on her heel to jab at the device on my belt.

"Jegrac! Give Aria the chronicler before she leaves." Neva places her hands on her hips. "And get whatever supplies you need from the caravan; it might not be in one piece when we see it next."

The archivist emerges from the depths of the carriage as if summoned. Several blankets trail behind her frail figure, dwarfing her in a cocoon of cloth.

"Don't worry," the old woman declares, "I've already got a second device ready to go. Bring the one you have to me, and we'll trade. Did you *really* think I'd let you three run off without recording another harrowing and thrilling tale about Honour's Stand's escapades? Yiatsu above, no! Just remember to turn on the spare chronicler before anything exciting happens. Now, Jegrac - please make sure your device is off before handing it to me, so I can start the transcribing process right away."

I oblige, thumbing the glowing gems as Aria reaches for the chronicler.

CHRONICLE 30
Recorded by Neva Oyii

The chronicler is secured to my waist before I do a final check of my outfit: my fans are glamoured and locked in place against my hips, hidden above my vibrant, high-waisted red leggings, which accompany the long sleeve crop top clinging to my skin.

Releasing a long exhale, magic seeps through the flexible fabric as I shimmer in and out of existence.

Excellent.

Isaac grunts as he adjusts the clasps on his armour. Peering at his position by the wall, he rolls his shoulders and catches my eye. His feet tap while he waits for me to finish stretching, but he doesn't tell me to hurry up. Ignoring his impatience, a smirk creeps onto my face when he reaches towards his toes, awkwardly imitating my routine. He struggles to copy my more complex stretches, so I switch to easier moves. Don't want my audience to overexert himself and pull a muscle. After a few simple poses, the clang of a metal barrier draws my attention and I drop into a more active stance.

Across the wide stone floor of the garage, Jegrac jogs towards us with Pall at his side.

The rest of the guild is gone.

Time to go.

My fingers linger on the patch Yuina sealed over my side. Toying with the delicate material, the wound throbs with a tender soreness, even though it should be healed by now.

"Everyone ready?" Isaac asks. Pall releases a sharp bark as he sprints to the Commander's side, and Jegrac nods. Waving at the door leading into the prison, I guide us onward. My guildmates fall into step behind me, while Pall manages to match my stride, his snout wiggling as he sniffs for any incoming threats.

"Never felt more prepared, Commander! This'll be a breeze!" I scoff. "All we have to do is stroll into the depths of this prison, dance past any security, greet the High Champions blocking our path, pick up our renegade dryad, and then head back home. Easy!"

Jegrac sighs. "We're also assuming Yuina properly memorised the maps she glimpsed while roaming these halls. I don't doubt her abilities, but it'd be good to find a similar document to check if she recommended the correct path. Which won't be easy; no one would be foolish enough to put such important information in the middle of-"

We pass a map plastered on the wall, and I match Jegrac's surprised grin. He snorts while we backtrack to get a better look. Several generous labels cover the image, making it easy to interpret.

Jegrac rolls his eyes as we resume our steady pace through the prison.

"Tells us a lot about this organisation, to leave something so vital in such a public place."

"Poor planning, perhaps?" Isaac suggests.

Our heads perk up when the crackle of static fills the hall. The dull crystals embedded in the ceiling flicker to life, accompanied by an emotionless, metallic voice.

"All available personnel to Area Twelve. I repeat, all personnel please proceed to Area Twelve. We are initiating a code Scarlet. I repeat, code Scarlet."

Isaac swears under his breath. "*Rift.* They must know we're here."

Jegrac tilts his head as we sprint around another corner.

"Are you sure?" he asks. "On the map back there, the number twelve was pretty far from our destination."

"Good point," I interject between measured breaths, "hopefully it's an unrelated crisis. Since it doesn't have to do with us, let's take advantage of this distraction and nab Liatris before anyone notices!"

Isaac nods.

"We better pick up the pace, then."

Dreary white walls rush past as we hurtle onwards.

A nearby sign catches my attention, and I grit my teeth.

"The cafeteria?" Isaac declares as it falls behind us. "Is this place going to be a problem?"

From his silence, I can assume he's talking at my back, so I just shrug.

If I could look ahead, I'd let him know. But the future is cloudier than ever, and straining causes a stinging pain behind my eyes. Like it or not, we're going in blind.

"The guards should be heading to Area 12, right? If they left anyone behind, we can handle them."

Jegrac rushes past us with Pall at his side, and the two of them ram their shoulders into the doors at the end of the hall, tossing the barriers aside with a harsh clang. Skidding past them, my momentum carries me up and onto an empty metal table. The bland grey walls of the large room twirl about as my fans slip into my hands. My skin grows cold as glamours pulse through it, covering me in a gentle glimmer.

The food court is nearly empty, other than the familiar High Champion waiting inside. She leans against the wall across from us, her fingers drumming against the curved scimitar clutched in her grasp. As soon as Isaac and Jegrac catch sight of her, their blades gleam beneath the bright Sun Shulls drifting along the ceiling.

"Hello, criminal scum!" Rahma announces, "Our seers predicted I'd have a satisfying future if I guarded this boring place, but who could've expected such a lovely surprise?"

The room creaks as boulders rumble and scrape against the walls, forming enormous golems with stone skulls that scrape the ceiling. The glowing shulls bump and spiral away from the heads of the giant elementals. The faint smell of a freshly tilled garden mixes with grease and oil, adding dirt to the lingering scent of hastily discarded meals.

"If you're looking for your dryad, you're too late." Rahma declares. She steps onto a metal table as her rock elementals lumber towards us. "Toxil is working on ... *it*. Reducing that *thing* back to the plant it's supposed to be. But you'll meet her again soon! Perhaps as a cute little decoration in your cell?"

The High Champion raises her blade. The wicked weapon is drenched in red and lined with ruby stones - *ones I'd barely noticed the first time it stabbed through my side.*

Rahma's grin curves like her sword when she sees my eyes widen.

Just as I suspected: she's the High Champion from the forest, excited to finish the job.

A pillar of rock hurtles towards me, forcing my thoughts away when the long limb of a nearby golem crushes the metal table on my left. The floor shrieks as the steel carcass gouges cracked and shattered tiles.

I flicker out of sight, although Rahma catches my gaze right before I disappear. She draws a thumb across her neck.

Good. *I'm going to enjoy wiping that smug grin off her stupid face.*

The ground shakes and another immense boulder strikes the place I'd been standing moments before. Unfortunately for Rahma, her golems are much too slow to catch me.

The High Champion's eyes narrow as she scours the room.

My smile widens when her golems ignore my leaps from table to table; their focus turns to Jegrac, Isaac, and Pall instead. My companions struggle to avoid and parry the stone strikes, forcing me to flicker back into sight.

"Hey!" Their heads snap my way, and I shout: "This one's mine - get moving. I'll follow you right after dealing with *her.*"

A stone fist strikes the place I'd appeared just moments ago, and I dance back into stealth, keeping an eye on my companions to check if they've heeded my advice.

Jegrac and Isaac scramble away, metal clattering and clacking as they sprint towards the other door, effortlessly dodging giant strikes while making their escape.

Rahma releases a satisfying string of curses.

Watching the golem's clumsy attacks, it's clear they've lost some precision. *Not as easy to hit targets who refuse to fight, huh?*

"Fine then - try and run! We'll hunt you down eventually - my minions won't stop until you're broken." Rahma snarls, waving her blade as her golems smash through tables and chairs in one final attempt to reach the other members of my guild.

A large trash can braces my weight as I balance on the rim. When the High Champion starts to speak, a mischievous idea worms into my head. *Perhaps with a little bit of encouragement, she'll focus on me instead of my companions.*

"Ready to watch your friends die, little *Seeth?* How ridiculous that you - a lowly seer - would dare to strike ME, the emissary of the Elders! And to consort with dryads as well? UGH. Those creatures will fall just like your people did, trampled into the dust for defying-"

Her curses turn into shrieks, seething words warping into a disgusted cry. The High Champion's hair is now sopping wet thanks to the hastily hurled fruit scrounged from the depths of the garbage can.

I dance away as the trash container is crushed behind me, her golems slowing and starting to hesitate, stone heads shifting to glance back at their master. I stretch one leg off the table to tap my feet against the floor, for a few beats of mockery, drawing ever closer, and the stone giants start to stomp away, their long arms encircling Rahma and hiding her from view.

Going on the defensive, huh?

Excellent. I've still got a few tricks up my sleeve, and a wall of stone won't stop me from teaching this arrogant High Champion a lesson.

My hands clutch the chronicler on my belt, and I flicker into existence to yell at Isaac. The golems shift their attention to me, following Rahma's rage.

"Hey, Commander! Catch this, shout out your undying gratitude, and get out of here!"

With one smooth motion, I fling the device across the cafeteria, turning away as it leaves my-

CHRONICLE 31
Recorded by Isaac Heathe

A nd I catch it right before it hits the floor. The chronicler is hastily strapped to my side as Jegrac whisks me away, his hand wrapped tightly around my elbow while Pall nudges me from behind. They guide me towards the door on the other side of the hall, away from Rahma and Neva's clash.

The lone golem guarding the exit attempts to block our way, but my blade is swift and heavy. A solid strike sends the stone creature crumbling across the floor.

Another splatter and a shriek echo behind us as Neva uses more scavenged food to irritate her opponent. I don't know why she hasn't gotten serious yet - since this fight would come to a quick end if Neva wasn't so intent on toying with Rahma - but she must have her reasons.

Glancing over my shoulder, I glimpse Neva flickering into existence, her fists clenched while a golem reels back. A spectacular dent has been carved into the middle of the stone, broken by a terrifying force. Neva shields herself from sight once more when the rocks crash around her hidden form.

The door snaps shut behind me, bouncing on its hinges as a great thud reverberates throughout the mess hall.

Rahma's muffled screams chase after us, and I shake my head.

She's just another arrogant enemy waiting to be humbled by our guild.

My attention snaps back to the present when Pall dashes in front of me, releasing a quiet bark as he picks up speed.

"What is it boy?" Jegrac exclaims. "*You sense - oh!* Isaac! We can smell Liatris! We're getting closer; pick up the pace!" The Nomad matches his hound's stride and hurtles ahead. They bound through dimmer and darker hallways, barely slowing as long stretches of shadow whisk past.

Gritting my teeth, I try to close the gap between us.

Pall suddenly skids to a halt.

His snout snaps to the ground, and we brace ourselves to keep from crashing into the crouching dog. Pall's soft whine whistles through the hall.

"No. Sniff again."

The Nomad's eyes widen.

"Oh, *Morrowfir. Pall, this can't* - no. *No!*"

Jegrac's voice cracks with a heart-wrenching pain, his eyes locked on the grimy white doors at the end of the hall. The barrier hangs limp off the pale walls, begging to be swung aside.

My companion stalks forward. His palms glint, deadly daggers slipping into his hands. Following suit, I draw my sword and run my thumb over the symbol on the hilt. It expands, sharp white runes glimmering across the brilliant blade as it grows longer.

We approach, weapons at the ready, until a horribly familiar voice calls out to us.

"Ah, Honour's Stand? Good timing."

Jegrac grimaces.

"Why so shy? Please, come on in!" Solaris bellows. "Toxil always appreciates an audience. Enter and admire his work."

I stomp forward and kick the doors aside, breaking the silence and stillness of the room with a loud slam.

The area on the other side is dingy and dim. Sun Shulls flicker against the ceiling and cast a dull light on Solaris, who grins as he examines us. His eyes flicker between Jegrac and I. He stands across from a stranger shrouded in dark green robes and a featureless black mask - another High Champion, likely the aforementioned Toxil.

Despite their threatening presence, I can't stop staring at the dryad strapped to the chair in the middle of the room.

She looks past us, her mouth hanging open, quivering and twitching like the wilting leaves on her slumped head. Liatris's emerald skin is faded and dotted with white; her dim violet eyes are unfocused, empty, and dull.

She doesn't move.

Does she even know we're here?

"*What have you done?*" Jegrac snarls. His voice rises into a tempest, boiling over with a strained rage, "MORROWFIR BLIND YOU! *WHAT HAVE YOU-*"

A blast of heat strikes me, so unbearably hot and cruel it forces my knees onto the floor, my chest heaving as sweat drenches my armour. Each breath is ragged and strained beneath the light burning my skin, forcing me to bite back screams as I raise my arms to shield my face.

"Quiet, *Nomad,*" Solaris sneers, "all we did was turn the plant back into a plant. Neutralised it. We're just trying to help.

Why not thank us for taking care of it? We could have shipped it back to Orion, but no - we kept it here for *you*." He releases a sharp laugh. "Though I'm certain those Dunefolk would have been *so* hospitable. Isn't *this* a much better fate?"

A dagger slices through the air, clattering against the wall as the luminescent blonde man knocks it aside. His grin widens.

"*Turn her back,*" Jegrac snarls, his words twining with Pall's furious growl. The two of them strain against the scorching light, dragging themselves across the dirty tiles as they glare into the oppressive brightness. "Heal Liatris before she gets worse. Before you can't undo what you've done!"

"Pardon me?" Solaris muses, casually pressing his fingers around a browned leaf crowning the dryad's head, crushing it in his grasp. "You *named* it?!"

Jegrac chokes back a pained cry.

"*No - please,* stop! You can't treat her like this, she-"

He hesitates.

Pall offers a quiet, troubling whine, but Jegrac ignores him. His eyes stay locked on Solaris while something shifts within him. The hostility begins to fade.

"I know what you want."

Solaris raises an eyebrow, but doesn't stop the Nomad from speaking.

Jegrac grits his teeth.

"It's not her you want. It's me."

The heat dissipates a little, just enough to make existence bearable again.

"Hmm. Is that so?" Solaris strokes his chin. "Fascinating. And why do you think that?"

Jegrac's voice cracks.

"I'll say whatever you need me to say," the Nomad mutters. Words evaporate in my throat when I try to interrupt his desperate plea. "I'll confess. *Please.* Just stop hurting her. Just... let her go."

A low chuckle fills the room.

"Finally, someone reasonable!" The blonde man abandons Liatris to saunter over to Jegrac.

The High Champion's expression twists into a wicked sneer.

My eyes flicker to Liatris. Is this our chance? Can I rescue her while Solaris is distracted by Jegrac's plea?

The stranger in green shifts his black mask towards me, answering my question. This second High Champion hasn't even bothered to threaten us yet. I doubt we could take them both on without extra support.

As Solaris draws nearer, the light grows stronger. Waves of heat batter against my skull. My head spins as the floor quivers, threatening to rush up once the brutal warmth breaks through my feeble attempts to stay conscious.

The glowing High Champion places a hand on his hip and points the other at Jegrac.

"A tempting offer, but one Nomad's confession might not be enough. However, the Head of the Council *has* been growing suspicious lately, and the Watchmen have been a little too prying, so this might be worth the risk. We're running out of options, and those fools don't understand our work."

He sighs.

"Unfortunately, I'll have to silence your guild. Can't have them spreading lies! Imagine the chaos if gullible people started believing High Champions are responsible for accidental rift attacks! Oh, the madness that would ensue!"

Solaris shudders, draws in a sharp breath, and then runs a hand through his hair.

"What I need from you, *Nomad,* is your allegiance. A commitment to Nexus. To our city! Though I understand such a thing does not come easily to your people, but... perhaps you can make an exception, to protect your guild?"

Jegrac manages a weak nod.

Solaris raises a thin eyebrow, ignoring my glare as he continues.

"Good. Because we..."

He pauses. His eyes flicker to the doorway, but then he frowns and shakes his head. Straining to peek over my shoulder, there's nothing to be seen.

Solaris looks down once more.

"Ahem. Where was I? Ah, yes. I have one other stipulation for our *deal*: I'll need those coins your companions found. You know, the ones with the four little scars? You seem to have stumbled across them by blind luck, though I have my doubts."

Solaris lets out another heavy sigh.

"In the end, it doesn't matter. The Council would rather stay ignorant of the rebellion right beneath their noses. But I suppose that's why they have us. *To do their dirty work.*"

The High Champion falls silent, his eyes distant for a brief moment. Then he shakes his head and peers down his nose at Jegrac.

"Enough talk. Nomad, tell me your choice. Struggle and die, or lower your head to serve a greater cause."

Jegrac snarls, and I reach for him, wanting to speak, to convince him that we'll be okay. He shouldn't have to lie for us. His lies might save us, but they will doom his people in the process.

There must be another way.

Sweat evaporates as it falls, tracing lines of salt down my crimson cheeks. Somehow, I find the words I've been looking for.

"Jegrac. Wait. You don't have to do this."

The wide-brimmed hat spins to look back at me. The green eyes hidden beneath are wide and sad.

Solaris sneers at me, but doesn't interrupt.

"This can't be your only option."

I draw myself upwards, bones creaking and muscles screaming as I rise onto my elbows, squinting through the harsh light at Solaris.

"What you're doing is wrong."

He scoffs, but makes no move to stop me.

"Targeting Nomads, torturing this dryad... I'm sure you have your reasons. Your excuses. But this great cause, this mysterious plan - how can you justify it? How many lives is it worth?"

The High Champion tilts his head, glances at the green-clad stranger lingering by Liatris, and then peers at me. He looks confused.

"In those camps-" I cough, and Solaris waves a hand. Some of the heat dissipates. My throat clears.

"Those camps aren't filled with rebels and foreigners taking space on Aegis soil - there are families. Children. Kids. What have those Nomads done to deserve such horrible fates?!"

Solaris's lip curls. He shakes his head.

"Necessary sacrifices," he snaps, though something in him seems to falter, if only for a moment, "a small price for the greater good. Their deaths prevent tragedies you cannot comprehend! The rift-"

A fire burns behind my eyes as my gaze sharpens into a glare, conviction filling each word with an unfathomable power.

"NO. *You* are evil. *EVIL!* There is NOTHING complicated about this. *YOU KILLED THEM.* HOW DARE YOU-"

A blast of light shoves me back. Solaris's hands glow with a piercing, bright intensity, ignited by rage. He snarls, then offers a cold, quiet whisper.

"Silence. *Ignorant brat.* No one understands what's at stake here. Keeping Nexus safe - keeping my people - no, *our* people, *Commander* - safe... it's the only thing that matters. And it requires sacrifice." He raises his arms to strike again. "But it must be nice, always watching from the sidelines. Never having to make a tough decision. What have you done for Nexus, Commander? Truly? Your sacrifices are nothing compared to the ones *we* have had to make."

I brace myself, skin burning as muscles groan in protest, the searing pain carving dry scars across my tongue.

"*Then help me understand.*"

The words are hoarse, strained, but somehow manage to break through the screams threatening to escape my lips. "What could be worth more than the lives of people who mean no harm? They just want to live, Solaris. Why can't we just leave the Nomads alone?!"

Solaris pauses and lowers his hands.

The heat returns as he shakes his head.

"We're wasting time," he declares. "Listen to me, you miserable fool - a High Champion has responsibilities you could *never* comprehend. So this charade ends now. After all, I'm just a senseless, *evil* murderer, right? It doesn't matter what I say. You've already made up your mind about me. Time to fulfill my role."

My face smacks against the floor, as if the warm tiles could grant relief from the pressure burning me alive.

But before Solaris can kill me, Jegrac reaches out, clutching at the High Champion's black trousers, leaving a red stain when the man smacks his hand away.

"Wait," Jegrac rasps, "leave him. I'm the one you want. Your scapegoat. You need me."

Drawing in a painful breath, I try to speak, but my throat is full of ash. Our Nomad coughs as he continues.

"Our Commander won't be a threat to you, even if you let him go. He'll make the smart choice. He always does. He'll stay silent if it keeps him safe."

The heat dissipates, allowing me to raise my head. The sadness in Jegrac's words makes me want to lower it again, but I face my guildmate head on.

He smiles at me, though his lips bleed as they curve upward, dyeing his long thin beard with a rusty crimson.

He nods, once.

"Goodbye, Isaac."

With Pall's support, he props himself upright. The loyal hound braces his weight against his back.

Jegrac stands tall and strong, as if bearing the burden of the entire guild upon his shoulders.

In the silence, words fail. All I do is think as loud as I can, as if Jegrac will somehow hear me.

You're more of a Commander than I'll ever be, Jegrac. Don't do this. We'll find another way. Please.

Solaris offers me a look of pity before turning to address Jegrac.

"Well done, Nomad. You made the right decision."

Jegrac doesn't respond, but keeps his gaze locked on the High Champion. He doesn't back down.

My fingers drag across the floor. If I could somehow stop them, if I could just reach him...

But he's too far away.

I draw my arms back to try and hold myself together.

There's nothing I can do now.

It's too late.

And if I speak up, I could get us both killed.

I would be wasting all of the pride and dignity Jegrac has tossed aside to keep me safe - to protect the guild - *to protect Liatris.*

I know it's not the right choice. But... it's the safest one, right?

It has to be.

And yet...

A gentle hand rests upon my back; a phantom, surely, as there is no one to be seen. My guilt, perhaps? Or is it the pressure to finally change; to finally pick the *right* choice instead of the *safe one?*

Every word drags through my throat like barbed wire, but it doesn't stop me. Nothing can stop me now.

"Jegrac. Wait."

The words startle Solaris.

"Commander?" he croons, "What are you doing? Your guildmate has already made his choice."

Muscles scream as I push myself upwards. Somehow I manage to raise my head just enough to meet my guildmate's gaze.

"Don't interfere, Isaac," Jegrac hisses through gritted teeth. "Make the right decision and *let me go.*"

No. Not this time.

"I'm tired, Jegrac."

The Nomad's eyes widen, and I continue.

"I'm tired of only making safe choices. And I know you are, too."

Solaris interrupts our conversation with a flare of heat.

"Careful, Commander - this sounds *treasonous*. And after I was so kind as to offer your Nomad a deal-" he turns to Jegrac, "-this is how you repay me?"

Jegrac's spit marks the floor.

"I'd rather die on my feet than live on my knees," he snarls. "A fate too good for the likes of *you*."

The High Champion's eyes blaze with fury, threatening to ignite the entire room. His lips curl, hands tense and wrapped in an immense, terrifying light.

"I tried to be reasonable," Solaris declares, "but you leave me no-"

He falters when a familiar woman steps out of her glamours and into reality, one arm drawn back while the other grips the High Champion's collar.

"Who dares-"

Neva's fist slams into Solaris's stomach. The High Champion folds like a rag doll, hurtling into the stone behind him, the wall releasing a resounding *crack* when he crumples against it.

Instantly, the heat disappears, and my energy returns. Muscles and bones shriek as I force myself upright, but I ignore the pain.

Pall leaps forward and clamps his jaws around Toxil's throat, knocking them to the ground. The High Champion goes stiff while Pall waits for the command to snap his fangs shut.

"You alright, Commander?" Neva says as she pats me on the back. She raises an eyebrow when I wince, and slowly withdraws her hand. "Hm. You two are in pretty rough shape.

Let's just get Liatris and leave; Solaris won't be down for too long, and we don't wanna' be here when he wakes up."

Jegrac is already at the dryad's side.

He stifles a sob as he cradles Liatris's frail body in his arms. Her fragile limbs are bound in place by rune covered chains, but Neva shatters the metal with a precise strike, her arms glimmering with magical energy.

She shares a look with the Nomad; their eyes are narrowed, dark, and worrisome. Beneath the silence is a dangerous, boiling rage - a feeling I share, but not something to get caught up in right now.

Our priority needs to be getting Liatris out of here. Revenge can wait.

The man on the floor whimpers, drawing our attention to the High Champion cowering beneath the bristling black hound. Pall peers up at us, his jaws closing a little tighter around the fallen figure's throat.

Jegrac starts to nod, but then hesitates when a voice breaks through.

"Wait! Just - *wait*."

Solaris stumbles upright, hand outstretched. Neva's strike must have hit hard, since he struggles to draw in slow, pained breaths. As he rises, the temperature rises along with him, adding a stifling heat to the room and reigniting my scorched skin.

"Should've stayed down," Neva hisses, bladed fans materialising in her hands.

Solaris attempts to speak, but is interrupted by an unexpected crackle.

The sound comes from the hallway, and Jegrac steps forward so that Neva and I can turn to gaze through the open doors. Rows of figures dressed in dark robes have congregated outside of the room, their faces hidden by white masks bearing two simple black lines that form an 'x'.

Oh no.

Why are the Watchmen *here?*

Neva curses under her breath, and leans closer.

"It's gonna' be tough to fight our way through them," she whispers.

Solaris pipes up before I can respond.

"Perfect timing, as expected of our dear Council. You there, Nomad! Ready to confess?" Solaris grips his stomach as he attempts to stand a little taller. He grimaces when he fails, the pain forcing his shoulders back down. "Now that the Watchmen are here, you have no choice but to give in. This little game is over."

His smug grin falters when the masked strangers make no move to arrest us, their empty gazes aimed at him as well.

He sighs.

"For all of us, it seems."

The High Champion steps away, offering us space while shifting into a fighting stance, his arms raised.

Jegrac's back presses against mine as Neva shuffles closer, her bladed fans poised and ready. Steeling my legs, it takes all I have to stay upright. Can I even swing a sword in this condition?

A hand loops under my elbow, supporting me; I share a quiet glance with Neva, and she just nods.

I know what she's thinking.

What we're all thinking.

If we fight, we lose.

Surrendering, however, will only keep us safe for a little while.

We have to fight.

And we have to win.

A solemn, emotionless voice breaks the silence. One of the Watchmen speaks.

"Stand down, High Champion Solaris," they declare. My eyes widen.

Solaris frowns, the heat in the room bristling, but then he lowers his hand. It dims slightly.

The Watchman continues, undeterred.

"The Council has revoked all charges towards the members of Honour's Stand, effective immediately. They are no longer your concern."

We keep our weapons ready, wary of a ruse, but the High Champion looks genuinely baffled, his head shaking in disbelief.

"What's the meaning of this?" Solaris snaps. He stomps towards us, barely hesitating as Neva brandishes her weapon against his throat. With a snort, he brushes it aside and walks past. Pall releases a rumbling growl, warning him not to come too close, his jaws tightening around Toxil's neck.

The Watchman who had spoken earlier shifts their attention to Jegrac. They are the only sign of movement amongst their peers, who stand still and silent like stone.

"Restrain your familiar. We will not hesitate to terminate it if it continues to threaten this Nexus citizen."

Jegrac grows tense, but he knows better than to challenge a Watchman. After a sullen whistle his hound releases the High Champion and skirts back to his side, guarding his master from this new threat.

The mask bobs up and down.

"Excellent. Now, on to other matters - the Council requires your presence."

The Watchmen shift in unison, gliding to the walls like clockwork dolls, sliding apart to create a path through the hallway. Solaris sputters in protest behind us, but quickly silences himself, not wanting to risk the Council's wrath. Neva pushes us forward before we can hesitate, and after a momentary stumble our walk shifts into a jog, and then an anxious run. I'm not the only one eager to leave this place behind.

The masked strangers fall into step around us, matching our pace as they escort us through the halls. Eventually, they slow, and we're forced to do the same to keep from bumping into them. An emotionless voice follows our path, echoing against the pale walls as we leave the High Champions behind.

"Solaris, you and your co-conspirators are currently under investigation for endangering the lives of Nexus citizens. The Council requires your immediate attendance."

As the High Champion's unintelligible response echoes at our backs, relief floods through me. At the very least, Solaris and his companions have other problems to deal with right now. Hopefully, these consequences will keep them from retaliating against our guild - for a little while, at least.

Pushing through the doors to the mess hall, we manoeuvre around broken stone and shattered tables as the Watchmen lead us onwards. A chorus of angry shouts burst from the corner of the wide room, and I spot Rahma. She is fuming, dried blood on her lip and a crimson bandage wrapped over her nose as she rages against another set of Watchmen. They refuse to budge when she tries to lunge at Neva.

And then she is gone, the door swinging shut behind us, leaving the furious High Champion to scream curses at our backs as we leave her behind.

We continue on for a little while, and then Neva finally speaks, filling the silence with something other than tired panting and hasty steps.

"How much longer is this going to take?"

She glances at Jegrac, Pall, and I. We're really struggling to keep up, and Jegrac has been carrying Liatris - he won't be able to stay on his feet for much longer.

"In case you haven't noticed," Neva continues, "our guild-mate is in critical condition. Will the Council turn a blind eye to her death?"

She frowns when there's no response, and so she adds, a little louder: "The citizens of Nexus won't be happy when word gets out that their beloved *Watchmen* were responsible for the death of an innocent dryad!"

We're met with silence.

The hall gives way to a large round room filled with active gates. Each doorway shimmers with a magical haze.

We're forced to a halt, and then the Watchmen slide apart, creating a path directly to the portal in the centre of the semi-circle of gates.

"Offer your complaints to the Council," one of them instructs. "You'll be speaking to them on the other side."

Jegrac nudges against me, and I manage to meet his eyes.

His face is burned red, scarred, and filled with worry. Together, we take another pained look at Liatris's frail condition.

He wants to help her.

We share another glance, and he sees the defeat in my eyes. He sighs, and then nods.

He understands. Right now, we don't have a choice.

"Commander?" Neva turns to me, her arms crossed, her deadly fans tucked in her grasp. She's ready to fight, if we need to.

But we can't. I shake my head, and she frowns. But she doesn't protest.

The gate beckons us onward.

With a sigh, I take the lead, and my guildmates follow me into the unknown.

CHRONICLE 32
Recorded by Jegrac

"It was off?" Yuina takes a second glance at the chronicler as it starts to glow. "Hmm. A security measure, perhaps?"

Aria nods, drawing her fingers away while I clip the device back onto my belt.

"Good work noticing it wasn't recording, Yuina," she whispers. "Now, let's not draw any attention to it, so they don't realise it's on. We have other matters to attend to, after all." Her eyes flicker towards the Council and the High Champions, who are focused on Solaris's testimony in the centre of the room.

The archivist waddles back to the ledge separating us from the Commander. Neva makes room so the two of them can continue whispering advice and information into Isaac's ears. He glances up every so often, his mouth set in a thin line as he prepares to represent our guild.

"Hey, Jegrac," Yuina mutters, "pay attention." I look down at the piece of parchment our historian has placed in my hand. When she gestures at a crisp brown bruise on Liatris's arm, I follow her lead, gently securing the rune-imbued bandage over the festering wound. It glimmers, draping over the dryad's skin like a wet leaf. Yuina lathers a few more of the magical bandages into place, and I watch Liatris's face, hoping for a twitch, a sigh, a groan - *something*. Anything.

Nothing changes.

Yuina frowns and yanks a notebook out of a hidden pouch, furiously flipping through pages and jotting down notes while she works. Since our historian is absorbed in her research, I distract myself with the nearby trial and the prominent people resting within.

Across from our guild, several High Champions sprawl behind a shimmering barrier. They appear to be split into two groups; those actively engaged in what Solaris is saying, and those acting like Frost. Our resident High Champion tempers his boredom by bending, moulding, and manipulating a piece of ice between his small hands as he ignores his associates.

An unfamiliar woman notices my stare and meets my gaze. She offers a quiet nod before returning her attention to Solaris. I search for a name; Damian had pointed out each of the High Champions when the trial first started, and he had called her... ah, yes. Dahlia.

Her pity is a welcome change from the hostility and indifference of her peers. I make a mental note to remember her name.

"...ALL I've ever done is try to keep us safe!" Solaris's tone strengthens as the head of the Council continues to question his actions. "You and I know *exactly* what will happen if these sacrifices stop - and we're not ready to face those consequences

- not yet. So why the sudden change of heart? The Council has eagerly turned a blind eye to these events for a long time. You made me - made *us* - High Champions for a reason! Why am *I* being punished for taking my role seriously?"

The Head of the Council shakes her head, the long brown locks framing her face shimmying as her eyes crinkle.

"Yes, Solaris, you've said this before, and yes, we understand your intentions. But we have policies and procedures for a reason. Regardless of the, ah... *challenges* these Nomads may cause, there are treaties and laws we *must* honour and uphold. And these recent allegations of you targeting people - regardless of their citizenship - are very concerning! Riftportals are monitored for a reason! What if you'd lost control? We - the Council - *your superiors, may I remind you* - cannot afford another disruption, especially at a time like this! Why, I - did you not think to inform me of your plans? Or one of us, at the very least?!"

Solaris falls silent, his gaze dropping to the floor. The room flickers, heat swelling as he rises into a glare.

"Well, I certainly couldn't have done this without support."

The Council falls silent. Some of their members, in fact, seem to have taken a sudden interest in their shoes, collars, and ties - trying to look anywhere other than Solaris.

"What are you implying?" The woman at the head of the table asks. Her voice has sharpened. She glances at her colleagues, some of whom make a noticeable effort to avoid eye contact.

She releases an annoyed huff.

"Oh, I see. None of you wish to verify this claim, hmm?"

When she receives no responses, the Head turns back to Solaris.

"Fine then. You are dismissed. *For now.*"

A wave of unintelligible whispers draws my attention away. Neva and Aria have leaned closer to Isaac, pelting the Commander with a barrage of last minute instructions before he's called upon to testify.

A sharp hiss snakes into my ears; Neva is annoyed by something our archivist has just said. Their words are too quiet to hear, but the old woman is persistent, eventually reaching up to place a hand on Neva's shoulder.

She shakes it off and turns back, her eyes narrowed when she spots me.

My foot slides back, head shaking at the unexpected hostility, but then the seer's face softens and she looks away. Aria peers over her shoulder to offer me a gentle smile, and then returns her attention to the Commander. She passes a piece of paper to him; Neva sighs loudly when he signs it.

"Jegrac?"

Yuina is holding out another glowing piece of parchment, which I take, mimicking her moves to plaster the paper onto the dryad's brittle skin.

A gentle cough blankets the room, and all eyes shift to the Head of the Council.

"Isaac Heathe, Commander of Honour's Stand. Your presence is required."

Neva and Aria whisper some last bits of advice before pushing Isaac forward, forcing him upright. The Commander's shoulders draw back, he takes a deep breath, and then his heavy footsteps echo until they finally settle on the round platform in the middle of the room. He turns to face the semicircle of ornate chairs housing the Council.

The stench of magic assaults my senses, and my fingers snap over my nose. The floor surrounding Isaac's feet glows, glimmering with runes, and a moment later the smell fades.

"Hello, ma'am. Present and ready, your honour." The Commander nods at the Head of the Council, who simply raises an eyebrow at him.

"Mr. Heathe!" she declares. "Your guild has submitted some troubling evidence regarding the recent riftspawn attacks."

Isaac nods.

The Head peers down at our Commander, her chin seated in the palm of her hand as she taps a thin finger against a withered cheek.

"Hmm." Her gaze shifts towards the High Champions. "Many of your claims line up with the information our Watchmen collected. While the exact circumstances and specific details are hard to prove, we cannot deny the vague truths in your submitted transcripts."

She sighs.

"However, even though we'd like to acknowledge your findings, we cannot publicly reveal the involvement of some High Champions in these recent... *accidents*. You understand this, yes?"

My fingers dig into my palms with such force I barely register when Yuina grabs my hands to pry them open. She keeps a hold of me, firm and understanding, anchoring me in place.

Rage builds at the blatant ignorance of the Council - *ACCIDENTS?!*

They don't care.

They never cared.

And-

"Of course, ma'am. I'd expect nothing less."

Isaac's voice rings through the room. My eyebrows rise at the quiet, unwavering force lurking beneath each word. The Commander continues to speak, undaunted, despite the clear displeasure etched into the faces of the Council.

"But, as *you* know, this is not a new problem! How many Nomads have been arrested without a fair trial? The Council is supposed to protect the people of Nexus, of *Aegis! What have we - and what have YOU - been doing this entire time to keep them safe?* Allowing rumours to grow, standing by while-"

The Head raises a firm hand, silencing him. Isaac's mouth moves, but no words come out, and he pauses.

"I understand why you think this way, Mr. Heathe."

The other Council members frown, glancing at the woman in the centre of their semicircle with nervous stares. She ignores them.

"You are responsible for a Nomad, after all. Unfortunately, their refusal to adapt to our ways and become registered Nexus citizens is a burden on our society. Are you feigning ignorance of this fact?"

Another hand taps me, gently, resting on my shoulder. I don't recognize it at first - for a strange moment I believe it might be Pall's paw - but the trembling touch reveals it's actually Damian.

He's trying to support me.

A small comfort, and a welcome one. Alongside my guildmates, I watch my Commander struggle against this corrupt system.

"Then explain it to me." Isaac hisses. His fists tremble against his side. "Because based on everything I've seen, the Council is also to blame for the deaths of-!"

The Head sighs, raising a finger to silence our Commander once more.

"Fine!" she snaps. "Let me offer some clarification."

The men and women beside her squirm in their seats, exchanging hushed whispers and anxious glances. The Head refuses to acknowledge her colleagues' discomfort.

"You must understand, Mr. Heathe, that these Nomads are a problem," she says in a calm, careful voice. "They are unregistered, living freely upon *Nexus* land, and actively occupying spaces claimed by members of our community. And yes, some might argue that no one *currently* lives within those areas - and others *could* declare that these Nomads are not *directly* harming anyone with their illegal residency - but such trivialities pale in relation to the Council's interests. The intrusion of these foreigners on our soil impedes the development of our economy! Not to mention how these Nomads threaten towns-" she hesitates, raising an eyebrow at the look of disgust on Isaac's face "-let me rephrase. At the very least, they make citizens *feel* threatened by their unwarranted presence. And, most importantly, due to their interaction - or lack thereof - with our Council and their refusal to adhere to Nexus registration laws, we have had no choice but to be wary of these potential threats living on *our* land."

Nonsense.

Everything she's saying, it's nonsense.

Yuina squeezes my hand, and I turn to her. Is she worried for me, or worried I might speak out? If so, I understand her concern; the safest option is to say nothing.

It's the safest, but...

It's not right.

A wet nose bumps against my palm as Pall brushes up against me, drawing reality closer and settling around my legs along with a sense of calm.

A reminder of the many reasons I hold my tongue.

My gaze drifts down to Liatris.

I wish to speak out, but I can't. Not yet. Not here.

A new voice echoes against the wooden walls of this giant chamber.

"Your Honour, you did say one thing which I - we - find quite worrying!"

One of the Council members has raised his hand to interrupt. The large man flicks his vicious, thin little eyes towards me. "This guild has a Nomad, does it not? I doubt *he* is registered as a resident of our city. Is that not cause for concern?"

The Head grits her teeth at the unwelcome interruption, but follows her colleagues' gaze.

"Yes. I'm aware." She snaps, brushing aside the man's comments. "And I was just getting to that, thank you."

She turns to Isaac.

"As the Commander of your guild, it is my duty to inform you of a complication regarding the pardoning of Honour's Stand."

In the front row, Aria stiffens and leans towards Neva to whisper something in her ear. The seer shakes her head furiously, pauses when Aria draws close to offer another hushed secret, and eventually throws her hands into the air.

"Fine! If it's our only option, then what choice do we have?" she hisses back.

If the Head notices the quiet outburst, she pays it no mind.

"Mr. Heathe, your Nomad - Jegrac - is not protected as a citizen of Nexus. A fact you must be quite aware of by now. The Council also has some suspicions regarding his transcripts. We have received claims - unsubstantiated ones, at the moment - declaring your records as having been intentionally edited or modified. And while most of your stories were verified by the citizens of Borderik and within the wreckage of Greyton, your Nomad's activities have not been consistently observed."

The room falls silent, all eyes in the room locking on me. Some steal glances, while others throw glares and suspicious looks my way.

Through all of this, the Commander remains silent. He is the only one who refuses to look at me, even though I cannot keep my eyes off him.

What will he say to all of this?

What *can* he say?

The man's shoulders rise once more, following a deep breath, and then he speaks.

"Let *me* offer a fact *you* must be quite aware of by now," Isaac muses. " I'm technically not a Nexus citizen either; my family resides in Borderik. As for this accusation about falsified transcripts: if such a claim is found to be true, that means anyone could have tainted these records. Some folks might even point fingers at the High Champions or the Council as possible suspects! To do so, however, is to admit that the chronicler - *a modified version of the recording devices you use and rely on for your trials!* - is a flawed and vulnerable tool. If you're admitting it's possible to modify a transcript, doesn't your fragile justice system fall apart? Our portable chronicler may have some minor differences, but it's based on the tools used by the Guild Registry to verify completed quests."

The Head twists her thin lips.

"Yes, I am aware," she mutters, "but this does *not* change your Nomad's status."

A long finger rises to jab at Isaac.

"As for *your* citizenship, Mr. Heathe? You are a Commander. All guild leaders are granted honourary residency within Nexus. Consequently, you have already received a pardon along with the rest of your guild."

Her eyes drift over me.

"But the Nomad is still on trial. Until we can prove his innocence, he will have to return to confinement."

A shiver runs along my spine. Pall whimpers.

But Isaac simply nods. He finally looks over at the guild, scanning the rows until he finds me.

A hint of a smile plays on his lips, despite the sweat dripping off the end of his nose. He locks eyes with me for a brief moment.

Then he turns back to the Council.

"So then, as the Commander, I'm a citizen?"

The Head raises an eyebrow.

"I already clarified: *yes.* Worry not about *your* safety, as we have already pardoned you. However, the Nomad will be imprisoned until his trial, at which point we will decide his fate."

Isaac raises a hand.

"Ah, well, that's alright then. You can go ahead and pardon him now." The Commander grins. "After all, *Jegrac* is the Commander of Honour's Stand."

He's met with stunned silence at first, and many slack, open mouths, and then a great sputtering erupts from the Council. The Head watches her peers as they fill the room with gasps and stammered objections.

"What?! A NOMAD, leading a guild?! Why, I- it- no, no, NO!"

"IMPOSSIBLE! Inconceivable!"

"Yes, we won't stand for it. If this is allowed, then - oh, *Yiatsu above!* What other nonsense will you let through?!"

The Head of the Council silences their babbles with a wave of her hand.

"*Enough*," she snaps before pointing a thin finger at Isaac. "We were informed that the Commander of Honour's Stand is *you*, Isaac Heathe. Explain. I am not in the mood for games."

The Commander shakes his head.

"At the time of my pardoning, I *was* the Commander," he says, "and now I'm not."

The Head raises an eyebrow, her attention shifting to Aria. Our archivist brandishes the paper Isaac had signed earlier.

"Ah," the Head mutters as she chews her lip. "Of course. Hm."

She falls silent, her gaze unfocused.

Perhaps it's a trick of the light, but for an instant, the Head almost smiles.

"I suppose a former member of the Guild Registry would have some understanding of how such things are done, though this process is a bit... unusual."

She thinks for a long moment, and then shrugs.

"Unprecedented, certainly, but not illegal. Well played, Mz. Stueck."

The Head returns to Isaac.

"So, Mr. Heathe. I have no choice but to accept Jegrac as the Commander of Honour's Stand, which means Jegrac is hereby pardoned of all-"

Two large hands slap against knees like wet fish, interrupting the Head's announcement. It's the man who had first pointed out my status as a Nomad.

"NO, Marjory! This simply *cannot* happen! We have been made into fools, as if we hand out pardons this easily, which is RIDICULOUS! We must *not* let this slight go unpunished!"

And with that, the room explodes into shouting. Solaris and some of the High Champions join in, yelling at each other and the Council in protest or with begrudging support. The ones who argue in favour of us openly challenge Solaris. I notice the woman who had smiled at me - Dahlia - refuses to back down.

The sound begins to die out, however, when a strange, unexpected giggling breaks through the cacophony. Wind-chimes of laughter lure all eyes onto Frost, who is seated against a wall littered with spirals of ice and snow.

"Wow! Oh boy, this is *hilarious!*" he gasps between chuckles, "All this *nonsense,* because of *Jegrac?* What are you *adults* doing?!"

One Council member rises from her chair, finger wagging at the boy, but then quickly retreats when the Head stands. An icy stillness blankets the room, although Frost continues to shake his head while trying to stifle his amusement.

"This child has a point." the Head declares. "We are wasting time on one Nomad, who by all means must be granted a pardon. If nothing else, we have no real proof against him beyond unfettered accusations. The members of Honour's Stand are free to leave."

Another Council member leans forward, to call out: "Certainly, yes, but some of us still believe the Nomad could have-"

The Head silences her with a glare.

"If you are suggesting *this Nomad* - the *Commander* of this guild - is responsible for the riftspawn attacks despite the evidence we've been provided, then I will have to take this accusation *seriously*. Which will mean a full investigation into *all* matters regarding the Nomads and the rift." The woman grins, but then falters when the Head continues: "And *yes*, this will include a full investigation and examination of our Council, if *any* of you decide to press this issue further! Do not think I am blind. *ANYONE* involved with unregistered riftportals *will* be brought to justice, *regardless of their social standing*."

She glares at her peers.

"So. Does anyone wish to pursue this matter further?"

Neva's hand starts to rise, but Aria catches it before it gets too high.

Everyone in the room wisely ignores Frost's eager wave.

"Well then!" The Head announces. "Jegrac?"

I stiffen as she looks at me.

"Yes, your honour?"

The woman offers me a pleasant nod.

"You and your guild are free to go. The gate is already set up to take you back to your guildhall."

Isaac doesn't have to be told twice. He sprints off the podium and over to our guild, jumping over the bannister to join Neva and Aria.

Yuina slips her arms under Liatris, carefully pulling her away.

"I've got her," she whispers as she steps out into the aisle. "See you back in the hall, *Commander.*"

Pall follows behind, hopping up the steps before disappearing through the portal.

Aria reaches across Isaac to pat my arm when she shuffles past.

Neva peers at me, pausing on the last step, her arms crossed as she stares down her nose.

"*Congratulations, Boss,*" she scoffs, "I'm looking forward to working with you. We're going to have a *lot* of *fun.*"

A shudder runs down my back at the unmistakable glee in her voice.

The Commander - no, not anymore - Isaac, *just* Isaac - pats me on the shoulder.

"Sorry to hand you this burden," he murmurs, "but it was our only option. Though, for what it's worth, I think you'll do well. And feel free to ask Neva for help! Between you and me, she's always been the *real* Commander."

He slips away.

"Er, excuse me," Damian says, skittering past. He peeks at me, nods, and then stops right in front of the gate. Turning, he offers two thumbs up and a shy grin, before being swallowed by the door's silky haze.

Rapid footfalls and annoyed curses draw my attention over to the High Champions' area. Our last member is attempting to push through the crowd.

"Oh! Oh, no no no. *Not you.*" The Head snaps. Frost frowns, mutters something rude under his breath, and then trudges back to his snow-covered bench.

The Leader of the Council glances at me.

"Why are you still here?" she sighs and waves me away. "Your guild is waiting, Commander. Go."

The wooden stairs creak as I sprint up them, holding my breath when the gate shimmers around me and draws me back to the guild hall.

Yuina and Pall are waiting on the other side, but the rest of Honour's Stand is nowhere to be seen. Isaac's voice echoes against the giant, colourless walls - he appears to be helping Damian settle into his new room - and Neva shouts at them to be quiet.

"So," Yuina says, interrupting my thoughts, "Aria had an idea." She points at the device on my side. "We'll leave the chronicler with Liatris and see if it picks up anything useful."

I lift the shimmering slab onto the dryad's stomach. The device threatens to fall while Yuina carefully shuffles Liatris into a better position.

"Think it'll do anything?" I ask, reaching across our co-matose companion to secure the device onto her dress. "It doesn't work when someone's asleep right?"

Yuina shrugs, her eyes wistful.

"We're desperate, Jegrac. Information on dryads is surprisingly scarce, so I'm ready to try anything at this point." She shakes her head. "Don't want to sound pessimistic, but..."

She trails off.

I clasp Yuina's shoulder and look down at my wilted, fragile friend.

"We'll figure something out," I mutter as the chronicler slips away, "we always do."

CHRONICLE 33
Recorded by Liatris Summerstep

...

...

...

...glass...

...

...

...

...root...

...

...

...no?

...

...home?

...

...
...the Glass...
...
...
...home?
...no.
... no no no no NO NO NO NO NO...
...NO. No. No...
...
...home?
...
...
...
...
...home.
...
...
...
...
...
...
Home.

CHRONICLE 34
Recorded by Neva Oyii

"Any progress?"

Aria shakes her head and sinks back into her chair with a grimace.

Yuina sighs, steps away from the dryad's wilted form, and wipes crumbled pieces of chalk onto her pants. Her shoulders drop. "I've imbued countless plant-related runes into her bandages, but her condition isn't changing. Is my script not advanced enough? *Rift*. I'll keep reviewing everything we've gathered on dryad biology, and throw ideas at the wall until something sticks..."

She shakes her stupor away, grits her teeth, and starts yanking journals, textbooks, and parchment paper out of the giant bags we hauled down from her room. Yuina settles on the floor as she scours for ways to aid Liatris's recovery.

A sticky leaf rests on the dryad's pallid forehead, and I find myself pushing it aside. It hurts to look at her, to be here again - after Ronan and Elise, shouldn't the loss of *another* guild member be easy to overcome?

Except Liatris isn't dead. Not yet.

Aria's quiet voice sneaks into my ear.

"This might be worth investigating," the archivist mutters as she shuffles through the piles of papers scattered across a nearby desk. I step towards one of the many tables and cabinets we've added to the centre of the guild hall.

Scanning the page, I search for answers within the sea of scribbles. Liatris's transcript is mostly unintelligible, though a handful of letters eventually rise out of the churning darkness. A simple message in the midst of a storm: *home.*

"It's a start, Aria. Nice work. Now we know she's thinking, at least. That's good, right?" My voice threatens to break.

Home, huh? Is Liatris aware of her surroundings? Has she found a gentle, fleeting happiness within her return to our guild hall?

A holler draws my attention away. Jegrac and Isaac emerge from the depths of the archives with scrolls and dusty tomes piled in their hands and strapped to their backs. A moment later, Damian appears, lugging an oversized knapsack behind him.

Jogging across the hall, I meet my companions and escort them through our makeshift infirmary. Damian lags behind, so I casually take a few books from his bag to help lighten the load.

"Find anything useful yet, Yuina?" Isaac asks as he drops papers and texts onto an already overstuffed desk. A few scrolls bounce off the wooden surface and down onto the floor with a soft clatter.

Our historian shakes her head, not bothering to look up from her studies.

"No. Not yet. Sorry." She shoves a book aside, growling with frustration before adding: "However, Aria just discovered that Liatris currently has some level of consciousness, and may be aware of her surroundings. Take a look at the chronicler reports and you'll see what I mean."

She glances at me, and I take the hint to redirect Isaac towards Aria's nest, where physical copies of the transcript are spread across a table. The archivist is hunched over them, but she shuffles aside when we approach.

"Oh?" Isaac whispers as he scans the recordings, "Oh, Liatris..."

Damian peers over his shoulder, and Jegrac joins him.

We linger in silence, broken only by the shuffling of papers and the occasional sigh.

My eyes drift shut, giving way to a familiar routine; sparks crack and shatter in the darkness as I reach for the future, letting *what is* give way to *what will be.*

The haze remains, but I force my way through and scour for details. White fog bends and warps to reveal familiar benches and colourful walls.

A sudden pain strikes behind my eyes, forcing them open. Still?

I still can't seer? Why?!

Is the Council trying to pressure us despite Aria's clever bargaining? Or am I simply losing this power? A High Champion could also be to blame; even if Solaris and his allies aren't strong enough to shroud my future, they have the resources to find someone who can.

And speaking of those stuck-up morons... a quick glance around the hall confirms that Frost hasn't returned yet. He's still trapped in the Council's chambers, waiting for his chance to escape.

I chuckle, remembering Yuina's joke about his High Champion status being removed, and how she had hastily clarified to Damian that *there's no way they would do something so stupid, when his status is the Council's only means of keeping him in check.*

Returning to the vision, I strain a little harder. Glimpses of our guild flicker into view, but a single image burns into my brain - Liatris, tucked in a corner, looking paler and sicker than ever.

The white haze creeps back, trying to cloud my sight, but I pour more energy into my eyes. My efforts lead to a new sensation: a terrible, humid heat. So incredibly scorching hot I'm forced to shove the future away as sweat trickles down my forehead and obscures my vision.

No one seems to have noticed my discomfort, and I throw a quick glamour over my face before they can.

Jegrac pipes up, drawing all eyes to him.

"How curious," he mutters, "Liatris keeps mentioning *home,* but why would she want to go back to Orion?" Our new Commander peers closely at the page in his hand. "If she's thinking about it, maybe we ought to listen."

Jegrac notices our confused expressions and raises his eyebrows.

"What? You know, Orion, her *home*land? The Dunes, the Oasis, the Glass?"

Before I can reply, a loud slam shakes the hall. The giant wooden doors on the far side of the room have been tossed aside by a blast of cold air.

Frost storms into the hall, arms crossed, ice cracking beneath his bare feet. His rampage comes to a halt when he notices Liatris, and with an annoyed huff he pulls the chill inwards, shivering as he restrains his rage.

Yuina glances up and gives him a quick wave before she returns to tending Liatris.

"They reprimanded you again, huh?" Her diligent hands replace the dryad's bandages with new, revised runes as she talks.

Frost shrugs. He keeps his distance, snow concentrated in a blistering flurry all around him.

"Unfortunately." He rolls his eyes. "Though I suppose my lecture was short compared to what Solaris had to sit through. The Council might not be fond of me, but right now, they *hate* him."

Jegrac snarls.

"So after all that - the riftspawn attacks and massacres of my people - nothing has changed?!"

Frost frowns.

"What did you expect?"

When Jegrac glares at him, he challenges the Nomad with a solemn stare and a dour reply.

"Don't be naive, *Commander*. The Council wanted to frame us. They don't care about you or your people. They're only punishing Solaris because he got caught."

Yuina interjects before Jegrac can: "I understand your frustration. But the Council has never been fond of Nomads, even though most guilds - including ours - actively support your people. Explains why they were so eager to target us...."

She shakes her head and gestures at Liatris.

"Once Foivos told the Council about our dryad, it was inevitable. We were the perfect scapegoat, and they had more than enough reasons to take us down."

Jegrac calms slightly, flexing his fingers out of clenched fists.

"Fine. Maybe I expect too much, but these High Champions are getting away with murder! They killed entire camps of people! *My people.* And even if the Council ignores those atrocities, Aegis citizens in Greyton - and Borderik too - were harmed because of the rifts Solaris and his group were opening! Where are the consequences for *that*?!"

Yuina clicks her tongue, and he glares at her. The sad, defeated look in her eyes douses his hostility.

"Jegrac, we understand how you feel. We're frustrated too. But we can't expect the Council to change; their only concern is Nexus. Solaris knew that when he started targeting Nomads. And thanks to years of suspicion towards your people - because of ignorance, mostly, and unchecked rumours - it's no surprise he and Rahma and Foivos have gotten away with this for so long."

"Excuse me," Damian interjects, and the group perks up at the reminder of his presence, "but murder's still illegal, right? We have laws in place! Even for a High Champion, it's still a crime!"

Now it's Isaac's turn to shake his head.

"Except for when the victims are not *citizens*. Usually, Nomads aren't bound to a realm or a city. This might come as a shock, Damian, but the Council has never helped Nomads beyond short-sighted schemes and empty declarations of support. They turn a blind eye to the hate they receive, even though they've done nothing wrong."

Damian's eyes go wide, his mouth hanging open as he searches for a response. Eventually, he just stares at the ground with his eyebrows furrowed.

"High Champions play by their own rules," Yuina sighs. "It doesn't matter what they're guilty of - the Council pardons them regardless."

My foot edges towards our new recruit to offer comfort, but something else itches at the back of my mind, a comment we'd dismissed, and I turn to Frost.

"Solaris acted like he was opening riftportals for reasons beyond just targeting Nomads. Do you know why? Actually, I've got a better question: *how?!*"

Frost shares a strange look with Yuina, and our historian nods.

He reaches into his cloak and pulls out a pulsing black and red gem.

The entire room lurches away, our eyes locked on the terrifying stone clutched in his hand.

Frost tucks it back out of sight.

"Calm down. It's inactive," he crosses his arms. "Every High Champion has one."

A stunned silence fills the room. Frost frowns.

"Oh, but not Solaris, Foivos, Toxil, and Rahma. Their rift stones were confiscated."

Jegrac snarls.

"So the Council took away some rocks as a consequence? A temporary punishment - *if you can even call it that* - after everything they've done?!"

Our High Champion shrugs.

"The Council has never placed restrictions on us before, so this *is* a change. And without access to the rift, your people won't be targeted - at least, not directly, and not for a while."

Yuina joins in.

"Don't forget, Jegrac: you're the first *Nomad* Commander! Now people have someone to rally around - a public figure to represent Nomads and dismiss ignorant rumours and assumptions. The guilds also have more flexibility with offering your people support - any threats towards Nomads now become threats towards *all of us.* This position comes with power; just wait and see."

Isaac draws Frost's attention with a wave.

"Did Solaris ever mention *why* he's so interested in the rift? Do you know what he's looking for?"

Frost hesitates.

He locks eyes with Yuina, who stares back at him with a pained expression on her face. For a moment - a very, *very* strange moment - Frost looks incredibly sad.

Then it disappears, and he shakes his head.

"I can't say."

"Can't, and won't," Yuina concurs. "I've already tried getting answers out of him, but apparently there are some secrets even High Champions can't share."

The new recruit has his hand raised, quietly waiting to break into the conversation. Isaac gestures at Damian, encouraging him to speak.

He stands a little taller, and then says: "I might be wrong, but... could the attacks be related to Nexus communities?"

When he sees my confused expression, he clarifies: "You know how Nexus is offering to connect independent towns to the main city? What if the attacks on Nomad camps and on places like Greyton and Borderik are meant to pressure people into joining, to stay safe and have quicker access to guild protections?"

"It's quite the theory," Yuina mutters. She rubs her temples wearily, smearing chalk across her forehead.

Frost sighs. "And likely correct – the Council does terrible things when they think no one's looking, all under the guise of protecting Nexus."

Our resident High Champion turns to Jegrac.

"But I tire of talking. Commander, you mentioned Orion. Why?"

Yuina responds before anyone else can. "Liatris needs to go there. Or, at least, we think she does..." She glances at Isaac, then Jegrac, and then me, her gaze uncertain.

Aria taps a small metal spoon against the cup in her lap. The quiet clink draws our attention.

"Those scarred coins, with the four lines," she declares, "Yuina, where did you say they were from?"

"Ah!" I exclaim, cutting off our historian, "This is what we're talking about, right?" My fingers unfold, revealing one of the coins. "Getting it back wasn't easy, but certainly worth it! Y'all should see your faces. Lotta' jaws to pick up off the floor!"

Yuina is the first to speak.

"The coin, Neva," she gasps, "look at the script!"

The object glints as it rolls over in my hand so I can get a better look at it. Ignoring the scratches, the metal inscription clearly reads: ORION.

"Well, that settles it." Aria declares. She rests her teacup upon a nearby desk, the gentle clatter underlining her words. "We have no choice but to head to the Dunes. I'll contact the Guild Registry, since we'll need a quest to hide our journey's true purpose."

A stunned silence settles upon the room, followed by a collective nodding of heads.

Frost, however, steps a little closer, his eyebrows scrunched in annoyance. When a shiver passes through us, the boy sighs and immediately steps back.

"I'm not going," he says, "Orion is too hot and too dry. I'll stay here and guard the guild hall."

Isaac starts to respond, but then pauses when Aria beckons to him, and he turns away to help her out of her armchair. She takes his arm and stands as tall as her weathered body will allow.

"This is for Liatris, you selfish brat! We're all going!" She begins hobbling away before he can protest, announcing over her shoulder: "So get packing! It'll be quite the trip."

Jegrac whistles at Pall, receives an eager bark in response, and then sprints towards the spiral staircase leading to the overgrown section of our guild hall. Halfway there, he skids to a halt, whirling on his heel to face us.

"Hey, Yuina? Mind helping me with the plants? We'll be gone for a while, so I'd appreciate it if you could show me how to add enchantments to keep them healthy. Liatris will be glad we're taking care of her little green friends while she rests."

Yuina hops to her feet.

"Sure, *Commander*, but in exchange, you're helping me pack."

"Ah, alright. Not a bad deal!"

"Oh, I'm not done - you have to help Neva, too."

"Is it too late to change my mind?"

Yuina's laughter echoes up the stairs.

Suddenly, it's just me and the newbie standing beside our broken dryad.

"Hello, ma'am," Damian mutters, "I can stay here with Liatris, if you want to start packing... I'm sure you have a lot of stuff to get ready."

I raise an eyebrow.

He shrugs, chewing his lip, and I offer him a gentle smile, which he takes in stride, his face brightening into a shy grin.

My feet tap on the floor, leading me away, but then I hesitate and unclip the chronicler from my belt.

"Here." The device rests on my hand, waiting to be taken. "Guild members only, as you know. So don't give it to anyone *not* in our guild, or you'll be getting a lecture from Aria!"

He hesitates.

"Damian, do you want it or not?"
The new recruit grabs it before the words have left-

Chronicle 35
Recorded by Damian Cappell

"**B**y the way, you need to learn how to fight if you're planning to stick around," Neva comments as she walks away, "ask Isaac and Yuina for lessons when you get the chance."

Her foot lingers on the first step of the spiral staircase. She glances towards me.

"Oh, and Damian?"

"Yes, ma'am?"

Neva points behind me.

"He wants to talk with you."

A chill brushes my back. Has Frost been watching us this entire time?

When I turn to face him, his emotionless silver eyes bore into me. His eyelids are lowered, and his mouth is thin and tight.

He doesn't say anything, until my courage and impatience pressure me to squeak out a pathetic: "*What?*"

I clear my throat and apply a little more confidence: "Can I help you, Frost?"

He stares at me.

I straighten out my back, standing a little taller. Even though the top of his head barely reaches my chin it feels like he towers over me.

Unable to hold his gaze, my eyes flicker downward.

Frost smirks.

"I saw your parents," he says, barely registering the confusion and shock on my face as his eyes drift to Liatris. For a brief moment his expression softens, before sharpening when it returns to me.

"They're fine," he adds, "if you care about such a thing."

I start to talk, but he shakes his head, silencing me.

"They talked at *me*," he snorts, "about *you*."

He rolls his eyes when I finally start to respond.

"But my mom and dad don't... I mean, why would they...?" I trail off, losing momentum. *Could they actually be concerned about me?*

Why?

Frost raises an eyebrow.

"They kept pestering me. Asking if you were okay."

For a moment, I wonder if he's joking. But then he sighs and adds: "I said yes so they'd leave me alone."

The boy begins to turn, signalling an end to our conversation. But I can't stop myself. The words spill out, forcing the High Champion to pause.

"I don't understand. After making me a scapegoat - putting me in danger, and using me to frame Honour's Stand - why are they *pretending* to care?!"

Frost shrugs.

"Your family owed the Council a favour. And when our guild was recognized as a possible threat to their plans, your parents were forced to take part."

He hesitates, eyes distant. Then he shakes his head.

"They could have placed you in *any* guild, but they picked us. The most powerful group in Nexus."

Frost glances at me again, a chilling emptiness underlining his dulcet words.

"Were they trying to protect you? Did they want *us* to protect you?"

He shrugs.

"Who knows? I certainly don't. And I certainly don't care."

Frost glides away, taking the cold with him. A trail of snow melts into puddles behind his bare feet.

The temperature rises, but my hands still tremble.

I want to ask more. To know more. I have to know if they actually care about me.

But Frost is already gone, slipping up the steps and out of sight.

Could it be true?

Was my family worried about me, for once?

I can't picture them talking to Frost. Any trace of imaginary concern dissipates like smoke, brushed aside by years of annoyed glances and unfilled promises.

If only I could believe him.

My mind will break if I spend too long thinking about this, so I search for a distraction. My eyes settle on Liatris.

The dryad.

Our dryad.

When I first joined Honour's Stand, she welcomed me.

She doesn't deserve this.

Whatever happens next, we can't leave her like this. We won't.

We'll fix her.

The hall grows bustling and loud, Neva's voice carrying across the balconies above my head, her shouts returned by Jegrac's irritated retorts.

Despite the sad reminder lying in the middle of the hall, this guild remains alive and well.

They accepted me, just like she did.

Quietly as possible, I whisper: "We'll bring you back, Liatris."

And then, even softer: "*Thank you.*"

Looking up to the ledges, I catch glimpses of Yuina and Jegrac milling about while Neva shuffles things in and out of her room. Frost slips out of sight behind an ice-encrusted door, and Pall pauses from his gallivanting to lap up a puddle the High Champion has left behind.

Echoes dance up from the archives as Aria and Isaac argue about putting a recliner in the caravan.

The sound swathes me in a great, unexpected comfort.

Jegrac calls my name, interrupting my thoughts, beckoning me to him. I look at Liatris, whispering one final promise to help Honour's Stand bring back her smile.

And then I turn to join my Commander, clicking off the chronicler as I go.

EPILOGUE CHRONICLE
Recorded by Aria Stueck

Silence blankets me as my eyes drift across the high ceiling and the tall white walls of our home. It's quiet; the guild is currently at the market, gathering last-minute supplies for a journey that will finally include me.

Isaac lingers nearby, resting on the floor, trying not to be a bother as he sharpens his sword.

My fingers skim through the records in my lap, compiling the events into a practical, completed transcript.

I pause at the chronicle describing the guild's visit to the Heathe homestead and sneak a glance at Isaac.

His eyes are distant, his mind elsewhere.

Is he thinking about his family?

Curiosity gets the better of me.

"Isaac," I say gently, and he perks up, "why didn't you stay?"

He tilts his head, confused, but then notices the chronicler on my knee. His eyes linger on the scribbles and lines covering the pages pressed against it.

"Honestly? I don't know." he responds. "It didn't seem like the right choice at the time. Although..."

He rubs a hand over his stubble.

"Okay, I'll admit it - I've been thinking about leaving the guild. Just... entertaining the thought. Not that I'd ever follow through with it!"

He chuckles.

"I've always worried my family might finally convince me to give this up." He gestures at the surrounding hall. "But I'm still here, so... yeah."

"You came back. Despite what your mother said, you chose to leave."

He shrugs his shoulders.

"Yeah, well," he mutters, "in the end, I wanted to come back here."

I raise an eyebrow.

"Even though you're no longer our Commander?"

Isaac sighs.

"Guess I don't have that excuse anymore, huh?"

My hand reaches out instinctively, and he takes it.

Always the gentleman, he offers me a small grin when I squeeze his fingers.

"Listen, Isaac. If you choose to return to the farm, we won't blame you. No one wants to guilt you into staying. And while it hurts to admit this - because *you know* we all love having you around - the guild would survive without you."

Taking a deep breath, I add: "Don't stay for us, Isaac. If you want to go, then go."

His hand slips away, drifting back into his lap.

"Yeah," he says after a long silence, "but..."

He waves up at the balconies.

"I *want* to be *here.*"

He gives me a weak smile, and I return his gesture in kind.

A clamouring outside the guild doors interrupts our conversation; Neva's voice clashes against Jegrac's shouts as they argue. Eventually, the noise fades, accompanied by the slam of caravan doors as hooves clatter on the stone street, heading off to fetch whatever item had been missed.

Isaac turns his attention back to me. This time, his words are soft and slow.

"Going back to Borderik... it helped me realise my family wouldn't let me go until I *told them to let me go*. It was a conversation I'd been avoiding for the longest time."

A little quieter, he adds, "I know my parents mean well. But whenever I find myself questioning whether or not this is the right choice - if I'm being selfish, for choosing to be here - I stop and remind myself that they don't have to understand *why* I want to be an adventurer. They just have to accept my choice, and trust in the life I've chosen for myself."

"...Isaac," I whisper, reaching out to take his hand again, "choosing the guild isn't the same as abandoning your family."

He looks away from me, though a hint of a smile plays on his face. He doesn't answer, but I know he's thinking about the guild, the newbie, and the life he's made for himself away from the family farm.

"Yeah. I know." Isaac turns to me, his eyes bright and warm. "My family will always want me to return to the farm; being close to home is the safest choice. But..."

His smile widens.

"The house in Borderik is where *my parents live*. It's not *home* anymore. And Nexus isn't my home either! Right here, right now - with the guild - *with Honour's Stand!* - I'm where I belong. I *want* to be *here*. *This* is my choice."

We sit in silence for a long time, thinking of the past, of things to be, of problems we still have to solve. I settle back in my armchair, resting my weary bones as I gather strength for the journey ahead.

When the chronicler slips out of my hand and clacks on the table beside me, the soft sound wakes a lingering thought.

"Isaac?"

My guildmate gives me a warm, familiar look, filled with the comfort of a well stoked fire.

I offer the sun in return.

"Welcome home."

ACKNOWLEDGEMENTS

Writing this feels surreal. Maybe it's because of my naive, new author spark (check with me on book 3 or 4... will I be cynical and jaded by then?), but it still feels like I'm jumping the gun by creating an acknowledgements page. And yet, here we are! The best part of this journey, though, has most certainly been the connections I've made along the way and the conversations I've had while sharing the first story of Honour's Stand with all my friends and family.

So, let me take a moment to recognize everyone who helped make this novel a reality:

First, a quick shout-out to everyone who volunteered to be a beta-reader, listened to me rant about my story, or offered support whenever I'd talk about the progress I was making. Thank you to Glenda Willcock, Corrine Codina, Jesse Grant, Pam Harman, Nicolas Pion, Sam Major, and anyone else I may have forgotten (sorry, lol – remind me to include you next time!). My drive to publish a book has been reignited many times thanks to all of you.

Much appreciation and gratitude to the head of my social media team and professional photographer, Rena Zhang. Looking forward to continued collaborations in the future.

Thank you to my lovely beta reader Olivia Hart; your comments and insight helped develop my characters to a new level, and your feedback let me revel in the joy of writing. An additional, bonus thank you for offering feedback on the final cover – it looks amazing! It also feels like you somehow love Liatris more than I do - and as a fellow plant-person she'd be honoured to meet you.

Haley McRae, my greatest rival and accomplice in this craft; without the late night calls, the one-sided conversations, and the brainstorming of plot lines and ideas, this novel wouldn't exist. I am very lucky to be friends with a talented writer like you.

To my mother, my number one cheerleader who got me into reading and writing in the first place through *home*work - I wouldn't be here, in this moment, without you. Sending all my love.

To my father, a huge thank you for scouring through multiple transcripts to raise my story from a second draft (and third... fifth... sixth...) to a novel. Thank you for believing in me and your faith that I could always do better. I greatly appreciate your support when editing my writing *and* my pictures - thank you, oh revered Master of Photoshop. You should try photography! I think you might like it! :)

And finally, a cliche thanks to you, the reader. I hope you enjoyed this story as much as I enjoyed writing it. Keep an eye out for the next book in the Honour's Stand series!

About the author

Micah MacCallum is a novelist and a teacher. He spends most of his days at school, but when not learning alongside his students Micah spends time writing, playing music, reading, and watering the great abundance of plants that *must* have been smuggled into his home, because he certainly does NOT remember buying this many.

He also likes writing long sentences.
Legacy is his debut novel.

www.ingramcontent.com/pod-product-compliance
Lightning Source LLC
Chambersburg PA
CBHW072317020726
47501CB00002B/548

* 9 7 8 1 7 3 8 3 2 3 0 1 2 *